WARRICK
TANNER
JACKSON

SEALs of Honor, Books 17–19

Dale Mayer

SEALS OF HONOR, BOOKS 17–19
Beverly Dale Mayer
Valley Publishing Ltd.

Copyright © 2018

ISBN-13: 978-1-773361-71-0
Print Edition

Books in This Series:

Mason: SEALs of Honor, Book 1

Hawk: SEALs of Honor, Book 2

Dane: SEALs of Honor, Book 3

Swede: SEALs of Honor, Book 4

Shadow: SEALs of Honor, Book 5

Cooper: SEALs of Honor, Book 6

Markus: SEALs of Honor, Book 7

Evan: SEALs of Honor, Book 8

Mason's Wish: SEALs of Honor, Book 9

Chase: SEALs of Honor, Book 10

Brett: SEALs of Honor, Book 11

Devlin: SEALs of Honor, Book 12

Easton: SEALs of Honor, Book 13

Ryder: SEALs of Honor, Book 14

Macklin: SEALs of Honor, Book 15

Corey: SEALs of Honor, Book 16

Warrick: SEALs of Honor, Book 17

Tanner: SEALs of Honor, Book 18

Jackson: SEALs of Honor, Book 19

Kanen: SEALs of Honor, Book 20

Nelson: SEALs of Honor, Book 21

Taylor: SEALs of Honor, Book 22

Colton: SEALs of Honor, Book 23

Troy: SEALs of Honor, Book 24

Axel: SEALs of Honor, Book 25

Baylor: SEALs of Honor, Book 26

Hudson: SEALs of Honor, Book 27

About This Boxed Set

Warrick

Brave, badass warriors who serve their country with honor and love their women to the limits of life and death.

Warrick Canton works with Mason's Navy SEAL team and he's going stir-crazy on the sidelines while he heals from an ankle injury. He longs for a relationship like the ones his buddies have, but, after his girlfriend of three years dumps him just when he thinks they're solid, he struggles to believe it's possible. He's invited to a backyard barbecue at Mason's house, where he meets up with the spitfire he's met before and knows won't give an inch. Warrick is intrigued, even though the she-devil won't stop arguing long enough to get to know her.

Penny Magnus loves her job as a clerk in the medical insurance offices, but trying to get stubborn men to fill out a few forms properly isn't her idea of a good time. With a fiery personality, Penny's open to starting a new romance but absolutely not with a difficult man, even if he is gorgeous. Her best friend got herself in an ugly relationship and had to ask Penny for help in escaping him.

Now, just when Penny and Warrick are calming down enough to actually connect, her friend's boyfriend contacts her. He blames Penny for the mess she created when she tore the love of his life from him. He goes on a rampage, targeting Penny—only he's thwarted by one big, badass warrior standing firmly in his way, protecting her. All he needs is for Warrick to make one tiny mistake...

Tanner

Tanner McGrath is the newest member of the team. Active in sports, particularly aerial types, he's training with a new military harness used in paragliding. The design was developed by Wynn Rider and her brother. As they run two SEAL teams through rigid training, Wynn's glider fails mid-flight, sending her plummeting toward the ground. Only Tanner's quick thinking saves her life—though it doesn't save her from losing her job.

Wynn used to compete professionally in the cutthroat paragliding industry before she walked away from it, but this accident is by far the worst she's ever had. Separating her gratitude from the growing attraction is nearly impossible.

Tanner has heard the old adage that saving a life makes you responsible for it. Having admired Wynn's career when she was a professional paraglider, he's more than a little interested in keeping a close eye on the fascinating lovely who almost literally fell in his lap.

When Wynn realizes her equipment had been sabotaged, she's worried her past has come back to haunt her. Tanner may be the only one who can help her against someone who's determined to put her and her brother out of business…permanently.

Jackson

A bullet takes out his rig, but a mechanic captures his heart…

When Jackson is forced to pull his rig to the side of the road as the radiator overheats, he's not impressed, but when a bouncy mechanic in camo drives back to help him, he's even less enthralled – with himself. She's smart, capable, single and knows a whole lot more about mechanical things than he does.

But when he hears that it's a bullet that's brought his rig to a stop, he knows exactly what to do – save the woman at his side and find the men who did this.

Deli was sent to assist Jackson and his sidelined rig. Only to find they are caught up in a double cross that has bullets flying and bodies dropping… some of them very close to her.

If only it was that simple… as the bodies start to fall, and their passion starts to heat up… who will be the final casualties in take the last shot in the final act?

Sign up to be notified of all Dale's releases here!
https://geni.us/DaleNews

WARRICK

SEALs of Honor, Book 17

Dale Mayer

WARRICK CANTON PICKED up another box of toys, shook his head, looked down at Joshua and said, "This is a lot of toys for one little boy."

Joshua danced in place. "No, it's not." He grabbed a small box beside Warrick. "Come on. I'll show you my new room."

Warrick chuckled and followed the little boy. In the ensuing weeks, with all the chaos and recovery behind them, Joshua was a whole new child. He no longer went to a private school and didn't seem to mind. He attended the local public school and was settling in. It would take him a bit, but he was young and resilient and had a lot of good times ahead of him to wipe out the bad memories.

His father was in jail and wouldn't be out anytime soon. The trial was scheduled but wasn't for another year. In the meantime, Joshua hadn't asked very much about him. Apparently he'd been awake and had seen his father try to shoot his mom. That had been too much for him.

They'd explained quietly what had happened, that his father had done something very bad and was in jail. Joshua had just nodded. Once he realized he would be staying with his mom, he was fine.

When he later heard Corey was moving into their new home with them, Joshua got really excited. And he'd seen plenty of Corey and Warrick. Even Mason had stopped by. Joshua had seemed pretty thrilled by all the men. It was a good life for a little boy. He would grow up with real men as role models—not assholes who used others for their own gain. And Joshua smiled all the time. The same off-center smile as his mother.

Warrick was happy for Corey, yet enjoyed being single right now. But it didn't make up for the three years he had been in a relationship with Sandra, where he'd thought he had had the real thing. He should have realized their breakup was imminent, but he'd been blind, not really aware of what was going on in her world. He didn't want to make that mistake again. But he hadn't found anybody else who he liked half as much.

Joshua led Warrick into the bedroom where Corey had set up his captain's bed. Corey took one look at the box in Joshua's hand and said, "Whoa, tiger. I don't think any more stuff will fit in here."

But Joshua just giggled and stacked his additional box atop the others off to the side. "We'll unpack later. I'll show you all my stuff then." And he raced back out again.

Corey looked up at Warrick and smiled. "Thanks for helping us today."

"A bunch of other guys just arrived too."

Corey nodded. "That's great. The more hands, the more gets moved in, and the faster this will go."

"Are you happy, dude?"

Corey looked up, his face beaming. "I'm so happy, I'm stupid with it," he admitted. "I hadn't really expected this."

"Sometimes you need to let go of your expectations and see what comes your way, instead of trying to control everything in your life."

Corey nodded. "How are you doing?"

"Outside of the concussion leaving me with an odd headache …" He grinned. "I'm fine."

"Time for you to find another woman," Corey said in a joking tone.

"No rush. I'm happy to watch you guys play house for a while."

"Here, give me a hand with this, will you?" Corey asked.

The two flipped the bed onto its four legs and finished off the last of the installation. They added the mattress and the drawers. And then stepped back. "He should like that."

Warrick slapped Corey on the shoulder. "That kid is in heaven."

"Yeah, I'm just a little nervous."

"Don't be. Just be you. It'll be great." Warrick smiled at his friend in all sincerity. "Don't forget his dad was an ass. It can't be too hard to beat that."

"Thanks," Corey said, laughing.

The two went back downstairs. And the house was full of men moving furniture and boxes. In the center of it all was Angela, her face flushed with excitement.

She caught sight of Corey and raced toward him, flinging her arms around him. "Your friends arrived."

He chuckled. "Yeah, hopefully so did the groceries."

Just then Ryder stepped in and held up a box. "I brought the steaks, potatoes and salads. Devlin's here with the grill. I think Mason is bringing a second one."

Warrick leaned against the doorjamb and watched as the chaos around him continued. This was what Corey had always hoped for. And Warrick was so damn glad Corey would finally get his chance at a home, a family and happiness. Warrick had watched his friend go through one lighthearted romance after another, never settling down. But, man, when Corey found the right person, he'd settled in a big way.

Ryder walked over, looked at Warrick and asked, "You okay?"

Warrick nodded. "I just think all the good women in the world are taken."

Ryder stared at him for a long moment. "I thought that way once too."

Warrick gave him a lopsided grin. "And yet look at you now," he teased.

Ryder nodded. "When it's time, when it's right, it'll happen. Until then, just enjoy life."

Warrick shifted from the doorjamb and thought that was a hell of a decent piece of advice. He could just enjoy life for a while. And, if he was lucky, somebody would cross his path and put a smile on his face to match the one on Corey's. And Warrick couldn't wait.

ELL, YEAH, HE could wait. He could wait for eternity until the right woman showed up if she was anything like the pugnacious terror in front of him.

It didn't matter that she was only five foot nothing, her fiery long red hair in a ponytail slightly off to the side and a face full of freckles.

She glared at him and had been for the last half an hour.

He'd filled out the paperwork incorrectly on his latest injury. And, damn, if she wasn't trying to hang him with it.

Warrick had a hard time stopping his jaw from jutting out, an imitation of her own actions. "Penny, I get that you have a problem with me," he said, trying for patience. "But honestly, I'm not trying to screw you over by messing up the paperwork."

She snorted. A completely unfeminine sound that both surprised him and intrigued him. She shook her head. "You might not be trying to be difficult," she said, "but you do it naturally. The instructions are so damn clear." She tapped the paperwork. "Why aren't you following them?"

Warrick sighed, took the papers from her, looked at them, and, sure enough, it gave exact instructions. He didn't know why he hadn't followed them. Then again, it was the third time he'd been in here with the wrong paperwork.

On one of the training missions a few weeks ago, he'd

hurt his ankle. It had pissed him off, and he had refused to get treatment until the guys had forced him to get it looked at. He had a hairline fracture and had severely strained his ankle, and his foot was in a cast, to keep the ankle immobile to heal properly. The doctor had been very clear how he felt about Warrick staying on his feet when he had long passed the point he should have gotten off of them before seeing him.

Warrick would be the first to admit he had more than his fair share of stubbornness. But then all the guys did. And nobody wanted to be sidelined with an injury. That just wasn't on anybody's to-do list. Not that he had a whole lot of choice. Not now at least.

He lifted his gaze from the paperwork and said, "Okay, I did it wrong. Sorry."

She blew out a heavy breath, directing it up where tendrils of red curls lifted off her forehead. Then she relaxed. "I just don't get it, Warrick. This is the third time in as many weeks."

He shrugged. "I'm really good at stuff I like to do." He plastered an engaging grin on his face, or at least he hoped it was. "You know? A lot of people don't want to deal with stuff that's boring and uninteresting."

"This is hardly boring and uninteresting," she said. "This is what gets you your medical. This is what gets you all that good stuff you need done so you can heal and get back onto the front line as fast as possible so you can go kill yourself again," she explained.

He chuckled. "It's not that bad."

She glared at him, her bottom lip jutting out. "You do remember you've got a fracture on your shin bone, right?"

"Yeah, but that's not a real break," he said, minimizing

the injury. "Besides, even if it was broken, it's not that big a deal."

"A break isn't a big deal?" she snapped. "Stress fractures, damaged tendons? Because somebody is an idiot and staying on his ankle well past the point when he shouldn't have been. Now that's a problem."

Under his breath he said, "Whatever."

Only she had heard him. And that was probably not a good thing. She turned and glared at him. "*Whatever?*"

He sighed. "How come I only ever see the prickly side of your personality?" he asked resentfully. "Everybody else says you're a sweetheart." She flushed, and he watched as the wave, almost shockingly red, rolled up her alabaster-white skin.

"*Prickly? Sweetheart?*"

He raised both hands in surrender. "What? So both of those are wrong or not allowed?"

"Not when they're complete opposites, no," she said in exasperation. "Fill out the paperwork properly, and bring it back again."

"We could do it right here and right now," he said hopefully. "Then I wouldn't have to come back."

She glanced at the clock and said triumphantly, "We can't because I have to close up the offices. It's four o'clock. You're too late."

He just glared at her. "Now you're being mean."

"Try to utilize an education level above a two-year-old and fill out the forms correctly."

Inside he fumed because, of course, his education was much higher than a two-year-old level. He was well known for his reports, but he wasn't sure why these damn medical forms were such a pain in the ass. He snatched the forms off the table and stormed out the room.

Behind him she called out, "Have a nice day."

He slammed the door in response. In the hall he tried to control his breathing.

Tanner walked up, took one look at his face and chuckled. "I told you Penny is a sweetheart."

Warrick glared at him. "How is that"—he jabbed a finger at the door behind him—"even remotely related to being a sweetheart?"

"She's a sweetheart, except when she isn't," Tanner said. "But she's the one who keeps everything flowing. So I wouldn't suggest you piss her off."

"Too late," Warrick roared. "Why is this crap so difficult?" He stormed toward Tanner, then swore as his ankle screamed back at him. He slowed his pace, taking several slower, more careful steps.

Tanner tsk-tsked. "Sorry, bud. That ankle's given you nothing but hell."

"Stupid thing. You know we had games last week, and I missed out on them. We were against the air force too."

"You missed out on the soccer and the water sports the week before." Tanner grinned.

"Damn it." But there was no help for it. He'd had a bad couple months with several injuries. Being so accident-prone wasn't normal for him. The latest was during a bout of outback survival training. After thinking it was all healed, he'd returned to work only to find out it was not only *not* healed but he now had a damn stress fracture. He motioned to Tanner. "Let's go."

"Sure," Tanner said amiably.

He walked like the cowboy he was. His voice had a drawl, his tone long and easy. It took a lot to rile him.

Warrick would have said the same for himself, but, every time he came in here, Penny managed to set him off again.

"So when do you get to see her again?"

Warrick looked at his buddy, confused. "See who?"

"Penny, of course."

He waved the paperwork in Tanner's face. "I have to fill out this shit again. And then take it back."

Tanner nodded. "Good. That'll be what? Monday?"

"Needs to be, yes. The doctor won't do anything else if I don't get the proper papers filed."

"Wow. You must've really screwed up."

"Apparently over and over again," Warrick snarled. "I can pull records off MI6's database without them knowing about it. I can write goddamn reports about terrorist activity in the US. I can write protocol procedures for how to deal with the rebels in Afghanistan. But when it comes to filling out this medical shit …"

"Did you ask her to fill it out for you?" Tanner asked. "I did that the first time, and, ever since then, she's filled it out automatically for me."

They were in the elevator. Warrick twisted and looked at him. "She *what?*"

Tanner nodded. "Yeah. Did you even ask?"

Warrick stared at him in surprise. "I don't know that I asked in as many words," he said slowly. "But she knew I was having a hell of a time."

"Yeah, but that's not the same thing as being courteous and asking her for a hand because you just don't understand."

Warrick shrugged. "She could've helped anyway."

"She *could* have, but obviously she didn't, so maybe you should try a little sweetness instead of all that anger."

Warrick nodded, but inside he was steaming. It was pretty shitty that she wouldn't help him. He could almost understand but, at the same time, not really. Still, he probably had gone in with a chip on his shoulder because it was the third time he'd filled out the forms incorrectly, and he was pissed not only at himself but at the system that required him to do as much as he had done. Surely, if he was off halfway around the globe fighting to save the world and somebody had found out he had filled out a form wrong, someone else could fix it for him. But apparently not.

The elevator opened on the main floor. He walked out slowly. "I don't think there's any way I can get her help," he muttered. "She was pretty pissed at me today."

"Honestly, she is a sweetheart. Everybody says so."

"Everybody can say whatever the hell they want," Warrick muttered. "It doesn't change the fact that she's not a sweetheart to me."

At that, Tanner just chuckled. "Are we heading to Mason's house for a barbecue, or are you going home and spending the evening working on paperwork?"

Warrick just glared at him. They walked over to Warrick's Jeep Wrangler. It was a manual, and he needed both feet for the clutch and the gas pedal. In which case, Tanner drove Warrick around most of the time. At least while Tanner was stateside. If their unit took off on a big training mission without him, Warrick would be pissed. And, if they went on an active mission, he'd be beyond pissed.

"How much longer?" Tanner asked as he got into the driver's side of the vehicle.

Warrick managed to get himself in on his side, relaxing slightly. "At least two more weeks. The doctor said he wouldn't even send me for more tests if I didn't get this stuff cleaned up." He waved the paperwork, then set it in his lap.

"So maybe you need to do that tonight," Tanner said. "How hard can it be?"

Warrick stared down at the multitude of colored papers. "It's too damn hard."

"Do you want me to stay in and help you?"

"Hell no. We're going to Mason's and having steak."

"Then we need to pick up some beer."

"Good. The liquor store it is. But I have to stop by the hangar first. I forgot my shit there."

They drove back to base, through the checkpoint, waved at the security guards, grabbed Warrick's gym bag and headed out to the real world. Or rather the other half of his world. Warrick had two worlds—the real world, which was his military life, and then the rest of the world.

He watched as Tanner, driving with almost a sense of joy, pulled the Jeep into traffic and headed to the liquor store only a few blocks from Warrick's house. As soon as he parked, Warrick hobbled out and walked in with Tanner.

"What do you think? Grab a twofer?"

Tanner nodded. "I tried to bring some food, but Mason said there was tons."

Warrick nodded. "The thing is, now that so many of the guys have partners, if anything, we're completely overwhelmed in food. There are always leftovers for days."

"And I get to have the benefit of that most of the time too," Tanner said with a smirk. "There are some advantages to being one of the two bachelors in our circle."

"Yeah, well, every time I meet somebody like Penny, I know why I'm still single."

At that, Tanner gave a shout of laughter. "Well, if you're not interested, I might be."

Warrick looked at him in horror. "Of course I'm not interested."

"Absolutely you are," Tanner said with a chuckle. "I see it as the only reason you've messed up the paperwork as many times as you have. It's also the only reason she hasn't stepped in and fixed it for you."

Warrick shot him a look but was at the cash register already. He paid for the beer, and, as they walked out the double doors, he muttered, "You're nuts."

"Nope, not nuts. She's helped everyone else."

"Exactly. If she was sweet on me, she'd be helping me, not putting me through this torment," he lamented.

"And, if you weren't sweet on her, you'd have done the paperwork in a heartbeat or at least asked for enough help to get through it so the process was over with. This way you keep getting the chance to visit her over and over again."

Warrick stared at him in horror. "Hell no."

But Tanner wasn't listening. He was too busy laughing. Instead of going back home to Warrick's place, he took several corners and put them on the road toward Mason's house.

As they pulled up in front, Warrick hobbled out of the Jeep, grabbed the beer he'd placed in the footwell and walked up to the front of the house. He was totally okay leaving Tanner behind. Warrick hit the doorbell and pushed the door open, calling out, "Hey, anyone home?"

Tesla, her face flushed and tendrils of hair everywhere and the cutest little apron he could ever imagine—a big tabby cat wrapping its arms around her waist—came racing toward him. "Put down the beer."

He obediently put the beer on the floor and opened his arms. She flung herself into them and hugged him hard. He held her close for a moment. "This is the only reason I would be interested in having a girlfriend again."

"What's that? Somebody to smile when you arrive?" she teased.

He rolled his eyes at her. "Not you too."

Tanner chuckled again, snagged the beer off the floor beside him and walked past the two of them. "Hi, Tesla," he said.

Tesla reached out, grabbed his arm. "What? No hug?"

"Warrick's suffering," he said. "He had another encounter with Penny."

Tesla turned back to see Warrick's face crinkling up in disgust. "I've told you that she's a sweetheart. How bad was it?"

He just glared at her.

She sighed. "Oh." She thought about it for a moment, and then Mason's gentle voice came from the kitchen, saying, "Don't bother about it, honey."

She turned a worried gaze his way.

Mason just shrugged and gave her a lopsided grin. "What will be, will be."

Warrick looked over at Mason. "What the hell does that mean?" Mason's bland look told Warrick nothing. But his instincts had already spiked, and he knew something was up.

He walked forward with Tesla exclaiming, "Are you still in that walking cast? When will you be back to normal again?"

He smiled down at her and patted her hand. "Anytime you want to fuss over me, you just ditch Mason. Then you can move in with me."

She beamed up at him. "Now if I thought you loved me like Mason loves me …" she said in a loud whisper, "I might take you up on that."

"How could I not love you as much as Mason does?" he asked earnestly. "Besides I'm twice the man Mason is." At that, she laughed hard, and he glared at her. "My ego can't take much more today."

And that made her laugh all the harder. She walked over to Mason, slipping her arms around him and laid her head against his chest. "Warrick, I keep telling you. You will find somebody."

"And I keep telling you that I'm not interested."

She grinned up at Mason and kissed his chin. "Should be a fun evening."

He gave a tiny nod, stepped out of the doorway, saying, "Warrick, we're getting the prep done for the barbecues. If you want to come out with me, we can sit and attend the grills. You won't have to walk around too much."

"Suits me." The kitchen was full of people, so he called out, "Hello, everyone, I'm here. Goodbye, everyone, I'm going outside with Mason."

There was an outcry of hellos and various other catcalls. He ignored them all, except to toss a big grin behind him, and walked out the double French doors of Mason's house.

There was a large pool, which was always nice. But off to the side was a huge outdoor kitchen area, and that's the one thing that Mason put to extremely good use. They were constantly having barbecues here. Who knew there would be so many of them who had become fast friends? And, if the men hadn't become fast friends, the women had. And that just meant the men came along and got to know each other a little bit better too. Every time somebody new joined the group, it seemed to shift and blend and then meld even better.

Warrick didn't understand it, but he was damn glad to be a part of it. He made his way to the two loungers Mason had set up by the barbecue grills and plunked his butt down in the closest one. Mason grabbed a cold beer and handed it to him. Warrick popped the top and chugged down one-third of the can, then sat back with a sigh of relief and said, "Now that is a hell of an improvement on my day."

"You were supposed to finish that paperwork."

"I tried," he said in an aggrieved tone. "I really did try." Then he told Mason his trouble from start to finish.

By the time he was done, Mason was laughing, his shoulders shaking so hard that the tongs in his hands were in danger of falling from his grip.

"It's not that funny," Warrick muttered.

"No, it's not," said a woman, her familiar voice coming from behind them.

He stared at Mason, his gaze going wide, and he shook his head. "Oh no, no, please no."

At this point, Mason gave up the ghost and howled.

Warrick slunk farther in the chair, picked up the rest of his beer, looked at it and thought, *What the hell.* He threw it back in one big slug.

He would need a half dozen more before he could turn around. But he didn't have to. He turned slightly to see somebody had stepped around into full view—somebody tiny, somebody with a fiery temper, somebody standing in front of him, her hands on her hips, glaring at him.

"Hi, Penny," he said in exaggerated politeness. "How nice to see you."

She leaned over and said, "Not so much."

He glared right back, shoving his jaw forward until their noses were almost touching. "You could have helped me," he roared.

"You could have asked for help," she roared back so the two had everyone's attention, but neither noticed they were so locked on to each other.

And suddenly Warrick could see the humor in the situation, and his lips twitched.

She shook her head. "Oh, no you don't. No laughing."

Too late. As soon as he lost control, he couldn't get it back.

Now she just got madder by the second. She looked at her beer, looked at him and reached out, as if to pour it over his head. But he caught her hand, twisted her around and pulled her into his arms, so she was seated in front of him in between his legs on the lounger. Then he snatched the can out of her hand and poured it into his mouth.

She struggled to get away, but there was no use. His arm was an iron grip around her tiny frame. Instead, all she did was get madder.

But, at this point, he was laughing so loud it was a struggle to regain control. Finally he calmed down. "Thank you. I needed that."

She glared at him, spun in his arms and punched him on the shoulder.

He looked at her and, in an injured voice, said, "Mason, you've got mosquitoes here."

She gasped and hit him again.

And Warrick chuckled again. He said, "If you do that a third time, I'll have to retaliate."

She leaned forward, her chin jutted out again. "Yeah? What are you gonna do? Hit me back?"

He dropped his voice to a serious tone. "Try it." He didn't mean to make it a challenge, but, at the same time, he couldn't resist.

She balled up her fist, swung back and hit him hard.

"Mason, definitely mosquitos." He grabbed her jaw, pulled her toward him and kissed her hard.

All around them, cheers broke out. She sagged against him, and he couldn't pull back. He kissed her again and again until she was completely compliant in his arms. Then he lifted his head and whispered, "Go ahead. Hit me again and see where we end up."

PENNY WAS MORTIFIED. As shrieks of laughter, clapping and cheers broke out around her, she realized how the two of them must have looked. She didn't know if she should run home where she could hide away in mortification and hopefully never see these people again, or if she could somehow brave this out. She wasn't sure how to do that.

In the meantime, she was completely tucked in Warrick's arms against his chest, his arms wrapped around her, holding her tight, and she lay sprawled, weak against him. She'd been kissed many times. Hell, she'd had several long-term relationships. But never had a kiss knocked the stuffing out of her like this one had. Of course, with the compound effect of her temper being pricked and the challenge from him …

At his last words about daring her to punch him again and to see where they ended up, she knew exactly where they'd end up. Making love right here, without a care for wherever they were. And that was a hell of a thought. She'd never been so lost in passion that she didn't know exactly what was going on and where, and she was afraid that, with him, she would completely lose herself. Not something she was prepared to do. And yet the draw, the attraction between them, was hard to ignore.

"All right, folks, give us a moment. Then we'll be up for round two. The play will begin after a short intermission," Warrick joked.

At that, there was more laughter from everybody around her, but, at the same time, it was friendly teasing. Most of the people moved away, giving them a little bit of space. She didn't want to move at all. She hoped everybody would assume they had had a prior relationship, and she hadn't just let a stranger kiss her silly …

And finally, when almost alone, she tried to sit up, but he kept his arms firmly around her.

"If you stay where you are," he said in a low voice, "we might be lucky to pass this off as a lovers' tiff."

As he wasn't really giving her much of an option, she relaxed back against him. "That would be giving them the wrong impression."

"After that kiss, sweetheart, I don't think so."

"What the hell was that?" she asked, but she kept her voice low so only he could hear her. She felt his head shake and heard the confusion in his voice.

"I am not sure."

"Well, that's good to know," she joked. "I hate to think it was just me."

"That's another reason why I don't want you to move yet," he said. "Otherwise the entire crowd will get to see just how I feel about what happened here."

She caught his meaning and realized the hard prodding against her hip was something she hadn't even considered. It had caught her sideways. She giggled.

He looked down at her, aghast. "Funny, is it?"

"Well, it is for me, yes. But not for you. Sorry." Then she giggled again.

He grinned. "At least I know I'm not dead."

She stared at him. "Hardly. You're one of the sexiest men I've ever met."

He looked at her and shrugged. "Since my last relationship broke up, I've been trying celibacy."

She stared up at him. "*Trying* celibacy?"

He nodded. "Trying. As in I haven't had a girlfriend in a while. I've gone out with friends. But I have deliberately avoided deepening the relationship."

"And why is that?" she asked, curious in spite of herself. She was pretty damn sure that was the first time she'd ever heard anybody say something like this.

He shrugged. "I didn't want it to be the basis of a relationship," he admitted.

Just then Mason walked in front of them, holding two beers. "After that show," he said, "I think you both deserve these."

Penny rolled her eyes at him. "Thanks." She took one. She watched as Warrick reached for his next one too. "I think that means you're ahead of me on the beer count."

"You were just very generous and shared yours," he said with a grin.

"If that's what you call it." She popped the top on hers and took a drink. She was still muttering over his words. "How's that working out for you?"

"How's what working out?" he asked, sliding her a sideways look.

Knowing Mason was fairly close by, she kept her voice low. "Celibacy. Trying to find a real relationship."

"Strange. Different. Nowhere near as exciting."

She could see that. Sex was often heated overwhelming passion. Fun, but then when gone, often a hollowness was left behind. "Would you recommend it?"

He shrugged. "Only if you're the kind of person who's okay being alone. Because often, if you're celibate, you're going to be alone."

"And here I thought a woman would say that."

"I think women do say that a lot, and I think you're right. It's less common for men to think that way. But it certainly is the way I've been thinking."

She took a sip of her beer and settled deeper into his arms. "Am I hurting you?"

He grabbed her hips, placing her slightly off to the side. "That's better." His voice was a little breathless.

She nodded. They sat there in the quiet for a long moment. "Is that why you kissed me?"

"Is *what* why I kissed you?" He stared at her in confusion.

Her lips twitched. "Yeah, that wasn't very clear was it?"

He shook his head. "No. Why the hell do women always have to question everything after a kiss?"

"I don't have to question everything after a kiss," she said. "But you've got to admit that, as a first kiss, ours wasn't exactly common or normal."

He nodded. "So what is your question? What do you want to know?"

"If you kissed me like that because you've been celibate for so long."

He froze, twisted slightly so he could see her, caught her chin so she was looking up at him and said, "Are you really asking if I'm so starved for sex that that was just an over-the-top kiss because I'm desperate?"

She frowned. "No. I'm not sure *desperate* is the word but maybe … *hungry*."

His eyebrows shot up. "I'm definitely hungry. But apparently it's you I'm hungry for. And that means I need my head examined."

She stared at him, hating to feel hurt. She understood what he meant though, as five minutes earlier they'd been fighting like cats.

Then, as if realizing what he'd said was inappropriate—or at least came across in a way he hadn't intended—he said, "Sorry. I don't mean to make it sound like you're not somebody I would choose, but you have to admit we haven't been exactly lover-like."

"*Lover-like*," she said, tasting the word slowly, rolling it around in her mind. "No, definitely not." Her voice was purposefully cheerful. "Maybe sworn enemies, yes."

"Definitely on two sides of an issue." He nodded in agreement.

"Two sides of a counter, for sure," she said, chuckling, parroting him.

"I really want that damn paperwork done and off my plate."

She nodded. "So do I. Because, if we don't do it properly, it ends up on my plate for way too long."

"Everybody says you're such a sweetheart and will help. And yet you never help me."

"You never asked for help."

He glanced down at her. "And yet you knew I was struggling."

"Yeah, sure did. But look at the job I do, and look at the men I deal with. Most of them are blockheaded, macho mouths who never ever, ever think they need help." She knew she'd hit home when he winced and turned his gaze away. "So the last thing I'll do is help you if you can't ask for help."

"Are you telling me that everyone else who deals with you, who says you're an absolute sweetheart, who got your assistance to fill out those forms, asked for your help? They came right out and asked you directly for help?"

"I don't know about everyone," she said cheerfully, "but lots of people did."

He sighed. "I might have a problem with asking for help," he admitted.

"*Might?*"

He glared at her.

She shrugged. "See? We're back to that temper again."

At that, he laughed. "Talk about a temper. You're a fine one to talk."

"Yep, I have a hell of a temper," she said. "But I wouldn't hurt a fly."

"You punched me. Three times."

It was her turn to wince. "I know. I don't quite understand why that happened. I've never hurt anybody in my life."

"Then you pick on me."

"You hurt me," she muttered.

He froze again, turning to look at her. "I'm sorry." His tone was low. "I didn't mean to."

"What you said to Mason though, that wasn't very nice."

He nodded. "But it's how I felt."

She thought about that and then said, "Well, I guess honesty is worth something."

"Hell, yeah, at least with me. I'll always be honest."

She'd had relationships where a couple men had said, "I'll call you in the morning," and, of course, she had never heard from them again. Those were lies. But then she thought of her last boyfriend, who'd said he was staying at a friend's, when what he meant was, he was staying at *her* friend's house. In her bed. Those were bigger lies. And she considered all the times she'd been hurt because of those lies and deceptions. "Honesty is worth a lot. It's very hard for me to trust people."

"That's because you have to have an honest relationship for trust to develop."

"I'm not sure I've had one of those before."

"Exactly. Hence the celibate part too."

She sighed. "That sounds fun and all, but I do like sex."

A rumble ran up his chest, but he managed to control it before it came out as an amused laugh.

She glared at him.

"I do too," he said gently. "I'm just choosing the time and place a little more carefully."

Then Tesla walked over. "Is it safe to talk to you two now?"

"Sorry about that," Penny said. "I don't normally make a display of myself."

Tesla flashed her a beautiful smile. "Best be yourself from the get-go," she announced. "Saves a lot of time and trouble sorting through the layers of who you really are later."

Warrick stared at her in surprise. "That's very insightful."

"Oh, I read it somewhere," Tesla confessed. She grinned at them. "Do you think you can help Mason with the steaks now?"

Penny tried to get back up again, but Warrick kept his arm around her. "I can, or somebody else can," he said. "Are you short on men?"

Tesla snorted. "Nowadays we're never short on men."

Just then Corey stepped forward, his grin a mile wide as he studied the two of them on the chair. "That's all right. I'll take Warrick's place. He's obviously busy at the moment."

At that, Penny struggled again to get up, but Warrick clamped his arm tighter around her and pulled her closer to him.

"Relax," he muttered and nodded at Corey. "Thanks." He looked over at Tesla. "Is there anything you need help with?"

She was trying to smother a grin. She shook her head. "I'll let you know when dinner is ready." She took off, chuckling.

Warrick glanced back at Corey to see his grin was still huge as when he gave Warrick a thumbs-up. And then Corey walked over to Mason, and the two of them layed the steaks on the hot grills.

"We have about six minutes," Warrick said, "and then it'll be food time."

"How can you tell?" she asked suspiciously. "That's a very specific time frame."

"Steaks, if they're done right, take about three minutes on each side. Of course, I like mine on the medium-rare side."

"So you're gonna let me out of your arms in six minutes?"

"I have to," he said. "It's pretty damn hard to eat a steak with one hand."

She smiled. "Unless we work as a team. I could cut it,

and you could eat it."

"Sounds a whole lot better than being at odds with each other."

She agreed. He let his arm relax, and she shifted slightly as she twisted a little more to look at him. "Do you think he's right?"

"Who?"

"Tanner," she said. "I heard him talk about the reason you kept coming in to see me."

He stared at her, flummoxed. "Honestly I don't know. I don't want to insult you, but I didn't think so."

But there was almost relief inside her as she agreed. "It confused me because, if that's what you were doing, and that's what I was doing, why were we playing games?"

"I'm not much of a game person," Warrick said.

"Neither am I." She thought about it for a minute. "But then I'm not big on trust, remember?"

Warrick nodded. "Since my girlfriend broke up with me after a three-year relationship, I guess I'm not either."

"So probably we should agree that *maybe* that's what we were doing, but we wouldn't want to think that's what we were doing." For her, that was an offering of an olive branch. But did he understand that?

He studied her, and the smile that dawned was enough to steal her breath away.

He nodded slowly. "I agree. So what are we doing about it?"

She smiled as her olive branch had been accepted. "We could try lunch sometime. Or even coffee."

His lips twitched. "Or we could try coffee one day, lunch the next day and dinner the day after that."

She glared at him in mock horror. "That might be a little too far, too fast," she joked.

"You're right, but it's better than jumping straight into bed."

She stared at him for a long moment, her lips twitching as she tried to hold back a big grin. She leaned forward and said, "After that last kiss, I'm not so sure about that." She hopped up. "I'll see if the ladies need any help." And she raced inside.

CHAPTER 2

MONDAY MORNING, PENNY was in her office when a phone call came through. "Warrick is here to see you."

Her heart jumped, and then she tried to school the silly smile off her face. She got up, grabbed a pen and walked out front. Warrick stood at ease at the counter. His gaze lit up when he saw her, and then immediately a shadow moved across his face. She understood how he felt. They hadn't exactly had the easiest beginning.

She smiled. "I hope you have the paperwork."

He shrugged. "I need help."

That startled a laugh out of her. "Come into my office, and let's take a look." She snatched up his paperwork, studying it as she walked back to her office with him following. She motioned toward a chair. "Go ahead and sit down."

She walked around to her side of the desk, sat on her chair and went through the paperwork. At least, if she focused on it, she might manage to get through this. All she wanted to do was hop back into his lap and let him give her a kiss like he'd given her before. She'd been unable to think about anything else since.

She worked her way through the pages, asking him questions about the couple boxes he had left blank. Before she knew it, it was done. She flipped it around and put an *X* on the signature line. "Sign here."

He signed it and looked at her. "Is it over?" he asked with relief, his expression hopeful.

She nodded. "It's good." She put it back on her desk. "Now you're off the hook, at least until we get this processed."

He sagged back in his chair and grinned. "May I take you out for lunch as a thank-you?"

She stared at him. "You may take me out for lunch but not as a thank-you."

He frowned. "Why not?"

"I don't want anything to make it sound like it was a bribe to do my job."

He nodded in understanding. "Well, I came in because it's almost lunchtime. So, if you're free, maybe we can go now."

She glanced at her calendar and nodded. "I think I can do that." Grabbing her jacket and purse, she walked him back to the outer office. It was empty except for Sally off in the corner. Penny called out, "Sally, I'm heading out for lunch."

Sally didn't even look up. But then Sally was sixty-five and working her last thirty days until she got to retire.

In the elevator, Penny and Warrick were silent. As they walked through the lobby, Warrick asked, "Where would you like to go?"

She glanced at him. "Did you have a place in mind?"

He shook his head. "Not really. But I'm always up for a burger."

"Of course you are," she said drily. "That's definitely man food."

"Nothing wrong with man food," he protested.

"No. But we could go to a place where there's man food and woman food."

"Don't tell me that you want us to eat rabbit food?"

At that, she laughed. "Well, at least I like a salad with my burger."

"I think you can get that at the man places I go."

She shrugged. "Maybe, maybe not." Just as they walked outside, she said, "If we're driving, we need to take my car." She pointed at his cast-covered foot.

He glared at it and nodded. "I forgot. I got dropped off as it is."

She laughed. "Come on. My car is over here." She led the way to a small Kia.

He got into the front, feeling like the sides were closing in on him.

She motioned at the seat and said, "Push back so you can get some leg room."

He adjusted the seat backward and that helped some.

She turned on the car, pulled out into the traffic and headed toward Bob's Burgers.

"How did you know I was talking about this place?" he asked when they pulled into the parking lot.

"It's very much man food." She laughed.

It was also very busy. They had to wait a good ten minutes for a table. When they finally sat down, one of the waitresses walked over with menus and said, "Hey, Penny. Haven't seen you in a while."

"Hi, Kathy. How you doing?" She exchanged pleasantries with the waitress whom she'd known for a couple years. "May I have a burger with a Caesar salad?"

Kathy nodded, wrote it down and turned to look at

Warrick. He ordered the house burger and fries. She took the order and disappeared. Just as they were about to start a conversation, she returned with coffee.

And instantly the awkward space that they'd been in before returned.

When Warrick's phone chimed, he pulled it out, looked at the message and said, "An officer lost his temper and emptied his handgun at stationary cars on base this morning, The MPs are trying to track him down but say it's possible he got off before security locked it down."

She raised an eyebrow. "Really? I hope they catch him fast."

"Me too."

"Is Mason on base himself?"

Warrick nodded. "He is at the moment and will keep us in the loop. Not to worry."

Just then her phone went off. She glanced at it. "It's my boss. He said there's a shooter somewhere close by. He heard the man escaped the base. He wants to know where I am." She sent a text back as to where they were and frowned. "How often does this happen? Maybe once a year?"

"It's been a little more often than we'd like, but, yeah, once a year maybe."

But something was in his tone. She glanced at him. "Did you know about this?"

He shrugged. "I heard a rumor this morning from one of the men in my unit. But it was never backed up."

"A rumor?" she asked, her tone low. "What kind of a rumor?"

"That somebody went on a rampage this morning. He then disappeared, and the base was looking for him."

She thrummed her fingers on the tabletop and studied

him. "But obviously you didn't know it would escalate."

"Of course not," he said. "Unfortunately there's been a lot of escalation lately. An awful lot of very unhappy people are out there."

She thought about that. "I think they're unhappy all over the world."

"I know. With all this unrest, I'm hoping to get back on my feet before my unit heads out for any missions. I'd hate to be sidelined with medical issues."

"How long for the ankle?"

"A couple weeks." He flashed her a smile. "Maybe faster if I can get in to see the doctor once that paperwork is processed."

She laughed. "Could've done that days ago."

He nodded.

Just then Kathy returned with their orders and asked, "Did you hear about a shooter?"

Penny nodded. "Hopefully they've caught him by now," she whispered.

The waitress nodded, disappeared and came back with ketchup a moment later. She said, "You take care of yourself."

Penny nodded. "You too."

"I can't see this having anything to do with either of you," Warrick said. "Although, if this guy's got to fill out paperwork like I did, I can see him getting mad enough to kill someone."

It wasn't a very good joke. Particularly considering the offices where she worked were near the base. Many servicemen and women from the base came through her claims processing division when they required more specialized medical care than the navy could provide locally. As long as the shooter was on base, then she was free and clear. "Still, it's not good news."

"No, it isn't." Warrick picked up his burger and took a big bite.

She realized he was right. They could deal with only so much at one time. And right now, there wasn't time to do anything. They didn't know anything yet. They would find out soon enough.

She'd just finished her burger when her phone went off. She wiped her hands and face, took a quick sip of water and then answered. "Hello."

And her boss's voice was strident. "Are you still at Bob's Burgers?"

"Yes. Why?"

"The shooter has taken some hostages."

"Who?"

"A couple doctors, a nurse and a patient at the hospital."

"So what's that got to do with me?"

"He mentioned you specifically. So the cops are looking for you."

"What? Who mentioned me?" she asked in bewilderment. "And I haven't heard from the cops."

"You will. I gave them your number. As to who's asking for you—it's the shooter."

"Why?" she asked, raising her horrified gaze at Warrick, who was obviously listening in. She held the phone out a little bit more so he could hear more clearly.

"He says you need to get your ass down there. Or he'll take out the patient first."

"Who's the patient?"

Her boss sighed. "It's Nina." And her boss hung up.

"Who is Nina?" Warrick asked in a hard tone. He put

down his french fries fast, as if realizing they were leaving in seconds.

She stared at him. "A coworker who was in a really bad relationship."

"And what do you have to do with it?"

"I'm not sure. I didn't even know she was in the hospital." She turned to look around the restaurant.

Just then the waitress came racing back. "Here's your bill."

Penny looked at Kathy, confusion on her face. "How did you know?"

Warrick said in a low tone, "I waved for the bill after that call."

She nodded blankly as her phone rang again. Sure enough, it was the cops asking her to join them at the hospital.

"We have security set up. Identify yourself, and you'll be let through." The policeman hung up, leaving her staring at Warrick.

He got up, tossed enough money on the table to cover the bill and reached out a hand. "Come on. Let's go." He led her outside to the car. He stopped, then said, "Give me the keys."

She looked at him in surprise. "I can drive."

He shook his head. "You can explain while we go."

Mute, she handed over the keys and got in on the passenger side. Maybe it was for the best after all. She was still adjusting to the news. He got into the car, pushed the seat back for more legroom, started the engine and reversed the car out of the parking lot. "Tell me about Nina."

"She was engaged to a naval officer," Penny said. "But he was very abusive."

"How abusive?"

"He threatened her with a knife, punched her in the face a couple times, broke her ribs."

"And she stayed with him?"

A wealth of disbelief resided in his voice, and Penny understood because she'd had that conversation with Nina several times, trying to convince her to leave George. "I know it's hard to understand why an abused woman goes back to her abuser," she muttered. "The thing is, the last time I convinced her not to go back."

"Okay, now we're getting down to the real reason you're the one involved."

She shook her head. "I don't know about that. There's no reason for him to want to see me." But she knew on the inside there was. "Nina must have told him something about me."

"If he's holding her hostage along with a couple doctors and a nurse at the hospital, then that would make sense."

"Nothing like this ever makes sense," she said. "I tried to convince her for years to leave him. And it was always the same story. *He loves me. He needs me. He'll never do it again.*"

"What was the trigger this time where she did leave him?"

"He broke two ribs," she said. "I convinced her to leave, but she was walking and talking and definitely not in the hospital the last time I spoke to her."

He shot her a glance as they sped through traffic. "Do you think she went back?"

"I hope not. But it's possible," she admitted. "It's also possible he tracked her down and beat her up."

"But didn't kill her. She managed to get to the hospital, and he came after her again?"

Penny shrugged. "You know as much as I do."

As they approached the security perimeter, he pulled up. When the police officer walked over, Warrick explained the gunman was asking for Penny.

The police officer nodded, picked up his radio and then motioned to him. "Head toward the hospital. They're expecting you."

Penny asked in a worried tone, "What does that mean?"

"It means, they're looking for this vehicle. We'll pull over when they tell us to. Then we'll get out. We'll do whatever they say."

"What if the policeman wants me to go inside the hospital?"

"They won't let you," he said. "They won't put another person in danger."

"But I can't let George kill those other people," she cried out.

He shot her a look. "Are you skilled in any manner that'll stop this from happening?"

She shook her head. "No, I work in the medical department. I'm a clerk. Okay, maybe a little bit above a clerk," she said, trying to muscle up a smile. "But I'm not a soldier. I'm not in any way armed or skilled with weaponry. I don't have a clue how to deal with a hostage situation."

"Which is why we'll follow everything they tell us to do," he said calmly. "Trust in the system."

"And sometimes that gets the hostages killed," she muttered. "Nina doesn't deserve that."

He didn't say anything. She hoped he wasn't judging Nina for being in the situation she was in. It was also just as possible that George had tracked her down and beat the crap out of her. If she'd managed to escape and get medical attention, he could have again tracked her down to the hospital as well.

"Are they still engaged?"

"I'd like to think not, but she did refer to him still as her fiancé."

"That implies she's still emotionally attached to him."

"I know. She always kept making excuses for him."

"That's also very common in that situation."

There wasn't a whole lot she could say to that.

As they drove nearer to the hospital, a police vehicle drove up beside them and motioned for them to follow. Warrick quickly fell in behind him. They drove around behind a large barricade. There were vehicles, armed men and crowds kept behind the barricade with what appeared to be some communication system setup in the front.

"Wow, I didn't expect this," she said. "For some reason I thought this would be pretty low key."

"This is low key," he said curtly. "Stay with me when you get up there."

Startled, she looked at him. "Why?"

"I don't want them pushing you to do anything you aren't comfortable doing. If they think you're alone, they might try to push your emotional buttons a little more."

She frowned at him. "I want to help. I want to get Nina out of there."

"I get that. But, in this instance, you're not alone. Remember that."

She wasn't exactly sure what he meant by that, but she was willing to go along with it. She got out of the vehicle, and one of the men walked over, asked her to identify herself. When she gave him her name, he said, "Come with me please."

She turned to Warrick, and the officer pointed to the others to stop him. And she realized that she wasn't comfortable going without him. She understood this was a chaotic situation, but Warrick was right. The last thing she wanted was to go into this alone.

"He's with me," she said in as firm a voice as she could manage. "Warrick stays with me."

The officer in front of her glared at Warrick, who stood there with his arms across his chest. Two more officers stood at his side. Everybody froze, waiting for officer to give an order. Finally he nodded. "Fine, he can come with you."

WARRICK DIDN'T SAY it out loud, but in his mind he was muttering, *Damn right I'm coming with her.* He fell in step at her side, and she slid her fingers into his hand. He clasped hers firmly and smiled at her. "It'll be fine."

She didn't appear to believe him. They walked up behind a large van and several other vehicles. Another man turned and looked at her. "Are you Penny Thornton?"

She nodded. "Has he said what he wants?"

"He wants you."

"Did he say why?"

"He blames you for some reason."

Her shoulders sagged, and Warrick understood exactly. The man looked at Penny and asked, "Why does he blame you? What does he blame you for?"

She glanced at Warrick, her shoulders straightening, and said, "He beat the crap out of Nina. He's been abusing her for years. I convinced her to leave him."

"When was this?"

"Six days ago," she answered. "Approximately," she added hastily.

Warrick watched and listened as the man asked several more questions. But she didn't have a whole lot of answers. He glanced at Warrick. "Do you know these people?"

Warrick shook his head. "Nope, I don't."

The officer frowned, his gaze going from one to the other. Warrick placed a large hand on her far shoulder, gently tugging her toward him so she stood right in front of him. She came willingly.

"Will you talk with him?"

She nodded. "Absolutely. I want to do anything I can to help. I don't want him to hurt her anymore."

The officer nodded. "We heard gunfire, so we're not sure if it's too late for that."

Warrick winced. If that was the case, they might as well storm in there and take out the gunman. But it was a hospital. And that meant an awful lot of innocent people were in a vulnerable position.

The officer brought out his cell phone. When it was answered inside the hospital, he said, "Penny is here." He turned to Penny. "He wants to talk to you." He held out the phone.

It was on Speaker. "Hello?" she said. "George, is that you?"

"What the fuck did you tell Nina?" he cried out. "She said she's leaving me."

"You keep hurting her," Penny said. "You know that's not … nice." She stumbled over the word as if realizing it was a weak word but couldn't come up with something else.

"Nice?" he roared. "She says the damnedest things. Things that hurt me too. So, of course, I hit back and hurt her. If she would smarten up and not always lash out at me, it wouldn't be so bad," he protested.

Of course he had the typical blindfold view of somebody who wanted everything his way and was prepared to beat up people to get it.

"You need to let everybody go," she said. "You're in a hospital. You'll hurt people."

"Since I'm in a hospital, and I'm going to hurt somebody, we're in the right place, aren't we?" he said sarcastically. "I want you in here. I want you to tell Nina what you told her was a lie. That you want her to come back to me."

Warrick shook his head. "You have to be careful."

She hesitated and looked over at the officer. He shook his head too and mouthed no.

"I can't come in," she said. "The officers won't let me."

"Well then, you tell them you are either allowed to come in or I start shooting people. Remember what you just said. This is a hospital. I'm not short on targets. You've got five minutes to decide." And he hung up.

She handed the phone back. "For what it's worth, I do think he'll shoot people."

The officer nodded, but he was obviously in a quandary. "If you go in there, he's likely to shoot you."

She nodded. "I know. But he's also got a lot more people in there to shoot if I don't show up. Let me go in."

"No," Warrick said, his voice hard. "It won't help Nina to have you get killed too."

"But if there's anything I can do to stop him from shooting the others …" she said, letting her voice trail off.

"Then I'm coming with you," Warrick snapped.

She stared at him. "Why would you do that?"

"Because I'm at least equipped to take him down if I get

an opportunity."

"He's likely to shoot you as soon as he sees you. Half the time I want to shoot you myself," she cried out.

He glared at her. "Definitely not the time. When we go in there, you're gonna follow my instructions right down the line."

She glared at him. "You're not the boss."

He poked her in the shoulder. "When we go in there, you will listen to everything I say. You'll do that, right?"

She turned to the officer and said, "Don't let him come in."

The officer stared at Warrick. "I want your name, rank, and why it is you think you should go in there."

When Warrick explained who he was and the training he'd gone through, the officer was already nodding.

"You might be our best chance. We've got snipers trained on the windows, but we need a clear shot. You'll have to maneuver him over toward that far window. I don't care how you do it, but, if we can get a clear head shot, we'll take him out."

Warrick nodded. "That's fine. If I can't take him down, I'll do the best I can to get him to where you can."

"You give us that, and we'll take the kill shot."

Warrick studied him for a long moment. "No taking out innocents. If you take out the wrong man, we'll all be dead."

"I know that." The officer walked to the front line and said, "These two are going through."

Instantly the men parted.

With his hand now clasping Penny's, Warrick asked, "Are you okay?"

"Yes, but you shouldn't be coming with me." She motioned to his foot. "You're injured. You won't be any help."

He snorted. "Even with my damn leg as it is, I'm twice the man that asshole is. You don't worry about me. I've got more tricks up my sleeve than that guy will ever know."

She shook her head. "You realize we'll both likely get shot as soon as we walk through that door."

"Not if he wants to get out of here alive, we won't be," Warrick said calmly.

But he also knew that too often the guys didn't want to get out alive. All they wanted was to create chaos, have a voice, and then they were happy to take out as many people around them as they could. Warrick would do his best to stop that. But he also had to take down this asshole—or at least get him in a position where a sniper could. Warrick understood the logistics of the problem, but first he had to convince this asshole that Warrick had a reason for coming in. "Make damn sure he thinks I'm your boyfriend," Warrick said.

"Why would I lead my boyfriend into a scenario like this?" she asked. "If I loved you at all, I'd do my best to keep you outside."

"Which, considering you've already tried to keep me out," he said with an interested tone, "means maybe you do love me, at least a little bit."

She snorted. "In your dreams."

"Sweetheart, you're already in my dreams."

They neared the front door. She reached up and knocked.

He looked at her. "Are you expecting him to answer that?"

She shrugged. "I don't know. I've never been in a position like this."

Just then the door opened, and standing far enough back

that Warrick couldn't lunge for him was a man holding a semiautomatic rifle. Warrick studied the rifle, looked at the man and said, "George, I presume?"

The rifle was raised and pointed at his chest. "Who the fuck are you, and what are you doing here?"

Penny stepped in front of him. "You wanted me. He wouldn't let me come without him. He's my boyfriend."

George snorted. "Sounds like you need to get some sense knocked into you too." He motioned the two of them inside. He looked at Warrick, saw the foot and sneered. "You're injured. What she'd do? Beat you up?" His tone was mocking, but he made sure the rifle was trained on one or the other. George motioned for the two of them to walk in toward the ICU. "Nina is over there."

Warrick stayed at Penny's side as she walked forward in a straight line. She could see nurses sitting on the side of the hallway, their hands and ankles taped. Nobody appeared to be injured; they all just stared, their gazes huge. They were so hopeful she was coming to rescue them, when, in actual fact, there was a good chance she would be joining them.

She pushed aside the designated curtain, and there was Nina, lying in the bed, her face black and purple. Penny raced to her side.

Nina took one look and started to cry. "You shouldn't have come," she said, sobbing. "You were so right. He's nuts. He said he lost his temper this morning because of me and shot up some cars on the base, then came after me."

Penny gently stroked her friend's face. "Hush. Don't talk like that."

"She better talk like that," came the voice at the end of the bed.

It was all Warrick could do not to give the man a hard

smack, but the rifle was pointed at Penny. Just one slight move on the trigger, and both Penny and Nina would likely be dead.

Penny straightened and turned to glare at him. "George, is this how you want her to love you?"

George drew his brows together. "What are you talking about?"

She pointed to Nina's face. "You did this. You beat her up. Look what she looks like now."

George shrugged. "She'll heal. That's just bruising." He lifted the rifle tip again so it was a little higher, pointed it at Penny's upper chest. "Now tell her."

She clasped Nina's fingers.

Warrick only watched with half a mind. He was studying the layout of the cubicle, the hostages tied up on the chairs in the outer hallway. He estimated the height of everybody around and determined the only ones vertical were the three of them. Nina was in bed, slightly propped up. So everybody was below George's ribs, which meant, as long as George kept the rifle high, the only ones in the line of fire were Penny, Warrick and the asshole.

Warrick would be totally okay if George went down in the process. Preferably forever. Assholes who beat up poor innocent women didn't deserve a chance. Warrick just needed the right moment. He listened as Penny tried to speak the right words that would make the gunman happy.

But Nina was beside herself. "No, no, no. He hurt me," she cried out. "I don't want to be with him anymore."

If she'd been at all herself, she probably would have realized she had to be conciliatory and tell George that he was the best and that she would be everything he wanted her to be. But, as it was, she was so terrified she couldn't think of changing her position, and it was all Penny could do to calm her friend down.

"See what I mean?" George said in disgust. "That's what I brought you here for. Talk some sense into her."

"Well, maybe if you weren't pointing the gun at us," Penny said in exasperation, "I could get her to calm down."

George glared at her, raised his arm and shot into the ceiling. "Watch your tone, bitch."

Penny's shoulders and spine locked down. She glared at him, then faced Nina. "Calm down, Nina. Crying like this won't help."

But George did change the angle of the gun so it no longer pointed at the two women. Instead, he turned it directly on Warrick. "Get her to stop that fast," George roared, "or I'll shoot your bloody boyfriend myself."

Instantly she turned toward him. "If you do that, then I won't help you at all. I'll tell Nina to run away from you as far as she can get."

George spun the rifle back in her direction. Warrick realized what she was doing. As long as the gun wasn't pointed at him, she was happy. But the minute it turned his way again, she did something to bring attention to herself. He understood, but he didn't think she did. She obviously cared more than she was willing to admit.

Warrick stepped forward at an angle as if toward the bed, but it also took him closer to George.

She glared at George. "Now raise that at least a little bit so she doesn't feel she'll be shot if she says the wrong thing."

"Maybe she *is* getting shot if she says the wrong thing," he roared, his hands trembling from holding the weapon.

Warrick noted George's trembling fingers. Also his emotional state was ricocheting him back and forth. Something else Warrick understood. It was hard to stay emotionally stable when the world was sending you one way or another.

George had taken a major step in the wrong direction. There wouldn't be a happy outcome to this.

Nina continued to cry, but it was a quiet sob. Penny leaned down, wrapped Nina in her arms and gently stroked her hair. "Take it easy, sweetie. Just take it easy."

Warrick watched George out of the corner of his eye, and he seemed to calm down now that Nina was just sobbing, not saying all those things he didn't want to hear. In his own way he cared for Nina. He just didn't know how to make all this work.

George lowered the weapon yet again. It almost pointed to the ground. Nobody else was around but the three of them.

Warrick judged the distance between him and George as over six feet. Warrick would have to move fast, grab the rifle and take George down. Warrick returned his gaze to Penny to make sure George didn't understand what was happening, and just then Penny turned to look at him. He gave her a harsh short nod, and he jumped.

He crossed the six feet in a single leap, his gun hand reaching for the rifle, shoving it into the floor as it fired, using his boot to keep it there as his hard right fist smashed George's face once. George stared at him in shock, his eyes glazing over, and he slowly sagged to his knees and then fell facedown onto the hospital floor.

Warrick leaned down quickly, picked up the rifle and unloaded it. Afterward he checked George for a pulse, found he was out cold but fine. Warrick turned into the hallway to speak to the medical personnel tied up there and said, "I need something to tie this guy up with. Anybody got something?"

One of the nurses said, "There's medical tape in the top drawer of the nurses' station."

He pulled out the drawer, and, sure enough, there was good solid medical tape. He bound the guy's wrists, then his ankles. He walked over to the front door, pushed it open and yelled, "Coming out."

He stepped outside, and, with his hands held up in front of him, he said, "The gunman is down. We need the police in here now." He walked back inside, headed straight to the hospital bed, pulled Penny up and away from Nina and wrapped his arms around her.

She hugged him tight and whispered, "You did that so damn smoothly."

He chuckled, tilted her head up and said, "Told you that I'm good." And he leaned down and kissed her.

CHAPTER 3

PENNY WANTED TO return to her office, but Warrick was having nothing to do with it.

"At least let's go for a coffee first," he urged.

She stared at him, troubled. "I can't just miss the afternoon. I've work to do. You remember all those forms that have to be filled out? It's not just you. Lots of people need these forms done."

"I know that," he said, "but you've just been through an ordeal. Nobody will expect you to go back after that."

She was of two minds. She pulled out her phone and called her boss. "Crisis averted," she said in a low tone, hating to hear the weakness in her own voice. "I went into the hospital. Warrick came with me and disarmed the gunman."

Her boss shrieked. "What? Who's Warrick?"

She gave him a brief explanation. "I was coming back to the office, but Warrick doesn't want me to. And I have to admit, I'm feeling a little shaky."

Swiftly her boss said, "Don't. Don't come back. Take the rest of the afternoon off. You'll probably have to make a statement anyway. So that'll take time."

She winced. "Yeah, I know. I'm not thinking clearly. I probably should do that first. Warrick suggested we go for coffee, and then see how I felt."

"Do your statement, go for coffee. Or just go home, put on a pot and relax."

She put her phone away and turned to Warrick. "He reminded me that we'll have to give statements."

Warrick nodded. "Stay here. I'll talk to the police." He walked over and had a short conversation with one of the men in charge. He nodded a couple times, then came back. "We can do the statements right now." He hooked his arm through hers and nudged her toward where the officers stood.

They asked her a few questions, wanting to know exactly what had happened, what she knew about the relationship between Nina and the gunman. Penny was as honest and open as she could be, but every question exhausted her, feeling more worn down by the minute. By the time she was done, she couldn't control the trembling in her legs.

Warrick, as if sensing how close to the end she was, wrapped an arm around her shoulders and said, "If you're done, I need to take her home."

The officer bent a little closer, took a look at her, likely saw the pale skin and the wide pupils. "Do you need medical attention?"

She managed a wide smile and shook her head. "No. I didn't get hurt. I may be a little in shock."

He nodded understandingly. "After adrenaline comes the low. Go home and rest up. If you think of anything else important, you can always contact us. He pulled a card from his pocket and gave it to her. Then he nodded at Warrick. "You guys can leave."

Warrick squeezed his arm around her shoulders and nudged her toward the vehicle. "I'll drive," he said.

She shot him a look. "I'm not an invalid, you know."

"Of course you aren't an invalid," he said, "but that doesn't mean I can't help you."

She smiled. "Thank you."

"I'm staying with you at home to make sure you're okay. Do you want to pick up coffee on our way or put on a pot there?"

She thought for a moment and said, "I'd like to put on a pot and sit on my little balcony and recuperate."

He nodded. "Perfect."

It was a short drive to her home, but it still felt like it took forever. At least fifteen or twenty minutes. By the time they pulled up in front, she was more than a little exhausted. They walked together to the front door.

She was amazed at how heavy her legs felt, how much effort was required for every step. She managed to get to the front of the apartment building where she fished for her keys in her purse. They walked toward the elevator, got in, and, when they got off on her floor, she handed him her keys without a word.

He took them, read the number stamped on the key, walked toward her apartment and unlocked the door. "How long have you lived here?"

"Four years," she answered. "It's not a bad place to be."

"Second floor is not the safest, but it's way better than the first floor."

That surprised her. "I get why the first floor is bad news, but why is the second one also bad?"

"Because a lot of men are quite capable of climbing up to the first balcony." He stepped out on her balcony, motioning for her to come beside him. They looked down to the ground below. "See that grassy ridge? It would take nothing for somebody to reach the balcony from there."

"That's if they were already in here," she said. "But if they're trying to access my apartment by the balcony, surely that's not so easy."

He glanced at her and smiled. "I could be inside this apartment in less than five minutes."

She frowned at him, obviously not believing him.

"You want me to prove it?" She hesitated, and he smiled. "You stand right here."

Only after he'd gone did she remember his foot. He shouldn't be doing any of this shit. She went to call for him, but, of course, he was long gone. As she stood here, waiting, he came around the side of her building.

The patio below her had very large planters. He hopped up on one of those. He had some small tool in his hand. The tire iron from her car? He hooked onto the bottom of her balcony and effortlessly gripped one of the railing bars. Pulling himself up, and using his legs, he kicked up and over.

She was dumbstruck. "Are you kidding me?"

He was breathing slightly heavy, but he smiled. "Now, if I'd been prepared and had the right tools, I could've made it up here soundlessly. And, of course, if I didn't have a bum leg like I have, I wouldn't have landed quite so heavily."

She glanced at the railing, then back at him. "You realize now you've destroyed any possibility of a good night's sleep in my apartment forevermore, right?"

He shook his head. "No, because hopefully it'll never happen."

"Now my mind is filled with possibilities of how it could happen," she murmured. She stared at the place where he came over the rail. "I can't believe it."

"It's not that hard. And, in a heartbeat, I'd be out on this balcony and gone again."

"Now *that* I can believe. But now that I have seen what you did, I'll never be able to unsee it," she complained.

He wrapped an arm around her shoulder. "Time to move?"

"I like this place." Her voice was grumpy, tired.

He nudged her toward the couch. "Sit down. Get your feet up and relax. You can direct me to where the coffee stuff is so I can put on a pot."

She summoned up the energy to tell him where the coffee was kept in the cupboard. He fixed everything and had the coffee dripping. He pulled cups from the cupboard and turned back to her. "Do you want any cream or anything?"

"You can fill mine with Bailey's," she said in a dry tone.

He turned to look at her. "Do you have any?"

She laughed. "No. It's not that bad. I'm just exhausted now."

"A normal reaction," he said, trying to comfort her with his words. "It'll all be good."

"How can it all be good? Did you see how fast you did that?"

"Did what?" he asked absentmindedly as he searched in her fridge for something.

"What are you looking for?"

"I was looking for something for you to eat. It's been hours since lunch, and you've been through quite a shock. A little bit of sustenance wouldn't hurt. Especially if it happened to have a bit of sugar in it."

"Cookies are in the cupboard beside the one that you got the coffee from," she said.

He found the airtight container, pulled it down and opened it. "Are these homemade?" he asked hopefully.

"Yeah, two days ago."

"Good to know." He brought the container to the coffee table.

"I used to always bake, but it's hard to cut down a recipe enough for just one."

"I've heard that from several other people. It's much more fun to cook or bake for someone. But, if it's just yourself, although it's nice to have good home-cooked food, it's a little hard to get motivated."

As soon as the coffee was done, he poured two cups and set them on the coffee table beside her. He sat to the left of her and clasped her hand in his.

She sagged a little deeper into the couch, just happy to be home. "You didn't answer me about how fast you acted."

"Well, of course I can't answer that. I do it automatically. It's not like I have to put much thought into it or check a timer. Don't forget how much training I have gone through."

She nodded and pushed gently against him. "Well, I'm very glad you were there."

"You're the one who insisted on going in to see a gunman who had a hate on for you."

"I couldn't let him kill her though, could I?" Her voice was faint. She could feel her eyes closing.

He gave her a gentle nudge. "Do you want a nap?"

She checked her watch and found it was four-thirty. "If I do, I'll never sleep tonight," she murmured. She straightened and gave her head a solid shake. "I'll try to get this coffee down. That should wake me up."

"Okay, that would help. Also get some sugar into you." He pushed the cookie tub toward her.

She reached in and pulled out a big fat one. She held it up and looked at it. "They are really good." She motioned at him. "Have some."

He snagged two. When he finally could speak, he said, "They are good. I'm all about home cooking."

"You can always cook or bake for yourself," she said.

"I could, but, like you said, it's kind of a waste. Besides, if I bake an entire batch of cookies, it leads me to eating an entire batch."

She understood. She had a hard time with that too.

After a few minutes he asked, "Do you feel any better?"

She took another sip of coffee, loving the way the warmth filled her stomach, giving her a little bit of comfort inside. "Yeah. I'm starting to…"

"He's behind bars now."

"They won't let him go, right?"

He shook his head. "I doubt it."

"It's not like he didn't do this in front of a lot of people," she joked. "I feel like I should contact Nina though."

"I don't know that we can contact her through the hospital. But I can always find out, see if I can get an update on her condition."

"If you could do that, I would be very appreciative." She looked up at him gratefully. "If there's any way I could visit her that would be even better."

He nodded. "Do you think you're up for it?"

"I want to be," she said. "It's way too early to go to bed, and, if I just stay here and relax, I'm likely to fall asleep."

He nodded. "That might not be a bad thing."

She sat back, sipping her coffee as he contacted the hospital for an update. Every once in a while he'd glance at her and nod.

"Okay. If there's any chance we can come tonight, I know Penny would love to make sure her friend is all right."

He smiled. "Good. That's perfect. Thanks. We'll be there at seven."

He ended his call, placed his phone on the coffee table and picked up his coffee. He twisted slightly on the couch so he could look at her. "She's doing okay. They're treating her for shock on top of her injuries, so they're keeping her in the hospital overnight at least."

"We can go see her?"

He nodded. "Seven o'clock."

"So just over two hours from now."

"Can you wait that long?"

She smiled. "Yes. Besides, by the time I have a couple more cups of coffee, I'll need food for all the slushing going on in my stomach."

"That's what I'm talking about," Warrick said. "But first we'll stay here and relax, and we'll let all that stress calm down."

"Are you used to dealing with people after a shock?"

"Not used to it," he said. "But I have certainly seen a lot of people in very difficult circumstances. And the resilience of the human spirit always surprises me. We can go through so much shit and come out totally fine on the other side."

"I hope so," she said. "I'm really worried about Nina."

"She will be fine. If she actually left him, and he caught her again, then of course she'll be terrified. But as long as he stays locked up, then she should do fine. I don't know how she'll handle a trial, if there is one. Because George is a naval officer and was shooting on the base, NCIS will work with the local police. The MPs on base did a full-on search for him there, but, after he escaped, the local police stepped in. Now that George is in jail, I can't say who gets jurisdiction."

Relieved, she sank back. "As long as he is in jail, that is

good to know."

"Nina'll need some support though."

She smiled. "Of course. That's no problem."

"There is also a good chance she may want to leave the area, depending on the circumstances of how he found her again."

"After watching you jumping on my balcony, I'm considering a move."

"That's not necessarily a bad thing either." His voice was cheerful. His phone rang just then. He picked it up and took a look at the screen. "It's Mason." With the phone at his ear, he said, "Mason, what's up?"

She listened in on Warrick's part of the Mason conversation.

"It's already hit the news here or at least a local grapevine. Yeah, she's a friend of Penny's. Her boyfriend was very abusive. Nina broke up with him, but he talked her into going to her house so they could talk and things turned ugly. Beat the crap out of her. She managed to escape, got to the hospital, and he tracked her down there. But then he turned his ire on Penny, thinking she's the reason his girlfriend was leaving him." He glanced at Penny.

She just smiled, put her empty coffee cup on the coffee table and curled up in the corner of the couch, listening to Warrick's soft voice. And drifted off to sleep.

"SHE'S ASLEEP NOW. We're at her place. She did really well in there. She had insisted that she go in and try to calm him down. Way too many people were in the hospital for him to start losing it."

"Good thing you were there," Mason said. "I'm surprised they let you in though."

"Back to Penny again. She didn't want to go in alone. And honestly, I didn't want to let her go in alone."

"Interesting. I'm hearing your and Penny's name a lot in this deal."

Warrick winced. "It's not what you think."

"Well, part of the gossip is the kiss at the end of the hostage situation."

A groan escaped Warrick's lips. "What would we do without gossip?"

Mason chuckled. "Well, I can tell you that Tesla's thrilled. She's known Penny for quite a while from their shared exercise classes at the Y. And Penny just never seemed to find a decent man. As far as Tesla is concerned, you're a decent man."

"I am a decent … What do you mean, as far as *she's* concerned? You sure as hell should be on the same wavelength in that regard."

Mason's laugh broke out free and easily through the phone. "Hey, that's not my deal. I don't assess my buddies as to whether they'd make great partners or not."

Warrick rolled his eyes. "Right, that's such a female thing to do."

"Anyway, what's the plan now? Is the crisis over?"

"It is," he said. "But Penny wants to visit Nina in a bit. They're keeping her in the hospital overnight. She was in pretty rough shape. I believe she's got a couple broken ribs. I'm not sure what else."

"I'm surprised Penny wants to return to the scene of the crime so fast."

"I think she'd do anything for her friend," Warrick said. "Not sure it has anything to do with the hospital or revisiting the spot where it happened as much as it's about making sure Nina is okay."

"Right. That makes total sense. Are you staying there overnight?" No humor was in Mason's tone now.

"Who's asking, you or Tesla?" Warrick asked in exasperation. "If I'm staying overnight, it would be to make sure she's fine."

"Sounds like a plan," Mason said, his voice cheerful. "How's the foot doing?"

Warrick didn't know how to answer that.

"Warrick?" Mason asked, his voice stern. "Did you reinjure it today?"

"No, I didn't reinjure it," he said gently, "but I'm sure the activities this afternoon weren't exactly helpful."

"As in, not conducive to healing?"

"Exactly," Warrick said. "But if I need an extra day then, at this point, it's not a big deal."

"Right, as long as you didn't hurt it so badly that you will be off it for several more weeks."

"No, Penny had the paperwork all filled out this afternoon, before we went out for lunch, so I'll get back to the doctor in the next few days."

"Oh, so you went out for lunch too?"

"Yes, it's the least I could do. I made her pretty miserable over those forms."

"Whatever reason works for you," Mason said cheerfully. "Tesla is calling me for dinner. You guys have a good evening, and, as long as George is locked up, she'll probably be okay. But you know what will happen if he gets loose."

"Not going to happen," Warrick said. "There were enough cops at that hospital this afternoon that I can't imagine anybody getting loose."

"Right. Take care of yourself. We'll talk in a few days." Mason hung up.

Warrick pocketed his phone, got up and poured himself another cup of coffee. If he was to babysit her while she slept, which was exactly what he wanted to do, then there was no reason not to have another cup of joe.

He sat back down again, grabbed the remote and turned on the TV. If there was any news coverage from this afternoon, he wanted to see it. As it was, he couldn't find anything on any channel.

He brought up the internet on his cell phone and took a look. The hostage situation was mentioned, but mostly the media was silent on this incidence. Maybe that was okay too. Never a good idea to give other criminals ideas or to toot the horn of the bad guys too loudly.

He put down his phone and snuggled in, shifting her so she wasn't lying in such an awkward angle, but stretching her out so she lay straight on the couch with her head in his lap. Sleep really was the best thing for her now.

When his phone rang again, he hoped it wouldn't wake her as he pulled it out to see Corey calling.

"What the hell?" was Corey's initial greeting.

Warrick grinned. "I know, right? Here I am, trying to take it easy, staying off my foot, just being a good calm citizen, and all hell breaks loose."

"That was pretty brave," Corey said. "Although I don't understand how they let you guys do it."

"I'm not sure they had a whole lot of choice. They were still waiting for somebody to make a decision when Penny more or less decided for everyone, said she was going in. She walked forward, and, of course, I wouldn't let her go alone."

"Didn't they call you back?"

"Sure. But when they understood who I was and with

her insistence on helping to protect all those other people in the hospital, well, you know what that's like."

"He could've shot her as soon as she walked through the door."

"I know. It did cross my mind as we went in."

"So I gather he wasn't really dangerous?"

"Everybody is dangerous in the right circumstances, as we know."

"But he was looking for attention?"

"No. What he really wanted was for Penny to convince Nina, his ex-girlfriend, to go back to him."

There was a hard silence, and then Corey said, "He really thought that would work?"

"Apparently. But, because he had a weapon, he held everybody hostage until Penny came."

"And then it wasn't hard to disarm him?"

"No. It really wasn't."

"You're lucky."

"I know." He glanced down at Penny still sleeping in his lap.

"And you and Penny?" Corey asked, much less than delicately.

"Everybody seems to be asking me that question," Warrick said.

"We're all concerned about you, dude."

"Let's just say, progressing nicely."

Corey chuckled. "Well, I can't really argue any of this if it puts the two of you on the same path." And he hung up.

Warrick had to agree. It wasn't exactly a typical courtship, but then, from what he'd seen with all his friends, typical hadn't worked out so well. Still this surviving-the-test-of-fire proved to be the best matchmaking system yet. And who was he to argue?

CHAPTER 4

PENNY AWOKE FROM her nap to find herself on the couch, her head on Warrick's lap, his arm wrapped around her chest. She twisted slightly so she could look up, finding him sitting, his head laying back. She couldn't see his eyes, but they were likely closed as his chest rose slow and steady.

She remembered bits and pieces of his phone conversation as she went under. She wondered if she could get up and move quietly enough that she wouldn't wake him. Her bladder insisted that she try regardless. She did her best sneaking out from under his arm and standing up. But, as soon as she turned to look at him, she saw his eyes were open, studying her.

She smiled. "I have to go to the ladies' room," she said by way of explanation.

He nodded. "I don't know if the coffee is still hot, but there should be some left, if you want to get a cup on your way back."

She walked to the bathroom, used the facilities and then took a moment to wash her face. The nap had done her a world of good, but she still felt groggy. It had been a hell of an afternoon.

She walked into the kitchen. The coffeepot had automatically turned off a while ago. She wondered how long she'd slept. She reached for her phone and realized she'd been asleep for just over an hour. "You should have woken me," she exclaimed. "I wonder if I'll even sleep tonight."

"You'll sleep," he said comfortably. "That nap was just enough to get you through the next four or five hours. Then you'll crash again."

She smiled as she sat down on the couch. "Well, it's almost six-thirty now. About time to leave and see Nina."

He nodded. "What do you want to do about dinner?"

She frowned. "I'm not really sure. We don't have time beforehand." She looked out at the evening sky. "You don't have to come with me, you know."

He smiled. "Nope, I don't," he said.

She studied him for a long moment. "You don't have to stay here with me either. I'm fine. You know that, right?"

He nodded but didn't say anything.

Realizing he would likely be stubborn, she turned to face him. "I'll probably come straight home after a visit with Nina, make a sandwich and just go to bed."

"That's probably a good idea."

"What will you do?"

He raised an eyebrow. "Does that mean I'm not invited to see Nina, come back here, have a sandwich and go to bed?" He was teasing her.

She could feel the heat flushing over her cheeks. She glared at him. "No. You're not."

"Ah," he said in a humorous voice. "Okay, in that case, I suggest we see Nina, and afterward we go out for dinner, and then I'll drop you back home again."

She frowned. But at least he was talking about leaving her alone at her place afterward. "I probably won't eat very much," she said.

"Nobody said you had to. But I highly doubt going to bed on an empty stomach is a good idea either. If you want, we can pick up some Chinese food and sit in one of the parks to eat."

"Or at the beach." She brightened. "That sounds pretty nice. Chinese food, pizza, a sandwich or something."

He nodded. "In that case let's head to the hospital, and then we'll go out and eat."

She glanced at her clothes. "If we're doing that, I'm changing. I'll only be a minute." She hopped up on her feet and walked over to the bedroom.

Once there, she closed the door and changed into something a little nicer, then grabbed a cardigan. If they were eating at the beach, the wind could come up, and it got quite chilly. She walked back out, slipped on her flats and said, "Two vehicles or one?"

"In order for there to be two," he said with a grin, "we have to go back to me not having my foot in a cast."

Her gaze went to the walking cast on his foot. "I keep forgetting," she confessed.

"And that's okay too," he said. "Keep forgetting. I can't stand the thought of it myself. I'll be grateful when it's gone."

"In that case I'm driving this time." Her voice was firm.

He shrugged as if it didn't matter to him.

She locked up the apartment and headed downstairs toward the parking lot.

Once in the vehicle, she directed it toward the hospital. "Do you think they'll still have crazy security?"

"No. I would think it's back to normal by now."

"I hope so. I'd like to never see that again." He didn't say anything, but then she remembered all the training he'd been through and the missions he did and realized this was stuff he saw on a daily basis. "How can you stand it? Seeing that side of humanity and dealing with it day in and day out, month in and month out, even year in and year out?" she asked.

"You never get used to seeing what evil mankind can dish out, but we learn to compartmentalize it, then to shoot some hoops, down a few beers, take a grueling run, swim, whatever. You have to be grounded in the reason why you're doing what you do, and then you realize that, day in and day out, there will always be a situation that needs your assistance. If people would stop fighting for the stupidest reasons, it would be a wonderful place to live. But, in the meantime, people are killing each other, and they need our help to make it stop."

"Yet it never stops," she muttered. She pulled up to the red signal light at the next intersection and stopped, waiting for it to turn green. She shivered lightly. "I didn't put on my sweater. I was expecting it to be warmer outside."

"It's not so much that it's cool," he said, "but you're still tired, still dealing with shock from this afternoon."

"It's amazingly debilitating."

"The minute you're afraid, you've given away all your power, and it's very hard to mentally deal with the crisis situation."

She thought about that. "Most people don't talk about giving away their power."

"More people should," he said shortly. "It's important to remain grounded. To understand what you're doing, why you're doing it. If you come from a victim's standpoint, you are incapable of doing anything or making a reasonable decision. You're too easily swayed by everybody around you."

"That hasn't really been an issue in my life yet."

"Good. Keep it that way." His voice came out almost determinedly cheerful.

"Do you have any family?"

"Yep, I do. I see them every once in a while but not too often."

"My family is all back East," she said. "I haven't been there for years."

"Not interested in seeing them?"

"My parents divorced after my brother's death. Both have since remarried. Both have families. I'm supposed to belong to both of them, but, in actuality, of course, I belong to neither."

"You don't sound too bothered by it."

"Not now. They divorced when I was eighteen after we lost my brother. They both remarried when I was twenty and twenty-one, respectively. It's an odd thing to realize how much everybody else has moved on. I know my parents still love me, but they have other priorities now, and I'm an adult. So it's not like I need anything from them."

"*Need* is one thing. Maybe *wanting something* is a different issue."

She shook her head. "I'm pretty happy out here on the opposite coast. I'm not sure I'm ready for little kids. And every time I think about them, and the brood they've produced, it's pretty scary."

"How many?"

"Three and four … respectively," she said.

He raised his eyebrows.

"Right. My father married somebody quite a bit younger, and he's the one with four now. My mom had another daughter, then twin boys. I don't think the twins were really in the plan, but life sometimes gets ya."

"Isn't that the truth?"

She pulled into the hospital parking lot and found an empty spot. As she got out, she said, "I hope Nina is okay."

"We'll find out soon." His tone was soothing.

She looked up at him. "Are you always so nice?"

"Is there another way I'm supposed to be?"

She shrugged. "Maybe nice is boring."

He snorted. "And yet, if I was yelling or screaming or hitting you, you wouldn't like it much either."

"No, of course not." She shrugged. "I'm being foolish."

"Right. I'd really like to get into the psychology of what you were asking about, but I'm not sure you know."

"What are you talking about?"

"I'm wondering if you're looking for negative traits in order to not like me as well."

His thinking was a little too close to the truth.

She picked up the pace, putting herself just ahead of him as they walked into the hospital. At least it kept her face out of his view. Interesting comment. There was something very different about Warrick. Maybe because he'd had just come out of a long-term relationship, but then she'd dated recently divorced men before who didn't have words of wisdom for her.

Warrick was definitely his own man.

She walked up to the receptionist and said, "Nina Foster. Do you have a room number for me, please?"

"Two twelve," the woman said with a smile. Her gaze went from one to the other. "You two were here earlier today, weren't you?"

Penny nodded. "Yes. Not much fun for any of us."

The nurse nodded. "No, it wasn't."

On the second floor they found Nina's room number and opened the door to see a ward of four beds. There were curtains around each of the sections. "Nina?"

"Over here."

Penny walked toward the end of the room and to the last curtain on the right. She stopped and smiled. "Hey. How are you feeling?" She bent to give her friend a gentle hug. She studied Nina's green and purple swollen face and winced. "I hope you are feeling better than you look."

Nina gave a choked laugh. "I look that bad, huh?"

For a moment Penny was not sure what to say. "Honestly I don't even know what to say, but it looks pretty rough."

"That's how I'm feeling too," Nina said as her gaze lifted to Warrick. She stared at him, and then, as if recognition hit, she beamed. "You're the man who took down my ex, aren't you?"

He nodded. "Yes. He's a pretty upset young man."

"He's an angry young man," Nina said ruefully. "About everything. It didn't matter whether it was his laundry that wasn't done, his supervisor who wanted him to do something shitty, his coworker treating him terribly, the guys teasing him, the sun wasn't shining … It didn't matter," she said. "He was always angry."

"I'm sure he'll get some help with that when he's in prison," Penny said gently. "Anger management is huge."

Nina sighed, her fingers busy pulling the sheet over her chest. "I hope he does. He's a good man inside."

Penny withheld judgment on that. An awful lot of men were angry at the world, but they didn't take it out on innocent bystanders, and they certainly didn't take a hospital hostage. "Did you talk to him at all?"

Nina raised her gaze. "He called me, and, not recognizing the number, I answered. I was at a coffee shop, trying to figure out what to do with my life, where to move. I guess he heard the background noise and recognized it. Next thing I know, he was in the coffee shop, standing in front of me. He wanted me to go home, just have a talk with him. He was calm and friendly, normal like. So I did. And of course that went badly." She clenched the sheets in her fingers. "I managed to run out of my house, screaming. He came after me, but the neighbors were already calling the cops. He disappeared. The cops brought me to the hospital. The next thing I know, he shows up here with a weapon." Tears rimmed her eyes. "I knew he had several weapons, he's always kept them locked up. It's not as if he can carry them around on the base. Besides, I never considered them an issue as I didn't think he'd ever get this bad."

"No, but you knew it was bad enough," Penny said. "I'm not trying to be heartless, but we can't wash this away as being one of his episodes."

"I know." Nina's voice was tearful, soft. "I was so hoping he would improve."

"Here, take a seat, Penny," Warrick said.

She turned to see he had placed two chairs close to Nina's bed so they could both sit down. She sagged gratefully into one. "I'm still really tired from everything that happened today too."

Nina squeezed her friend's hand. "Thank you so much for coming into the hospital. He kept saying he would get you here, and I knew the cops wouldn't add another hostage, but then, just like that, the two of you walked in, and I couldn't believe it. He seemed to be really surprised too."

"I didn't want to come in alone," Penny admitted. "And

Warrick wouldn't give me that option either."

Nina smiled, her gaze going from one to the other. "I didn't know you were seeing someone," she said. "But at least you found a protector and not an abuser."

Penny winced. "What will you do now?" She was trying to get Nina to focus on her future, not her past.

"I don't know. I finally called my mom and explained what happened. She's pretty upset. She wants me to go home. I'm not so sure I'm ready to do that."

"Where is home?" Warrick asked.

"Mexico City if I had a choice," Nina said with a smile. "It's a very different world there and I have some family there now."

"True, but it would get you away from everything that's happened here."

"I know. I can see going maybe for a week or two, but I'm not sure that's the life I want anymore. I have a decent job here. It pays well. I have friends. The problem with that is that he knows where I work and live, and who my friends are."

"You don't have to make a decision right away," Warrick said. "It's a good time to be sensible and give yourself a little time to recover and then make some decisions about your life."

After that there was some small talk, and then finally Penny stood. "We're going out for dinner. Then I'm going home and catching some sleep. Hopefully by tomorrow I'll be back to normal."

"What about our boss? Now we're both not at work."

"I already told him what happened today. He told me to take the afternoon off, but I'll be back at work tomorrow. It's Friday, and I have a bunch of paperwork I need to file and submit before the week is over."

Nina nodded. "I think I have more sick leave coming. I don't know."

"Talk to the boss. I'm sure he won't have a problem with you taking time off. You've been through a lot already. Besides that's the kind of paperwork we do, so, if you need a hand with it, you can let me know," she joked.

Nina waved goodbye, and Warrick and Penny headed outside.

Penny checked her watch. "That was only about forty minutes."

"Right, so it's still early." Warrick wrapped an arm around her shoulder and gently tugged her a little bit closer as they walked to the parking lot. "So Chinese, pizza or sandwich?"

"Chinese," she said. "In one of those take-out boxes with chopsticks."

Her decisiveness made him stop and stare at her.

She shrugged. "And I want to sit on a log and feel the wind in my hair. I want to watch the sun go down."

"Okay," he said with a smile. "I think I can handle that."

She chuckled. "Pretty sure you said you were damn good at everything."

He chuckled. "Challenge accepted."

HE DIRECTED HER to his favorite Chinese restaurant and said, "You sit here. I'll go in and get our orders."

"It'll take time though," she said. "We may have to wait ten or fifteen minutes. You only ordered it a few minutes ago."

He shook his head. "They are really fast here." And

without waiting for her to reply, he hopped out, closed the door and walked inside.

Even with a walking cast, he moved with a lion's grace. He was big; he was lean; he was muscled, and there was just so much power radiating from him. She was pretty damn sure George had taken one look and realized it was already over, and, even though he held the weapon, no way in hell he would get away from Warrick. She watched as he had a quick conversation with the clerk, and the next thing she knew, a large bag was placed on the counter, and Warrick was at the cash register taking care of the bill. He was outside and getting back into the vehicle in no time.

She smiled. "I thought you're supposed to be off your foot."

He chuckled. "I am. Who knows, besides you, that I'm not being as good as I should be?"

She rolled her eyes.

He said, "Now let's head to the beach."

There was a spot in her mind that she wanted to go.

On the way he pointed out a Starbucks. "Let's swing by there and grab coffees to-go."

They hit the drive-through and soon had hot steaming coffees beside them. She drove the last leg to the parking lot above the beach.

As she got out and collected the coffees, she said, "Can you walk in the sand in that thing?"

"Don't you worry," he said. "I'll be just fine."

She wondered if she'd insulted him. From his tone of voice, she thought she might have.

She deliberately headed toward a large log that overlooked a section of rougher beach area where the ocean slammed in waves against the big rocks, leaving seaweed behind. On the log they were far enough back to get a little spray from an exceptionally large wave, but most of the time they would be dry. She had her cardigan wrapped around her tight. She figured they could start on the log, and, if it got too cold, they could sit on the sand up against the log and be out of the wind more. She deliberately didn't watch Warrick's progress as she worked her way toward the log. She scrambled up on top, closed her eyes and sat with her face tilted into the wind and the remaining sunshine. Immediately she could feel the stress and tension of the day drifting off her shoulders. It felt so damn good to get out and have that fresh air and warm sunlight wafting over her.

When she heard him sit down beside her, she smiled and said, "Isn't this beautiful?"

"You're beautiful."

His words surprised her. She opened her eyes and smiled. "That's not quite what I meant."

"Maybe not, but it's what I meant." He opened the bag and pulled out a box with a little metal handle on the top and set it at her feet. Then he gave her a pack of chopsticks. At the same time he took his coffee from her hand and buried it partway in the sand, so it wouldn't fall over. Then he pulled out his Chinese food.

It looked like something still remained in the bottom of the bag, but he put it down on the other side of him. She followed suit with her coffee and then opened up her Chinese food. She didn't know what the heck he'd ordered, but the smell was intoxicating.

She took her first bite and moaned in joy. "This is perfect."

He chuckled, and they sat in amiable silence enjoying the moment.

Every once in a while she gave her head a shake and let the wind ripple gently over her face, her eyes closed. "I needed this tonight."

"It's always good to have something like this," he said. "There's a sense of wildness, a sense of freedom out here."

"*Freedom.*" She nodded, mouthing the word again. "I like that. That's exactly what it is." She went back to her Chinese food, and, when it was gone, she sighed and stared at her empty carton. "I guess I was hungrier than I thought."

"Are you still hungry?"

There wasn't any surprise in his voice. As if he'd expected her to polish off the whole thing. "I wouldn't normally eat that much," she confessed. "But I think you're right. After everything today, I have an appetite now."

"I'm almost done with mine." He took the last couple bites of broccoli and folded up the two empty cartons, put them back in the bag, then pulled out a tinfoil container with a cardboard top.

She stared at it. "More food?"

He took off the lid, and, sure enough, inside were several egg rolls.

"Oh, now that's a good idea."

Ignoring the chopsticks, she reached into the container and pulled out a big fat one. Then she picked up her coffee. With coffee in one hand and the egg roll in the other, she munched her way through it. And, when she was done with that, she had a second one. After that she was full. She waved the rest of them at him. "Those are all yours."

The wind had picked up. She pulled her sweater a little bit closer around her shoulders.

"Are you cold?"

She shook her head. "Not really. I was thinking, if I got

much colder, I could sit in the sand, but that will be cool too."

Just then a big gust blew through, and she shuddered and hunched a little lower. Warrick polished off the last of his food, cleaned up the garbage, turned so he was straddling the log, and then pulled her into his arms, under his windbreaker, so she was a little more protected from the wind.

Tucked against his chest like that, no way she could be cold. The man was a bloody furnace. She snuggled happily, let her head rest against his chest and smiled. It wasn't exactly what she thought the evening would bring, but she was all for this. "He won't get out, will he?"

"I hope not."

"I keep thinking he'll escape, or they'll let him off on a technicality or something stupid."

"The only way he could get off or get out is if he escaped."

"That doesn't bear thinking about. Poor Nina. She needs to heal and recover."

"So do you," he said. "There's never an easy answer after something like this."

She nodded and smiled.

They stayed like that, wrapped in each other's arms for at least another forty minutes. She kept thinking it was time to go home, but she never wanted to break the moment. She couldn't remember the last time she just sat and relaxed, enjoying being with a man.

When his phone rang, disrupting the silence of the evening, she shifted so he could pull out his phone. When he answered it, she felt the change come over him immediately. His body stiffened, and, though he kept an arm wrapped around her firmly and kept her tugged tightly against him, she could only hear his part of the conversation. But what she heard was enough to set her blood running cold.

She tilted back her head when he hung up and said, "Did I hear that?"

He nodded. "Yes. The asshole got loose."

CHAPTER 5

"**H**OW THE HELL is that possible?" she cried out.

"He was escorted to jail by two men. Somehow he managed to strangle both with his handcuffs on."

She stared at him in horror. "Are you saying he just killed two police officers?"

"And he now has their weapons." Warrick's tone was grim.

She shook her head. "Oh, no, no, no. That's not good."

"None of it's good," he said.

"What about Nina?"

"The hospital is on full alert. The police are sending extra men to help protect the staff and the patients at the hospital. They have even enlisted the navy's help to safeguard all those people. But that was a warning phone call for us. It's not just about Nina. It's also about you."

She stared at him and frowned. "But I did what he asked me to do," she said.

"No, in his mind you're responsible for Nina leaving him, then bringing me in, and I'm the one who took him down. You started this chain of events—in his demented mind. So now he's likely to come back after you, and he's likely, as we all know, to go back after Nina."

"Dear God," she whimpered. "This is not at all what she or I need."

"Given that scenario, I highly suggest I sleep on your couch tonight."

She brightened. "Now that would be something I'd really appreciate because he might show up there."

"Why's that?"

"Because he has been to my place. With Nina. He knows where I live."

"In that case, maybe we should go to my place," he said thoughtfully.

"Would he know who you are? Would he be able to check the navy's database and find out where you live?"

Warrick frowned. "If he had my training, the answer is *absolutely.* I'm not sure what his clearance is, but it's possible. He's going to be well trained regardless."

"So maybe we shouldn't go to either place," she said. "The last thing I want is to face him again."

"I'm not sure we'd be facing him at all," Warrick said quietly. "There's a good chance he'd shoot us in the back, instead of facing us, so that we can't see who it is or when to evade the attack."

She stared at him. "Why would he do that?"

"Because now he's got some dedicated purpose to his madness. I don't think he wants to reconcile anymore. He's moved from wanting Nina to be with him to killing two cops."

"Maybe we need to figure that out. We need to go where he isn't."

"That's a good point." He pulled out his phone and sent several texts. "I'm trying to get more details right now."

"If he was shooting wildly on base earlier today targeting parked cars in an apparent temper tantrum, then escaped capture there, surely he's not returning to the base now, right?"

Warrick nodded.

"So, if *we* were to go on base, since George would be avoiding the base now, where the hell would we go?"

"I could find us a place," he said. "Even though I live off base, I still spend a lot of time there."

"Still, to play devil's advocate here, if we're off base, won't we have a better chance of hiding from him?"

"Not really. He just made the dumbest move of his life. Once he killed those cops, every law enforcement officer in the city is after him."

"So we need to lay low," she said with a nod. "I think we can do that. We could pick a hotel anywhere in the city. George won't have time to track us with so many possible locations to check."

"That's true enough. So," he said with a grin, "where do you want to go?"

She thought about it and said, "I haven't a clue. But I do know I no longer want to go to work tomorrow."

"I'd be all for that."

"I've got an idea," she said. "How about I just sit here all night and listen to the waves?"

His arms tightened around her, and he pulled her even closer. "I don't have a problem with that."

Her phone rang. She sighed. "Of course somebody is trying to get hold of me." She pulled it out. "It's Nina." She hit the Talk button. "Nina, how are you?"

"He's free," she shrieked into the phone. "He's free! He'll be coming after me."

"I heard that, and the police and the navy have men coming to protect you and the other patients and staff," Penny said, trying for a soothing voice. Obviously that wasn't working though. Nina screamed even louder. "Calm down, please. I can't understand you."

"You have to run. He's coming after you too."

"I know that," Penny said. "Warrick is here with me right now. We're just figuring out what to do next."

"Somebody needs to go to my girlfriend's. She doesn't deserve to come home and find him there."

"Tabitha?"

"Yes. I was staying with her. She's not answering her phone. I'm afraid he's already there."

"Did you tell the cops?"

"Yeah. They said they'd get somebody out there, but they didn't think he'd go there. They figured he would either come here after me or go after you."

"We can go and make sure she's okay. And then we'll probably get a hotel room or something for the night so he can't find us."

"Oh, good," Nina said with relief. "I also heard how they're bringing cops and navy guys down here, and security is on high alert. But he got in before, so I don't know how good that'll be. I won't sleep again until he's caught and put away."

"I know. I can't say I'm feeling very secure at the moment either." And yet later, as she put her phone away, she knew that was a complete lie because, cuddled up in Warrick's arms like she was, it was hard to imagine anything more secure than being right there.

"Who's Tabitha?"

"The girlfriend Nina has been staying with this week after George broke her two ribs."

"So we need to make sure her friend is okay. He might or might not know where Tabitha lives but he'd have no trouble tracking the address down as one of many possible places she'd run to."

"Did he take the cop car too? Or did he find something a little more subtle to drive around town in?" she asked.

"I doubt he took the cop car. Too obvious." As he was busy sending texts, more came in with tidbits of information. "He did take the cop car, and it had been found abandoned. They suspected he'd picked up another vehicle." Warrick added, "I'll let them know we'll run to Tabitha's place and take a quick look. The last thing we want is another friend involved in this."

"God no," Penny said. She hopped to her feet on top of the log. "Let's go. The sooner we find this guy the better."

"We're not trying to find him," he corrected. "We're making sure Nina's other friend is safe."

With that, they walked to her car.

"I'll drive."

She stopped, turned and looked at him with a frown. "Why?"

"In case he tries to track us down, or we accidentally come up on him."

It took her a minute to realize what he was saying. Then she handed him the keys without a word.

He dropped their garbage into the trash can on the side of the parking lot and went back to the car to find she was already inside, buckled up.

JUST THE THOUGHT of him even considering driving for that reason made her cringe. She wasn't a scaredy-cat. But a psycho with a gun, well, anybody with a brain should be terrified of that.

He pulled the vehicle out of the parking lot and asked, "Where are we going?"

She gave him directions and hoped Tabitha wasn't even home. Trying to explain this nightmare wasn't something Penny looked forward to.

They pulled up to the front of an apartment building. Tabitha's apartment was on the third floor. They got out and hit the number on the intercom. There was no answer.

The door to the apartment building opened, and somebody came out. He held it for them, and they walked in.

She glanced at him. "I suppose you think that's not a good thing either, or is it?"

"Of course not," Warrick said. "Security exists for a reason. What's the point of it if you'll just let in every stranger when they come to the door looking to enter?"

She shrugged. "Honestly I hadn't thought of that."

"No, most people don't."

Upstairs on the third floor they walked to Tabitha's and knocked. When there was no answer, Warrick knocked several times hard. On his third knock the door unclasped and slid open.

He shoved Penny against the hallway wall and placed a finger to her lips. She stared at him, her eyes huge. He whispered, "Stay here."

And she realized what the unlocked and open door meant.

WARRICK STEPPED TO the side of the hinges and gently pushed open the door. No lights were on inside. He couldn't hear anything. He didn't have a weapon and had no way to know if somebody was inside or not. He dared not call out, but, at the same time, now that he had knocked, somebody on the inside knew he was here. He waited, listening.

When he thought he heard a *thump*, he slid in through the front door and assessed the small hallway ahead of him. As soundlessly as he could with his bloody walking cast, he made it to the living room and peered around the area. There was no sign of anyone. A light was on in the hallway down at the other end. Knowing this was likely where the gunman—and/or Tabitha—would be, Warrick approached cautiously.

He hadn't heard another sound since he'd first entered. A bathroom was beside him. The door wasn't fully closed, and there was enough of a halo light for him to see in.

Crouching down low, knowing the gunman would likely shoot at chest level, he gently pushed on the door. No shot was fired. He stood and peered around the corner. And his heart sank. Lying facedown was a woman with blood pouring from the top of her head. A large pool surrounded her on the floor.

He quickly checked to make sure she was dead, knowing in no way could she survive that kind of blood loss with her head injury. He checked the master suite, checked the en suite bathroom, did a quick sweep around the rest of the apartment and then brought Penny inside. She took one look at his face and cried out.

He shook his head. "She's been shot in the head. No way to save her." He already had his phone in his hand and called it in. He motioned to the couch. "Sit down and don't move."

She sat like a little schoolgirl, her hands on her lap and just stared at him.

He answered the questions as fast as he could, saying he

could already see the intruder was gone. He needed to find out where he'd go next and how long since he'd been here. They would need the security cameras' feed from the apartment complex, though that wasn't his job. He wouldn't have access. The city police would completely shut out all navy personnel and would have nothing to do with Warrick. At least not until there was evidence George had killed Tabitha.

The cops were at the door within minutes. Warrick let them in. He gave a statement; then the police wanted them to leave the apartment, and that was fine with him. He pulled Penny's hand, helping her to her feet, and led her out in the hall again.

By then she was shaking. She'd caught a glimpse of Tabitha on the floor, and it wasn't a pretty sight for anyone to see.

He led her back out of the building, down to the car. Once inside, he sat and just held her close.

"Now what do we do?"

Her voice sounded more frozen than terrified. He'd rather she kicked and screamed and cried than this numbness. "Well, let's see. We have a killer hunting us. What we have to do is be smart."

She stared at him. "What does that mean?"

"We need a place to go that's safe. I'm not sure exactly which direction to go. You need to let me think about it for a minute."

Just then a vehicle ripped through the parking lot and tore onto the main street ahead of him. Instantly Warrick pulled out in the traffic and chased him.

"What are you doing?" Penny yelled, buckling up and grabbing for the dash. "Why are you chasing that car?"

"Did it ever occur to you it might be George?"

"Did it ever occur to you it might not be? Don't you wait until you confirm something before you go after somebody like that?"

"Hell no. A lot of criminals stay at the scene of the crime to watch what happens."

"It makes no sense."

"Of course it does. He saw you arrive. For all we know, he was coming up Tabitha's hallway after us, but I called the cops, and he heard them arrive too fast and chose to get away then."

She stared at him, dumbstruck at the concept.

He wasn't thrilled either, but it was all too possible. If the killer had been there not very long ago, they might have just missed him. If he'd seen them go up or pull in or recognized her vehicle, George may have wanted to return and kill them at the same time.

For all Warrick knew, George was already on the stairs coming up to Tabitha's apartment again when he heard the sirens. The fact was, Warrick was following somebody who didn't want to get caught, and that meant Warrick was interested in who he was. "Do you know anything about George's family?"

She shook her head. "No, I don't. Why?"

"Call Nina and ask her to find out if he has a brother to go to, a mother to go to, somebody who would give him a bolt hole to hide out in."

"Why would anybody do that?" she asked.

"Because often family doesn't believe the stories about their own relatives. And then consider that a gun is mighty persuasive."

She pulled out her phone, and he listened as she talked

to Nina. "Nina says he has a brother who's a drug addict, but he doesn't live in this area. He lives down in the skid row section of San Diego."

"Get an address if you can," he said. "I don't feel like being a sitting duck until this guy finds us."

"Do you really think he'll come after us that fast?"

"It's hard to say. If he's trying to annihilate everybody even remotely associated with Nina, he's got a lot of targets to choose from."

"But you're thinking we're at the top of the list."

"Or Nina is. In his mind, she could be the betrayer, or she could still be the person he loves. There's no way to know."

"Down on Dondi Street," she said. "It's in the commercial area by the docks."

He nodded. "I don't know the area. See if you can bring it up on the city map."

"We can't go down there on our own," she said.

He glanced at her. "I'll have to call for some backup."

"We need to call the cops."

"Then do so," he said calmly. "Tell them where we're headed."

It was obvious the vehicle was trying to shake him. Warrick let him get a block ahead and calm down, and then he pulled in behind him again. The driver was getting rattled. He took a left-hand turn, almost causing an accident as he darted through traffic.

Warrick swore. "Damn it."

Then there was a break in the traffic up ahead. He pulled a U-turn and took a right, going after the guy again. It took him a few minutes of wandering the blocks to find him, but he came up behind him again. The guy hit the gas and tore off, getting back onto the main highway. This time he headed in the right direction toward his brother's.

Being a naval officer, George could disappear in an awful lot of places. And those were places that, although Warrick was navy himself, he might not know. The trouble was, everybody knew who George was, and everybody was looking for him.

"The cops aren't happy. They want you to stop chasing him."

"I thought you decided it wasn't him I was chasing," Warrick said.

"Are you trying to piss off the police?"

He shrugged. "Not necessarily trying to, but I'm not prepared to let this guy go either."

"Well, you don't even know who he is." She tried to speak in a reasonable tone.

"If he'd stop, I'd ask him," Warrick said with a smile.

Just then the guy up ahead took a quick right and then a quick left. Warrick followed suit. He was determined not to lose him.

"Maybe you didn't understand me. The cops ordered us to stop chasing him."

Warrick considered it and then discarded it. "Unless the cops are here to take over, I'm not letting go."

She groaned. "Are you always this stubborn?"

"Yes," he said with a nod. "I think I am."

They kept up the chase for another ten minutes until he saw the docks up ahead. The vehicle had slowed. Warrick had let several vehicles get in between them. As he watched, the car headed toward the warehouses on the left side of the dock area.

"This is definitely not your typical nice neighborhood,"

Penny said quietly. "There are prostitutes on the corners, homeless people sitting on the sidewalk."

"Yeah, interesting choice for him."

"Again you don't know it's him." She was frustrated.

"Well, if it's not George, then the cops can't be upset with me, can they?"

"Whatever."

He kept his eyes peeled as the vehicle pulled up and around the block just a little bit ahead. Warrick killed the lights and drifted into the turn after him. The vehicle was parked halfway down the next block. Warrick gently braked, trying not to move so as to remain undetected. He watched the driver get out, dashing across the street. Once he entered the building there, Warrick drove the car a couple more blocks, then pulled off to the side of the road and parked, killing the engine so no one would see brake lights either.

He looked at her and said, "Now I'm in a pickle."

She looked at him in surprise. "Why?"

"I want to go after him."

"I don't like the idea of that at all," she said. "That's not safe."

"I'd be going after him regardless of that issue." Warrick's voice was hard. "But I can't leave you alone. Because, if I lose sight of him, he can backtrack and grab you."

She gave him a bland smile. "Then I guess you can't go after him, can you?"

He pulled out his phone. "Who were you talking to in the police department?"

"I don't know."

He wasn't sure he believed her, but, at the same time, he already had somebody on the phone talking to him. He pulled out the card that the cop had given him earlier in the day and asked for him. The city police and NCIS were working together on any George-related developments.

Within a few moments the call was transferred over. "Who is this?"

"I'm the guy who walked into the hospital earlier today and disarmed the gunman."

"What do you want?" But the aggression was gone; instead there was just curiosity.

"I tracked a vehicle from Tabitha's house, who was Nina's friend and murdered within the last hour," Warrick explained. "We're down at the docks at what appears to be an empty warehouse building a block away from the Willow area, which is where your suspect's brother lives."

"You followed him?"

"I did," Warrick said baldly. "He took off out of Tabitha's apartment parking lot as we were leaving. The cops had just arrived. I didn't know who it was, but, given his behavior, I decided I would give chase."

"Exactly where are you?" the officer barked.

Warrick gave him directions. "The vehicle is parked on the block behind me. I can see it in my rearview mirror."

"Don't move. Keep an eye on that vehicle."

Warrick agreed. "Are you coming yourself?"

"I'm sending black-and-whites first. I'll be there as soon as I can. Probably in about fifteen minutes."

"Good, we'll be here." Warrick hung up and turned to look at Penny, who was staring at him.

"How come they didn't talk to me like that?" she protested.

He grinned. "There's a language. And you don't speak it."

"What language?"

He chuckled. "A language between protectors." And that's all he said.

CHAPTER 6

TWO CRUISERS PULLED up behind them in half the expected time. Several men exited and swarmed the vehicle they'd tracked. Penny watched in the rearview mirror. Several of the men then disappeared to search the neighborhood, and one man walked toward them. Warrick opened the door and stepped out.

Penny huddled in her corner, content to listen to the men go over the recent chase. The cops were less than pleased, and Warrick wasn't giving an inch.

"Did you see George leave the vehicle?"

"Yes, he crossed the street, but I haven't seen him since."

"We've got the vehicle but are searching for him in the area. It's best if you leave now."

"And if we don't want to?" Warrick challenged. "He's the asshole who killed Tabitha and the two officers. And he's after Penny here."

"Penny?"

Warrick motioned to the interior of the car. She sighed as the officer bent and stared at her. She gave him a half-hearted smile.

Warrick leaned down beside the cop. "He'll need to ask you a few questions. Come out for a moment."

Opening the door, she stepped out and walked around to Warrick's side. He tucked her up close. She couldn't help leaning in closer to absorb some of his strength. To the officer standing in front of her, a frown on his face, she asked, "What do you want to know?"

Penny answered all the questions fired at her. To think she was going through a second event like this in such a short time period was a living nightmare.

"No, I don't have a clue where he might have gone." She'd seen enough to know her nightmares were just beginning.

"Do you know if he has any close friends nearby? A place where he might lay low? We already know about his brother. Do you know anyone else close to him?"

"No, I didn't know him that well. You'd have to ask Nina. I can't believe he killed two cops and Tabitha. She was completely innocent." She looked over at Warrick, tears never far from her eyes. "This will destroy Nina."

"Nina needs to get better, and she needs to find another place to live a long way away from here," Warrick said seriously. "Even when they catch her ex-fiancé"—he let out a heavy sigh—"it'll be hard for her to deal with the guilt."

Penny nodded. She stood taller, her arms hugging her chest. She was chilled through and through. More cruisers arrived as a large-scale manhunt began. She thought it was somewhere around two in the morning already. She understood that Warrick had been okay to wait until all the local people had been interviewed, but the police had taken the information she'd given and then asked her to stay so they could ask her some more questions later.

But now she was chilled and tired. She was heading back into the shock zone, and all she wanted to do was go home, curl up with a heating pad and cry. It was too unbelievable. She looked up at Warrick. "Can we leave now?"

Warrick glanced at the cop.

The cop nodded, handed them both cards and said, "Let us know if you think of anything else."

"It won't be tonight," she said, stifling a yawn. "I'm too exhausted to do anything but sleep."

Warrick walked her back to her car. His gait was not normal. Then again, he'd been on that damn foot all the time he should have been resting with his leg up.

"You'll be held back from working yet another week if you don't get off that leg," she warned him. She automatically went to the driver's side. Inside, she reached a hand out for the keys.

He handed them to her. "I know."

She drove slowly toward her apartment. The roads were empty. There was an eerie silence to the world around her. "Is he coming after me next?"

"I wouldn't be at all surprised," Warrick said.

"So shouldn't we go straight to a hotel now?"

"I just had a better idea. We're going on base."

She shot him a startled look. "We are?"

He nodded. "A friend of mine has an apartment there. He had to go back East. His father had a heart attack. We'll stay at his place. Take a left there."

"I could use clothes."

"Tomorrow. We're too tired for anything else."

She thought about that for a moment, then realized he was right. Tomorrow. It was already tomorrow, dammit. She took the corner and drove back toward the base. They remained silent until she pulled up to the security checkpoint. She rolled down the windows on both sides, explaining who they were.

Warrick handed over his ID and gave the address for

where they were heading. The men nodded, wrote down their names and lifted the bar.

She drove through, then said, "I didn't expect to get through that fast."

"I sent Mason a text, asking him to clear it for us."

"Oh." She should have thought of that, and she would have if her brain wasn't so fuzzy.

Following his directions, she ended up outside an apartment building. "Is this personnel housing?"

"It sure is. Singles, usually men," he said with a smile. They walked inside the front door, and he led her to the elevators. "My buddy, Morgan, lives on the top floor."

"How will you get in?"

"Mason again. He has Morgan's keys. He came in and unlocked it for us and left the key on the counter." Sure enough, the apartment was unlocked. Warrick stepped in front of her, making sure she waited at the entrance, did a quick search of the apartment, came back and nodded. He led her inside, locked the door behind him, picked up the spare key sitting on the counter and pocketed it.

He took one look at the couch and sighed. "I'll take the couch. At least this one is big enough for me to lie down on."

She walked through to the small bedroom and saw a huge bed. "Forget it, Warrick. The bed is way too big for just me. We'll both sleep here. At least we can get some real sleep." She took off her shoes, dropped her sweater on the chair. "Or do what you want. I'm too damn tired to even argue." She kicked out of her jeans, folded them and placed them on the chair, pulled her T-shirt over her head, then went to the bathroom, came back out shortly and crawled under the covers.

All the while he stood in the doorway to the bedroom and watched her.

She gave him a half wave. "Just take care of yourself, and both of us will reconvene in the morning." And she closed her eyes.

The trouble was, she couldn't quite relax until he decided what he would do regarding his sleeping arrangements. She heard him in the bathroom; then the bed sagged as he sat on the other side. She heard rustling movements, as if he was undressing, then clips, and she realized he was taking off the hard plastic walking casing around his plaster cast. With that, he stood, managed to get his jeans off and then lay down on the bed.

"Get under the covers," she said. "You have to have a good night's sleep too, or you'll never heal." She could feel his hesitation.

Then he stood back up, pulled the blankets down and slid under the sheet.

She smiled. "Good. Sleep." She heard his muttered goodnight back to her, and then she let her eyes drift closed.

When she woke the next morning, bright sunshine streamed into the room. She could hear birds chirping and even dogs barking outside. She lay here for a long moment, remembering exactly where she was, only to envision the scene at Tabitha's place.

Dry-eyed after shedding so many tears last night, she could still feel the burn as they wanted to tear up with all the injustices in the world. She'd had such a wonderful evening on the beach and for it to end with Tabitha's murder was too much. She thought about how the families of the two cops must be having the worst day of their lives. How damn unfair. George had a lot to answer for.

She sighed and shifted in the bed. And then remembered Warrick was supposed to be here with her. She rolled over onto her back and frowned. "Of course you're not here." After another moment she sat up and made her way to the bathroom. After using the facilities, she did a quick wash, longing for a shower, but, even more than that, a change of clothes. She did the best she could to braid her hair so it was a little neater. She opened the bedroom door and smelled coffee. She dressed quickly in the same clothes she'd worn last night and grabbed her sweater, putting it on too. She remade the bed the best she could, mentally noting she needed to thank the man whose apartment it was.

She walked into the kitchen to find Warrick sitting down, a cup of coffee beside him, his fingers busy texting on his phone.

He looked up and smiled at her. "How are you doing?"

She shrugged, then plunked her butt down on a kitchen chair. "I'm doing as well as I can. I slept decently."

He nodded. "Ditto."

She stared at him for a moment. "Any news?" she asked hopefully.

He shook his head. "If you're asking if they found George, the answer is no."

She sighed. "Of course not." She glanced around the apartment. "As much as I appreciate your friend lending us this space to get some rest, I'm not sure what our next step is," she admitted.

"As soon as business hours officially start," he said, "I'll phone the police and get an update. I did leave a voice message earlier, but nobody has responded yet."

She nodded. "I don't imagine we're on their priority list."

"Not to mention they were up all night too," he reminded her.

She winced. "Like we were." She glanced at her phone. "I don't know if I should go into work or not."

"Why would you?" There was no condemnation or judgment, just curiosity in his voice.

She looked up at him and smiled. "Two reasons. One, there are a lot of forms that need to be processed, yours for example, and it gives me something to do that keeps me busy. Two, while I'm at work, I'll be 100 percent focused on getting the job done, and I won't be worrying."

He rapped his fingers on the table as if thinking deeply. "Both of those are good reasons. It's nice to see you're dedicated to your job."

"It's not even so much dedication. I like my job. I like seeing things get processed and completed. I like knowing I'm helping others. For many people, the type of work I do is boring, dull, a necessary evil. But there is an occupation for everyone out there, and I'm quite happy with mine." She gave him a bright smile. "But, in order to do that, I need to go home and get a change of clothes. And, before I show up at the office, I need food."

"Do you have to make the decision right now?" His voice was low. "Let me check with the police. See if they have any problem with you reporting to your job. If they suspect you're in danger, they may feel obligated to put a detail on you. And that won't be good for anyone. They may also forbid you to go to work in order to protect those you work with. The fact that Nina works there too just adds to the danger factor."

She stared at him, that ugly twisting in her gut intensifying. "I hadn't considered that," she admitted.

He smiled. It was gentle and reassuring. "You're not alone here. I won't turn around and desert you while this madman is making our lives difficult." He had his foot resting on the chair, but he swung it to the floor now. "This makes my job a little more difficult, but we'll manage."

She groaned. "The thing is, it shouldn't be your job." She emphasized the last word. "It's not that I'm against having a little more security around me, given what happened to Tabitha, but this really hasn't got anything to do with you." She caught his gaze and saw a glint of anger there. She frowned and demanded, "Why are you getting mad?"

"Stop insulting me, and I won't get angry," he snapped back.

She glared at him.

He glared right back.

She sighed. "This is a stupid conversation."

"With you it often is."

She shook her head, decided now was not the time to start another fight with Warrick and stared around the kitchen to avoid setting him—or her—off. "So what do we do until you call the cops?"

"See if there's any food here. If not, we can go out for breakfast."

"I don't really want to take advantage of your friend's generosity any more than I have to."

"You're assuming you'll sleep in your own bed tonight," he said with a headshake. He lifted his phone and waggled it at her. "It'll take an okay from the police to convince me that's a good idea."

"I want my life back."

"We all want our lives back." He lifted his ankle. "This has had me sidelined for weeks now. If I had my druthers,

I'd be back on active duty, out training with my buddies. But I'm not. I have to do my best with that. You've been targeted by a madman. You have to do the best with that. Mine is an inconvenience. Yours could be the end of your life."

As a rebuttal it was pretty damn effective. And there wasn't a whole lot she could say in response. "I get that. I just don't know how to handle it. I don't know what I'm supposed to do."

"I highly doubt your boss wants you at work if you're bringing danger to anybody else," he said. "Isn't there anyone who can handle the files on your desk?"

"Sure," she said. "But they're all on my desk, and I feel responsible."

"But, if you aren't replaceable, you can't be promoted."

Her jaw dropped. "I hadn't ever heard that before," she said slowly. She rolled the idea around in her mind and shrugged. "I'm not exactly a career woman. If I get promoted, I get promoted. If I don't, I don't."

"Is it what you want to do long-term?"

She frowned. "I have no idea what I want to do long-term. I fell into this job. I enjoy it. It makes me feel good, but it's not like it's a passion. But then I don't have any of those. I'm not an artist or a musician or a writer or anything like that. I don't have a driving need to coach anyone, so this gives me something to do with my life." His lips quirked, and she could feel her ire rising again. "There's nothing wrong with being an average person."

"Absolutely not," he said. "But there's nothing average about you."

Inside, she admitted to being pleased at his comment. But she didn't see anything special about herself. She really did enjoy her work. "The thing about the job I do is that I can be productive. I can mow my way through a ton of files, and, at the end of the day, I can see I've accomplished something. The fact that what I'm doing is helping people makes it that much better. But there's another factor. I get to close the door at the end of my day, and I don't have to think about it until I go into work the next day. It doesn't come home with me. It doesn't keep me awake at night. I have a life to live the rest of the time."

"What do you do with the rest of your life?"

She grinned. "Lately I have been teaching yoga to little kids."

His eyebrows shot up.

"Right? It's a moms-and-tots type of class I teach at the community college. I love yoga, and I used to teach classes for adults. But then I realized so many people offer those kinds of classes, and I wanted to hit the other age groups who didn't have access to the same kind of training."

"So moms and tots?"

She nodded. "I also teach at two senior centers on Saturdays."

"Would this George character know about them?"

She frowned. "I wouldn't think so. I highly doubt Nina said anything about it. I also haven't been doing the senior centers for all that long. I've been teaching at the community college for two years now though."

"And what about at the Y?"

She nodded. "I don't currently have classes there, but I start again in July. I do yoga outside. We all go on the front lawn where there is sunshine and fresh air. I teach classes for relaxation, for health, for back pains ..." She shrugged. "I do a lot of different classes."

"And yet you don't want to do it full-time?"

"I never really thought about it," she said. "I have a job that gives me a nice paycheck. That allows me to not have to worry about making my hobby a full-time career."

"Interesting. A lot of people would prefer to do it the other way around, take the hobby and turn it into a career."

"And then there's that money-making pressure. Maybe I wouldn't enjoy my hobby as much anymore."

Just as he was about to respond, his phone rang. "It's the detective answering my call." He got up and walked a bit away.

She sipped her coffee as she listened to Warrick. It was a short call.

He returned and sat down. "They don't have any leads. Your office is under surveillance just in case George does approach. The detective wants you to lie low for today and for the weekend."

"And the yoga classes? I have two tomorrow at two different senior centers."

"I mentioned them. Told the detective how you didn't think George knew anything about them. The detective said, as long as you didn't feel anybody would be in any danger, and George doesn't know about them, and if you are smart getting there and leaving, it should be fine. I also told him that I would be attending your sessions with you."

"Oh, you'll love that," she joked. But inside she was thrilled. "I need to call my boss though."

"That's a good idea. And make sure somebody else gets all those priority files to work on."

"And then we have a full day ahead of us," she said with a frown. "What do you want to do?"

"Mason is running by my house to grab me some

clothes. Do you want Tesla to go to your place and grab some clothes too?"

"Can't we go?"

"The cops don't want us to. They've got your apartment staked out."

"Well, I'm certainly not letting Tesla put herself into any danger." Penny frowned. "If we can leave, I suggest we go out for breakfast, maybe do a little shopping. I could use a new set or two of yoga pants and tops anyway. I do have a favorite shop at the Bradbury Mall."

He nodded. "In that case, we'll do breakfast, shopping and make more plans after that."

She chuckled. "Is everything so easy with you?"

"There's no need to make this difficult," he said gently. "I will do most of the driving, so you can keep a low profile and still enjoy the day."

"And hopefully the cops will pick up George soon."

"They're on it. We have to trust they'll do what they can to make this all go away."

"Can we see Nina?"

He frowned. "In theory, yes. But I will check in with them first to make sure that's still okay."

"Did anybody tell her about Tabitha?"

"I don't know. That'll be up to her doctor to decide, whether news like that could set back of her progress. Her healing has to come first."

Penny pulled out her phone, found her boss's number, checked the time and said, "It's after eight. He's usually in the office by now. She tapped her Contact entry for him and waited for him to answer. When he did, she explained the situation. "The police aren't expecting him to show up at the office, but please be extra careful."

"I can do that," he said. "We do have a ton of work here, so it's not great timing, that's for sure. But we need to keep you safe."

"It's more than just me," she said. "You need to be safe too."

"If you have a picture of the gunman, that will help."

"I'll have Warrick send you something." At that, she rang off. "My boss wants you to send an image of George, if you've got one, or if you can get one from the detective. My boss will give it to building security and have them go on high alert." She stared restlessly out the kitchen window. "And, if that's the case, surely it would be okay if I was there."

"No. He could be watching for you to arrive. If you don't show up, he won't likely go after anybody there."

She still hated the thought of it, but there wasn't a whole lot she could do to make this any easier on anyone. "I don't have my laptop." She frowned. "I wish to hell I had gotten that from home. It's got my schedules and everything on it."

"I can ask the cops to pick it up from your apartment if you want."

She spun. "It'll take cops to go in there?"

He nodded. "I would highly suspect so. I was thinking Tesla might be able to get in because Mason would be with her. But I think a police officer should go in and grab you a change of clothes and your personal belongings."

He pulled out his phone and called the detective again. While Penny listened, they made arrangements for one of the men on standby to get a policewoman to go into Penny's apartment and collect a list of items.

She nodded. "I still want to go shopping though."

"We can. They'll take the clothing and laptop to the

police station. We can swing by there and pick it up after breakfast."

She turned and glanced around the kitchen. "We could be here for a few days, couldn't we?"

He nodded. "We could. Good thing we have the apartment then, isn't it?"

She smiled. He was right. It was much better to be grateful for what they had than to rail against the circumstances she was forced to live with.

HE WAS GLAD she could see reason amid her currently more emotional state. He understood her frustration, but, at the same time, Warrick knew it was not a smart idea to be moving about with a crazed gunman out there. Warrick was willing to go to a restaurant and do some shopping in a mall, but he'd already tagged Mason, asking if anybody with days off could act as a backup. Mason had responded quickly, saying Tanner had two days off. Warrick had agreed that Tanner would be ideal. He was relatively new to the SEALs unit. He had come in from back East months ago. But he was a good man. And there was a good chance nobody would know his involvement with Warrick.

"Did you send a picture of George to my boss?" Penny asked.

"The detective did," he said absentmindedly as he put the key in the engine. "I also sent it to Mason, who sent it out to everybody we know. His photo should be up on all the social media sites and on the news platforms too."

"Good," she said with relief. "I don't want my boss and coworkers to be sitting ducks. George could pull that same stunt from the hospital, taking everyone at work hostage and demanding that I appear again."

"Even if he calls your office and gets your voice mail saying you aren't there right now, he'll wonder if you're there and not taking calls."

"Do you think he'll try to get in?"

"He can try, but, with the security beefed up, hopefully he'll see that as a deterrent."

"Which means he'd try to get me at my home."

Warrick shot her glance, hearing the despair in her voice. "And maybe that's a good thing. The police are on this. For all I know, they've got a policewoman set up in your apartment as a trap."

She stared at him, biting her lower lip. "And what happens if that policewoman gets injured? How am I supposed to live with that?"

"You'll live with it, like we have to live with everything out of our control, including Tabitha's death."

Her face crunched up, and she sighed, sagging back in the seat. "I know you've dealt with so much death in your career, but this is a new event for me—knowing people who ended up murdered. It's going to take some adjustment for me to get your level of guilt-free dealings when it comes to such brutality."

He pulled out into traffic. He knew of a favorite restaurant in the same mall she wanted to go to. Tanner was already there, watching for their arrival. He knew exactly where they were coming from.

"Can we drive past my place to see if there's any activity?"

He nodded and slowed as they approached her apartment.

"I don't see anyone."

"You're not supposed to, but they are there. Now for breakfast." And he drove past and on to the mall.

As he pulled into the parking lot, she looked around and said, "This is where I wanted to shop, but I thought we were having breakfast first." She opened the door and hopped out.

"We are having breakfast first." He walked around and wrapped an arm around her shoulders and tucked her up against him.

He moved smoothly but definitely kept an eye out all around them. He had George's face memorized in his head, but he also knew how easy it was for someone to disguise himself. And, if this guy had any skill at disguises at all, he'd already have made some major changes. Just adding or taking away facial hair and changing his normal hair color made a huge difference.

Inside the building Warrick relaxed ever so slightly. He motioned her down the front hall to another hall heading off to the left to another exit. "The restaurant is down here."

She followed at his side, looking around. "I don't usually come to this part of the mall."

"That's why you don't know about the restaurant then." He opened the door to the restaurant and smiled at the waitress. "Reservation for two for Warrick."

He felt Penny's gaze but ignored her. They followed the waitress to a booth with no window, just as he had asked.

Penny sat down and looked at the window tables. "Couldn't we sit over there?"

He shook his head. "No."

She frowned, looked at him for a brief moment. "Because it makes us targets?"

He nodded.

"Your mind must be full of horrid scenes and vivid

memories that I really do not want to deal with."

The waitress returned with coffee and water, then asked if they needed a few minutes to look at the menu.

He nodded and smiled. "Just a moment or two longer please." He picked up the menu and took a look. He had no idea what his day would be like, so he had to ensure he would have enough energy when he needed it. He glanced over the top of his menu. "Did you see anything you want?"

"All of a sudden I'm not hungry," she muttered.

"Doesn't matter if you are or aren't. You need fuel. If not for right now, then for later in the day in case we need to run."

Her gaze widened, and then she dropped her eyes to the menu again.

He could see the menu shaking in her hands. He closed his, reached across the table and clasped her hands. "It will be fine. But I don't want you getting hungry later when we can't get you any food."

She nodded quietly, closed the menu and said, "Then you order for me." She picked up her water glass and took a hefty drink. It seemed to stabilize her. She replaced the glass. "Make sure it has lots of meat in it."

He gave a bark of laughter.

The waitress returned, and he ordered two of the specials. It came with eggs, sausages, ham, hash browns and toast. He didn't know how much she'd eat but figured he could finish the rest.

They discussed the weather, friends, anything to do with something that wasn't their current situation.

When their breakfast finally arrived, she took one look and laughed. "I said I was hungry earlier, but there's still just one of me, not two of me."

"If you can't eat it, I'll finish it for you."

She stared at him in astonishment, glared down at his plate, then back up again. "Are you serious?"

He nodded. "Absolutely." He quickly buttered his toast with the extra butter they'd provided and dug in.

He watched with quiet satisfaction as she took her first couple hesitant bites and then seemed to forget all about everything else and focused on eating.

She managed to plow through three-quarters of her meal before she slowly eased back and said, "I didn't think I'd get this far." She picked up a piece of toast, spread jam on it and took several good bites.

"Adrenaline comes in a big rush, and then you crash," he said. "At that point, you need to build up your energy reserves again. Otherwise you stay exhausted."

"So from here we can go to shopping?"

He nodded. "Absolutely."

She groaned. "Eating a big meal is hardly conducive to trying on yoga pants."

"I don't think that will make much of a difference."

She shook her head. "You don't understand women's clothing. When I say they're snug, that means one thing, but most clothes are tight."

"You can always get a larger size," he said with a note of humor.

She shot him a look. "*Right.* You do realize, in order to make women feel better, they changed the size specs so a woman who used to wear a size fourteen now gets to wear a twelve and feel great about herself?" she said drily.

He stopped and stared at her.

She chuckled. "I'm not kidding."

"Why would they do that?"

"So every woman then gets to buy something smaller than what she used to wear. It's all psychological-mind-games stuff." She waved her toast around in the air. "But it works. Everybody feels better because now they get to buy a size smaller."

He didn't get it. "You're only deceiving yourself."

"That's where the mind-game part comes in. It's industry-wide, so nobody is deceiving anybody. The fact of the matter is, all of a sudden you wear a size smaller, and now you're not fat after all." She picked up the rest of her toast and looked at it. "I really want this, but I've already had more than enough of everything."

"Decide how full you are," he said. "If you're at 100 percent, stop. If you're at 80 percent, stop. If you're at 70 percent, consider having a little more."

She frowned. "Why stop at eighty?"

"Because stopping when not yet feeling full means you give your stomach a chance to get the message and to tell your brain you're full," he said. "Now, if you were me, you'd eat the entire plate and not worry about it."

"Why? What's the difference between you and me?" she asked suspiciously.

"It takes a lot for me to get full."

"Even injured?" she asked. "If you were in full training, I'd understand, but you're not doing all that much right now, are you?"

"Ouch." But he nodded. "You're right. I'm not doing as much. But healing also requires calories. And yesterday I can't say I ate very much compared to my normal consumption."

"Well, you're certainly not fat, so your normal consumption must be about right."

"I go up and down, depending on the type of training I'm doing."

"Are you really into all that fitness stuff?"

"And healthy living, healthy lifestyle, all that lovely happy-go-lucky stuff."

She chuckled. "You are the last person I would expect to be involved in happy-go-lucky stuff."

He just grinned and took another big bite of his toast.

She finished her meal, laid her fork down after the last bite of potatoes and moved her plate back. A half piece of toast remained, but he figured she'd had enough.

Finally she leaned forward, looking at him. "When were you going to tell me about the bodyguards?"

His eyebrows shot up. He leaned forward. "What are you talking about?"

She looked worried. "Are you telling me that they have to look after us?"

He dared not look around. He knew Tanner was slightly behind her to the left. "Who do you see?"

She motioned behind him. "Two big guys. I figured they were either cops, bodyguards or somebody you called for help."

He shook his head. "No, sure didn't." He thought about that for a moment. It was easy for her to misunderstand who might be here and why. This restaurant was very close to the base, so there could be any number of reasons why somebody looking like that would be here. Hell, the guy could be a bloody retail clerk at a doughnut shop for all they knew. Everybody made superficial judgments based on looks all the time.

She leaned forward again. "Are you sure?"

He studied her carefully. "What makes you think they're

following us?"

"They keep looking at us," she said, her tone low, worried. "Or maybe they're just looking at me."

At that, his grin widened, almost splitting his face. He leaned forward, so he whispered almost against her nose. "Sweetheart, there are a hell of a lot of good reasons why every man in this room is staring at you."

She flushed bright colors and pulled back, giving him a hard frown. But he knew she was trying to get him to change the subject, and he wasn't so easily persuaded.

"Are you sure you haven't met them before? Maybe they've asked you out," he said.

She glanced at the two men and shook her head. "I think I'd remember them."

"It's possible you made a bigger impact on them than they did on you." He chuckled. "You're a beautiful woman, and men notice."

She shrugged irritably. "Whatever."

He finished his meal and motioned for the waitress. She came back with the coffeepot, filled their cups and took away their dirty plates.

"You do that the same way Mason does. It's like, you lift a little finger, and somehow the world around you jumps."

"Have you seen Mason do that?" He certainly had, but it was normal for Warrick as he spent a lot of time with Mason.

She nodded. "I met Tesla for lunch one day, and Mason joined us. It was the same damn thing. As soon as he looked around for assistance, people jump in to help him."

"I think it's that air of confidence," he said.

She nodded thoughtfully. "It's possible, but I don't know. I sure wouldn't mind having that same sense of presence."

"Why? So you can have people do your bidding?"

"No, of course not," she protested. But then a twinkle entered her gaze. "Maybe a little."

The waitress returned with the bill. He picked it up and handed her his credit card. She had the machine in her hand. She quickly ran the card through; he punched several keys and cleared the bill. She handed him a receipt, which he folded up and tucked in his wallet with his card.

"Do you want to finish your coffee?"

She nodded. "I do. Not to mention those two guys just paid for their bill too."

"Interesting." He gave a general look around, turning to see who she was talking about. His gaze drifting past them before coming back again. He didn't recognize either of the men. He returned his gaze to her and shrugged. "No idea." His phone rang. He checked to see a text coming in from Tanner, asking if he knew the two thugs. So he'd seen them too. He sent a response back. **No, do you know them?**

No.

They could be after Penny because she's cute.

That's what I was thinking.

Warrick put away his phone, tossed back the rest of his coffee, stood and held out his hand.

As she scrambled over the bench seat, she said, "Do I need to hold your hand?"

"You don't want to?" His voice held a mock-injured tone.

She rolled her eyes, slipping her hand into his.

He tucked her close and wove his way through the tables out to the front door. He opened it and waited for her to pass through. His gaze checked the restaurant, but he saw no sign of the two men. Outside, he led her to the left and said, "We'll head to the mall through here."

Unperturbed, she nodded. Then she said, surprising him, "So can Tanner join us for lunch this time?"

CHAPTER 7

SHE WATCHED THE surprise light his eyes. "Yes, I saw him. Obviously he was our backup. Did he know the two men?"

Warrick shook his head. "No, he didn't."

"So they're nobodies then." She gave a nod of satisfaction. "That works for me." She slipped her hand out of his fingers but slid her arm through his.

Together they walked to the store she had wanted to go to. She stopped in front of the windows and exclaimed at the pretty colors.

He looked at the leggings and wondered how they could possibly make so many prints and patterns all on the same type pants—all patterns he couldn't imagine 90 percent of the men of his acquaintance ever wearing. But she appeared delighted.

She laughed and said, "They've got the new colors. I want to go in."

He walked in behind her. She headed to her favorite racks and pulled out leggings, looking for matching tops. She twisted with two in her hand and looked at Warrick. "Which ones do you think?"

He looked down at a geometrical teal and black, then another one that appeared to have pink flamingos all over it.

She chuckled. "I guess the teal and black, huh?"

"I didn't say that," he protested.

"No, but your face did." She laughed gaily. She put the flamingos back and wandered to another rack.

It was all women's clothing, mostly yoga wear from what he could see. Some of it was pretty minuscule. They even had something he thought were lined leggings. But surely in this California climate it wasn't necessary. He waited and watched while she went through rack after rack.

The salesladies kept approaching him, asking him if he wanted help with anything. They obviously thought he was here to buy gifts for a girlfriend. Finally Warrick said in a gentle but firm voice that he was with her and pointed over to where Penny stood. Immediately the saleslady stepped back, gave a nod and disappeared into the background.

Warrick walked over to join her. "So do a lot of single guys come in here?"

"No clue," she said cheerfully. "But I should bring you with me more often. I never get service like this."

He glared at her.

She picked up several other outfits she wanted to try on. "You might as well make yourself comfortable. I have to go into the changing room." Seeing the dread on his face, she laughed, pointing to a chair. "If you sit there, they'll probably not bother you."

He walked over and sat down. "How long will you be?"

"Only long enough to pull on a few outfits and check them out."

One of the salesladies walked over. "Do you want to change, dear?"

Penny nodded and took the first one in the row of changing rooms. She could hear the saleslady stopping and talking to Warrick. It really irritated her how much attention the man got. She wasn't kidding when she said she never got his kind of service. She'd been in the store half a dozen times. It was all she could do to ever get anybody to answer any questions when she was here. Yet they were fawning over Warrick. She had to admit, as she pulled off her jeans and shoes and socks, that he was a hell of a good-looking man, and it made sense people were all over him. The fact that he was nice to boot just added to it.

She pulled on the geometric teal and black and looked at it critically. It wasn't bad. She took off her shirt and bra and tried on the sports bra. Together they were quite eye catching. She frowned, not sure about it. And then she heard Warrick.

"Sweetheart, come out and let me see."

And she froze. She glared at the mirror. "That's okay. I'll stay in here," she called back, her voice floating up and over the walls.

"That's not fair. You told me that you wouldn't buy anything without showing me first."

She gasped. That weasel. He was either trying to embarrass her or he really wanted to see what she looked like in her yoga attire. Considering how skintight her outfit was, she wondered if it wasn't the latter. But then, if he was coming to her class tomorrow, he would see her anyway. Deciding he deserved a dose of his own medicine, she opened the door and stepped out, sauntering toward him. He looked up, caught sight of her, and his gaze widened, a flush rising up his neck. She stopped right in front of him and said sweetly as she did a slow turn, "What do you think, sweetie?"

He studied her form, his gaze slowly going all the way to the floor and back up again. If she hadn't just given him an invitation to do exactly that, she would have smacked him.

He nodded, his voice hoarse as he said, "I think you should get that."

She chuckled, reached out and stroked his cheek. "Really?"

He just nodded.

Purring like a kitten, she sauntered back, making sure she added a little bit of sway to her hips as she walked into the small room. "Maybe I should try on the others and show you."

"Yes, I think you should do that." His voice was gravelly.

She chuckled. "But maybe you won't like them. You could end up sitting here while I try fifty different outfits."

She could hear a strangled gasp as he tried not to protest. She quickly changed out of the teal and put on a bright pink outfit that had lots of white on it. The sports bra top was even skinnier, and it had a wider band around the ribs. She frowned, not sure if she liked it or not, and decided he deserved to see this one too.

She unlatched the door and walked out to find Tanner standing with Warrick. She raised her gaze and said, "Well, two votes instead of just one."

Tanner whistled. "Wow. You are something. That fits you like a second skin."

She had to admit he was right, but then it was the nature of yoga pants. She turned to Warrick. "What do you think of this one versus the teal?" She did a slow turn again.

But Warrick was already nodding his head rapidly. "You know something? I think you should get both."

She chuckled. "I don't know about that. I still have a couple more to try on, but they're a little different."

She turned and walked away, hearing their voices drop as they whispered back and forth. But she didn't think it was about her or about her outfits. And then she was mad because she was stuck in here getting changed. Still, she'd come for that reason, and she needed to pick out something not only to wear at their temporary apartment, just in case they didn't get her clothing from the police, but also because she had planned on buying a couple yoga outfits anyway. She wanted something not quite so revealing for the old folks' home. The old men always appreciated it, but some of the women took umbrage at her lack of clothing.

She tried on several more outfits, not even bothering to show the men, and came to one that had a long crop top, so very little belly skin showed, and she decided that one and the teal one would be perfect.

Dressed again in her street clothes, she took the clothes she wanted and left the others behind. As she stepped out, she realized Warrick was no longer sitting there. Frowning, she walked through the store to see both men standing at the entrance. She headed to the counter and paid for her purchases, wishing she could hear what the guys were talking about.

The saleslady smiled at her. "Your boyfriend really seemed to like these, didn't he?"

Penny chuckled. "They're skintight, don't leave much to the imagination. What's not to like if you're male?"

The saleswoman nodded. "We don't get many men in here who are happy to wait for the women."

Penny could understand that. She didn't think she'd have the patience to do very much of it either, but then she wasn't much of a shopper. She tended to go to the store she wanted, pick out exactly what she knew she needed and leave.

With her two purchases wrapped up in a bag and the

receipt stuffed in her wallet, she joined the men. Tanner nodded toward Warrick, and the conversation between them stopped.

Warrick turned to look at her and smiled. "Tell me you got the teal one."

She nodded. "I did, but I didn't get the pink one." The sight of his crestfallen face made her smile. "Although I could go back and get it, if it's really a deal-breaker."

He shook his head. "You look dynamite in the teal one. But there was just something about that pink and white …"

"Hardly appropriate for the old folks' home though, I think."

Tanner asked, "Old folks' home?"

She explained about the yoga classes she gave for the seniors.

He whistled. "That's a really good idea. Not only is the exercise good for them but I'm sure it makes them feel much better."

"They love it. I have two classes tomorrow, and Warrick will take me from one to the other. Since my apartment is apparently under siege, I thought I should pick up some new outfits. I was planning on getting two new outfits anyway. It seemed like this was good timing." She looked around at Warrick. "So, update?"

Tanner turned an innocent face toward her, and she shook her head. "Oh, no you don't. No way you get to pull that look on me." She watched him try to control the laughter moving through his gaze. "I've spent too much time around Warrick to not know when you're pulling a fast one. You have news. I'd like to know what it is." She looked from Tanner to Warrick and back to Tanner, waiting for one of them to answer her.

Warrick glanced around the mall, but nobody appeared close by. The saleswomen in the store were a good ten or twelve feet away. He nudged her out a little bit farther. "The gunman was sighted a block from your apartment building."

The color bleached out of her skin, and it was all she could do to not gasp.

Warrick clenched her hand tight against him. "Breathe. Just breathe. It'll all be okay. I told you that."

She glanced at him hesitantly, then up at Tanner. "And, of course, they didn't catch him, right?"

He nodded. "That's right. They didn't get him."

She could feel every hope inside her melting away. She'd been so optimistic that this really would be over quickly. She nodded and turned toward Warrick. "Where to now?"

He smiled. "Tesla's off today. She suggested we go spend the afternoon by their pool."

Penny stared at him in surprise. "Really? Because that would be absolutely awesome."

He nodded. "That's what I thought. But we'll head to the police station because they did pick up a bag for you, and they have your laptop there."

She beamed. "Perfect."

"Is there anything important on your laptop?"

She shook her head. "Not really. Just, you know, emails and stuff like that. I feel disconnected if I don't have it."

"What about your phone? Isn't your world connected to your phone?"

"I don't have much in the way of data," she explained. "My schedule and everything is on my phone, but I prefer a bigger format to look at. I find phone screens awfully small."

Tanner nodded. "I'm with you there."

They walked slowly through the mall, back past the restaurant and took a nearby exit. Once outside, Tanner moved ahead as if he didn't have anything to do with them and remained about ten or fifteen feet in front of her at all times.

She glanced at Warrick. "Any news on those two guys in the restaurant?"

He shook his head. "No. We haven't seen them since. Is there any reason why they would be involved?"

She frowned. "I can't think of any. As far as I know, George was a bit of a loner."

"Would he be in trouble with somebody like that? Any reason why they would follow you to find him?"

She almost stopped in her tracks at the thought. She turned to look at Warrick. "Now that's a very disconcerting thought. Why would you put that in my head?"

He raised an eyebrow. "We have to consider this from every angle. The truth is often just outside of what we're considering. So you have to get very real about it."

"Right." Her insides were torn. "Nina did say he had a gambling problem. But I don't know how bad it is."

Warrick stared at her in surprise. "You didn't mention that to the cops. Does Nina have any money?"

She looked at him and nodded. "Actually she does. She comes from a wealthier family."

"We're heading to the police station anyway." His tone was brisk. "We'll update them with that information."

"What difference does it make?" she asked.

"If George is in trouble with somebody, like a loan shark, or has a gambling debt he has failed to pay, then there could be other angles we're not thinking about, you know? If it's just a case of revenge, then he'll be coming after you, but what if it isn't that simple? What if he's hoping you have money, so he can pay off these guys, and he knows they're on his tail? Desperate circumstances make for desperate men."

"He already killed two cops and a woman. How much more desperate can he get?"

Warrick shot her a look. "He can get a hell of a lot more desperate and a hell of a lot more dangerous," he said, and then he was quiet.

WARRICK PULLED INTO the police station lot, got out, waiting for her to join him. He constantly searched his surroundings. Tanner had arrived ahead of them and kept watch as well. But Warrick couldn't get the feeling out of his head that this information she had would change everything. Regardless, a crazy gunman was still on the loose. That's what they had to focus on. But, if something else was going on with George, the cops needed to know that too.

He walked into the police station and, at the front counter, asked for the same detective he'd spoken to earlier. The woman nodded, told him to take a seat. He turned to find almost all the benches full. Two empty spots were on the far side. He'd just sat down when a door off to the side opened, and the detective walked out.

"Warrick, come on through." He smiled at Penny. "How are you doing today?"

"I'm okay," she said. "But Warrick thought maybe I should tell you something I had forgotten about."

The detective's gaze lit with interest. "C'mon in. We have clothes for you and some other personal belongings."

He took them to a small room, motioned for them to take a seat and said he'd return in a minute. They sat down and waited.

She glanced around and spoke in a low voice. "Is this an interrogation room?"

Warrick shrugged. "Maybe. Ask him when he comes back, if you're interested."

She wrinkled her face at him. "Have you ever been arrested?"

He shook his head. "Not in this country." His grin was a bit off-kilter.

She considered him and then shuddered. "I don't think I want to hear that story."

"Nope, you probably don't," he said smoothly. "Sometimes our missions go a little sideways."

She nodded, grateful when the door opened and the detective returned. He had her overnight bag from her closet and a reinforced paper grocery bag. She checked the overnight bag, smiled when she saw several outfits, including shoes and a sweater, and then reached for the paper bag. Inside was her laptop, charger cord, cell phone charging cord—which she would never have thought to ask for—and the book that had been on her night table. She smiled. "Hey, that's very thoughtful of you."

"You can thank the policewoman. She thought of the extras."

There wasn't room for the laptop in her overnight bag so she just laid it on the floor beside her bags.

The detective looked at her. "What is it you think you need to tell me?"

She shrugged. "I don't know that I need to tell you anything, but Warrick thought it might be important."

Warrick nodded. "It is important," he insisted.

"We went to breakfast this morning. Two men were watching us," she began.

Warrick listened to her version of the events. When she was done, he added, "What that really means is, it's possible George's also trying to outrun a loan shark or somebody he owes money to for a gambling debt, and maybe those two bone-breakers are chasing him down via Penny."

The detective looked interested in that for a moment. "How would they have known you were in the restaurant?"

"They wouldn't have," she said immediately. "That's why I didn't think it was very important."

"Did anybody know of your plans to go to the sports store today?"

She stared at him in surprise. "I don't think so. I didn't write it down on my schedule. Although my yoga classes are in there. But that's not exactly something anybody would have had access to."

"Where's your schedule kept?"

"In my purse," she said, lifting it up. "It's also on my laptop, but they'd have to have my log-in and password to get in."

"Most hackers could get into your e-data. Whether on your phone or your laptop. But we don't have other illicit computer activity going on in this case." The detective frowned and drew question marks in a row across the page.

Warrick knew, when you had odd information, that you tried to fit it into the facts as you knew them presently. The trouble was, you often didn't know enough until the end, when you got the fuller picture. Even more frustrating was when you never got those final answers, and you were left wondering how the last pieces fit together. "We stayed at a friend's place on the base last night," Warrick offered. "So nobody would have known where we were, not even to follow us to the mall."

"Right. So chances are, those men weren't following you."

"Not likely, no. We did run by my place earlier," she said, suddenly straightening in a chair. "I didn't see the police there, but Warrick just drove past."

The detective nodded thoughtfully, tossed down his pen, stretched out his legs on the nearest empty chair, crossed his arms over his chest and said, "But these guys could have seen you there, at your apartment, and followed you to the mall?"

She shrugged. "Maybe. But, if these two know George, then they probably know about Nina. If they know about Nina, they probably know about me too. From the hospital siege."

"Good point," he nodded. "We can take a look at his back history and see if we can roust anything on gambling debts or any other kinds of illegal activities he might have been involved in. But I don't think it changes the scenario all that much. He's still a crazed gunman on the loose. He's killed two cops and murdered a woman. I'm not sure having two bone-breakers, as you called them, after him will change anything much."

"Except maybe make him a little more desperate," Warrick said. "It's always dangerous to forget a hidden element in this kind of deal."

The detective studied him for a long moment as he rubbed his jaw. He nodded. "You're right. Any other elements mean our plans can go haywire because we weren't expecting them. I don't have a problem with the pair showing up and killing him. Lord knows I don't want this George to take out any more innocents, but we have to run him to ground before we can find him."

"How is it that you didn't catch him at my apartment?"

"He saw the officers standing at the front door. It took them a moment to register that he was using a cane until he got further away when he tossed it and ran. By then, he was already half a block away, getting into a vehicle. He took off, and, although the officers followed him, he was too far ahead, and they lost him."

She nodded, staring out the window. "It seems like we always get so close, and he has just enough good luck that he slips away."

"That's the thing about luck," Warrick said. "He will run out of it eventually."

But the look in her eyes as she stared at him was somber. "And how many more people have to die before then?" she asked quietly. She turned to the detective. "You need to talk to Nina. She could to tell you more."

He nodded. "I can do that. I was about to head out and run down a few other leads we've got. I'll stop by the hospital first and see if she can confirm this gambling debt angle. You didn't take any photos of the men you saw at the restaurant, did you?"

Warrick shook his head. "But Tanner might have." Warrick pulled out his phone and sent Tanner a text. Almost immediately a photo showed up on his phone. He lifted it so the detective could see it. "It's not great, but this is the one we've got."

The detective looked at it and whistled. "Wow. Okay, that changes the game entirely."

Warrick stared at him. "In what way?"

"Those two are part of the Monroe gang. They run drugs, prostitutes and, yes, gambling. They do every kind of gambling you can imagine, from cockfights to dogfights to illegal casinos in back rooms. Their eldest brother runs the outfits. These two are more the hired muscle."

"We still don't know they were interested in Penny for any other reason than the fact she's an attractive woman," Warrick said thoughtfully. "But the coincidence isn't something I'm real comfortable with."

"You told me it was nothing," Penny said. "You told me that I had to tell the detective, but you said not to worry about it."

"We didn't see them again though, did we?"

Relief washed over her face. "That's right. We never saw them again, so maybe they decided whoever they were looking for wasn't me, or I wasn't a threat."

The detective's lips twitched. "Or they decided you weren't as easy a target, now that you have Warrick with you."

She stared at the desk, then slouched against the back of her seat. "There is that."

"What are your plans for the rest of the day?" the detective asked.

"We're heading to a friend's house for the afternoon." Warrick gave him the address and names. "You can always reach me there."

"How secure do you feel at that place?" the detective asked.

Warrick smiled. "Mason works with me, as do several of his friends. Considering it's Friday, I know some are coming over for a barbecue this afternoon. So I'd have to say, I feel as safe there as I would inside your jail."

"Good enough. We'll keep in touch. And tonight"—he stood as he looked at the two of them—"where are you staying?"

"We'll return to the apartment of the friend I mentioned

earlier," Warrick said. "Nobody knows where it is, and I'm keeping it that way."

"Just make sure you're not followed."

"Not a problem."

Outside the station Warrick led the way to the car, looking for signs telling him if Tanner was still here.

"Are you expecting us to be followed from here?"

"Until George is caught, I'm expecting everything," he said quietly.

"That doesn't help me to calm down and to stop worrying, Warrick," she said.

He tucked her back into the car, walked around to his side and sat down. He turned on the engine and heard his phone buzz. "Tanner says the coast is clear."

"Hearing that makes me feel better," she said. "I don't live in the world you guys live in. But it's nice to know you help each other out when you need it."

"That's what friends are for."

"Before we go to Mason's, can we visit Nina?"

"Not sure that's a good idea," Warrick said. "You heard the detective. He's heading down there now himself."

"Right. In which case we can't talk to her right away, but she'll be upset after she talks to him."

"Why don't we wait until tomorrow?"

She nodded. "I am glad to have some clothes and my chargers and laptop though."

"It was thoughtful to get your cell phone charger. I hadn't considered it," he admitted.

"Neither had I. How sad is that?"

He drove in the direction of Mason's place.

"Are you sure it's safe to go to Mason's?" she asked. "I don't want to put them in any danger."

"I highly doubt we'd find anyplace safer than there."

She sighed. "Well, I could certainly enjoy an evening without worrying about it."

"So let's make a pact. Let's go there, have a good afternoon, not talk about this, not worry about this and just have fun."

She smiled up at him. "Is that possible?"

"It is if you make it possible," he said seriously.

She thought about it and nodded. "In that case let's do it."

CHAPTER 8

A S THEY GOT into the car to leave that night, Penny hugged Tesla. "Thank you for a lovely afternoon and evening."

Tesla beamed. "I'm really loving these barbecues with everyone. Sometimes it seems like a lot of work, and then everybody comes with some dish I haven't tasted before, and I realize how great it is to be together, sharing a meal."

"It was lovely." Penny got into the car with Warrick and realized Tanner already sat in a vehicle off to the side. She frowned. "Why is Tanner still on guard duty?"

"Why not?" Warrick asked.

"He's got to get rest sometime."

"And he'll take it when he needs it," Warrick said. "Don't worry about Tanner. He's an old hand at this."

"An old hand at what?"

"Tracking people."

"Yeah, but he's tracking us, and we're not exactly hard to find," she said in exasperation. "Surely he should be tracking George."

Warrick turned to look at her and smiled. "He already is."

"What do you mean? Has he located him?"

"He's got a line to tug. We're just waiting for a couple other men to show up to give us a hand."

She glared at him. "*Give us a hand.* What do you mean by that?"

"I mean, we don't want Tanner heading off on his own, do we?"

She frowned. "No, he might get hurt that way."

"And I can't leave you. So we need somebody to back up Tanner."

She sighed. "When did life get so complicated?"

"I wouldn't worry about it," he said. "This is what we have right now. Don't worry about the what-ifs or make any decision about anything else."

She shrugged. "Easy for you to say. Who are you waiting for to go with Tanner?"

"Corey. He's been out all day with Angela, his new partner. But her sister and husband have just arrived, so he's coming out for the evening to give us a hand."

"You really want to go after George yourself, don't you?"

"Of course I do, but I'm not doing anything that puts you in danger."

"But we don't think anybody will find me at your friend's place, so why don't you drop me off there, then go help him?"

He smiled. "Not happening. I have no intention of leaving you alone."

The trouble was, she didn't want to put anybody else in danger either. "It's really an uncomfortable situation to be in," she said.

"Yeah, it is, but you're doing really well with it."

She laughed. "Hardly."

They approached the base's security gates again. She watched as Warrick handled the man with the ease of long practice, and before long they headed back to his friend's apartment.

"I'm under really good security here," she said. "Why can't I stay here alone, and you can go off with Tanner?"

"Oh, break my heart with all that gratitude," he said.

She gazed at him in exasperation. "What is it that you want me to say? Of course I'm appreciative of you looking after me."

He shook his head. "Not an issue."

"You see? That's part of the problem. It's as if you would do it for anybody."

"And maybe I would," he said. "I would certainly help anybody in need. I mean, if a situation wasn't of your choosing, and it descended on you, obviously I'll do what I can to help."

And with that she had to be happy. But, at the same time, something about his response pissed her right off. As she sat and steamed all the way back to the apartment, she realized how intensely angry this whole thing made her. She hopped out of the vehicle before he could come around to her side and slammed the door harder than necessary. His eyebrows went up, but she stormed past him into the front doors of the apartment building. "I'll take the stairs and meet you up there."

But he drew her inexorably toward the elevator.

She tapped her foot on the floor with her arms crossed over her chest as they waited for the elevator to show up. When it did, several people got off. They got in, and now it was just the two of them. In close quarters again.

He punched in their floor number, and she never said a word.

She felt his gaze on her but ignored him. She knew being angry was unreasonable. The man was just helping her out.

And she didn't fully understand her reaction either, except for the unrelenting presence of her pent-up anger rushing through her.

"We're almost at the apartment."

She shot him a look. "I can tell what floor we're on."

He didn't say anything further.

When the door opened, she got out and marched toward the apartment. Then, being ahead of him, she had to wait for him to catch up. He unlocked the door, and she went in. She dumped her stuff in the bedroom, pulled out her laptop, walked to the kitchen, laid it down on the table, plugged it in and tried to bury herself in her emails. She looked up to see him heading toward the bedroom and on into the en suite bath. And she realized how late it was.

But she was still so pissed off that she didn't figure she'd get to sleep anytime soon. And yet, at the same time, she also knew she was being childish. She stood, went in the bedroom and checked her bag, and, sure enough, she had a pair of baby doll pajamas in there. With relief, she headed to the hall bathroom and got changed.

He still wasn't out by the time she returned, and she thought she heard the shower going. Now a shower would be nice, but no way could she handle that right now.

It had been a very long day after a very short night. Her toiletry bag was in the overnight bag as well. She went back to the other bathroom and brushed her teeth. As she walked past her laptop, she closed the lid so it would go to sleep. On her way back to the bedroom, she realized Warrick still wasn't there.

Finally she got into bed on her side and thought maybe she'd find a way to calm down before he came out and she blasted him. She knew it wasn't fair, and she knew she needed to shut her mouth and just accept the situation. Trouble was, that wasn't exactly her way. She turned out the light on her side and tucked under the covers. She should be tired.

She'd only gotten a few hours' sleep the previous night, and today she'd been a bundle of nerves. It was bad enough to think George was out there looking for her, with at least two more guys thinking she could lead them to George.

By the time Warrick opened the bathroom door and came into the bedroom, she had herself pretty calmed down.

And then he did it. "Still pissed off at me?"

She stiffened in bed as he sat down on the edge, but he didn't lie down. She had no idea if he was planning to sleep here beside her or on the couch. In her mind she was quite prepared to let him stay here like she had last night. But being waspish as she was, she wanted to snap at him and tell him, if he was a gentleman, he'd sleep in the other room. So she refused to answer him, knowing if she spoke now, she would end up feeling foolish later when she finally calmed down. Numerous times she'd let her mouth run off in the wrong direction, and she'd regretted it majorly afterward.

"Quite a little temper you've got in there, don't you?"

She bit her lips together, refusing to let him get her all riled up. Trouble was, she was already there.

"What's the matter? You didn't like me saying I'd help anyone?" He slipped under the covers, stretched out beside her. "Of course I would. It's what I do."

And then he rolled over, presented her with his back, turned out his light, and it seemed like he relaxed. But the longer he relaxed, the less she did. Finally she straightened up and looked over at him. "But you didn't have to make it sound like I was just anybody on the street."

She studied him for a long moment because no answer came. "He can't be asleep can he?" she whispered to the room. And then she realized the bed was moving. His shoulders were moving; in fact, his whole damn body was moving. He was laughing at her.

She bounced to her knees, reached for the pillow and whacked him over the head and body. She didn't know how long he had been silently laughing at her, but it seemed like he'd been laughing out loud at her forever. She hit him and hit him and hit him, and he let her.

Finally she expended all her energy and tried to catch her breath, him lying on the floor, still laughing uproariously at her. She stared at him. "When the hell did you get on the floor?" she asked in bewilderment.

"A few minutes ago. You were so busy wailing on me that you didn't even notice."

She groaned. "I do have a bit of a temper. And you seem to be really good at making me mad."

He bounced back onto the bed, retook his spot where she'd been hitting him and said, "Of course your situation is very different than me helping anybody around the world."

She shook her head. "It's no different at all. I wanted to be special. I wanted it to be maybe the sign we were getting along okay, and you wanted to help me because you were helping *me*, not just because you were helping *someone* in need." She flung her pillow on him and stretched out, almost falling flat on her face on the bed.

He was chuckling so hard, and, at this point, she felt very sad. Since when did she become such a complainer? But she really liked him. Even if he did spark her temper more than he should.

"It doesn't matter if I would help everybody else in the

world," he said, "because the one person I am helping right now is you."

"That's not helping," she announced.

He whispered against her ear. "I know. What you really want to hear is that I'm doing this because I want to help you, because I want to keep you safe. And I *am* doing it to keep you safe."

She shook her head. "Oh, no, that's too little, too late."

He rolled her onto her back and glared down at her. "Oh, it is, is it?"

She nodded. "Absolutely. If you wanted to make me feel better, you could have done that a while ago. Not now."

"I have no intention of trying to make you feel better," he said.

Her heart lurched as she sat upright. "Why not?" Her temper spiked again. Her argument even sounded foolish to her as she realized she was going on the attack again.

"Why not what?" he asked.

And then she caught the glint of laughter in his eyes. "Why aren't you wanting to make me feel better?" She glared at him. "You know you're making me nuts, right?"

He shook his head. "Sweetie, you're already nuts." And he leaned over and kissed her.

IT WAS ALL Warrick could do to not cry out as she pulled from his embrace. His body had hit the flashpoint, and he knew sex with her would be incredible. Hot, fast, furious. And his body was already screaming as she withdrew from him. He reached out and held her once more.

She shook her head. "No way you'll woo me into having sex with you," she declared.

He could see the resistance in her. But he wasn't sure if it was resistance of her, of the situation or of him. "Isn't there?" he asked, his body responding to the term *sex*. Just like any teenage boy, his body was more than ready to take the next step.

She glared at him. "And none of those hot slumbering gazes my way either, please."

He chuckled. "Well, I didn't know that's what I was doing. It's an interesting concept though."

She shook her head. "No, no, no. Not the time, not the place and probably not the right person."

That surprised him. As far as he was concerned, they were moving toward this point very rapidly. He frowned. "And here I thought we were becoming much more than friends."

"I don't know if we are or not. But remember your vow of celibacy?"

He stared at her. He dared not laugh. But it was hard to contain the twitch of his lips. "I said I was *trying* out celibacy. I certainly never made a vow of celibacy."

She shook her head. "No. No way you'll let something like this stop a much deeper path."

It took a moment to figure out what she was talking about, and then he said, "Are you trying to say you don't want a flash-in-the-pan sexual encounter to derail my celibacy attempt?"

She gave a clipped nod. "Exactly."

Once again he was hard-pressed to hold back the humor. The last thing he wanted to do was insult her. *Again.* "I tried out celibacy," he said gently. "But since meeting a firepot whose kisses I can't seem to get enough of—neither can I stop touching whatever part of her body she'll let me touch—therefore, celibacy has been the last thing on my mind. I made a decision to try it, and now I'm making a decision to not have celibacy in my life." He stroked a finger across her cheeks, around the edge of her chin and then down the nape of her neck. "But that's my decision. Not yours."

"I don't want to be responsible for taking you off a moral path."

At that, he had to chuckle out loud. When he calmed down enough, he whispered, "I was looking for more than a one-night stand. I wanted sex that would make me feel fulfilled. A relationship with a woman I can hold in my arms past that initial night. I wanted to wake up in the morning to see the person beside me and smile. What I didn't want was that emptiness. Finally I figured out that a lot of that emptiness was inside me—my selection process, my take on what is a relationship. I wasn't choosing to have deeper, more meaningful relationships. I think having a lot of relationships, if that's what both parties want, is fine. But, at some point, I wanted something else. And I needed to do some work. On myself." He made sure there was no confusion here. "And now I've met somebody who not only am I attracted to, as is obvious"—he rotated his hips, leaving her no doubt about how he felt about their current position—"but she's also somebody I admire and respect. I also seem to have a penchant for freckled redheads who have tempers."

"No stereotyping me please." Her voice was softer.

He could see her resistance already easing back. And that worried him. "I didn't choose celibacy as a vow against sex. I chose celibacy as an option to find out what I really wanted in a relationship."

She gave a happy sigh and sank down against his chest,

her arms crossed over his back muscles. "Not many men would talk like that."

"I'm not many men," he said.

"Most men are turned off by my temper," she admitted.

"Of course they are. Makes them feel threatened. There's a time for every emotion. The worst thing we can do is keep it all stored up inside. Much better to have a healthy outlet than to keep it bottled up where it'll cause disease over time."

"My mother was like me. But she was very Italian. She and my father fought all the time. But they always made up just as nicely."

He grinned. "And I bet many times your father pricked your mother's temper just so the makeup sex would be fantastic."

She stared at him for a moment, and then he could see the memories filtering in, and she chuckled. "I can so see that happening. Never thought about it before, but my dad was one cagey guy."

"And I bet they had a very physical loving relationship."

"They were always hugging, holding hands. They never went shopping without touching all the time." She smiled. "It's the first time I've felt good about that whole family thing in a long time."

"Due to the loss of your brother probably." He stroked her hair off her forehead, letting his finger run through her scalp. "Loss is one of the biggest, probably *the* biggest, heartache any of us can go through."

She nodded, and a heavy sigh reached up from deep inside, as she lay on his chest.

He held her close, wondering what she must have gone through.

"It was," she admitted. "When I graduated, I took a job

as many miles away as I could because I didn't feel like I had a home anymore. The relationship between my mom and dad, although still close, was no longer the relationship I remembered. And, of course, my brother was no longer there, and he's the only sibling I had."

He could see how painful this was for her, and it was an interesting look into her family history. She lay limp against his chest. He slowly brushed her hair back, stroking her scalp, gently massaging it, easing away the tension and the worry. Everybody had a different perception of an event. Her mother could very well have decided she had lost her daughter at the same time too and would have taken on the guilt from that relationship breakup.

"I feel like I should call her."

"I'm sure she would love that," he said quietly. "There's nothing like making peace with your past to let you see the future in a whole different light."

"I wanted what they had, but I can't trust it anymore," she said, "because they broke up."

"For their own reasons. You can't judge them for it, if it's what they needed to do."

She stayed quiet for a long moment, resting against him quietly.

He wished she'd fall asleep, but he could see the wheels in her mind were turning.

She shrugged finally and said, "Maybe tomorrow."

He wrapped his arms around her and hugged her gently. "Go to sleep. When you wake up in the morning, maybe you'll have the right answer for you then."

He watched as her eyes drifted closed again. He kept massaging the back of her neck, then let his fingers drift up and down her scalp. Finally her breathing eased into a deep heavy alpha sleep. With any luck she'd slip into a beta sleep and completely relax.

She hadn't gotten much sleep last night, and she'd suffered one shock after another. But there was nothing like facing your own mortality to have you take a look at the relationships you either had or lost.

More than a few instances in his own life found him staring down a gun barrel and wondering if he would make to it the next day. He had a kid sister who he hadn't called in a couple weeks. He had told her about his leg but hadn't followed up. And, just like Penny, he thought maybe he should give her a call the next morning. With that thought uppermost in his mind, he drifted off to sleep himself.

CHAPTER 9

PENNY AWOKE THE next morning, amazed at her position. She lay atop Warrick, her arms draped over his chest, her legs mingled in between his, but he slept beneath her unaware or not bothered by her weight. She'd met a lot of strong men in her life, but he was one of the few who was so natural with it, so completely accepting of the gift of a strong healthy body. She lay here for a long moment enjoying the peace of having his chest raise her frame and lower it. At first she'd been mortified, but now she had such a serene feeling this relationship could actually happen.

Normally she slept on her side, so it was a sign of the depth of her exhaustion last night that she'd slept in this position. And, of course, with that came the thought about her mother and father and all her past relationship woes. And Warrick's magical acceptance of what she felt was a horrible trauma in her life, one that caused no end of guilt.

She lifted her head and studied Warrick's face. He lay solid, not unlike the rock he was. And that was what he'd been for her so far. Solid, steadfast, dependable, protective. She could come up with a dozen more synonyms, but those covered it pretty well.

He also had not tried to persuade her to have sex with him. She thought about that phrase for a long moment and realized just how wrong it was. Because it wouldn't be sex.

Making love with Warrick would be a whole new experience.

She wasn't sure she could ever have unattached sex with him because her heart was already engaged. It was too early to know how deep or how well it was engaged, but no doubt he had touched her on many, many levels—even though she hadn't wanted to go that direction.

Her fingers itched to explore the massive body beneath her. She crossed her hands over his chest and just studied him. The square jaw, the heavy five-o'clock shadow already arising overnight, thick brows, wide forehead, hair brown with a bit of curl to it, just long enough that it flicked off his head toward the pillow because of his position.

She gave a happy sigh.

There was a rumble under her chest, and he whispered, "What are you looking at?"

She chuckled, her voice soft, dreamy. "You."

His gaze opened slowly, and then he tried to blink the sleep away from his mind. "Why?"

She grinned. "Because you're beautiful. Because I've never really had an opportunity to study your face. Because I couldn't help myself."

His gaze widened as he took in her words. But she also felt another response lower down. She considered her options. She could get up, go to the bathroom, put on coffee in the kitchen and carry on with her day. Or she could take a step that would move them both into a whole new territory. She whispered, "I was thinking about your words last night."

His forehead creased as he obviously cast his mind to their earlier conversation. This probably wasn't fair to him because he was still sleepy. But she figured it was the best time.

"And I realize that sex has nothing to do with this." His

hips lurched beneath her. She smiled gently, reached up a finger and traced the outline of his lips. "It's all about making love."

She leaned down and kissed him. Soft butterfly kisses at first, her tongue tracing the outline of his lips, sliding between them, tasting, teasing, gently meeting his tongue before she deepened it. His hands were on her back, not holding her close, just resting there, letting her do as she would.

She lifted her head and smiled. "You're a miracle, you know that?" His eyebrows shot straight up, and she could see the confusion in his eyes. She chuckled. "I'll explain later. I'm a little busy at the moment."

She lowered her head again, this time kissing him with all the passion that had been building since she'd first met him. She remembered her parents, their fighting, their making up. Then she thought about all the times she'd been fighting with Warrick, realizing that had been the same mating game. The same wanted outcome, but she'd been too scared to take that step. She kissed him hard, deep and long.

By the time she lifted her head, her breathing was ragged, and then she smiled. Because so was his.

"Lady, you pack a mean punch," he said, his voice hoarse. He rolled over so she was beneath him. "Now it's my turn."

And he lowered his head and took her to the depths of a passion she'd never known before. She wrapped her arms around his neck and hung on tight.

She'd been wearing a few pieces of clothing, and so had he. But somehow, in the next few minutes, she realized all of it was tossed to the floor, and now it was just heated skin against heated skin. She couldn't stop whimpering, and he wouldn't let her hold back.

She was begging for more when he suckled her breasts. Her back arched, she cried out as she held him tight against her when he moved to the other one. She whimpered because she wanted to feel his lips again and again.

When he slid his way down to the apex of her thighs and tasted her, her legs wide open and weeping with joy, she was beyond thought. She grabbed his curls and pulled on him hard, but he couldn't be shifted. He was a mountain. There was nothing she could do but accept his ministrations, but she didn't do it quietly.

"Warrick, come to me. I need you now. Damn it, I want you. I want you inside me."

At that, he moved up the side of her body, spreading her wide, plunged deep and whispered, "I've got you."

With his large fingers wrapped around her backside, he plunged and rocked and rolled gently, and then more forcefully. Sex would never be the same again for her. There was no plunging desperately, waiting for, driving toward an outcome that both wanted. This was a playfulness, a journey, an experience she'd never had.

When he finally moved with that ending purpose behind it, all she could do was hold on tight. As he drove deeper and deeper, faster, longer, she tightened her legs wrapped around his hips until he sent her screaming into her orgasm. Through her own cries, she heard his moan as his release swept over him. He crashed down beside her, ever careful to make sure he didn't crush her with his weight.

After a moment he whispered, "Are you okay?"

She was sobbing. She rolled over, seeing his worry and a hint of fear in his eyes. "Happy tears." She wrapped her arms around his chest, buried her face in his neck and whispered,

"Never been better."

He crushed her against him, and she thought that maybe, just maybe, there was such a thing as perfection. She was exhausted; she was energized; she was mesmerized.

After they lay here for a few minutes, his hands gently stroking up and down her body, she whispered, "You know, if we'd started this last night, we would have had the whole night to play."

"We could have," he said, "but somehow I think this was much more special. Besides, I don't think we're limited to one night, are we?"

She lifted her head and smiled up at him. "God, I hope not. Personally I'd like to have as many nights as we want together."

"Well, that's what a relationship is all about," he said comfortably.

He shifted her in his arms, and she asked, "You mentioned celibacy. How long has it been?"

He shrugged. "Not all that long, I had a three-year relationship that she broke off, but we'd been having problems for weeks before that, and I had wondered then if she hadn't been seeing somebody. She didn't want *us* anymore. And that's always a big sign."

"I'm sorry. After three years you think you're there. You think you've found everything you want."

"And instead what you find out is that, for some people, it's just comfortable until they find something better," he said. He tilted her chin and said, "But I'm good. In fact, I'm better than good."

She reached up and kissed him. "You do realize the world is about to intrude on us?"

He nodded. "Shower?"

"Absolutely." She shifted to sit up. "Alone or together?"

He chuckled. "Absolutely together."

She slipped off the bed, walked into the bathroom, shut the door to use the facilities in private, and then opened the door for him. She turned on the water and stepped inside the flow.

The naturalness of being with him amazed her. She was the kind of woman who normally would grab her clothing to hide her body as she raced to the bathroom to get dressed. But there was none of that with him. What he hadn't explored of her body already, she knew he would take a lot of time to explore the next time.

And she welcomed it. She wasn't ashamed of who she was; instead she reveled at his response to being with her. It was so damn freeing to see acceptance and enjoyment on his face. She stood under the water, letting it wash over her face as he stepped in behind her and picked up a bar of soap. She smiled when he gently used the bar and washed her from head to toe. Then he picked up the shampoo and did her hair. If there was a thought of how he had learned to do this so well, she squashed it with a follow-up thought that she was reaping the benefit of all his practice.

When he was done with her hair, he turned and kissed her, his tongue taking long, deep, sweeping strokes. She wrapped her arms around him and said, "Not sure we can do this in the shower."

He chuckled. "Remember? I'm the guy who gets things done."

She was lifted and pinned in place, and he slipped inside. So natural, so calm, so damn powerful that it brought tears to her eyes yet again. If the last time had been like a rock 'n' roll orgy on the stage, this was like a symphony of tenderness and gentleness. And she couldn't get enough.

When they were finally done, she whispered, "I hope your friend doesn't have to pay the water bill here."

Warrick chuckled. "I'll ask if he does. Believe me. I'll toss him some money for it."

She smiled and whispered, "Can it get any better than this?"

He wrapped his arms around her and hugged her close, whispering against her ear, "I hope so. I highly suggest we give it our best to find out."

She nodded. "For the first time in a long time, I'm totally okay to see what the future brings."

He reached down and tilted her chin. "It already brought you to me. I can't imagine anything better."

She kissed him yet again. She thought she could spend a lifetime doing that, just touching and kissing him at odd times because she was so damn grateful he had walked into her life. Maybe she'd been screaming at him like a shrew back then, but she'd obviously recognized this man was for her. It was all good.

WARRICK CAUGHT TANNER'S expression, his grin a mile wide as he looked from Warrick to Penny. Inside he cringed because he knew exactly what Mason and Tesla would say. And Warrick knew he was in for some ribbing from the guys, but he really hoped they'd be at least respectful. Immediately he chastised himself. The men were always respectful of the ladies. And honestly, he'd given as good as he expected to get at this point too.

There was such a thing as payback, and he'd certainly ribbed a lot of them over their fine partners. He'd been jealous as all hell all that time. And yet, for a while, he'd been together with Sandra, and he'd been plain happy for them. But, since he knew something was missing in that relationship, he'd been worried about how to fix it, how to change it, what to do. When Sandra took the decision out of his hands, he realized their relationship had been done and gone for a long time. And he had been really worried about nothing he could change or fix. Now he knew the guys would have a heyday with him.

Tanner, however, didn't say a word. He just nodded toward Penny and said, "You look like you got some sleep for a change."

She beamed. "I did indeed. It's been a rough couple days."

Tanner looked at Warrick. "I spoke with the police this morning."

"Oh? Any update?" Penny asked.

He nodded. "They spoke to Nina. She gave them some names. They checked it out, and apparently George does have a gambling debt of well over six figures."

Warrick whistled. "That's not a small debt. It still doesn't explain all this."

"No, but according to Nina, she does have that kind of money. It's sitting in a trust. It's one of the reasons why he wanted her back in his life. Instead of trying to find the money elsewhere, he wanted her to give it to him."

"And he couldn't force her to do it, so he needed her to do it because she loved him." Warrick nodded. "Makes a sick kind of sense."

"Isn't that the way?" Penny murmured. "Is she still safe?"

"I haven't checked in with her this morning." Tanner looked around the small café they'd chosen to meet in for breakfast. "There is some concern that the two thugs might be following you."

"I haven't seen them at all this morning," she exclaimed.

Warrick watched as she nervously glanced around. Had the cops found George yet? He was haunting Nina's house and the hospital. Warrick knew he would get resistance from Penny by refusing to go to the hospital. She really wanted to see Nina again. Originally he'd thought it would be fine, but, with George still on the loose, no place was safe. "I wonder when Nina's being released," he murmured.

"Whenever she is, she needs to get the hell out of town," Penny said. "She's the one who'll be the real target."

Again he kept his next thought to himself because, of course, Penny wasn't thinking like a desperate madman. Yes, George was after Nina for the money, but he was also after Penny for revenge. And those two guys were after George. If he was supposed to give them money, the two goons wouldn't want to kill George, at least not until they got the money first.

"I'm not sure there's any reason for them to keep following Penny," Tanner said to Warrick. "Except, if they're still looking for George and figure he'll target her, then it makes sense to keep an eye on the target too. And, when he shows up, get the money they want and either take out George or leave."

"But I can't get the money for them," Penny said in a matter-of-fact tone. "So really the target is Nina, not me."

"Except that ..." Warrick let his voice trail off.

She turned to him, narrowing her gaze until she was staring at him. "Why did you stop talking?"

He tried to give her a bland innocent look, but it hadn't been working very well with her.

She shook her head. "Oh no, hell no. You're not keeping that from me."

"I don't want to use scare tactics, but there are all kinds of reasons for the men to continue to follow you."

She held out her hands. "Like what?"

He loved the challenge in her voice. She just didn't want to back down. He kept his voice low when he said, "What would make Nina hand over the money to George?"

"Only if she loved him."

"Or to save somebody's life she cares about."

She stared at him for a long moment and then nodded agreeably. "Yeah, of course."

And he waited. And waited. And when her face broke with the realization of what Nina would do if George held Penny hostage, the shock was almost too much to bear. She hyperventilated right in front of him. He reached an arm out, tucked her firmly against his side and held her close. "I won't let them get to you," he said. "You've got to remember that."

She swallowed hard several times.

Just then the waitress returned with the coffeepot and menus. He grabbed a menu for the two of them and held it up so it half concealed her face. And he kept talking to her. "Remember all we've been through so far. We're not giving up the ghost now."

Slowly she started to relax. "You must think I'm really stupid," she muttered.

Surprised, he looked down at her. "What are you talking about?"

"I didn't get what you're trying to say at first."

"That's because you see the good in people. I've spent a lifetime dealing with the bad."

She stayed nestled against his chest, not even looking at the menu.

"You should be hungry," he said, looking at the listed items. "How about pancakes?"

She gave a half shrug. "I don't think I can eat."

"Too bad." When the waitress returned, he ordered two stacks of hotcakes and eggs on the side with two sausages.

She sat back up after the waitress left, turning to look at him. "So, are you trying to eat my breakfast again too?"

He stared at her uncomprehendingly.

She rolled her eyes. "I told you that I'm not very hungry. I don't think I can eat."

"And?" Tanner asked, his voice confused.

She gave him a drawn smile. "This way, Warrick gets to eat his breakfast and mine."

Tanner chuckled. "Some of the women in our acquaintance can eat pretty damn well," he said.

"And I guess, at the right time, I can too," she said. "But, right now, just the thought of what he ordered is enough to make my stomach heave."

"Don't worry about it," Tanner said, giving her an easy smile. "You're not alone. You need to remember that."

Warrick appreciated Tanner's support because it was the one thing Penny really had forgotten. She wasn't alone. This really was not just about her but more about everyone rallying around her.

She nodded and smiled. "If Warrick hasn't said it, let me say it. Thank you for looking after us."

Warrick protested. "He's not looking after me."

She snorted. "Bullets will kill you too."

"Like hell," he said good-naturedly. "I have been shot several times. I'm still here."

She glared at him. "That's not funny."

"Actually it is," he said chuckling. "At least at this point in time."

Tanner reached across and patted her hand. "He's a good guy."

She nodded. "He is a good guy. He's also irritating. He's frustrating. He's …" She ran out of words.

Warrick leaned closer. "Yes?" He turned a devilish grin on her. "Don't stop now."

She turned so they were almost touching nose to nose. "Very irritating."

"You already said that," he said helpfully. "Surely you have another synonym."

"Adjective?"

"Both work." His grin widened.

She groaned. "I'm not sure I'll ever get used to having you around. I used to get mad, and it was a good feeling. Now I get mad, and you're right there in my face, trying to make me madder," she complained.

But there was humor in her voice, and he appreciated that. "Temper is definitely something you need to let out," he said. "Emotions need to be released and preferably before they become uncontrollable."

The waitress arrived with steaming hot stacks of pancakes on three plates.

She looked at the four pancakes stacked high. "No way I can eat all this."

Tanner and Warrick exchanged looks as they each accepted the same overloaded plates themselves.

Warrick handed her the butter. "You better take what you want because we'll finish it."

She sighed, took what she wanted, and the men cleaned

out the rest of the butter and slid it over the top of their pancakes.

Then Warrick handed her the syrup. "Better get what you want."

She shot him a look of disbelief but poured a generous helping over her pancakes. As soon as she was done, he handed it to Tanner first. In one swoop, Tanner damn-near emptied the bottle. When Tanner handed it back, Warrick completely emptied it.

"Oh, my God! Can you guys really eat that?"

Even as she finished speaking, the waitress returned with plates of eggs and sausages and set them down on the side. Warrick carefully put the eggs and sausages into the swimming pool of pancake syrup and butter, and, catching the look on her face, he tossed her a devilish grin. "Want a bite?"

She shook her head, put down her knife and fork, and said, "I want to watch you guys eat this."

They both looked at her in surprise. Warrick cut cleanly down the center of the stack, cut off a wedge, topped it with a piece of sausage and popped the whole thing in his mouth. Tanner wasn't far behind with pancake, egg and sausage all on the same fork to disappear into his mouth equally as fast.

Warrick watched Penny's look of startled surprise change to amazement. After chewing this bite, he said, "Aren't you eating?"

She muttered darkly and turned her attention to her stack.

He plowed through his food with great enjoyment. After all, he'd worked up a hell of an appetite this morning. Given a choice, he'd have the same exercise every morning and a breakfast like this to follow. He kept an eye on Penny as she worked daintily through her stack. It seemed like four pancakes were too much, and she kept cutting just the top two. He knew she would need more butter and syrup for the two in the next layer. She also ate one egg and one sausage.

When she was left with two pancakes, she put down her knife and fork again, and said, "Okay, I'm done. But I could really use more coffee."

Warrick called the waitress back over, and, as she cleaned up his and Tanner's empty plates, he asked her, "May we get more coffee, plus more butter and syrup please?" He scooted Penny's plate closer to him. He ate the last egg and sausage and waited for the butter and syrup before devouring her last two pancakes.

Just as he was about to eat the last bite, his phone rang. He glared at it and said, "It could've waited five more minutes." He handed his phone to Tanner. "Looks like it's Mason."

While Warrick finished off his—Penny's—breakfast, he listened as Tanner talked.

When Tanner ended the call, he said, "Nina has been released. She's heading home and then apparently to the airport this afternoon."

Warrick studied Tanner. "Did the cops send anybody to escort her?"

Tanner shook his head. "She didn't tell anyone but hospital staff. One of them called Tesla. Nina said she wouldn't be home longer than five minutes, and then she'd be on her way to the airport. Which, of course, we know won't work at all."

Warrick looked up, caught the waitress's eye, and within seconds they were paying the bill and rushing out of the restaurant.

"Why would she do that?" Penny asked. "She knows he's

still out there."

"She also knows he's not trying to kill her. He wants the money."

"Sure, but what'll he do to get it?" she asked bleakly.

With her tucked into the car, Warrick pulled out of the parking lot and following her directions toward Nina's house. He already knew it would be bad before they got there. He didn't know how long it had been since Nina had been released, but it was too damn long, and he was pretty damn sure George was already after her, if he didn't already have her.

CHAPTER 10

PENNY WATCHED THE houses race by. She pulled out her phone and sent Nina a text. **Where are you? Why didn't you stay at the hospital?** There was no response. She hit the Call button. "Pick up, damn you, pick up."

She caught Warrick's glance and shook her head as the ringing went on and on. Penny was going to be sick with that heavy breakfast sitting in her stomach as she worried over Nina's state.

"Surely he wouldn't have hurt her already," she said.

"Depends if he snatched her or not."

She hung up the phone when Warrick's phone rang. He looked at the screen. "Answer that, please. It's Tanner."

"Tanner, this is Penny. What's up?"

"I just talked to the police. They didn't know Nina had left the hospital. She was afraid somebody from the hospital or somebody from the police station would let the cat out of the bag, and somehow George would find out."

"I've been calling her and already sent several texts," she said, "but there's been absolutely no response."

"I'm not surprised," Tanner said. "We're on the way. Just stay positive."

She hung up, placed the phone back on the dash between them and relayed the gist of the conversation to Warrick.

"I can see her doing that more than I can see her saying, *I don't want security*," he admitted. "She'd have to slip out, grab a cab, get home, grab a few things, and then maybe stay with the same cab and go right to the airport."

"I guess. She can always come back later and clean up the house, sell her car or drive the car to wherever she is going."

"Exactly."

He pulled up outside Nina's house. The drive had taken longer than she had expected. Just enough Saturday morning traffic slowed them down.

She checked her watch. She'd canceled her first yoga session today. There wasn't enough time now for that. She raced to the front door and pounded on it, hitting the doorbell several times. But there was an empty, desolate look to the house.

Warrick was behind her, walking up and down the veranda, looking in the windows. "Do you know how to get into her place?" he asked.

She nodded. "Reach up to the top of that doorframe, will you?"

He dragged his fingers along the top and nodded when he pulled down a key. "How many people know about that?"

She shrugged. "I did, and probably George did. She was forever losing her keys."

He shook his head but unlocked the door. He stepped in front of her. "You wait here."

She reached out and grabbed his arm. "You wait for Tanner."

He looked down at her in surprise.

She shook her head. "I'm serious. Remember? George's already killed two cops."

"She's got a point," Tanner said from behind them. Of course he had a cheeky grin on his face. He looked at Warrick. "You go high. I'll go low."

The men jumped through the front door. She stayed pinned in place outside, hating that she couldn't see what was going on inside.

Just when she was ready to peer in, Warrick's head popped out the door, scaring her. She gave a shriek, clasping her hand to her chest. "Oh, my God. You scared me."

He grabbed her hand and tugged her into the house. "Nobody seems to be here. I want your help in determining if she's taken anything, if she's managed to get home and is gone already."

She wandered through the lower floor. "It all looks normal here." In the kitchen a couple cups were on the side counter with a dish in the sink. She opened the fridge and found nothing fresh or new. Or was there? She stopped, took a look at the side door and frowned. "There's milk here."

Warrick looked at her in surprise. "And?"

"Nina can't drink milk. She has a dairy intolerance."

He closed the fridge, put a finger to his lips, snagged Tanner, who was going through the cupboards and told him about the milk. In a low voice Warrick asked, "Is there a basement?"

She frowned. "Yes, I think so. This home is one of the older houses. I don't even know that it's earthquake proof." She leaned forward. "Did you guys look upstairs?"

They nodded. "Checked the closets and under the bed too," Tanner confirmed. He looked at the back window. "What kind of car does Nina have?"

It took her a moment. "A Volkswagen Beetle, last year's model I think."

Tanner nodded. "It's parked in the back toward the alley gate."

She walked over and peeked out the back kitchen window. "Well, that's it. But she never parks there. She always parks on the street."

"That's if she's driving," Tanner whispered. "But what if somebody else was? Somebody who's trying to keep a low profile?"

Warrick had his phone out, already sending a text.

She leaned over to see he was letting the police know. She glanced at the two men and swallowed hard. "Are we seriously thinking he's still in the house?"

"I don't know," Tanner said, "but we need to make a big show of leaving so he feels secure."

Warrick nodded. "We also need to get Penny somewhere safe."

"What difference does it make where I am?" She frowned at them. "Because I'll be with you guys."

Both men just looked at her with those straight bland faces she was coming to hate.

"You mean, I'm not coming with you?"

"We'll come back into the house and wait for him to come out of his hiding spot," Warrick said quietly. "He's got weapons. We don't. We need to catch him by surprise."

They motioned her to walk toward the front door.

They made lots of noise and called out, "Nobody is here."

"Okay, good enough."

On the front step Warrick whispered to her, "Now go straight to the car and lock yourself in."

He handed her the keys and waited until she got down the stairs and to the vehicle. The car was just around the corner, two houses down.

She slid into the passenger side, locked the door, slumped down on the seat and groaned. Damn men. She knew they were doing what they felt they needed to do, but she was really tired of them always putting themselves in danger. She crossed her arms and tried to still her panicky breath and waited.

AT TANNER'S NOD, the two of them crept back inside. They spread out on opposite sides of the living room, keeping to the wall where the main view would be better. They didn't know how long it would take but figured they'd need at least ten or fifteen minutes before anybody would exit whatever hidey-hole they had found. Hidden around the corners, out of sight as much as they could be, they waited.

Warrick had a good view of the upstairs staircase and the basement door going downstairs across from him. On the other side, hidden behind a massive armchair, was Tanner. They could see each other and send text messages or even hand signals as they waited.

It only took eight minutes before the basement door slowly opened.

Warrick held up his finger to Tanner. When a disheveled man slipped around the corner, Warrick realized the man living in Nina's house *was* George. That was the good news. What they really needed to know was where the hell Nina was.

George walked quietly forward, carrying two pistols in his hands. He walked up to the front of the house and peered out the living room window. Warrick hoped to God that Penny had slouched down in the vehicle so she couldn't be seen.

As George stared out the living room window, his face twisted into an ugly dark sadistic mask. "Bitch." And he headed for the front door.

He must have seen some sign of Penny in the car. And they were out of time. As soon as he put one of his weapons into his belt at the back in order to reach for the front door, Warrick jumped him. He took him down, slamming his head against the doorjamb, the gun going off aimlessly into the flooring. As soon as George was down, Warrick pulled his hands behind his back and disarmed him. "Call the cops."

Tanner picked up both weapons and made the call.

George was only stunned, however. And he started swearing and resisting. But, with Warrick's knee in the center of his back and his hands twisted behind him, George couldn't do a whole lot.

With the call over, Tanner raced into the kitchen and came back. "She has zip ties." He looped several together until they were wide enough to get around George's ankles and wrists.

When Warrick rolled him over, George spat at him. Warrick grinned down. "That's all you can do now." He shook his head. "Wow, aren't you a badass?"

And that set off George. With Tanner and Warrick standing guard, George lost it, screaming and yelling obscenities and threats until he finally ran down and lay gasping on the floor. "Let my arms go. They hurt," he whined.

"No. No way I'm letting you loose again," Warrick said. "If for nothing else, for Tabitha's sake and the two cops you killed."

George glared at him, but he was still heaving, his breathing rough and agonized.

"Where the hell is Nina?" Warrick asked.

George's gaze lit up with a maniacal light. "No fucking idea," he roared.

But Warrick wasn't so sure he believed him. He looked at Tanner. "You good here?"

Tanner nodded. He rolled George over and sat down on his back. "He's not going anywhere."

George shouted obscenities again, but Warrick headed for the basement door. Turning on the lights, he raced down the stairs, and, sure enough, there was Nina, blood pooling underneath her body. But it wasn't a ton. She did appear to be conscious. He dropped to his knees beside her. She moaned.

"Nina," he whispered. "Easy girl, we've got you. You're safe now."

Nina opened her eyes and groaned. "George caught me at home. I think he was living here," she said, her voice full of fear.

"We caught George," he said. "Tanner has him tied up in the living room, and the cops are on the way."

She sagged back onto the floor. "Oh, thank God. He's lost it. He's completely psycho."

Warrick checked her over and found she had a head wound, and she'd ripped open her stitches on the side of her neck. "Back to the hospital with you."

She sobbed quietly. "I just wanted to get away. I felt like I would get caught any minute at the hospital. Every time the door opened or there was a voice outside my room, I was petrified it was him coming after me again."

Warrick understood. "But now you've got to heal from

this latest attack, and, as long as he's in jail, you should be okay."

"I hope so," she said. "But those loan sharks … He was worried about them before. He said they were coming after him and would take me hostage to get the money if they couldn't get him."

Warrick winced. "Let's just be grateful you're okay."

She sat up slowly, holding her head. "I don't feel so good," she said.

He laid her back down again. "You just wait here. We'll get an ambulance for you."

He had his phone out and called the detective on the case. "We've got George tied up at Nina's house, and I found Nina in her basement. She's injured, and we need an ambulance for her."

"Just talked to Tanner," the detective said. "Officers are on the way. I didn't know about the ambulance though."

"Nina's got a head wound. Some of her previous stitches are ripped open. I'm not exactly sure what else." He swore as he checked her over further. "She's got a bullet graze on her shoulder. Still looking." He moved his hands over her body, doing a quick search. "I think that's it."

"We're all on our way. Just hold down the fort until we get there."

He stayed at Nina's side until he heard the cops pull up. He asked her, "Are you okay if I go greet them? I need to direct them here to you."

She smiled. "I'll be fine."

He raced up the stairs, pushed open the door and called for two cops to come down to the basement. The others were handcuffing George, who was still lying on the floor. Warrick called out to Tanner, "I found Nina. Though injured, she's alive."

"Awesome," Tanner said. He stepped back, and an officer led George outside. They weren't being terribly gentle, but then why should they? He had killed two of their own.

Warrick raced back downstairs to help Nina. "I've called for an ambulance," he said to the cops already downstairs. "I don't really want to move her. Every time she moves, it hurts."

The men nodded and asked him questions about what had happened. He gave as much information as he could, but, when he heard the ambulance, he bolted back upstairs. When he saw an EMT pull a gurney inside, the other racing ahead with a medical bag, he called them down to Nina's side. Then he was asked to step out of the way. Seeing she was in good hands, he worked his way through the crowd, back up the stairs where he found Tanner. The detective had him pinned in the corner, getting as much information as he could from him.

The detective looked up and said, "Warrick, I need to talk to you."

Warrick nodded. "Give me a minute. I'm getting Penny from the car."

He ran outside to the car, feeling freer and happier than he had in a long time. This was exactly what Penny needed. And now that Nina didn't have to worry about George anymore, everything was good. He pulled open the passenger door and froze. She wasn't here. He crouched down and looked inside the front seat and then into the back. The car was empty.

He spun around. "Penny," he called, but there was no answer. "Penny," he called again. No answer. He picked up his phone and texted her. To his horror he heard the responding *ping* from inside the car. He found her phone sitting on the floor just under the passenger seat. But there was absolutely no sign of Penny.

He ran back to the detective only to have cops holding up George's phone. "This is ringing."

Warrick snatched it from the detective's hand and answered it. "What do you want?" he snarled. He clicked Speaker, and the voice on the phone filled the air. "If you want your bitch back, you'll make sure you get the money we need."

"What bitch?"

"We're not stupid. We know perfectly well George is in the cop car, and you're the one talking to us. We can see you."

Everyone turned and saw a vehicle drive off in the distance.

"We've got your lovely Penny, as she calls herself. But we need a hundred Gs. We need it now."

"Where?" he said urgently. "Where do you want to do the drop?"

"We'll call you back in an hour. Make sure you're the one who answers the call."

Just then Nina was brought up the stairs into the living room. Warrick turned to her. "The loan sharks have taken Penny."

She cried out, "On, my God. George's damage is never done, is it?"

"We have to get Penny back."

She nodded. "I don't know how I can help though."

"They want the money that's owed to them."

She winced and looked at the detective. "I have money, but it's not something I can access easily. I don't know how much George has. Can you take his money?"

"We have money," the detective said. "But it'll have to go with GPS trackers. And I have to get a hell of a lot of authorization to make this happen."

"Well, you got fifty-five minutes," Warrick said in a hard voice. "Or I'm contacting my navy buddies, and we'll do a private mission. It might look like money passes hands, but it'll be a hell of a lot uglier as soon as we arrive."

The detective stared him down. "This is a police issue."

"It's my girlfriend's issue," he said. "And I'll be damned if I'm letting these assholes keep her. Not now that I found her. Penny's coming home safe and sound. No other ending is allowed."

CHAPTER 11

PENNY WOKE SLOWLY, lying facedown on a floor. The pain in her head pounded at the back of her eyeballs, as if someone was screaming to get out. She moaned softly, her hand going to her temple. When her fingers came away sticky, she stared in disbelief. Her brain was fuzzy, struggling to comprehend what had happened. She'd been sitting in the car, waiting for Warrick and Tanner. She'd slunk down low, hoping not to be seen by anybody passing by.

Then cops had arrived, and she'd opened the window to get some fresh air, believing it was all okay now.

As she lay here in the darkness, she cast her mind back to remember what had happened. She vaguely remembered a shadow approaching, and the door opening. And then pain exploding on the side of her head. She shuddered as ripples of agony shifted up and down her head. She let her hand drop to hit the floor, the movement itself jarring her body and sending yet more waves of pain through her head. A greasy sick feeling wafted up her throat. She struggled to hold back the bile. She breathed deep through her nose, desperate to control the vomit from spewing.

As she quietly lay on her stomach, trying not to move, she listened for sounds of anything to determine where she was. Was she alone? Was she guarded? Had somebody else been taken hostage with her? Nina?

Her gaze flew open as she studied her surroundings without moving her head. It was a dark room, like a basement. No furniture was in front of her; the walls were gray, and a window brought in a little light but not much.

She studied the floor she lay on. It was cement, painted gray, again like a basement. But there was good news—her hands weren't tied together.

She shifted her feet cautiously, aware every movement jarred her head and whatever injury she'd sustained there. But her feet shifted freely back and forth so, again, no ties around her ankles.

She rolled over superslowly until she was on her back. Her body relaxed in relief, and just the change in the position made her muscles cry out for joy. She stared upward, and the dusky light revealed a single bulb hanging from the center of the ceiling. A fixture was supposed to go over it, but nobody had bothered. She rolled her eyes gently, trying to see more of the room.

There were no ceiling tiles, just open rafters. Past her feet was a door in the corner that she hadn't been able to see at the beginning of her search. So she'd been tossed into a room, and the door closed. Obviously nobody was afraid she'd get away so her hands and feet had not been bound. Given her head condition, she could see why.

She didn't know when anybody would check on her again, but she wanted to have her head fully focused. She searched her pocket for her cell phone, swearing softly when it wasn't there. She didn't know if her pockets had been turned out, but, from the looks of it, she had nothing on her. Moving cautiously with one hand to her head, she used her other to push herself gently to a sitting position.

As soon as the room stopped spinning, she got to all

fours and slowly stood. She gasped as the greasy waves of pain crawled up the back of her throat once more. She took several deep breaths and stumbled toward the window. She had no idea what time it was—thinking it was somewhere around eleven, maybe ten this morning, that she'd been taken.

It was still daylight outside; the odd light was from the dirt on the window. The ground was just below the windowsill, confirming she was in the basement of some building. Outside there wasn't much grass, mostly weeds and brown dirt. She saw a busted fence in the distance. She struggled to open the window, but it was old, the latch rusty. If she had something to break it, she could possibly get it open, but she wasn't sure, with her head like it was, if she could jump in order to climb out. Although she'd give it a damn good try if she could.

Another window was on the opposite wall. She made her way slowly to it and looked out. More broken fence. The yard was filled with someone's garbage. She pushed on the latch and managed to get the window unlocked, and slowly she dragged it open. The trouble was, the windows were small. She wasn't sure that, even as small as she was, she could get her shoulders through. But, if she could get up there, she thought she might be able to wiggle out far enough. Even though she knew it was futile, she turned once more to search the room, looking for a chair or a stool, a cardboard box, anything to give herself a boost up.

She was pretty damn short, and this was one of those times she knew it was a flaw. But she was fit—other than the damn blow to her head—and the cement wall had been painted but wasn't terribly slippery. She wasn't wearing any shoes, which she thought was odd. But still, it gave her an idea. Maybe her bare feet would make it easier to climb.

Knowing that the pain would explode in her head anytime now and that the men could return in a split second too, she grasped the window frame itself and clambered up, shoving her head and shoulders through the opening, the pain in her head be damned.

It was a tight squeeze, and she worried she might get stuck in the middle. But when she heard a sound below, she panicked and pushed herself fully through, scraping her arms in the process. Her hips came through easily, and she tumbled to the dirt on the other side. She groaned, gasping her temples once again as blackness threatened to overtake her. She closed the window and hurriedly slipped into the sparse shrubbery beside the house.

With no idea where to go but knowing she had to choose a route that wouldn't cross anybody's line of sight from inside the building, she snuck around to the side of the house and took a look out front. The fence was broken, and several trees were off to the left. If she could get there, she might make her way around the fence into the neighbor's yard, then dart to the cars and thereafter disappear.

It was only a half-assed escape plan, but she had to do something fast before somebody found out she was missing. Because then the search would be on, and she knew she'd never get another chance.

Putting her plan into action, she nimbly sprinted across the grass and slid into the tree line. Her head was booming now. She reached up to find fresh blood pouring down her cheek. But there was no time for it. She made her way around the fence and contemplated her options.

There was a car close by. If she could sneak to the other side of it, she might be able to sneak up that side of the road.

More trees were up ahead. She slipped behind them and leaned against one, gasping. A car drove down the street, slowed to look at her but kept going. She realized how she must look. But she didn't dare stop just anybody driving by in this neighborhood. With her hand over her head wound, she stumbled forward, knowing she was leaving a bloody trail behind her. But that couldn't be helped either.

At the corner she had to choose left or right. She could hear traffic more on the right, so she crossed the road towards it and kept going. She walked and walked but never saw anybody. There was nobody to ask for help, nobody to ask for a phone. She was hoping for a store or a gas station. All the houses in this area were dilapidated, the yards unkempt, weeds overgrown. It looked like a pretty rough area. This was the last place she wanted to be.

She kept walking, even though she passed a couple people. They were either laughing or jeering, but nobody stopped to help her. Neither did she ask them for help. She made it to the corner and found a cement barricade. Needing to sit down for a moment, she sat on the other side, hidden from view, while she caught her breath.

Her head was really bleeding now.

She was at a dead end. The city had obviously put up these barricades to stop people from driving through. Instead of looking like a better neighborhood, the houses looked even worse.

And that was as much of a worry as anything.

She tried to recollect her thoughts, knowing she needed to contact Warrick or the police. If she could just find a gas station, a corner store, or someplace where maybe somebody would give her a hand. She didn't dare knock on any of these doors. And, although vehicles drove past her every once in a while, nobody stopped.

Feeling slightly better when the nausea calmed down, she slowly stood, looked around and saw an intersection up ahead.

Walking gingerly because of the damage done to her bare feet from running on cement and rough stones, she made her way to the intersection and read the two street signs. She was at Laurel and Willow. None of that made sense to her dazed mind.

She tried to figure out where she was, but nothing came to mind. A vehicle stopped at the intersection. There was a woman driving. Penny reached out a hand and waved at her.

The woman went through, passed her, then stopped. She hopped out of the vehicle. "Are you okay?"

Penny shook her head. And then cried out from the pain. It sent her to her knees.

"I'll call the police for you," the woman said.

Penny waved her hand this time in acknowledgment. She could hear the woman talking, but then the woman got in the vehicle and drove off.

Penny groaned.

It was probably due to the neighborhood as much as anything else. But what was Penny to do now? Sit here and wait? How long would it take for the police to come? And had the woman called the police or had her husband told her to get the hell out of there before somebody came after her? Penny didn't know and wasn't sure what to do. But her brain kept slamming against her skull so badly that she knew she would vomit any second. She sat huddled on the street, waiting for the waves of nausea to ease back.

When they finally did, she used the fence beside her to stand back up. She leaned against it, figuring out what to do.

The intersection gave her hope. It meant traffic, not deserted roads ending up nowhere.

This was important; she just didn't know how to make good use of the knowledge yet. Just as she crossed the road, a truck came up behind her. There were shouts. She turned, saw two men racing toward her, and she cried out, starting to run. But she wasn't fast enough. One of the men grabbed her. The truck pulled up behind her, and she was tossed into the back, her head bouncing on the bed. She cried out in pain and screamed, "No! Stop! Leave me alone. Let me go."

And then a blow smacked her up the side of her head, and darkness claimed her.

WARRICK STARED AT Tanner. "Did you just say the police got a call?"

They drove Penny's Kia through the known territory where the drug lord/loan shark operated, searching for any place where they might have taken Penny. It was the only hope they had. They were due to meet said loan sharks in fifteen minutes. The cops were doing their thing, but Warrick and Tanner decided not to sit idly waiting.

They had the location for the drop. They had scoped out the area. It was a park, and, as much as they liked parks for things like this, it also meant a lot of people and a lot of places to hide.

Tanner said, "That was a detective. Somebody just called in. A woman needed help at the corner of Willow and Laurel. But, when the cops got there, nobody was there."

"Did they get a description?"

"The woman who called it in took a picture, and it was Penny."

Warrick hit the brakes, pulled off to the side of the road. "Are you sure?"

"He's sending me the photo." His phone buzzed. He brought up the photo, and Warrick heard him suck in his breath.

Warrick took a look to see it was definitely Penny curled up in a ball on the street, blood flowing down the side of her head. She looked lost and terrorized. "Why the hell didn't the damn woman do more to help her? Just get her in her car and drive away with her?"

"She was scared. It's a pretty rough neighborhood, and she was afraid whoever had done this would come after her. The cops have already contacted her. She led them back to where she'd seen Penny, but there's no sign of her. There is, however, blood. They're tracking it back to where they might have kept her."

Warrick stared at him. "What the hell are we supposed to do now? We don't have enough time to track Penny, get to the park in time for the drop-off. I gather she tried to escape."

"The kidnappers are supposed to be bringing Penny to the park. Keep that in mind," Tanner said.

"It's not enough." Warrick's voice went dark. "We should have gone after her."

"Gone after her where? We didn't have a clue. The getaway vehicle was too far ahead of us to follow them. Even the souped-up black-and-whites that came around the block right at that time lost her, remember?"

Warrick sat here for a long moment, his eyes closed, remembering the black-and-white cop cars taking off behind the vehicle that had been taunting them, knowing Penny was likely with them. But to think she had escaped from her kidnappers was massive.

"Do you think they're searching for her?" Tanner asked.

"Oh, hell yeah, they're after her. They need her for the exchange."

"And what if they don't find her?"

"Then we're in trouble. Not only that, they'll know *they're* in trouble."

"They do have cops at the scene, trying to track the blood back to where she came from. But the trail goes for blocks." Tanner read the text from the detective that just came in.

"Tell the cops to stick with it. It'll be one of those run-down houses. She came from somewhere."

"You're a better tracker than they are," Tanner said.

Warrick nodded, hit the gas, and, within four minutes, they were at the location she'd been found. "Give me six minutes. We have to get to that damn park on time."

Up ahead he could see the cops talking to each other, but he ignored them. He ran as fast as he could, easily picking up the blood drops as Penny made her way that far.

He could see where she had stopped and sat against a cement barricade and kept on down the block. He moved as fast as he dared. Time was beyond being a limitation here. Even if they found the house where Penny had escaped from, it didn't mean she was there anymore. If they'd picked her up, then they could already be on the way to the park with her. Warrick tracked the trail back to where he lost it at a wooded fenced-in area. On the other side was a pretty run-down house. He noted the address, and, when Tanner pulled up beside him, he hopped into the front seat. "I lost the trail here."

Tanner turned the car around and drove toward the

park.

Warrick called the detective. "I tracked the blood back to a house." He gave them the address. "I looked but didn't see any sign of her. I imagine they have her and are on their way to the park."

"I'm at the park now," the detective said. "We have a policeman doing the drop. He's in plain clothes, sitting on a park bench. The exchange is due to take place in ten minutes. But I'll send men to the address and check."

"We'll be at the park in five," Tanner said.

"We'll set up a perimeter search," Warrick told the detective. "Make sure you don't hand over the money if you don't see Penny."

The detective's voice was hard. "We'll do our job. You stay out of our way."

Warrick gave a hard laugh. "Hell no. I'm not leaving until I know Penny is safe. And, if these assholes have her stashed, you can bet they're not leaving until I know where she is." He hung up the phone.

"It's not too wise to piss off the cops," Tanner said.

"Then he shouldn't say something so stupid," Warrick snapped. "No way I'm leaving until I've got Penny back in my arms."

Tanner nodded. "Understood."

"Exactly," Warrick said. "This is just too unbelievable. To think she escaped and then was picked up again."

"But we don't know that for sure."

Warrick gave him a hard glance. "I know. That makes it almost worse. What if some other asshole took advantage of her situation and picked her up? What if she's fallen into a ditch somewhere, and I missed the blood trail?"

"Trust that she's damn smart enough to have escaped in

the first place. She's not just a smart cookie, she's got a lot of common sense. Let's give her a chance." Tanner pulled into the park, driving around to the far side. He parked beside a black-and-white.

They hopped out and disappeared into the tree line. Warrick could see the plainclothes man sitting on a bench with a briefcase beside him, playing on his phone. It was hard not to miss a cop, even when they weren't dressed like one.

"Do you think he really doesn't see how obvious he is?" Tanner asked.

"Maybe he means to be. Keeps everybody else at bay."

They quickly did a search around the area, their gazes moving constantly. What Warrick was most concerned about was a gunman, snipers, anybody hidden who could take out the cops—or Penny.

That wasn't these goons. They were after their money, and they didn't give a shit who paid, just so they got it. But sometimes everybody had to take a loss. As far as Warrick was concerned, the loan sharks would take the loss tonight.

As they approached the parking lot again, two vehicles pulled in, both black, both with dark tinted windows.

Tanner grabbed his arm.

"I see them."

Two men got out, one from each of the vehicles. They headed toward the center of the park and sat down on the bench beside the guy with the money. He talked to them; both shook their heads. They pointed to the briefcase; he shook his head and pointed to the cars.

One man pulled out his phone and called somebody. The back doors on the second vehicle opened, and, sure enough, two more men got out. One was from from the restaurant. He reached back inside the vehicle and pulled out a limp form, carrying her like a child.

Warrick's breath caught in the back of his throat. Anger curled in his gut, and his fingers clenched as he realized it was Penny, unconscious, limp in the man's arms. Warrick knew that, when he was done talking, he would just drop her on the ground, and her head would get smashed yet again.

Tanner gripped his forearm. "Easy."

A growl came from the back of his throat. Warrick would rip that man in two for what he'd done to Penny. "How many in the other car?" he gritted out.

"I'll find out." Tanner disappeared.

The man carrying Penny walked toward the bench and, in front of everybody, propped her up so she was leaning against the plainclothes detective. The detective's face held anger and pain. Warrick worried there was a good chance Penny wasn't alive.

She didn't move—her body just dropped where it had been placed. He'd never felt an anger driving through him like it did right now.

He watched Tanner come up behind the car on the driver's side. He knew from the hand Tanner held up one more man was inside the car.

As Tanner crouched down, he opened the door only a slight bit. Warrick didn't think the man sitting on the park bench had any idea what was going on. Just as suddenly the door clicked closed again. And Tanner was behind their car. Two men and Penny had come out of the other vehicle. How many more were there? Warrick waited for Tanner to make that assessment.

If not many, there was a good chance Warrick could take out those assholes too. He waited and watched. The men on the bench discussed something. One of the goons had a weapon. It was held against Penny's side. Instead of being angry, he felt nothing but relief because, if they were holding a weapon on her, that meant she was still alive.

CHAPTER 12

PENNY SLUMPED AGAINST the poor man she'd been propped on. She'd been awake since the vehicle had stopped moving. When she'd been hauled out unceremoniously, packed like a two-year-old and taken across green grass, she had deliberately pretended to be unconscious. She needed every opportunity she could find to get free.

They were in something like a park. She could hear voices, but, for the most part, the area was silent. When she was propped up on the bench, leaning against somebody, she couldn't figure out what the hell was going on.

But any change was good as far as she was concerned, and anybody else in the world, hopefully, would be better than the assholes who had thrown her into the back of the truck and kept hitting her head. She didn't remember getting transferred from a truck to a car. Her head even now was pounding. She tried hard to stop her face from scrunching up in pain or gasping.

It was important for them to think she was unconscious. The element of surprise was the only benefit she had right now. Voices rolled around her. The man she'd been propped against was angry, talking about her condition, worried that maybe she was dead. But when a gun was prodded into her waist, she realized her situation was still no better.

A briefcase and money, as per the discussion going on

around her, was handed over. These were hard voices, ugly talk she had trouble discerning.

And then the man beside her held up his hand and said, "Go. Take your money. Just go."

The men snorted, turned and walked away. Peering through her lashes, she was shocked as one of the men turned, raising his gun and pointing it at the man beside her. She froze in a panic.

When the gunman's head exploded, and his body crumpled to the ground, she gasped in shock, struggling to sit back up again. The man beside her reached around and held her in place.

"Don't move," he said. "One gunman took off with the briefcase."

But the man who'd been ready to shoot them was down, dead on the ground. There were shouts in the area, screams and yells as everyone chased after the man with the money. She looked up. "Who are you?"

"I'm a police officer," he said quietly, giving her a wry smile. "Almost a dead one apparently."

"Two of those assholes took me out of my car and hit me over the head. I woke up in a basement. I escaped, but I couldn't find any way to get help, and they caught me again, threw me in the back of a pickup, slammed my head down so hard I lost track of everything until I just woke up in the parking lot a few minutes ago."

"No need to worry," he said with a smile. "We've all been fighting to get a hold of you."

She sighed. "I never even heard what happened to Nina."

Helping her stand, he said, "George is back in jail, and Nina is fine. Well, not fine exactly," he corrected. "She's back in the hospital."

Penny stared up at him in a haze. Now that she was on her feet, the world spun around her. She sat back down abruptly. "I don't think I can stand, much less walk."

He nodded. "We'll just sit here until help comes."

She shook her head, then cried out. She gasped several times, waiting for the booming agony in her head to calm down. "Are we safe here?"

He frowned and looked around. "I presume everybody is after the other gunman. As long as they keep him away from us, we're as safe as we can be."

"I don't know about that. There was somebody else in the car." She looked up to see Tanner walking toward her. But no sign of Warrick. "Is it safe?" she asked.

Tanner nodded. "We still haven't caught the two men trying to get away with the money, but both vehicles have been disabled."

She wasn't exactly sure what he meant and needed it spelled out. "Did you kill them?"

The cop beside her stiffened.

Tanner chuckled. "I don't need to kill anyone these days. I just knocked him out," he said carelessly. "We needed the numbers back down for our benefit."

She asked, "Warrick?"

"He's after the gunman. We figured he's one of the two assholes who kidnapped you. Warrick is planning on getting to him, making him pay for what he did to you."

She thought about that. "I hope he gets him too."

Tanner's grin widened. "Look how bloodthirsty you can be."

"They hurt me," she said plaintively. "They didn't need to do that."

"No, they certainly didn't." Tanner nodded solemnly. He crouched in front of her, holding up two fingers. "Tell me how many fingers I'm holding up."

She glared at him. "Two."

He moved his hand around, making her track his fingers so he could see if she had a concussion.

"I don't know what I have," she said, "but I think I'll need stitches. My head is killing me."

"We'll get an ambulance to you," the officer said.

She slumped against the bench. "God, I hope they get him. I want this over with."

"Nina is in the hospital, getting looked after. Maybe we can get you in the same room with her."

"Will she be okay?" She looked up, searching Tanner's face. "How did she end up hurt again?"

As she listened to Tanner explain what he knew, she raised her hand to her throat. "It's scary to think they'd both been inside the house the whole time we were there. He could have killed us anytime."

"Absolutely. But you were supposed to be safe in the car."

"And I thought I was. I was sitting in the front seat, looking at all the cops at Nina's house, when somebody opened the door, slammed me in the head."

"Did you feel them doing that?"

"I don't remember. I just went numb."

"How did they get the vehicle door open?" Tanner asked in exasperation. "You were supposed to have locked it."

She looked at him and scrunched up her face. "All the cops had arrived, so I figured I was safe. It was hot in the car. I didn't even think about it. I had the window open to watch."

Both men stared at her. Tanner palmed his face, then dropped his hands and said, "You should come up with a better excuse before Warrick finds out what you did." He just laughed.

She frowned. "He won't yell at me, will he? Because he'll just make my head hurt more."

"He won't deliberately hurt you. But you're due for a good telling off for not following orders."

She shot him a look. "He better not. He's supposed to be nice to me."

"Why is that?" Tanner asked, barely holding in his laughter.

She glared at him. "Are you laughing at me?"

He shook his head. "Of course not."

She sniffed. "Of course you are. It's either laughing at me or prodding my temper. That's what the two of you do."

"No, that's Warrick. I laugh at both of you. As for Warrick, he doesn't have much of a temper to prick. So no point in trying there. Unless it has to do with filing medical forms."

She nodded painfully. "It's only me with the temper. And he does like to make me blow."

"Only because he loves you," Tanner said lightly.

She turned and looked up at him. "Promise?"

He remained crouched in front of her. He gently stroked her muddy cheek. "Absolutely I promise."

She beamed. "Then you better go get that sorry ass of his right back here so he can take me to the hospital because I'm not feeling very good." She looked at him, and the world started to go crazy funny. "I'm really not feeeeeling ..." She pitched forward into his arms and knew no more.

WARRICK DODGED TO the left, hoping to cut off the asshole as he ripped around the parking lot. They were several blocks away from the park entrance. Four cops were running after him, and he wouldn't let up his chase either. He wanted to pound this asshole's face into the ground and keep stomping so he'd never get back up again. He'd put his injured foot firmly into the back of his mind, but he knew he'd pay for this later.

When his phone rang, he ignored it. But it was persistent. He pulled it out to see it was Tanner. "What the hell?" he roared. "I'm in pursuit."

"It's Penny. She collapsed again. I'm taking her to the emergency room right now. We don't have time to wait for an ambulance."

Warrick came to a screeching halt. He stared ahead at the man he wanted to pound into the ground, then at the four cops behind Warrick. "We're really close to catching him."

Tanner hesitated. "Dude, I don't know what's wrong with her. She looked funny, and her eyes rolled up into her head, and she pitched forward. She's got several head wounds from when they banged her up."

Warrick had already turned around and raced toward the park. "I'm coming. I'm at the corner of Match and Warden. I'll be there in about three minutes. I'm heading toward the main intersection off Plymouth. Pick me up there."

He put away his phone, then pulled it back out again and called the detective, still running. "You got four cops in pursuit. Make sure you catch that asshole. I've got to get Penny to the hospital."

"We've got several blockades in the direction he's heading. We'll get him."

"Make sure you do," Warrick said in a dark tone. "There's no contest between grabbing that guy or getting Penny safely to medical attention. But I don't want to turn around and find out you guys lost him." He hung up, stuffed the phone back in his pocket and picked up his pace.

He was flat-out pounding the pavement. He knew there would be hell to pay because the walking cast was already splintered around his leg. He knew the damage on his ankle would be just as bad. A vehicle blew its horn right behind him. He came to a stop to see Penny layed out in the back seat of her car. Tanner was driving.

Warrick hopped inside, closing the door. Tanner immediately drove off. Warrick leaned over the seat and checked Penny's pulse. Blood still seeped from one of her head wounds. He could see her chest rising and falling, but it was shallow. "What the hell?" he roared.

"I know," Tanner said. "We'll get her there. We'll get her some help."

Warrick didn't want to turn around, but, with the corners Tanner took at top speed, Warrick was flung around. Finally he turned around and buckled up.

There was a hard silence, and then Tanner said, "From the looks of it, we'll have to get a room for the three of you, damn it."

Warrick looked at Tanner in confusion. "What are you talking about?"

"Nina, Penny and you." He motioned at Warrick's foot.

Warrick stared down at his ankle and the shattered walking cast. He groaned. "I know the doctor will take one look at that and give me no end of hell. So will Penny."

"You better know what happened before she wakes up,

so you can deal with it and not ream her out before she has a chance to recover."

He listened in disbelief as he heard what Tanner had to say. "She was sitting there in a locked vehicle with the window wide open, watching everything happening at Nina's house?"

"She said she didn't even think about it. She was just waiting for you and me to come back to the car."

Warrick groaned, falling against the back of the seat. "It's so like her. Way too damn trusting."

Tanner chuckled. "I don't know. She figures you'll tell her off, and she says it's not fair."

"Hell, yeah, I'll give her a telling off. And it might not be fair, but it won't stop me," he said in an ominous tone.

At that, Tanner chuckled out loud.

Warrick glared at him. "You don't believe me?"

"Nope. You'll get started, take one look at her, fall down beside her and apologize yourself silly because you don't want to upset her."

"Hell," Warrick said in disgust. He turned to stare out the window moodily. "I've got it bad, don't I?"

"You do," Tanner said cheerfully. "The good thing is, she does too."

Warrick turned to face his buddy.

Tanner nodded. "Yes, I'm serious."

Warrick once again twisted in his seat to see how she was doing. She didn't even appear to have moved. "She sure as hell better make it through this," he said, "or I'll reach into the other side and pull her back so she stays with me until we're old and gray."

"That's one of the nicest things I've heard from you in a long time," Tanner said.

"Then help me make it happen," Warrick snarled.

"I'm doing it. I'm doing it." He pushed the gas pedal even harder. The car shot forward, cutting through an intersection, just making another green light. Several turns later, he headed for the hospital, pulling up outside the emergency entrance.

Warrick was already unbuckled, getting out. He opened the back door, took one look at Penny and sighed. Very gently he bent and struggled to lift her in his arms. He carried her into the hospital, ignoring all the protests of the other people waiting, nurses and doctors intervening, going straight into the emergency room, laying her down on one of the beds. Then he gasped for breath as his foot pounded with pain.

A doctor came around and took one look at him. "Are you the patient, or is she?"

He glared at the doctor, seeing somebody with salt-and-pepper hair. He had age and a lot of experience on his face, which calmed Warrick some. "Her first. And then I guess maybe me."

"You must be Warrick," the doctor said.

"The detective must have called you."

"Yes. Besides we all know your face. You're the one who saved the hospital staff. So you definitely get treated. And this young lady was with you. What the hell happened to her?" The doc was busy checking things over as he spoke to Warrick. "We'll talk as soon as I get her run through an MRI. I don't like those head wounds at all. We're gonna get a CT scan too."

The next thing Warrick knew, Penny was wheeled out of the room. He sagged down in a chair.

The doctor took one look at his leg and said, "Please tell

me you didn't run on that?"

"Somebody hit her in the head, locked her up in a basement. Then, when she escapes, the same asshole comes along, picks her up, and throws her into the back of a pickup bed and slams her head yet again. And, if that's not enough, then he packs her to the park and uses her as bait for money." Warrick's voice snapped hard and ugly. "Damn right I chased him down."

The doc stared, jaw open. When he finally recovered, he said, "Then at least please tell me that you got him?"

Warrick's phone rang. He pulled it out, checked the text and grinned fiercely. "Yeah, he's in custody."

The doctor nodded. "In that case you're next."

A nurse came around the corner with a wheelchair. She smiled and said, "Hop on, big guy. Time to get that leg X-rayed again."

He groaned. "Maybe we'll be lucky and the cast was ready to come off anyway. I can't say I felt any pain when I was running."

The doc chuckled. "Nope, you wouldn't have. You're blockheaded at both ends."

The next thing he knew, Warrick was wheeled down to X-ray. He had to wait in line. Finally he was led into another room, assisted onto the table where his leg was stretched out. The tattered remains of his cast were cut off, and then X-rays of his ankle were completed. He was sent back to the emergency room.

He was still sitting on the chair next to the bed where Penny would be upon her return when Tanner came in. Warrick looked up and frowned. "Where the hell have you been?"

Tanner sighed and held out a cup of coffee for him. "I

thought I'd tell you the officers picked up the guy, and he's down at the jail."

Warrick nodded. "Yeah, I got a text from the detective. They've X-rayed my leg, and they're running tests on Penny's head right now."

Just then Penny was wheeled back into the small room. She was still unconscious. Warrick stared at her and wanted to cry. "She is so damn small," he whispered.

"She's also a fighting terrier, so don't you worry. If anybody's beating this back, it'll be her."

They waited and waited. Not only did the test results have to be typed up but the doctor had to read them.

Finally the doctor came in and said, "She's got a skull fracture on the left side and a couple lumps on the right side. We'll keep her overnight because we want to make sure there's no bleeding on the brain. She'll be checked into the hospital. You can stay with her once we get her into a room. But she needs to stay calm, so we're giving her a light sedative to keep her under while we keep a close watch on her brain."

Warrick's heart stopped as soon as he heard *brain bleed*. He nodded mutely. After that was controlled chaos until she was settled in a room in Intensive Care. He was allowed to sit beside her.

At least until a nurse came and said, "Time for you to get a new cast."

He looked at the nurse in dismay. "Maybe check the X-rays again?" he asked hopefully. "Maybe the bone has healed by now."

Her grin was wide and fat. "Running on an injured ankle is not good for it. And it's guaranteed not to heal if you don't get it casted again. So buckle up, big guy, and let's go."

He groaned.

Tanner took his spot and waved goodbye. "I'll let you know when she wakes up."

Warrick muttered to the nurse, "You could've let me wait until she wakes up. I really don't want her to see his face first."

"Sweetie, if you don't know it by now, that girl is super-sick in love with you already. I was here when the two of you came to deal with the gunman. I can see the signs. She watched every move you made and hung on every word you said. In fact, I'd say she sees you as her hero. At least as keeper material." The nurse chuckled. "Besides she won't be waking up until tomorrow morning, guaranteed."

"Seriously?" he asked.

"Seriously."

In fact, she was dead serious because Penny didn't open her eyes until well after seven the next morning. His own eyes were gritty from sleeping in the chair, waking every time a nurse came in to check on Penny. He stared at her open eyes for a long moment before he realized she was looking at him.

"How are you feeling?" he asked as he hopped to his feet, shuddered and then hobbled over to her.

Her gaze shot downward, studying his foot. "You hurt yourself," she said. "Why? You were supposed to be getting better."

"Chasing bad guys on a walking cast is not a good idea apparently," he said cheerfully. "Don't worry. I've already been lashed out at by the doctor for having done something so stupid."

She smiled. "So then you can't get upset at me for having done something stupid either, can you?" she said triumphantly. She winced as she shifted in bed. "I can't say I feel very good."

"You've got a skull fracture, so move gently."

Her gaze widened. "What else did they say?"

"Oh, nothing much," he said cheerfully. "Except the nurse said you think I'm a keeper."

"I never said anything like that," she cried out, then shuddered at the pain. "You just made that up."

"Nope." He paused. "Does that mean you don't think I'm a keeper?"

She snorted. "You protected me, kept watch over me when I was in danger, tracked me down after I was kidnapped and then went after the asshole who did it, and you made it to my hospital bed before I woke up—all on an injured ankle." She smiled up at him, her fingers gently stroking his cheek. "Definitely a keeper."

He grinned and kissed her fingers. "I would suggest that, as soon as you get released from the hospital, maybe we go home to my place and stay in bed for at least a week," he said.

She froze in the act of shifting her position and looked up at him. "Can we?" she asked hopefully.

He chuckled. "Well, if we want to work it that way, we probably can."

She nodded. "I so want that." She raised her arms, and he leaned down to hug her. "Especially if we get to stay in bed together."

He leaned closer. "You still have a head injury. You've got to take it easy."

"You still have a foot injury," she whispered. "You've got to take it easy."

They looked at each other and beamed.

"In bed is perfect," they both said, and he kissed her gently. She wrapped her arms tighter around him and kissed him as passionately as she had before. And Warrick knew he was the luckiest man alive.

TANNER

SEALs of Honor, Book 18

Dale Mayer

PROLOGUE

T ANNER MCGRATH WATCHED Warrick and Penny from the doorway to their hospital room as they cuddled on the bed. Tanner couldn't believe that, once again, another relationship had sprung up out of nowhere. As intense and as true as this one was, he had no doubts these two would make it. They were a perfect match. Yet, if anybody had asked who would have been perfect for Warrick, Tanner would never have picked somebody like Penny. And, in the same manner, if he had been looking for somebody for Penny, he'd never have picked Warrick for her either.

Damn good thing Tanner wasn't a matchmaker because he would suck at it. But, as he thought about his own life, he realized he sucked at it anyway. He hadn't had much luck picking someone for himself.

His phone rang, and he pulled it out, checking the Caller ID. "Mason, they're both in the hospital. They'll need at least a week off," he said. "Warrick cracked the damn cast off his ankle running down the guy who beat the crap out of Penny and put her in the hospital. And, of course, she's got those three separate injuries to her head so …" He let his voice fade away.

Mason chuckled. "I'm sure there are a lot of reasons for the bed rest. I certainly don't have any problems with him getting it."

"Right. Honestly I'm jealous as hell," Tanner announced. He turned and walked down the hall, giving the two a little privacy. "Although I've had more than enough of hospitals for a while."

"Yep, me too," Mason said. "Since Warrick will be off on medical leave for at least another couple weeks, we need you back full-time."

"I only had two days off," Tanner said. "I have to admit, they've been pretty full days." He took a step around a laundry cart and also a group of hospital staff before he could speak again. "What are we up to next?"

"Paragliding. Trying out new harness designs. We'll do three or four jumps tomorrow, if we can get them in. We'll work on these for the next couple days."

Tanner grinned. "Awesome. I love jumping. Seems like I never get enough of it."

"Or, when we do any," Mason said with a laugh, "it's nighttime, and we're in silent mode, jumping into unfriendly foreign terrain."

Tanner nodded. "Isn't that the truth? So where will we be jumping tomorrow?"

"In California," Mason said. "Sorry about that. Nothing exotic for you."

"Hey, that's okay. Who's doing the training?"

Mason hesitated. "The message I got said it's a civilian trainer."

"Who is he?"

"Wynn Rider." He hesitated, then spelled the first name. "W-Y-N-N."

Tanner stopped. "Really?"

"Do you know him?"

"Nope," Tanner said. "Because it's not a him. It's a her."

"Really?"

"Yep. I saw her working with some other guys a while ago, when I did my last recreational jump. I heard she's really good. But no one from our unit has had a chance to work with her yet."

"Tomorrow your unit and one more are it. This time you get to check her out firsthand. Maybe she'll suit you."

"Nah, I doubt it. Besides, if somebody suits me, chances are it's not somebody who's good for me. I watched Warrick and Penny come together. I'm not sure I would even recognize what suits me."

"Leave it in the hands of fate," Mason said. "It hasn't failed us yet."

CHAPTER 1

B RIGHT AND EARLY the next morning, Tanner piled into
the back of the transport truck as the eight SEALs in his
unit headed over to the paragliding training session. San
Diego was a well-loved paragliding location. But the SEALs
had a private cliff edge for today's training jumps. Tanner
had done a fair bit of paragliding in his life. Always found
the experience a step above *exalted*. There was no way to
explain the sense of freedom that flying and soaring in the
sky gave him. It was seriously magical.

He wished everybody had a chance to try it at least once
in their life. He understood his unit and another SEALs unit
were trying out new harnesses today, offering better control
and able to carry more weight with extra straps for hooking
up packs. Tanner wasn't sure about the constantly changing
designs, but he was willing to go with whatever just for a
chance to soar in the sky again. At their destination they
found the other SEALs team had arrived before them. As
Tanner bailed out of the truck, Macklin called out, "Hey,
Tanner. How's that idiot Warrick doing?"

Tanner gave him the thumbs-up as he walked over to his
buddy. "Happy as a bug in bed," he said. "Especially now
that he's not alone."

Everybody else gathered around gave smug nods.

"Understood," Macklin said. "Mason's matchmaking

magic is still working."

Tanner nodded. "Warrick's healing nicely, but it'll be a while yet."

"Well, glad to have you back. Although I gather your days off weren't terribly relaxing."

"No, they weren't," Tanner said with a grin. He pointed to the blue sky above. "But this is an absolutely perfect day to be out here. Can't think of anything I'd rather do."

"Unless it's being like Warrick and stuck in bed with someone special," Macklin said with a big grin.

Tanner had to give him a point for that. "You would know. You've spent plenty of time there yourself."

"I have, and it's fantastic," Macklin said.

Shadow, with Jackson at his side, stepped up to Tanner, nudged him and said, "I think we all have, except for Tanner and Jackson here."

Macklin frowned, slid a sideways glance at Tanner, who waited, knowing the inevitable was coming. Macklin asked, "You looking?"

"Nope. Don't get me into this."

Macklin shook his head. "I wouldn't knock it. Fate has a habit of turning around and smacking you in the face."

Tanner nodded. "I watched Warrick and Penny come together. I tell you that was almost cataclysmic. It doesn't happen like that for everybody though."

"It sure hasn't for me," Jackson said in joking manner.

"No, probably not," Shadow said. "But, when you find the right one, there's nothing like it."

Shadow rarely spoke, and, when he did, it was something to listen to. *Big, silent, indomitable* was how Tanner always thought of Shadow. The SEAL groups were made up of all alpha males. They had to be just to do the kind of work they did. But there was something about Mason's team. Tanner was part of the expanded unit. So many guys were working together now, regardless of their unit assignment, that it was hard to know sometimes who worked with who. But that was what made all the units work so well, whether alone or on a joint mission.

Over thirty of them had trained together closely. Across the country were over two thousand men like Tanner. His brother SEALs. He counted himself as one of the lucky ones to be a part of this unique and select brotherhood. And maybe, if only on the inside, Tanner wondered about finding someone special, like what Mason's team had found, well, who could blame him? Watching Warrick's relationship with Penny evolve had been pure magic. Tanner was really happy for the big guy.

The training session started. They were called to attention, separated into groups and brought over to various paragliders already laid out. These were some of the biggest out there, with the silks spanning forty feet when fully opened or otherwise engaged in flight. Sometimes the silks were called wings, like *a pair of.* But these were just one continuous swath of silk. Regardless, these were some kind of beautiful when aloft in the air.

Then fifteen minutes of safety instruction followed and thereafter another fifteen minutes just going over the differences between these new units and the old ones they might have used before. Apparently the newer versions allowed their riders to get closer to the cliffs, to land faster, presumably without crashing.

Tanner would soon find out.

When instructed to, Tanner stepped up to the blue-and-white unit in front of him near the cliff's edge. He had a huge grin on his face; he'd always been partial to blue. It was a great color for the sky, and today, well, hell, it was just a damn good day to be outside doing anything.

Twenty minutes later it was his turn. As he soared off the cliff, the single swath of silks on each paraglider already billowed high above him as the wind lifted him to join them. This was where he got to really live. Man had been trying to fly ever since they first saw birds in the air. What freedom this was.

Immediately a breeze caught Tanner's paraglider and lifted him higher and higher, sending him soaring well above everyone else. It was absolutely perfect. He soared and dipped, coasted, experimenting to understand how the new controls worked. These were fantastic.

He glanced over to see a bright purple-and-white unit. It was Wynn. He gave her a single hand wave, and she smiled at him, waving back.

If he couldn't be alone up here, being silent with the others was the next best thing. He watched the other gliders circle around toward their designated landing target. Following suit, sad to come down, he slowly angled his way lower and lower to the big zone marked off on the beach below.

This was the first of several trips today. He needed to understand how these controls worked, so that, by the end of the day, he had it down. With that thought in mind, with each jump, he played around a little more, understanding the controls, swooping left, then right. He could make a bit of a nose adjustment too, which was interesting. He played with that a little, and the whole time Wynn stayed close to him.

Finally he circled, lowered himself, using the brakes, and came to a clumsy stop on the ground. He laughed out loud, loving life. He turned to watch Wynn execute a perfect landing with her purple silks billowing to rest beside him. He called out in admiration, "You've obviously done this a time or two."

She laughed and nodded. She walked over, unclipping the harness around her chest, and held out a hand. "I'm Wynn Rider. You were working with one of my assistants earlier. I didn't get a chance to introduce myself."

He shook her hand, happy just to feel her firm grip beneath his. "These are quite the gliders." His smile was still full of joy.

"And you're obviously one of those who loves to be up there."

He nodded. "I can't think of anything better."

Her smile beamed. "Then we're agreed. You ready to go again?"

He laughed. "Absolutely."

Not only did he get to go again, but again and again, trying out one of the gliders with some specially designed aluminum framework to hold weapons. By the end of the day, heading off for his last trip, he stood in line and waited, watching as they headed off the cliff's edge, going three at a time. He glanced over at Mason and said, "Today is just one of those days you can't ever forget."

Mason chuckled. "Isn't that the truth? We haven't had a day to do this in a long time."

"Hard to believe we're getting paid for it too," Tanner said with a big grin. He caught sight of Wynn on the far side of Mason, making adjustments on Shadow's harness while talking to another instructor. They were using different harnesses this time. He frowned as he looked over to see if there was a problem. He nodded to Mason and said, "Do you think that's an issue?"

Mason turned, glanced and shrugged. "I'll have to trust the instructors in this case."

Tanner nodded.

Mason roared off the edge of the cliff, in perfect form as always. He was one of those guys who did well at everything.

Tanner was less so. He had a little bit more of the country farm in him. Big, rugged, raw-boned, so not everything came easy. Things like dancing were damn hard. His feet wanted to do anything but. Yet, when it came to karate and judo, his feet danced just fine.

He stepped up next and saw Wynn step up beside him. "Any reason you're tacking onto me again?"

"You have this tendency to be last," she said with a smile. "And I will always be with the last one."

He glanced around and realized she was right. He shrugged. "I don't want it to end. This is the last run of the day, and it's been glorious. Thank you very much for your part."

She shrugged and said, "Hey, I'd do this every day all day if I could." She kept shifting her harness, checking her lines.

"You and me both," he said with feeling. "Any problem with your paraglider?"

She shook her head. "One of the instructors had a bit of an issue with the harness earlier, so I'll take it down myself. See if anything is wrong with it."

He frowned. "Is that safe?"

"We'll find out," she said, laughing as she raced off the cliff beside him.

Her answer was likely meant as a joke, but he couldn't quite relax. These paragliders were absolutely stunning. The ride was freeing, like being one with the world, but the minute there was an issue, it was as unforgiving as the rest of Mother Nature. Still, Wynn appeared to have no problem as she caught a thermal updraft and floated above him. Close by, the two of them glided gracefully through the sky. He twisted and turned, dancing on the wind, absolutely loving how the paraglider responded. He'd have to remember to say something to her when they hit the ground.

If she had anything to do with the design changes on the harness, he was all for them.

He was still smiling, his eyes closed, his face in the wind, reveling in this moment, when he heard a strangled exclamation. He turned to catch sight of Wynn struggling. The frame of her paraglider had folded, causing her silks to collapse, and she plummeted. He dove down beside her and could see her struggling even more to hold on. The strings were likely tangled, but he couldn't tell from where he was. She pulled hard to right her rig but started to crash-dive. He dropped the nose of his glider, tilted his unit and dove deep. Paragliders were generally meant for one, although there were special harnesses for tandem flights. Tanner had done plenty of safety trainings in tandem but hadn't undertaken any midflight rescues.

Until now.

And it was damn hard to do a rescue in these paragliders. He'd never had any training for something like this, and it definitely required fast thinking. He maneuvered under her, hoping for an unorthodox tandem midair hookup, expecting to feel the blow when she fell into his silks, knowing they would tumble twice as fast with twice the expected weight. He could see her above him, still struggling inside her silks, but he couldn't see what she was doing.

Had she pulled her parachute? Did she carry a spare? Or was she flying light without a reserve chute?

He couldn't communicate with her. He could only hope that she understood he was underneath her, like a safety net of sorts. Although she might prefer to take the blow herself, to avoid injuring anyone else, and slam into the ground alone, she could inadvertently take him down with her if she just didn't realize he was here. But he couldn't open his chute, or he'd pop up above her. Then he'd lose his chance to try a tandem maneuver. He slipped off to the side of her, watching her progress.

She caught sight of him and gave him a worried glance, and he slipped back underneath her. If her glider completely failed, she wouldn't have any choice. She'd plummet on top of him.

By now the people on the ground could see they were in trouble. He was trying to stay directly under her, but she was in a nose-dive pattern while he had to circle to lower his unit down, and that made it much harder. He took one more chance at shifting to the side to see what she was up to. Her wings had fully collapsed and sent her plummeting.

He dove down underneath, catching her just as she slammed into his wings. But her added weight folded his silks, with both ends drooped uselessly toward the ground, and Wynn bringing down the center point. Yet it brought her closer to him. He felt for her harness through the silks and grabbed on tight before he pulled his chute. This was like yanking on the parking brake when the foot brakes wouldn't respond in a car. Not the best thing but the second-best thing at the moment. They were jerked back and up, and he heard her cry out. The chute was tangled in the mess above him. It slowed their descent but not enough.

She shouted, "Hit the water."

He glanced around to see a river below them to the right. It would still be a hard blow of a landing but was their best option. He adjusted his angle as much as he could, hoping it was enough. The wind caught and dragged his disabled mess toward the water. He fought for control. Yet again, he could hear her yelling something above him, but he couldn't make out her words.

By now the wind had really twisted up his own silks, and they went down faster and faster. He had to worry about them drowning, tangled in the lines while underwater. He kept his focus on the river as they came in hard and fast. Before he was about to hit, he reached up and unhooked from his harness. It wouldn't do much for him—or even for her—but it might cut down Wynn's speed at the moment of her impact with the water.

He let their rigging soar above him as he dropped below, and *smack,* he hit the river hard. Instantly he drove up to the surface, searching for Wynn. His and her silks were a tangled mess on the surface, the frames dragging them down, the current already catching one section of it. He could see everyone on the river bank racing toward them, but there was no sign of Wynn. He pulled out his knife from his boot and swam toward the swirling mass of purple and blue and white silk in the center of the river. He grabbed a big gulp of air, went back down underwater and luckily spotted her immediately.

When he caught her up in his arms, she struggled, her panic instinctively already taking over. Tanner pinched her hard to grab her attention, then slammed his mouth over hers and blew his oxygen into her mouth—then started cutting. She relaxed as if understanding he was here to help and that her struggles made that worse. As it was, she'd gotten herself into a hell of a tangled mess.

He popped up to get another gulp of air, went back down, transferred more air to her and back to work cutting lines. The water churned around him as the others came in to help. Finally she was freed.

When Tanner broke through the surface again, he could see her gasping for air, but Shadow had her in a firm grasp as he moved her toward the shoreline.

Tanner called out to her, "Are you okay?"

She raised a hand with a thumbs-up sign.

Mason appeared beside him. "What about you? That was a pretty hard landing."

Tanner nodded, gasping for breath. "I'm okay. We need to get this mess out of the river though."

"The guys are on it," Mason said.

They made their way to the shoreline and dragged themselves up the steep embankment to collapse on the grassy edge. Tanner sat there, soaking wet, catching his breath as he studied the wreckage in front of them. "I'd sure like to know what happened."

"You're not thinking sabotage, are you?" Mason asked. "In our line of work, we tend to get caught up in that thinking a little too easily."

Tanner chuckled. "She said one of her assistants had an issue with the harness, so Wynn was flying it to check it out herself. She started off fine but then not so fine. I just know, at the end there, her lines and wings were completely tangled, and I thought I saw some loose lines flying free."

Mason's frown was instantaneous.

Tanner nodded. "Right. To me that sounds ominous already."

"Take a closer look into that."

"I'm on it."

A truck drove up behind them. Jackson and Kanen hopped out. They ran winches from the back of the truck and were already in lighter gear, out of their boots and jackets, heading into the water to hook onto the paragliders. Sodden silks now were entangled with debris from the river. It took a few minutes, and, with Mason and Tanner helping, they had both paragliders and the silks on shore, up on the side of the river.

Mason turned to look at Tanner. "Was your unit okay?"

"It was fine, until we tangled coming down." He turned and walked to where Wynn remained on her back, staring up at the blue sky. He collapsed beside her. "Close call."

She rolled her head toward him and gave him a half smile. "Thanks for the rescue."

He shook his head. "I think it was more of a guided crash than a rescue."

"The problem with coming down on top of you is getting your silks all caught up too," she said. "It would have been better for me to go down alone than to kill us both. But honestly I *really* didn't want to smack into the ground at that speed."

"Neither did I. Good call on the river."

"It was a last-minute thought," she said with a half laugh. "By the time I hit the water, I realized I was between two sets of gliders with a mess of tangled lines."

"But I had my knife on me, and we got you out of there, so it's all good." They lay there quietly for a long moment. "Changes your view of life, doesn't it?" he said.

"It sure does."

"Scared to go again?"

She shook her head. "No. But I want to know what happened to that harness."

"Ever had an accident before?"

She nodded. "Sure, just a couple, but they were a long time ago," she admitted. "I've been doing this for ten years professionally. First competing and then training. I've never had an accident like this."

"What are you thinking?" Tanner asked.

"This may sound weird and totally unrelated, especially since I wasn't paragliding. But, in the last couple months or so, I've had three odd incidences leading up to this."

"All of them this bad?"

She shook her head. "No, not even close. Makes me wonder if this one today wasn't supposed to be the finale."

As her words settled in his soul, he stared at her with a grim realization. "You think all four of these recent *incidences*—paragliding or not—were on purpose?"

"Yes. *And* no. I don't know, … but I really don't want this one in particular to have been premeditated. Yet, I don't know what else to think," she said. "Like I said, ten years, nothing out of the ordinary. Now this." She shook her head, bounded to her feet and brushed the debris off her wet clothing. "Time to do a postmortem." And she turned and walked away.

WYNN COULDN'T STOP the shaking. She hoped Tanner hadn't noticed. It was hardly a sign of confidence if the instructor went to pieces in front of her students. Yet, these SEALs were probably better prepared for this kind of emergency than she was. Like she'd told him, *ten years*. Sure there'd been a couple mishaps over the life of her career—

and now a few minor things of late, mostly concerning her personal life—but nothing while paragliding that was anything like today. What she hadn't told Tanner was how the parachute she always wore hadn't opened earlier. Whoever had intended for her to go down had planned for her to go down and to stay down. That was a sobering thought.

Her legs were still wobbly as she made her way to the school's truck she'd driven out here. In her heart she knew today had been no accident—it had been sabotage. But she'd have to go over the glider in order to prove it. This was her personal paraglider, her own specially designed harness. This had to be a personal attack.

She hadn't gotten more than twenty feet when her arm was grabbed roughly. She spun, surprised to see Tanner glaring at her. She raised an eyebrow. "What's the matter?"

"What do you mean, *incidences*? Explain." He spoke slowly, enunciating each word carefully. "And do you realize what you're saying?"

She shot him a hard look. "I know what I suspect, yes. Three *incidences* before this are three too many. And this one almost killed me." She glanced around. "I could have died several times over on this flight. If it wasn't for you, I probably would have," she said boldly. "But I did survive, and that won't make somebody very happy, will it?"

"Who?"

His tone was harsh. As if he were still coming to terms with the fact that somebody evidently was trying to kill her. "I'm not sure," she said honestly.

In the back of her mind—what with the road rage incident and the break-in at home and the falling pillar narrowly missing her at work—she'd wondered, so she'd fully checked her equipment today with extra care. Then Trish had wanted to try Wynn's personal rig, so Wynn had let her do one flight. When Trish had worried that something was wrong, Wynn checked it over again quickly, then decided the best way to figure out the problem was to take it for a flight.

"I work with a lot of people. I wouldn't have said I had any enemies." She shrugged. "I have a lot of friends, but of course nobody is perfect."

"You have no idea who could be trying to kill you?"

Kanen stopped the truck close to them. "Do you guys want a lift?"

Wynn shook her head, pointing. "That's my ride there." The school's logo was on both sides of that truck.

"Good enough." And he drove off.

Tanner walked, his boots wet, his clothing completely soaked, and yet he didn't seem to notice, whereas she could already feel her thighs chafing, her ankles blistering inside her shoes. She wanted nothing more than to go home and to have a hot bath, curl up in bed and think about what just happened. No, actually she'd rather go to sleep and forget about what just happened. But it was well past the point of pushing this off as being her imagination. Today, whoever had tried to kill her had almost succeeded.

CHAPTER 2

TWO HOURS LATER Wynn arrived at the school, wet and shaken. She entered the front office building, heading toward the showers and her locker. Luckily she had a full change of clothes still here, including underwear and shoes. She didn't feel much better afterward, but at least she was dry. She left the office building, locking it up behind her, crossed the huge tarmac area and entered the warehouse.

She stood alone in the school's warehouse—really two adjoining hangars with storage in loft areas above and in various corners below or on shelving units all around its perimeter, leaving the main square footage open and unobstructed. She stared at the skeleton of her paraglider, now on the floor of the warehouse. She'd had this one for a couple years. And it had certainly done its time and more, but she'd always been very strict about its maintenance and safety. It should have lasted another several years. It wasn't the only one she had, but it was by far her favorite.

It was late, and she was tired, but she knew she would never get to sleep tonight without at least *some* answers.

The crash itself had caused more damage to what had already been wrong with the glider—per Trish's earlier remarks—not to mention the lines that were cut to rescue her. How would she tell those helpful cuts from possibly those harmful ones? And then there was her chute. It had failed to open. Something that had yet to happen to her. Ever. That it would happen at the same time as the paraglider failing was more than a coincidence. She stood, rocking on her heels, her hands in her jeans pockets, as she stared at the crumpled mess in front of her. *Should I tell the cops? But it's just supposition at this point. Hard to find any evidence after the crash landing and the watery rescue.*

Proving sabotage, … well, that would be hard to do. Still she had to try.

She bent down and straightened out what she could of the glider and its silks. Once the pieces were relatively in the correct position and the wings were stretched out to their full forty-foot span, then she studied the remains. What was missing was her parachute. Not seeing it, she walked around to where Tanner's paraglider sat in a crumpled heap. He'd taken the brunt of her fall, both that of her accelerating body weight and that of her paraglider.

Since she and Tanner had both crashed, chances were his paraglider was done for too. As she searched through the remains, she found his parachute still attached but not hers. Frowning, she walked over to a nearby corner, where her jacket and personal belongings were, wondering if somebody had tossed the chute there. But there was no sign of it.

Walking toward her backpack, she pulled out her cell phone. Heading to the wreckage again, she took pictures from as many angles as she could to examine later on her computer. But she couldn't let go of the fact that her chute was missing. The best answer was it lay at the bottom of the river. Which meant she would never see it again.

She always packed her own chutes. That was just one of the many safety checks that she did. So what happened here? After she'd taken pictures, she bent down on her hands and knees and slowly examined the lines inch by inch. There were multiple cut lines, but, given Tanner's underwater rescue of her, that was to be expected. But what about the two slashes in the wings? Had these occurred before the crash landing in the water? Considering the branches in the river, likely not.

When she'd first noticed trouble, her wings were billowing, and a line had snapped up in the top right corner.

With heavy thoughts, she stood, snagged her jacket and backpack, took one last look around, shut off the lights and walked out, locking the door behind her. She crossed the tarmac separating the warehouse hangars from the front office building. Her deep-purple Jeep sat in the first parking lot, outside the main office door—the last lonely vehicle in the lot.

As she pulled away from the school, she glanced behind her, wondering what it would take to get to the bottom of this.

For so long, paragliding had been her life. She now taught paragliding classes at the school on a regular basis for the last two years. Although unnerved by today's events and grateful to be alive, she knew she didn't dare let the fear overtake her, keep her from going up again, or she'd lose her livelihood. And the way to get over that fear was to get back on that proverbial horse as soon as possible and also to get answers about what happened today.

Back at the apartment where she was temporarily housesitting, only a few miles away from the warehouse, she downloaded all the images from her phone onto her laptop. While the transfers took place, she made a simple sandwich and a hot cup of tea, then sat down to take a closer look. She was too tired to see any differences from what she had noticed in person. Knowing the pictures were all safe, backed up in the cloud, she shut down her laptop and headed to bed. But sleep wouldn't come easily.

She kept waking up as she relived the crash over and over again. Lying under the covers, soaked in sweat, it seemed like her initial shock had receded, and now her body's full reaction to the trauma had settled in.

She huddled, letting the tears flow as she realized just how close she'd come to not even lying in this bed anymore. Finally exhausted, she'd slept, but the last thoughts in her mind were *Who hated her enough to want her dead? And why?*

TANNER CALLED THE paragliding school, looking to speak with Wynn.

"I'm sorry, she's not in yet," came the chipper voice.

He frowned. "I left a message earlier. When she gets in, could you please tell her to call me?"

"Is this Tanner?"

"Yes. Please pass on the message. I'll keep calling until she answers me."

"Persistent, aren't you?" But the woman on the other end of the call had said it on a happy sigh, as if that was the best thing somebody could be.

Tanner shook his head, not quite understanding the attitude. "In this case, yes," he said briskly. He clicked off his phone, pocketed it and walked into the impromptu meeting. He hoped he was on time, but he couldn't let go of talking to Wynn to make sure she was okay. He still wasn't happy at having to leave last night with the rest of the teams, but, without wheels of his own and still on duty, he couldn't avoid it.

Mason glanced at him as he walked in. Kanen was here too. "Did you get ahold of her?"

Tanner shook his head and took his seat as the commander stepped up to the front of the helicopter hangar where they'd been working. The next hour was a rehash of so much of the same old stuff that it was hard to pay attention. At one point, Kanen smacked Tanner on the leg, and he bolted upright. The commander caught the movement and gave Tanner a half glare. He returned it with a small smile.

Finally the meeting was over, and they filed outside. Kanen said, "You were really lost in there."

"I can't get over Wynn feeling the accident was no accident," he muttered in a low tone for only Kanen's ears.

But true to form Mason heard. "Are you sure?"

"Hell no. That's what I wanted to talk to her about," Tanner said. "Apparently this is her fourth *incident* in several months."

The men stopped.

Tanner nodded. "This one was by far the worst. She's afraid it was sabotage."

"Why didn't she say anything yesterday to us?" Mason exclaimed as Jackson joined them.

"I didn't have a chance to ask. I suspect she wanted to find evidence first."

"After a crash like that, I'd be surprised if anything is left to find," Jackson said. "Are you sure somebody didn't follow her home and finish the job?"

Tanner shot Jackson a horrified look. "I called the school's main number several times last night but got no answer. So then I searched for her cell number. Called it a couple times. Still no answer. But, with her in the air as much as she is, her cell's probably sitting in her Jeep. And

I've called the school three times already this morning, speaking with their receptionist," he said.

"Somebody went to a lot of trouble, if they're responsible for all four attempts on her life in the last several months," Jackson warned. "This one would definitely have killed her if you hadn't been there with her."

"She had said something about the assistant instructor having trouble with Wynn's unit earlier, and so I stuck with her. I just had this feeling …"

"Did she say what the original trouble was?" Kanen asked.

Tanner shook his head.

"Sounds like nobody should have taken it up," Mason said. "It was a pretty grim end to an otherwise great day."

"True enough," Tanner said. "But we've done enough paragliding to know it's a relatively safe sport."

"As long as maintenance is done on all the equipment," Jackson said. "And I have to believe somebody who does this for a living knows how to look after her gear."

"Not only does she look after her gear but she's been working on new designs and prototypes for a long time," Mason said. "Normally we would have had this training within our own ranks, but, because this is one of her designs, we were test bunnies for a civilian."

"Personally I thought her gliders were dynamite," Tanner declared. "So much more control. I could have floated for hours up there. The second run was particularly good. With all the warm air funnels, I was up for almost an hour."

Mason agreed.

Tanner asked Jackson, "Did you see anything odd about Wynn's run yesterday?"

"You mean, other than the fact she crashed and burned

in a spectacular way?"

"And we're sure it's not something else?" Kanen asked cautiously. "I know she seems sane and normal and all that stuff, but you know what? Going down like that could certainly have been a suicide attempt."

The other guys just stared at Kanen.

Kanen shrugged. "I know that's not the first thing that comes to mind, but we've certainly seen it happen and been surprised each time."

"We might have, but I don't see her as that type of person," Tanner said quietly, his mind refuting the idea.

She was so full of life and had struggled so hard to hold the paraglider in the sky. And then she'd been determined not to take him down with her. For those who wanted to believe it was a failed suicide attempt, they would probably take that as a confirmation of their theory. Yet, in his view, it showed an instructor who was bound and determined to not take another life down with her. Never an easy thing to do.

He shook his head. "I don't see it." Just then his phone rang. He pulled it from his pocket, noting the ID on his screen, calling out, "It's her." He took several steps away. "Wynn, are you okay?"

The light laugh on the other end of the phone reassured him, and he relaxed slightly and rocked on his heels. "Glad to hear you're laughing. I was more than a little worried about you last night. I felt terrible leaving."

"It was quite chaotic, and you were on duty, so it makes sense."

"How late did you stay?"

"A couple hours," she admitted. "I took a lot of pictures after I got my equipment stretched out, trying to figure out what happened. But there's so much damage and so many cut strings from not only the crash but from untangling me and then from getting it loaded back up again that honestly I'm not sure I can tell anything. That's the conclusion I came to last night anyway," she said, but her voice was quiet.

In the background he could hear a lot of noise. "Are you at work?"

"Yes, I am. That was my personal paraglider, but yours was company-owned. So, of course, I have meetings coming up this morning about the accident. Postmortems are never fun. Yours is damaged to the point it's a write-off, and the school's insurance will cover it, but that's not the issue."

"It could have been worse," he joked. "We both could have crashed and burned on the ground."

"Believe me, that joke's been tossed around a couple times already this morning." Her tone turned brisk as she added, "So you don't need to keep calling me. I'm fine."

"Except for the fact somebody's trying to kill you ..." He growled. "And I really don't want anything to happen to you."

"Just because you saved my life once," she said on another laugh, "does not make you responsible for it ever after."

"Well, there's definitely a line of thought that says exactly the opposite." He didn't know how to make her realize how serious this was. Finally he said, "If something happened to you, and I didn't do anything about it when I could have, I'd never forgive myself. I get that you don't know me and maybe don't particularly care to know me, but I do feel like we've bonded over a near-death experience that's just a little too horrific to relive."

"I hope to never relive it," she said. "I don't mean to make light of it. I just don't think there's anything you can do."

"Are you going to contact the police?"

"I'm not sure what I can tell them. I had a paragliding accident. Was it possibly sabotage? Yes. Did a line snap, even though we do the best we can to change them out after so many flight hours are logged? Yes. But accidents do happen."

"What about your chute?" He heard her catch her breath and frowned. "Please tell me that you just couldn't get to it or something like that."

"I got to it," she said, her voice soft, barely above a whisper. "But it wouldn't open."

"Shit," he whispered. "You see? Now that's just another one of those major things happening to you recently that make this all too real."

"How do you think I felt about it?" she said. "Particularly at the time. The thing is, I haven't found my chute. All the equipment came back to the warehouse, but there's no sign of my chute. I figure it's at the bottom of the river."

Now he *really* didn't like to hear that. "Who packs the chutes?"

"I always do my own," she said, her tone weary. "So, in theory, there shouldn't have been a problem."

"And those do happen every once in a while," he said thoughtfully. "But when you add it all together, no way this is a coincidence."

"Exactly," she said, her voice getting fainter.

Then he heard somebody call out to her, and she responded with "I'll be there in a minute."

She came back to his conversation. "Look. I have to go. The bosses aren't very happy with me at the moment. *Bad press* and all that."

"Just how unhappy are they?" His voice was hard. "Are they unhappy you destroyed the equipment or unhappy you survived?"

"Good question," she said. "But I have no answer yet." Then she hung up.

He put away his phone, turned around to see the rest of the guys had moved off. He walked over to join the few left.

Mason asked, "Any update?"

"She went over the equipment last night, couldn't find any sign of obvious sabotage. However, there was so much damage after the crash that she's not sure she would have been able to tell. However, there is one other point that made me extremely leery."

The men looked at him expectantly.

He said, "Her chute also didn't open."

At that, everybody stiffened.

Tanner nodded. "Right. Too many *accidents* all at once."

"Yeah. And that takes it into the realm of attempted murder," Jackson said quietly. "And, of course, she's probably not going to the police without hard evidence, is she? Not to mention if she's the type to think the best of people, she's not going to believe she's actually in danger."

"Right. I don't think she's going to the police any time soon," Tanner said. "She was heading into a meeting with her bosses. Apparently they're not terribly impressed. Bad press, damaged equipment, etcetera."

But Mason put that in perspective. "And you have to wonder just how many people might want to see her in trouble with the bosses."

"Or how the bosses might want to see her fail, although I'm not sure just why they would want that," Kanen said.

"Hard to say. But, no matter which way you look at it, she's in trouble." Tanner agreed. "The problem is, what am I going to do about it?"

CHAPTER 3

B Y THE TIME the meeting with her bosses was over, Wynn felt rough. One of the owners, Curtis, had been pretty vocal about the damage to the school's paraglider. He had couched it in terms of *Oh, thank goodness Tanner was there to save you*, but, at the same time, Curtis had made her feel bad because the cost of these paragliders was pretty extreme. As if she didn't have a good idea of that, since she and her brother had their own business of designing and producing paragliders.

But her main boss, Charlie, had been the worst, saying the bad press would kill their business. And the whole reason for bringing her on board was to increase business. She was supposed to be the face of paragliding, to give them a whole new lease on life, a marketing uptick, so to speak. And now, with the bad press, her presence was a detriment—one he would like to put a quick stop to. She'd explained about the sabotage, but he wouldn't listen. And that's why she wasn't telling the police. They'd just brush it off as Charlie had.

He was angry it had happened at all. She understood that. She wondered if it was time to leave. She and her brother, who was an engineer, were designing new harnesses. They'd applied for patents on several new control systems. Still, she had hoped to stay here at the school for at least another two to three years, to pay the bills but also to fund their research while the patents went through, before they began producing their own paragliders. She needed this job. She needed to keep producing money.

On cue, her phone rang. She looked at the screen to see Todd's name. He had probably heard by now. Groaning, she answered it with a bright, cheerful voice. "Hey, how is big brother doing?"

"It depends if little sister held something back about her day yesterday, something that even still terrifies me to think might have been the truth."

She groaned, walked over to the big window, stared out over the tarmac. "Who told you?"

"Harry. You know how he likes to keep me in touch with everything you're doing, good and bad," her brother said caustically. "Why didn't you tell me?"

"Because I didn't want to worry you," she said quietly, making sure nobody could overhear. "And I'm fine, thank you."

"How bad was it?"

"Well, if one of the other paragliders hadn't helped maneuver me down safely, I would have smacked into the ground at about thirty miles per hour," she said, like speaking of someone else. "At my suggestion, we bailed into the river, and I almost drowned because I got caught up in the lines and between the wings of his paraglider and mine."

There was a shocked silence on the other end of the phone before he yelled, "What?"

"Yeah. So it was bad." She took a deep breath. "And you're right. I should have called you, but I was pretty shaken. My body's real reaction set in sometime in the middle of the night, when I woke up reliving the landing over and over again."

"How did it happen?" His words were stuttered.

It had been just the two of them for years. Their parents had been gone a long time now. So she and Todd were very close, and, of course, if she had died, he would have been left alone. "I'm sorry. I didn't mean to be quite so callous about it all. But I'm finding it's a little easier to deal with the pain and shock myself if I don't dwell on it too much. As for what happened, the corner right line snapped, and the wing billowed up and lost its loft. The framework came apart in midair."

"But that should never happen."

"I know," she said quietly. "I have lots of pictures of my crashed paraglider. I did stretch it all out in the hangar last night and took photos of everything."

"Send them to me," he said. "I want to go over them."

"One other thing you should know," she said. She took a deep breath. "I reached for my parachute. And it wouldn't open. And you know I was flying without a reserve," she murmured. "As I always do."

More silence passed, and then he exploded. "Oh, my God. Oh, my God. Oh, my God."

She leaned against the window; her heart warmed at her brother's reaction. "Right?" she said calmly. "And that can happen, as we well know. But not very often."

"About one in every ten thousand," he said.

Her brother loved data.

"Accidents do happen. Shit still goes wrong. But in this case …"

"Yeah, in this case, somebody wanted to make sure I did not survive that fall."

"Who?" he asked urgently.

"I haven't a clue," she said.

Two men walked toward her. She gave them a smile and stepped out of the nearby doorway, turning slightly so they would know and see she was on the phone. They walked on past.

With a sigh of relief, she whispered, "I just came out of a meeting with the bosses. Curtis is pissed off about the school's paraglider being damaged. And Charlie is pissed off at what he says is *catastrophic bad press.*"

"I don't suppose either of them expressed sorrow that you were involved in such a horrific accident," Todd said. "Isn't it time you quit that job?"

"I'm not sure I'll have a job to quit in a couple days," she said. "They weren't happy at all. If the media gets ahold of this, and it becomes a shit storm, then you can bet I won't have a job tomorrow."

"I'm totally okay with that. We'll make do one way or another."

She smiled. Her brother not only loved data, he loved engineering and building. But he did not handle the books, and he did not pay the rent or buy the groceries. "You know we can't afford for me to quit," she said. "As much as I would enjoy the downtime, I can't quit. We need the money."

"Do we though? Maybe we need to sell assets instead."

"You've got a good point there," she said cheerfully. "We've got to make sure that, whoever this asshole is, he doesn't succeed. No point in working for a living if I don't get to live."

"No joking," he snapped. "This is serious."

"It is. I know," she said gently. "I'm sorry. I'm just distancing myself from it all. It was pretty horrible."

"I'm sure it was," he said. "Are you coming home now?

Surely it's safer here."

"No," she said. "As much as I'd like to, I need to see this through. I've got a class in a couple hours."

"Call me if anything else turns up. And make sure you send me those damn photos."

"I will," she promised. Hanging up, she pocketed her phone and headed back into the hangar. They ran a lot of classes here with a lot of instructors, and there was always maintenance to be done on the equipment. What she didn't want was for anybody to assume she'd lost her nerve.

As she walked in, Bruce called out, "Shitty day yesterday, huh?"

She nodded. "One of the worst."

"You're going back up again?"

"I so am," she called out with a thumbs-up sign. In fact, she was due to go out in another two hours. She checked her watch and considered that. *Gives me time to go over my remaining paraglider to make sure it's not damaged.*

And, if people left her alone, she could get that done. She walked into the second hangar where her spare paraglider was, and this time she went over it with extra care, taking photos before she was due to head out.

Curtis came over and stood in front of her. "What are you doing?"

"Checking my equipment before I go out this afternoon."

"I changed your teaching schedule this afternoon," he said. "I figured you needed some time off."

She straightened and glared at him. "Why would you do that?"

He shrugged. "It was an unnerving experience. I figured a day off wouldn't hurt you."

As much as she studied him, she couldn't see anything deceptive in his face. But his tone was slightly off. She shook her head. "I'm fine."

"You might be fine, but what will you do if you damage this one?" he said, motioning to the paraglider in front of her. "You only own two."

"I'll get another," she said shortly. "What excuse did you use for my class?"

"Just that you're under the weather."

"Not good enough," she said. "These people signed up to work with me. A substitute is not the same thing."

"It's not like you can't be replaced," he said. "Maybe this is a good chance, a good opportunity, to figure out just how replacing you would look." And he turned and walked away.

TANNER DROVE HIS Jeep into the school's large parking lot and parked beside a dark purple Jeep. He hopped out and walked into the front of the office building.

The receptionist smiled. "We're just about to close," she said. "In fact, almost everybody's gone. Is there anything I can help you with?"

He smiled at her. "I'm looking for Wynn. Is she still here?"

The receptionist pointed at the purple Jeep through the big front window and said, "If that's here, she's here."

He cast a glance back and grinned. "Figures she drives something like that."

"Apparently she has driven nothing but Jeeps since she was sixteen." The receptionist laughed. "The guys bug her about it a lot. This is the first one she's had in a girly color, she says."

He twisted and studied the rich plum-hued Jeep. "I really like that color. It's more of a deep purple than a light lavender girly purple."

"I think it's pretty too," the receptionist confessed. "The warehouse doors are still open, if you want to walk over there. She's probably cleaning up."

"Did she have any training sessions today?"

"She was supposed to but was grounded after the accident yesterday. Another instructor went up in her place."

He nodded, turned and walked away with a wave of thanks. But inside he wondered. He was relieved she hadn't gone out, but, at the same time, it was better for her if she immediately did. The longer one took to get back on the horse, so to speak, the harder it was to do so. It was a good couple minutes' walk crossing the pavement to the open warehouse. He stood just inside the big open hangar doors and searched. It was gloomy inside. He took several steps in and called out, "Wynn, you here?"

Silence.

But when he thought he heard raised voices, he walked toward the back. As he got closer, both voices were definitely male, though Tanner called out again, "Wynn?"

Two men stepped forward and frowned at him.

Tanner held up his hands. "Hey, I'm not trespassing or anything. The receptionist told me that I'd find Wynn back here. Have you seen her?"

Both men shook their heads, one of them saying. "No, she's gone for the day."

Tanner pointed over his shoulder with his thumb. "But her Jeep is still here."

The guy who had spoken shrugged. "Don't know anything about that."

The second man shot the first one a hard look. "She's around here somewhere. I saw her about a half hour ago."

Sensing the tension and not liking it, Tanner nodded. "Well, either I can look around or you guys can point me in the direction where I'll find her." He said it coolly but with a tone that declared he fully intended to find her, and he'd go looking himself and, if they didn't want him to find something, too damn bad.

The first man gave a sound of disgust. "She's probably over in the other hangar. Just go through that door there."

He pointed to a door Tanner hadn't seen at first glance. He nodded and walked toward it. It was unlocked. He pushed it open, checked behind him and found the two guys were again in a heated argument, but this time their voices were muted, as if they didn't want him to hear. People argued. That didn't mean every dispute was nefarious or had to be broadcast for everyone to hear. It could be about who made the coffee that day. Too often it was something silly like that.

The next room was full of hanging silks, framework, parts and pieces, like a repair shop. He called out, "Hey, Wynn, are you in here?" From the far back corner he heard a muffled sound. He walked toward it to see her straightening up parachutes. "Hey, glad to see you're still here."

She turned, startled.

Her face lit up when she saw him, making him feel good.

"Hey, what are you doing here?"

He shrugged self-consciously. "I guess I wanted to make sure you're still alive."

She held out her arms. "As you can see, I am."

He nodded. "You didn't teach today?"

Her arms dropped to her sides, and she turned back to the parachutes. "No," she said. "The bosses thought I should have the day off."

"Was it the bosses' decision or yours?"

"Theirs." She shot Tanner a quick glance. "I wanted to go up. The faster I go up, the easier it is."

He nodded. "My sentiments exactly. Were they really upset?"

"One of them is," she said. "Maybe with good reason. I don't know."

"If it's sabotage, then they should be upset." His voice was hard. "But, if it was an accident, well, accidents happen."

"Sure they do, but nobody wants it to happen on their watch," she said drily. "Bad press isn't good for anyone, remember?" She turned back again to the parachute on a table.

"Did you ever find your chute or the main harness?" he asked.

She shook her head. "No. I asked around, but everyone's assuming it ended up in the bottom of the river."

He swore. "I'm sorry. I should have checked with Kanen about that." He pulled out his phone and dialed Kanen. "Hey, you were part of pulling those two paragliders out of the river. Did you happen to see her harness with her chute?"

"We pulled the one out," his buddy said. "Not sure I ever saw a second one. It was a mess of cut lines."

"Right. I just wanted to check. Thanks." He shook his head. "Kanen only remembers seeing one."

"With all the lines tangled and cutting the parts to lift them out of the water," she said, "it's quite feasible it dropped deeper into the river," she said calmly. "But my brother wants me to bring it home, so he can inspect it."

"Your brother?"

"Todd," she said by way of explanation, "he's an engineer. We designed the harnesses and the new framework. Patents are in progress," she confessed with a small smile.

"Wow. Good for you." And then he thought about that. "Who else knows?"

She stopped and stared at him. "It's not something we've hidden."

He crossed his arms over his chest. "Maybe you should though. Especially considering recent events."

"The first one was pretty minor," she said. "Somebody tried to run me off the road. As it was, the ground was fairly flat, so I don't know what he expected to happen. Todd and I were in my Jeep, so I just off-roaded for a while, watched the guy disappear and came back on the road again."

"Where was that?"

"I was driving back roads that weekend. Sometimes, when I want to get away from everything, I like to go for drives. I think he was just being an asshole."

"If that was the only thing to happen recently, then maybe," he said. "But what about the second one?"

She frowned, looked around, didn't say anything for a long moment. "One of the crossbeams in here, part of the struts that hold all the framing pieces up there in the warehouse …" She pointed to a loft. "One of the corner crossbeams came down, and everything dumped where I had been standing just seconds earlier."

He studied it for a long moment, his heart stalled at the thought of all those sharp aluminum parts coming down at an angle. "That could have killed you."

"I try not to think about it," she said with dry humor. "But you're right, it could have. I didn't let people know I was directly in the line of fire."

"You didn't say anything?"

She shook her head. "No. There is a catwalk up there, where we load stuff. It's certainly possible something might have, you know, happened when I wasn't looking. But I can't say for sure, and all the evidence is gone."

"Gone where?"

She shrugged. "The guys fixed it, built a new strut, new support. For all I know, the old pieces went into the garbage. They didn't say anything about it at the time."

"Well, if they'd set it up to look like an accident, they wouldn't tell you otherwise, now would they?"

"It's hard to imagine anybody I work with here would have done something like that," she said.

"I don't think we ever want to consider our friends as having those kinds of thoughts," he said quietly. "That doesn't mean they don't."

She turned, fisted her hands on her hips and stared at him. "What is it that you want from me?" she cried out. "I didn't even really consider it an issue until yesterday. Then it was pretty hard not to."

"Of course, but the fact is, now it's a little too late to see that evidence, isn't it?"

"Maybe not. The crossbeams were probably tossed out back." She walked toward the back of the building, stepping behind hanging silks. He followed her, admiring the quality of the cloth. Then she pushed open a door and walked to the back of the property. The weeds had gathered here, and definitely some odd pieces of wood were tossed out and stacked up against the building. She looked at the pile and said, "It was probably one of these."

"What did it look like?"

"Like one of those big eight-by-eight beams used as a pillar." She walked over, studying the debris. "But it doesn't appear to be here."

"So the crossbeams were just like the pillars extending from the floor up to the loft area?"

She nodded. "I think it was twelve foot long, maybe ten." She pointed back at the warehouse. "The same as the new one in there now."

"So they only replaced the one beam that fell?"

"Correct."

"What about the others? Did they check them out too?"

"I really don't know about that."

"They should have. If the one crossbeam fatigued due to nothing other than age, then the others should have been checked out too. If any beam or crossbeam is deemed structurally defective, it should be replaced," he said.

She nodded. "I agree with that theory. But I still have no idea if they checked all the pillars, all the crossbeams. However, I think they did something else to the new one, like attached more crossbeams. Someone said too much weight was on top of it. That's why something had come down. Maybe even loose plywood was across it originally, as some kinda flooring. It was pretty thin, as I recall."

"So again an accident that looked like an accident and was viable in terms of it being an accident, ready to happen at any time. But how convenient that you happened to be the person standing there when it did give way."

"I've already thought of all that." Her voice was low. "It still doesn't tell me anything about who though."

"You didn't see anybody on the catwalk earlier?"

"Quite a few people had been up there," she said. "They were unloading and moving materials around. The hangars have been kind of a mess, so we've been on this big kick to clean them up and to make better use of the space."

He nodded and turned to look around. "I don't see a beam that size here. From what you said, maybe the beam was fine. Maybe just one of the crossbeams failed. So it's possible that they used the same pillar."

"I didn't look at it that closely," she confessed.

And that made sense too. If she wasn't involved in doing any of the structural work on the building, then why would she? Out of curiosity, sure, but maybe it was more painful to watch something like that being fixed after her near-miss. He didn't know. He would have been in there, helping to fix it. But he understood her point.

He walked back inside and took a look around the hangar. Two storage areas were definitely up on top. He could see the one crossbeam had been replaced versus the old one, because the old one sagged. Definitely an accident waiting to happen. "I'm surprised they didn't fix both at the same time."

She glanced up at the other one. "I guess they figured it didn't need it."

"So another accident that could be planned," he said.

"It's possible," she said. "I'll have to remember not to stand anywhere close to that one."

"Do that," he said. He looked around again. "When are you done here for the day?"

She checked her watch. "Now," she said. "Why?"

He flashed her a big grin. "I was going to suggest dinner." The surprise in her gaze was almost insulting. And then he realized he had made an assumption he had no right to. "If you're not in a relationship," he said hurriedly. "I never even thought to ask. Sorry."

She laughed. "No, that's fine. I'm not in one, and I would love to have dinner. As long as it's not Chinese."

He laughed out loud. "You don't like Chinese food? You've got to be the first person who I've heard say that."

"My brother is addicted to it," she said with a laugh. "So we have it multiple times in a week."

"There's a special showing at the racetrack tonight. I don't know if that appeals." He studied her face, watching it light up. Inside he felt something settle. She really was into more unusual stuff. And that was cool with him.

"The auto show—I was going to see that," she said. "I love looking at the latest vehicles. Of course nothing quite compares to my Jeep."

He walked out of the warehouse, waited for her to lock up and said, "So what would you like for dinner then?"

"There's a barbecue place near the racetrack," she said. "If we go now, even with the twenty-mile drive, it would be a bit early though."

"I don't think that's an issue," he said quietly. "The thing is, we would have to take two vehicles."

She nodded and considered the problem. "I'm staying just a few miles from here. Where do you live?"

"About a thirty-minute drive away."

"In that case I guess we'll drive to my place, leave a vehicle and go together." She stopped and turned to look at him. "If that works for you."

He gave her a big beautiful smile. "It works perfectly."

They walked to the front of the parking lot, and she stopped again at the two vehicles. "Of course you drive a Jeep, don't you?" There was a sort of resignation in her voice.

He frowned. "Is that a problem?"

She shook her head. "No, not really a problem."

Something in her tone he didn't quite understand.

Then she brushed off whatever it was and said, "I suggest you follow me home. That's probably the easiest way to get there." She hopped in her Jeep and turned on the engine. "I'm on the 4200 block of Sunset Boulevard. In case you get lost."

"I won't get lost," he called back.

"I meant, in case you lose me," she said with a laugh. She raised her eyebrows, pulled the Jeep out of the parking lot and took off.

And that's when he realized she liked speed—just like he did.

CHAPTER 4

O F COURSE HE drove a Jeep. There was just something about men who drove Jeeps. Lots drove them for fun; lots drove them for show. But he drove it like he knew exactly what it could do. And that was attractive.

She'd always been an outdoor kind of gal. All the men in her life had driven trucks or Jeeps; almost all of them had been outdoorsy guys. She understood she had been training SEALs with Tanner's particular group and realized it was an unusual circumstance in that they were all navy personnel getting specialized training from civilians. But they'd been that badass can-do-anything-in-the-world macho group that she had expected of SEALs.

They'd been a little intimidating at the beginning. Her assistant instructor, Trish, had wondered just what the school was up against training a classful of SEALs. But it had been a long time since Wynn had been intimidated by anybody. Yet she'd stepped forward to lead the class with a total sense of confidence. The fact that she'd gone down in flames, as witnessed by all those SEALs, had not been a good way to end the day.

But Tanner was right when he had said they shared a connection now. Not the connection she'd have preferred, but, considering how damn sexy and attractive he was, it wasn't a bad way to start a relationship. She'd been surprised to see him when he had walked into the hangar today, and, yet, on the inside, she had had a sense of waiting for him.

Maybe knowing that, because of the way they'd come together, it couldn't be over quite so quickly. So he'd come to check on her, to make sure she was okay after a day of teaching, which showed how much of a caring person he was. Yet, when he'd suggested dinner, she'd been hesitant.

It had been two years since her last serious relationship, enough time to be looking again. But why bother? She was so busy with her own life—working as a trainer during the day, working on her designs at night and taking care of her brother—that she hadn't bothered. Literally she'd fallen on top of Tanner, so that gave them a combustible beginning.

After stopping by her house-sitting location, they'd decided to take his Jeep for the evening. She walked into the barbecue restaurant with him just several steps behind. This was one of her favorite places to eat. The food was hot, plentiful and reasonably priced.

Dani, the waitress, looked up, caught sight of her and waved. Within minutes they were led to a nice table by the window. As they sat down, Dani said in a joking tone, "Glad to see you. It's been at least a week."

Wynn chuckled. "It has been. At least this time I'm sitting in the dining room and not picking up takeout."

"Tell that brother of yours to get out of the design shop and to get back over here." Dani chuckled. "And who are you?" She turned to study Tanner.

He stood again, reached over and shook her hand.

Surprised, Dani gave him a second glance. "Wow, Wynn, your taste has moved up in the world."

Wynn could feel the heat rising up her cheeks. She leaned toward Tanner and pseudo-whispered, "Don't worry about Dani. She just lets anything trip off her lips."

Dani laughed a big booming laugh that echoed through the room. "Now that's true enough. You two take a look at those menus, and I'll be back in a jiff." And she took off.

With Dani gone, Tanner smirked. "I gather you come here a lot."

She chuckled. "One of my favorite places to eat. But then, it's also my brother's, so that makes this a nice solution for dinner."

"Your brother? The one who likes Chinese?"

She smiled, welcoming Tanner's natural curiosity that came out in an easy way. "Yeah. He does all the meticulous detailed work. He was a professional, like me, until he had a bad crash. That sent him delving into research to improve safety."

"How badly hurt was he?"

"Bad enough that we didn't think he'd ever walk again. He doesn't walk well, but he does walk. He has a wheelchair for when he gets tired, but he's getting stronger."

"How long ago was his accident?"

"Two years ago," she said with a sad smile. "He spent six months in the hospital, followed by physio. Now he works at home, where his design shop is. I'm staying temporarily where we left my Jeep, house-sitting at a friend's apartment while she's away. But I still go home to help him out all the time."

"That must be hard."

"You have no idea. I deliver food or cook, do laundry, … the whole works. I might as well be his mother." She gave a light laugh. "But losing him would be way worse than taking care of him."

"Are your parents no longer living?"

She shook her head. "We were raised by our grandparents. After we headed off into professional sports, there wasn't a whole lot for my grandparents to do. We were both very young, and they guided our careers as much as they could, but we had agents and lived abroad for a lot of our late teenage years to early adulthood. They live in Arizona, at one of those retirement communities, and they're pretty happy there."

Tanner didn't say anything to that, and she knew her family probably sounded strange, but professional athletes often lived like that. Maybe if she had parents still alive, they'd have had a heavier role in her life, but it wasn't to be, and she barely remembered her parents as they'd died when she was barely nine. It was hardly an issue for her. Hard to miss someone you never knew.

She turned the tables on him. "What about your family?"

"My dad is an accountant. My mom took early retirement and does a lot of volunteer work. They live back East, on the north end of Florida."

"That would be nice," she said. "What brought you west?" He gave her half a look, and she remembered the group he was in. "Of course. You work with Mason, right?"

He nodded. "That's right. Been in the navy eight years now."

She smiled. "That means you like it, if you've been in that long. Isn't it physically demanding?"

"I could say the same about your occupation." He laughed. "Not too many professional athletes out there."

"Actually there are," she said, leaning forward. "But most people don't recognize one in their own neighborhood."

"Lots of people might want to be a professional athlete, but it takes a ton of dedication to achieve that status."

"You make a lot of sacrifices along the way," she said with a smile. "But I've never regretted it."

"So tell me what incident number three was."

She laughed. "And I had hoped you had forgotten about that." When he remained focused on her, she sighed. "A break-in at the house. We came in to see a figure fleeing out the back. Todd had been sleeping. I was only gone an hour or two. I figured it was someone looking for easy items to pick up. But he left empty-handed. After that we started locking the doors."

"So who do you think is trying to kill you?"

His words came out of the blue. She stared at him. "You don't pull any punches, do you?"

"I was there, remember?"

She nodded. "I don't know anybody who's trying to kill me."

"You do. You just don't want to see who it could be."

"How do you look at your coworkers and friends and consider that one of them wants to knock you off?"

"You start with those you have disputes with. You look at those you don't get along with. People who have complained about you. People who would benefit from your death."

"The only person who benefits from my death is my brother. But he would never harm me. Plus, he needs me alive on so many levels," she admitted. "So that doesn't wash."

"Is he the beneficiary of a life insurance policy if you die in an accident?"

She nodded. "Yes. And the patents we hold jointly

would become his then too."

"That makes him a prime suspect."

"If he was able-bodied and out there hating me, maybe. You'd have to meet him to realize killing me is the last thing on his mind."

She watched as Tanner leaned closer. "Does he have a girlfriend? Somebody who wants to get married? A business partner?"

She thought about it for a long moment. "No, not any longer. Not since his accident. His girlfriend took the easy way out and ditched him while he was in the hospital."

A whisper of sadness crossed Tanner's face.

She nodded. "It was way worse for him, believe me."

"I hate it when people do that," he whispered.

"I hated her for a long while, but, at the same time, she also gave him a gift. If she wasn't long-term-girlfriend material, she sure as hell didn't need to be here for the short-term." Her tone was curt. "And beyond that, I can't think of anybody else who would benefit from my death."

"What about the school you work for?"

She raised her shoulders. "I can't see any way they would. An accidental death would be a black mark on the school."

He strummed his fingers on the table.

She watched with fascination. Well-manicured nails, strong and capable hands. She presumed the tempo of his strumming also matched the speed of his thoughts.

Finally he spoke up. "There are very few motives for murder, but the most common are power, sex and money."

"I'd add revenge to that."

His gaze lit up. "That's a good one too. So who would want revenge on you?"

"I haven't a clue."

Just then Dani returned with large plates of ribs.

Wynn felt her mouth water. "I hadn't realized how hungry I was until I saw this."

Dani chuckled, came back shortly and refilled their water. "Enjoy your dinner." And she left them once more.

"Back to that whole revenge thing," Tanner said as he picked up his knife and fork, tackling the ribs on his plate, "how about somebody you might have beaten out in a competition?"

At that, she laughed. "I haven't done serious competitions for a couple years. Surely they wouldn't wait this long."

"The timing is their issue. Maybe they just found you again. Maybe they were injured, and they're back on their feet now. Who knows why somebody is doing what they're doing?"

She cut into her rib and took a big bite. As soon as the mouthwatering juicy taste filled her senses, she almost moaned in delight. When she swallowed the bite, she gave a happy sigh. "I swear I could eat these seven days a week."

"They are good," he said.

They ate in companionable silence while she thought about what he'd said. "I was at the top of my field until I retired. Lots of people were coming up behind me. But we're talking a lot of names. And there's no reason for anybody to want to take revenge now."

"Were there any close calls? Were there any rulings where you might have won out over somebody else due to a technicality? Did you ever experience this kind of nastiness when you were competing?"

"Not really. It's not cutthroat. So I don't imagine doping being a factor or, you know, government backing or anything huge like that coming into play. Sure, I had sports sponsors, and that was always nice."

"Did you take any sponsors away from anybody? Or, after you left, was somebody expecting to get the same backing and didn't?"

She didn't even want to think about that, not when she was eating such a great dinner. But he wasn't likely to let her off the hook. "I can't think of anything like that. Are you enjoying your dinner?"

"I am, but I can talk and eat at the same time, so stop changing the subject."

With a heavy sigh she put down her fork and picked up her water glass, taking a sip.

As soon as she set down her glass, he asked, "What about lovers, ex-husbands or ex-girlfriends?"

"God, I hope not. No, I'm not married, have never been married, so no ex-husbands. Yes, I've had relationships that ended a little abruptly, but more because I wasn't interested in quitting my competition circuit. The last one was more of a mutual 'Hey, we're not going forward in our life. Let's split up and go find other people' kind of a breakup."

"So … no big fights with anybody, no big blowups. So you never had an affair with a married man, and his wife is trying to kill you?"

She stared at him, fascinated. "Is that how your mind runs?"

His big shoulders rippled with laughter. He calmed quickly and said, "Not necessarily but I've seen an awful lot, mostly the negative side of life …"

"Well, if there's no money involved, and I can't see that it's related to any sex issue, that only leaves power and revenge, and I don't think revenge plays into this at all."

"There's always a reason," he said calmly as he started back in on his ribs. "You just have to dig deep enough."

"Do these kinds of things ever happen between strangers?"

"Absolutely. But, in this case, it would have to be somebody trying to get away with tampering for fun, or because he didn't like the color of your hair or something else equally stupid."

"The color of my hair?" she asked in a dazed tone.

He waved his fork around. "Meaning, he selected you for an arbitrary reason. I can't imagine that because this guy knows the layout of the school's warehouse. He also has access to the loft in the warehouse as well as your gear …"

"I was considering that problem because having access is huge. As you saw today, the two hangars—or the warehouse—regardless of what you call that building, it is not locked down during normal working hours. Even afterward if someone is staying late. So it is not illogical to consider a stranger did come through."

"And parked where?"

She frowned. She was almost done with her ribs, and she was slowly losing her appetite as the conversation about possible sabotage refused to abate. She'd hoped for an evening out, away from her troubles, but this was just more inquiries into something that he felt responsible for. "Normally they would park in the front, and Mindy would see whoever is there."

"Would it be completely normal for somebody to park out front, then walk around to the warehouse and look for you guys?"

"That *would* be totally normal," she said. "And that's what I mean. Almost anybody could get into the back building without raising red flags."

"How long would it be before anybody noticed if one of the riggings was being tampered with?"

"I'd like to think immediately, but, of course, that's not quite true."

"No. Not only is it not true but I was in one hangar for a few seconds while two men were fighting in the back. And it didn't sound very pleasant. Even then I had to call out to them several times to get their attention so I could ask where you were."

"Who were you talking to?"

"The names on their shirts read Kirk and Tom."

She nodded. "Those two fight all the time."

"It doesn't help me though, does it?"

"And then they probably pointed in the direction where you should go, right?"

He nodded.

"See? That's part of the problem with the lack of security there. It is way too possible for somebody to have come in the warehouse and damaged my equipment."

"But it's way more likely it's one of the people who works there," he reminded her. "Having access is one thing, but knowing which gear was yours, which you were going to use, and making it look like they weren't doing anything when actually they were doing something wrong, that takes talent. And it's a whole lot easier if the bad guy works there and if he gets to pick his timing for his acts of sabotage."

She stayed silent, not wanting to consider that concept.

Dani returned then and took away their plates. "Do you want any dessert?"

Wynn shook her head. "But I'd love a cup of coffee."

Tanner agreed to a cup of coffee himself and before long

they were left alone again. "How many people work for the school?"

She frowned and pinched her nose. "I think close to twenty now. But not everybody is there all the time."

"That's more than I thought," he said in surprise.

"We're one of the largest paragliding schools in all of North America," she explained. "So, there are not only office workers and trainers needed but also warehouse workers. There's delivery, transportation … all these other secondary issues as well."

Tanner nodded thoughtfully but didn't say anything. And yet, his fingers rapped on the table again, mirroring his anxious thoughts.

"What are you thinking?" she asked curiously.

"Trying to figure out how this works together," he said.

Dani returned with coffees for both of them.

Wynn waited until their waitress was gone and said, "We could talk about something more pleasant."

Tanner stretched out his long legs so they kicked out to the side of the table. As he leaned against the chair, he picked up his cup of coffee and stared at her over the rim. "We could, but the chances of us doing that are slim."

"Why is that?" she asked lightly.

"Because the next attempt could kill you."

TANNER STUDIED HER over the table. The setting sun made a long shadow that caught her face ever-so-slightly. But even that couldn't dim the life force that shone brightly from her eyes. He leaned forward and said, "I really don't want to see anything bad happen to you."

He watched the surprise light her gaze, and then she almost slumped forward.

He leaned across, clasped one of her hands in his and whispered, "And I mean that. No, I'm not making a move on you. Unless you want me to," he said with a lethal grin. "But you're a beautiful woman who's talented and capable, and I'd hate to see that snuffed out early."

She winced. "You don't leave a girl much chance to ignore this, do you?"

He shook his head. "No. If it had been one incident, then maybe. Two incidences, no. Three, now four? Hell no."

She groaned. "So what am I supposed to do? They weren't all paragliding accidents. It's not like I can stop driving my Jeep, so why stop paragliding? That's been my life for a long time."

"I can imagine. I'd really like to see you go back up as soon as possible, but I am a little worried about you taking your rigs up."

"I thought that would be the safest."

"Anything that identifies the equipment you use will be the equipment that's tampered with," Tanner said. "So, if you are teaching one morning, it'll be obvious which is your gear. If you take two, one as a decoy, chosen at the last minute, then chances are good that the second one will be just fine."

"I can do that for my next class. And I see your point. The logical thing to think is that the tampering likely happened in the warehouse," she said.

"But you don't *know* that, do you?" Tanner asked. "And that's causing you to doubt what your gut says otherwise?"

"No, of course I don't *know*. I have no proof. Plus, I know these people. And my emotions don't believe anyone there would do something like this. My God, Dave drove the truck with the gear to the training spot that day."

"And what's your relationship like with Dave?"

"It's fantastic. He's like a second father to me. He's got a wife and three kids. I've been to their place for barbecues lots of times. He was pretty upset when he found out what happened," she admitted.

"That's all fine and dandy, but would Dave have any reason to tamper with your gear?"

The shake of her head was emphatic.

It made him wonder. "And did you consider something else?"

She raised her gaze until she stared at him.

"What about one of your students? Would any of them have had *any* reason to tamper with your gear?"

At that, her gaze narrowed. "Maybe you should look at yourself or at Mason because that's who I was teaching that day."

He sat back and thought about it. Indeed, it had been two of their units. Sixteen SEALs in all. "What about the other instructor working with you?"

"Trish has worked with me for the two years I've been here. So why now?"

"Would she take over your spot if you failed to do your job or if you died?"

"It's possible," she said cautiously. "But she doesn't have the experience for something like that yet."

"But it's hard to get the experience she needs if you're always ahead of her."

Wynn nodded her head silently.

They finished their coffee, and he took care of the bill, then walked her out into the evening air. "I guess at this point we've hashed it out as much as we can. Let's head off to the racetrack and enjoy ourselves."

She laughed, a bright freeing sound. "Now that's the best thing you've said so far tonight."

He grinned. "It's not all sad news all the time."

"I'm really glad to hear that because I thought this was a date. Instead, it became an interrogation."

He stopped, turned and looked at her. "Now that doesn't sound very good. It *was* intended as a date. I'm sorry. I'm just very concerned about your welfare."

The smile fell off her face as she nodded. "I understand that. I appreciate it. So thank you. You're the only one who asked any questions."

Instantly, his suspicions rose. "What about the paragliding school?"

She shook her head. "It was all about accidents being bad for publicity and the monetary loss of equipment. I don't think they gave a damn about what happened to me."

"Then I suggest we check out the new models at tonight's car show and have a good time. We'll forget about the rest for now. Tomorrow's a new day, and the investigation can pick up then," he said smoothly.

She nodded and smiled. "That sounds good to me."

CHAPTER 5

THE NEXT MORNING Wynn walked into the main hangar to find a meeting already ongoing. She rushed over to the circle, frowning. She checked her watch, but she was in at her usual time. She glanced at Bob, one of the other instructors, and softly asked, "When did the meeting start?"

He leaned in closer and whispered, "About ten minutes ago."

She crossed her arms and tuned into the discussion, trying to figure out why she hadn't been included. Maybe they thought she wasn't coming in today—or maybe they'd *hoped* she wasn't coming in today. When the meeting finally broke up, she walked to Charlie and asked, "Why in such a rush to have the meeting that you couldn't wait for me today?"

He looked at her in surprise. "I figured you wouldn't be here."

Unnerved, she slipped her hands into the pockets of her windbreaker. "Why wouldn't I be here? I'm due to go out this morning. I come in every morning at this time, particularly if I'm teaching."

He patted her shoulder. "Yeah, I want to talk to you about that. Let's go into my office."

She thought about her options, thought about what Todd had done earlier this morning; then she nodded her head. "Fine. By the way, the police should be by soon for their investigation."

Charlie had taken two steps, but, hearing her words, he spun and froze. "What are you talking about? … Police?"

"Just in case you were planning on firing me right now and giving me the helping hand out the door," she said smoothly, her eyes glinting with anger, "I'm fully prepared to go to the police to open an investigation into this mess." She'd wallow in denial that this was a police matter but it was impossible to do so now. But it's not a step she wanted to take.

The color leeched out of his face, and he shook his head. "You can't say a word about that."

She snorted. "I'm not only going to say something about it but I'm going to scream it from roof to roof. You were about to fire me for something I had nothing to do with. Do I really have to remind you that I was the victim of a glider crash?"

He glanced around, as if making sure nobody was listening in. "I was going to ask you to take time off, so we could recover from the bad press."

"What bad press?"

He frowned at her. "You know, anytime an accident happens, the media gets wind of it."

"But have they? No." She shook her head. "You were just trying to get rid of me." She thrust her chin out in his direction. "Maybe you were behind the sabotage. Maybe you thought that was another way to get rid of me. Permanently."

He stared at her as if she were something he loathed.

She nodded. "I can see the real Charlie inside there now. And what about your partner? Is he in on this too?" She pulled out her phone and texted Tanner. "You know that last group I took up? The one when I had the near-death *accident?*"

"Yeah. What about them?"

"Do you remember what those guys do for a living?"

He crossed his arms over his chest and glared at her.

She nodded. "I'm presuming you do then. Because I certainly found out. Not that they advertised the fact they were SEALs, part of that elite team, but they're protectors. And they've already got several of their men asking a lot of questions. So far, not only have you not even asked about my welfare but you're only concerned about giving me the boot. Very suspicious." As soon as she sent off her text message, she hit a Speed Dial number, put the phone to her ear, turned and walked away. When her brother answered, she said, "I've been fired."

Her brother gasped. And then laughed. "Of course you have. How else do they get rid of bad press? Idiots."

Just then her shoulder was grabbed, and she was jerked around, hard.

Charlie got in her face. "I did not fire you," he roared. "You've certainly given me lots of reason for you to be fired though."

"Yeah, give me those reasons right now," she snapped, holding out her phone to him.

He stood, glaring at her and then her cell, but he didn't have an answer.

She snorted, pulling her phone back to her ear. "Todd, you hear that? Charlie's got nothing to say."

"I've already contacted the lawyers," Todd said. "Tell him that they'll be in touch."

"Todd says our lawyers will be in touch." She turned on her heel and left Charlie, the worry evident on his face.

Todd added, "The cops should be there soon. I don't know why I had to call them. You should have two days ago. Someone tried to *kill* you, Wynn. We need all the official help we can get. And I'm attaching my trailer to the truck as soon as I hang up." Which he promptly did.

Wynn pocketed her phone and walked outside, just to clear her head. As she stood by her Jeep, her phone rang again. She glanced down, smiled and answered it. "Hello, Tanner."

"You're fired?"

"Yeah. Now Charlie's backtracking and saying he didn't fire me, but he never gave me my job back again either."

"I'm only about ten minutes away."

"What will you do here?" she asked in disbelief. "I wasn't texting you for assistance."

"No, but I can help you get your gear out of there. *All* of it. I also want to take a full 360 in photographs to ensure I understand how the layout of those buildings work, so we can do a timeline as to how somebody got in there to sabotage your gear."

She thought about that for a moment. "Todd's coming with his truck and trailer. I've brought a lot of my own stuff into this place over the last two years," she said morosely. "It may be more than I realize at the moment. But I don't intend to leave behind any of my designs for the likes of Charlie to try to steal my intellectual property. I'm still here, currently outside by my Jeep. I haven't been forcibly removed *yet*."

"Sometimes life happens," he said quietly. "All you can do is soar on the winds of change."

At that, he hung up, leaving her laughing. "Great line, Tanner. Great line." She turned, reentered the hangar and walked to her designated corner, where she had her gear, including an older spare laptop and a bunch of her tools. Todd called her back. Her phone hadn't seen this much activity in … forever.

"I'm already hooked up to the trailer and hopping into the truck now. Be there in about ten minutes." And he hung up once more.

She rolled her eyes. Just in time for Todd to meet Tanner.

Curtis raced toward her and said in a jovial voice, "Hey, hey, hey, hey."

She stopped and gave him a stone-faced look. *Like he didn't already know that Charlie was firing me today.*

Curtis held up both hands. "Look. I'm sorry. I didn't know Charlie was planning on firing you this morning."

This morning. "Right." It's not that she didn't believe him, but, well, she didn't believe him.

"We can't handle any bad press right now. The school is not doing all that well, and we still haven't got any of the new designs up and running," he said.

Frowning, she realized he meant *her* designs. Just because she worked for them as an instructor did not mean her intellectual property—past, present or future—was part of her employment package. Her written contract with the school clearly stated that. Her attorneys had made sure that was very clear, and it was repeated in several sections therein. Said contract was signed by her and the two owners and also by two of her lawyers as witnesses. The contract was written to stand up in court, if need be.

While she may design a few things for the school, she sold only the equipment to them, not her IP behind it. Again clearly spelled-out in her contract. Now, if Charlie and

Curtis wanted to hire her as a technical consultant or as an actual designer for them and the school, that would be a separate deal to consider. Plus, Curtis just said they weren't doing well. No way they could afford her as a designer.

As she took stock of where she and Todd had been on some of the design changes, she half smiled inside. Because, of course, they didn't share much with the school, and she had already applied for patents covering all their designs. She turned and walked away from Curtis. "Sorry business sucks. I wonder how many other people are getting fired by the end of the day."

She said it just loud enough that several people working in the warehouse stopped and looked.

Kate came running. "No, no, no, no. Don't even start talking like that. Charlie didn't mean what he said."

"Charlie absolutely meant everything he said. He wants me gone. He wants me out of the way. And I wouldn't be at all surprised if he wasn't behind the sabotage that was a deliberate attempt on my life two days ago. The cops have already been notified."

At the strangled sound coming from the man behind her, she spun and looked at Curtis. "So does that mean you had something to do with it too?" Her voice was gimlet steel. She had absolutely no sympathy. She stepped forward and poked him in the chest. "Not only did you not ask if I was okay but you didn't even ask me what happened. Why is that? Because you already knew? You also didn't take any time to investigate the state of my equipment or what might have gone wrong."

"Why would I?" Curtis cried out, his palms up. "You're the expert."

"That I am. And that's why I'm telling you right

now"—as she gave him yet another poke to his chest—"that my equipment was sabotaged." *Poke.*

He stared at her and shook his head. "I know you're overwrought. I'm sure, absolutely sure, that when you take another look at the situation, you'll realize you're just seeing ghosts where there aren't any."

She gave a strangled laugh. "I wonder if that's what your line will be when the cops get here. After all, I'm *just a woman.* Right? I mean, I'm *overwrought,* right? Isn't that how women handle emotional situations? *We go to pieces. We make up stories to get more attention.*"

Curtis tried to backtrack, and she wasn't having any of that.

"Somebody tampered with my gear. The most common and likeliest place was here in this warehouse. You can bet that the drivers, the trainers, the students, and everybody else who works for this school—past and present—will be investigated. Along with the school's *co-owners.*"

"I think you put too much faith in a simple accident," he said, his voice turning surly. "You're wasting police time."

"The police will decide that on their own." Tanner's hard voice washed over them. "But she sure as hell isn't wasting mine. And I have an incredible arsenal of tools and personnel behind me for everything I need. I was there when her rig collapsed. I was there, watching her lines snap. It was me that she landed on. It was the two of us tangled up in our gear in that river. And, if you think I don't know the difference between a simple accident and equipment failure at a monumental level, you have no idea who the hell you're insulting." Tanner stood straight and strong as he strode toward them, his voice carrying loudly.

They had collected quite an audience by now.

Curtis put up his arms in mock surrender. "I don't know who you are …" he started.

Tanner shoved out a hand and said, "Tanner McGrath, US Naval Service. As a SEAL, I've been part of sensitive international investigations for the last eight years. And I'm telling you right now, that event two days ago was sabotage."

In front of them all, Curtis wilted.

She snorted. "Oh, so because a *man* says *sabotage,* you believe him?" She shook her head and walked past Curtis. "Tanner, since you have such a profound effect on him, maybe you can get information about where Curtis and Charlie have been for the last two days and who the co-owners have had through the hangars and close to my equipment. Obviously I can't trust them anymore." And she kept on walking.

She didn't know what Tanner was doing behind her, but she could hear the men talking, and Curtis was no longer belligerent with Tanner. Yet, Curtis had really pissed her off. That was the way of the world. A lot of men wouldn't even listen to a woman, but the minute another man stepped into the argument, they completely changed. And there was no doubt that Tanner was a full-blown alpha. Curtis was so not. But she would take Curtis over Charlie any day.

Up until now, she hadn't had a problem with either man. She'd worked for the school happily for two years. The co-owners had had lots of plans as far as she was concerned, but apparently something had happened that she didn't know about.

As she stepped in front of her desk area in the corner of the warehouse and looked to see just what was here, besides her computer equipment with design software, Trish ran toward her. "Oh, my God! Are you sure?"

Wynn spared her a quick glance and then nodded. "Yes, absolutely."

"So you're saying I could have died on the previous run?"

Wynn straightened and remembered Trish had taken Wynn's rig out first. Trish had been the one who had said the equipment wasn't operating properly. Wynn reached out with both hands and said, "Oh, my God! I would have been devastated if you had crashed."

Tears already welled up in Trish's eyes. "Oh, my God! Oh, my God! How could somebody do that?"

Wynn said, "I have no idea, but I intend to get to the bottom of it. I've had accidents before, but they were minor, and they certainly weren't caused by somebody else."

Several of the training assistants who worked here came toward her. They had equally tense frowns. "So what's this we hear? You got fired, and we could be getting fired next?"

She shook her head. "I don't know about you guys, but, yes, I've been fired. My crash the day before yesterday was the result of sabotage. Curtis and Charlie have decided the bad press is more than they can handle, so they're taking the opportunity to fire me."

"But that's totally unfair."

"That's awful."

She agreed and sat with a thud in her desk chair. "Maybe it's for the best. I don't know what happened to my gear, but I can't trust this place anymore. The troubling fact is, Trish had taken my rig on a preflight run that day and could have been the one to crash instead. The last thing I want is for any of you guys to have been hurt using my equipment just because someone wants to kill me."

Trish, at that point, sniffled harder.

Wynn opened a desk drawer and pulled out a box of Kleenex. She handed her several. "It's a good lesson for all of us. Even though we check our gear before we head out, we need to check it again after it reaches its destination. Another preflight check. And just as complete and thorough."

"We all checked out the gear first thing in the morning though," Trish whispered. "And then onsite we did the same cursory checks we do every time. I couldn't figure out why yours was funky at the time."

"Exactly, and that's why I took it down. I had to see what you were explaining to me in action, in the air." She slumped farther into her chair and looked around. "For two years I've been really happy here. I'll be sad to leave you all."

A sobering silence filled the group.

"What was that about us getting fired?" Fred asked again hesitantly.

"After they fired me, I worried you all would be next," she said. "Charlie's excuse was that business has been really poor. So they didn't want to pay me any longer, and they couldn't afford to take any more bad press and suffer a further drop in sales." She glanced around at the inventory in the warehouse. "There is a lot of money tied up in the business. But still, I wouldn't have said we were any less busy now than we have been for the last six months."

"I haven't heard anything, but then we don't know if anybody got wind of the accident either," said Dave, the driver who'd hauled the gear up to the top of the hillside.

"True enough. But, honestly, at this point, I don't care about the press or Curtis and Charlie. You guys get to go on without me. This is no longer my life." And she pulled out the bottom drawers and started emptying her desk.

The men just stood and watched while Trish sobbed.

TANNER WALKED OVER. He'd already dealt with Curtis, and he'd deal with Charlie in his own way. Tanner couldn't believe they had fired her. There had to be some rules or laws against that. But he also knew Wynn wouldn't back down from her position, no matter what the police decided regarding any sabotage.

He watched as she unloaded her desk, packing it into an empty cardboard box, along with her laptop … and maybe her laptop contained the reasons why someone would want to kill her. Anybody around here that was a techie could have stolen her IP designs work from that very laptop. He wanted to ask but not while a group of her coworkers stood around.

One of the men turned and looked at him. "Hey, who are you, and what are you doing here?" The man stepped in front of Wynn, as if to defend her.

Noting the gesture, Tanner smiled. "I'm a friend of Wynn's."

Trish looked up and gasped. "He's the guy who saved Wynn in that accident."

At that, everybody crowded around, wanting details.

"We heard some of the story, but, wow, that's pretty horrific. What made you think of the river?"

"It was Wynn's suggestion," Tanner said. "And a good one."

"Except I almost drowned as I got caught between the two wings and tangled up in the lines," she said with a laugh. "It's one thing to face an imminent death. It's another thing to tell your mind—all within seconds—how it would be better to possibly survive a drowning rather than hitting the ground going too fast."

That brought up a ton more questions. By the time

Tanner was done with those, he noted she had packed up another boxful from her desk and had gathered together a backpack and what appeared to be several jackets and some work boots. He heard a noise behind him and turned to see a trailer backing into the hangar.

She smiled at Tanner. "Come and meet my brother, Todd." They each took a load from her desk area and headed to the truck and trailer. A big fancy Silverado with some serious pulling power turned off. Wynn and Tanner deposited the boxes and backpack and windbreakers in the trailer.

The driver's side door opened, and a young man exited slowly. Tanner remembered Wynn talking about Todd's accident, how he was mobile but not as good as he could have been. Tanner stuck to Wynn's side as they walked over to greet her brother.

Todd looked at her, smiled and glanced around. "I guess it's time, huh?"

Wynn nodded. "I guess."

They shared a knowing look, and she turned to Tanner. "I want you to meet Tanner. He's the guy who saved my life."

Tanner watched as Todd took several steps forward. He walked with the help of crutches, giving him added support. He leaned forward and held out his hand. Tanner took a step forward and shook Todd's hand. "Nice to meet you."

"Ditto. Thanks for saving my sister's life," he said. "Would you help us load up?"

At that, Tanner said, "Let's get her stuff and her outta here."

Behind him came a hard voice. "Her gear and only her gear."

Tanner realized Curtis and Charlie were standing side by

side, their arms crossed. Tanner glanced at Wynn, and she nodded.

"Of course," she said. "We're taking away my damaged paraglider. I know the police will want to see it. Let's load that first."

The word *police* caught Tanner's attention. He looked at her, but she shook her head to forestall any questions from him. He wasn't sure what she was up to, but, as she gave instructions, he followed. She had two of her own gliders and then two prototypes she'd been working on. All four were packed into the trailer, taking little space when folded; then she went back and separated out harnesses.

At that, Charlie protested.

"Sure I'll leave them here," she said, "*providing* you pay the invoices, which you have not done. So cut me a check right now, or they go with me."

That shut him up, and he glared at her. "But sixteen were on that invoice."

"Exactly."

Together Todd and Tanner separated them, taking her designs, leaving the outdated stuff, and loaded up all sixteen. Then she headed to the wings.

"Those wings are not yours."

She spoke over her shoulder as she continued directly to the wings. "Same damn thing. Sixteen of these wings are mine. You were supposed to pay me because I brought them in special. But you did not." She spun and glared at Charlie and Curtis, her hands on her hips. "Cut me a check right now—provided it won't bounce—or they leave with me."

The two co-owners looked at each other, had a hurried conversation and then spun back to face her. "They're overpriced anyway. Take them with you."

"They're not overpriced. They're cutting-edge technology. What do you expect in this business?" She shook her head.

Tanner helped her remove the hanging wings from the side beam. She stopped and looked around, then found several drums of rope she had marked as hers. He loaded up those and then the four boxes of parts that she handed him. He glanced over at Charlie and his partner, but neither said a word. So Tanner guessed they either realized this property was hers, or they couldn't pay to keep them. Interesting that they stood here to make sure she took only what was hers. Then that was to be expected with these guys.

And then she walked along the shelving, looking to see what else of her personal property could be here. Tanner turned back to Todd and said, "That's a lot of stuff she had here."

He nodded. "We were cutting them a special deal on designing particular items for the school and trying out prototypes. So she ended up having a lot of overtime as the situation developed. We had deliveries of parts shipped right here. So she needs to make sure she's got everything because, once we leave the property, there won't be any going back." He brought up his phone. "Here's one of the invoices, Wynn. Come and take a look. See if you've got all this stuff too."

She took a look at the image on his phone. "Right. Carabiners, all the stainless steel connections, straps, T-bars ..." She walked over to the other hangar making up the warehouse, leaving them all by Todd's truck and trailer.

Tanner glanced from the owners to Todd, asking quietly, "Do I stay here, or do I go help her?"

Todd whispered, "Better you go with her. A couple of

274

the guys who work here in the warehouse are much less than friendly."

He shot Todd a look. "Then your sister and I are going to have a second talk. I asked her specifically who she might not be terribly friendly with here, and she said she was friends with everyone."

Todd snorted. "Several of the guys were pissed when she rebuffed them. A lot of the paragliding lifestyle is pretty free-swinging. She didn't have eyes for anyone and has strict rules about not going out with anybody she works with. A couple of the revenge pranks got pretty ugly. I don't know that they'd have had anything to do with this current level of sabotage, but I'm happy to have her a hell of a long way away from here," he said quietly. "This isn't the first thing that's happened to her."

Tanner nodded. "She said three previous odd events in just a few months. ... Then this *finale*, as she called it."

Todd shot him a surprised look. "Then she trusts you, if she told you that much. She doesn't share much in her life."

"No. She's gotten used to sharing with you and nobody else," Tanner said absentmindedly as he kept an eye on the direction Wynn had gone. He wanted to go after her and help, but he was more worried about the partners standing here on guard. He pulled out his phone, walked over to one side and started taking pictures.

Charlie yelled at him, "You have to have our permission to take images in here."

He slowly lowered his camera. "Since I'm taking them in order to understand who had access to her gear and her equipment in order to sabotage her work, any protests on your part make you look mighty suspicious."

Charlie's mouth snapped shut.

Todd chuckled.

Charlie glared at him. "You don't belong here either."

Todd nodded. "Damn straight I don't. Neither does my sister. And we'll be happy to leave here shortly. You guys have been treating my sister like a piece of shit for long enough."

Curtis protested. "That's not true. She's been a welcome addition to the paragliding school."

"Yeah? Until you tried to blast her out of the sky, and then, when she survives that supposed accident, you fire her." Todd shook his head. "One of your best workers ever." He glanced around at everybody gathered here. "So who's the next person who does so well that they'll, you know, maybe have another accident and get fired. They don't like success here. Just try it."

The other employees stared at their feet.

Todd laughed. "Well, you know she's busted her ass for you guys for the last two years, and yet, Charlie and Curtis still treated her that way, so anybody here who's worried about their job, you should probably start looking for your next one now."

Charlie sputtered, "We're not firing anybody else."

"Oh, so you do admit to firing her?" Tanner said. "Very interesting. I'm sure the labor board will have something to say about that."

"We're not part of any labor board."

"Of course not. You wouldn't pass muster, would you? Besides, you don't need to be. There are laws governing companies who treat their employees like shit," Tanner said smoothly. "I'm sure I won't have any problem finding somebody to listen to her."

Just then he heard a shout. He raced in the direction

Wynn had gone. There, he saw her standing up against two big men. The two men he'd seen fighting earlier. With Todd's words still echoing in his mind, he raised his chin and said, "Hey, what's going on here?"

Wynn turned and looked at him. "They're being asshats."

"I thought I heard you cry out." He pointed to the wrist she rubbed gently.

The two men backed up slightly.

She shrugged and said, "One of them disagreed with me about taking two of my boxes here."

"That's school equipment," the man muttered. "She doesn't take nothing with her."

"That depends, I guess," Tanner stated, "whether your bosses will pay her for that equipment."

The men stared at her, then stared at him. "The bosses didn't pay her for it?"

"No," she snapped. "I tried to tell you that they owe me over ten grand."

The second man whistled. "Well, that's not cool. How long have they owed you that?"

"A couple months now," she said wearily. She brushed her hair off her forehead. "Now would you mind? I need these at the trailer."

They brought over a hand truck, stacked up the big boxes, and the four of them trooped to where Todd waited with the truck.

She glared at the owner. "So you didn't even tell them that you haven't paid me? They seemed to think I was stealing this stuff." She turned to face the crowd gathered around. "Do you guys realize the owners owe me over ten grand?"

"It's at least fifteen," Todd snapped.

She nodded. "Yes, it could be that high. I've forgotten how much I brought here," she confessed. "I do this because I love it. And I was willing to carry the cost for a little while. But this has gotten ridiculous."

At the muttering from the other employees, Charlie said, "We hit a bad patch. Obviously we were going to pay you."

"Obviously," Tanner drawled. "When was that, by the way?"

The men just crossed their arms over their chests and glared at him.

Tanner shook his head, bent down, grabbed a box and loaded it into the back of the pickup bed. By the time the latest boxes were loaded, he thought maybe they were finished, but, as he looked around, she'd already disappeared again. He sighed.

Todd chuckled. "Get used to it. Just when you think you understand what she's doing, where she is, she's gone."

"Has she always been like that?" he asked Todd.

"Absolutely. Stick her in a corner and she'd be on the other side of the room in a way that you had no idea was even possible. She has never been one to be caged in. She always has to fly free."

Tanner thought about that, thought about the work she did and understood. "So I guess she does this work because it's a real passion for her. Not a job. Not a hobby."

"A *passion* is the right word. Our father took her up when she was about eight years old. She's been trying to get her feet off the ground ever since."

Just then Wynn came back. "I think that's it." She looked around the warehouse, staring up, staring down, and then, as if she decided she had what she needed, she walked over to her ex-bosses, reached out a hand and said, "Thank you very much for the last two years." She shook both their hands, then walked over to Todd and Tanner, standing by the truck, and said, "Todd, you're free to go. Then I'm heading to my Jeep."

Todd hopped in and disappeared toward the main road, taking the truck and trailer with him.

She lifted a hand in goodbye to the training team she'd worked with for two years. "All the best. Happy windy days ahead for all of you."

There was a chorus of goodbyes as she turned and walked away.

Tanner followed her, then asked, "Do you have anything in the office building?"

She stopped and said, "Hell, yeah. There sure is. My locker, for one." She walked into the office and smiled at Mindy. "Just about gone."

Mindy looked startled. "You mean, for the day?"

Wynn laughed as she walked through to the back. "So not."

Mindy hopped up from her chair and followed her anxiously. Tanner stood undecided in the front room. He'd like to have a good look around the place. With a quick glance to make sure nobody else was close by, he strode through to the back in the women's wake.

The front office building wasn't terribly big. There was a lunchroom, a change room, a set of showers, lockers and an open cubicle areas for offices. Also a separate boardroom. He poked his head into each of the spaces, took several photographs, caught sight of Wynn emptying her locker, took several photographs from there and then, on his way back, took photos of the overall layout. Once he was back in the front reception area, he stepped outside and stood beside his Jeep. He pulled out his phone and contacted Mason.

"Hey, what's up?" Mason asked.

"I stopped by the paragliding center to speak with Wynn, to see if she'd managed to get back up in the air again and how it had gone."

"And?"

"She's been fired."

He caught Mason's sucked-in breath. "Really?"

"Yeah. Bad publicity and all that."

"It was an accident, or at least they should be thinking it's an accident, and bad accidents can happen to anybody. Are they holding her responsible?"

"It appears to be that way, yes. A little bit of strife when she packed up her stuff here. Her brother arrived with a big trailer and truck, and I'm here, so we managed to get hopefully all of her gear loaded. They haven't paid her for over fifteen grand's worth of inventory brought in for her to do some specialized product work for the school."

"Interesting," Mason said in a noncommittal tone. "How is everybody reacting to her leaving?"

"Well, the owners were half backtracking but now feel she needs to get off the property," he said. He glanced around and added, "The others appear to be having mixed reactions."

Just then Wynn came out from the back rooms into the front office, carrying a large duffel bag and a smaller back-pack. She smiled at him, walked through the glass front doors toward him and tossed the rest of her belongings into her Jeep.

He told Mason, "She's back now. I've got to go." And he hung up, pocketing his phone.

She turned to look at him. "You didn't have to get off the phone for me," she declared. "I'm fine."

"I can see that," he said. "Are you ready to leave this place?"

Mindy followed them outside, standing there, not knowing what to say.

Wynn stood there for a moment, her hands on her hips as she surveyed the property. "Once I leave, I'm pretty damn sure I won't be allowed back in again," she said with a sigh. "Which is really too bad. I spent two years of my life here. I hate to leave under these circumstances."

Mindy shook her head and walked up closer to them. "The problem is, I don't really understand what the circumstances are," Mindy said with a wail. "They said you had a terrible accident, but I don't understand why you're being fired for that, unless …" Her voice suddenly stopped.

Wynn looked at her. "No, I wasn't negligent. No, I didn't put anybody else in danger."

A look of complete relief washed over Mindy's face. "I'm sorry. I didn't mean to suggest you were …" She stood nervously before them, shifting from foot to foot, as if realizing she had said the wrong thing.

Wynn gave her a quick hug. "It's all good." She glanced at Tanner. "Are you heading to your house now then?"

"No, I think I'll be trailing you back to your place."

"What if I'm not going home?" she challenged.

"Then I guess you're not going home," he said. "Considering the strange events over the last few days, I don't think I'll be leaving you alone at the moment."

She narrowed her gaze at him, then, realizing Mindy watched their exchange with great curiosity, Wynn nodded. "I'm going to the shop. Todd will need help unloading all that stuff we packed up."

"That's another good reason for me to follow you."

"Don't you work today?"

"Nope. I've got two days off," he said. "Besides, even if I didn't, I'd take them off."

She rolled her eyes at him, but she had a big grin on her face. She smacked the side of his cheek. "Then keep up if you can." She gave him the address as she walked around, hopped into her Jeep, turned it on and reversed out of the lot.

With Mindy and now the rest of Wynn's paragliding team watching, Tanner got into his Jeep and followed Wynn off the property. Hopefully Wynn had all her stuff because he highly doubted her ex-bosses would give up anything after this point.

Passing several marked police cars as the cops drove onto the school's property, Tanner followed Wynn onto the frontage road. Tanner wondered if the saboteur had expected this to be the way for things to end. Or maybe that had been his plan. Right from the beginning.

CHAPTER 6

SHE DROVE STEADILY toward her home and the shop. Her mind was still consumed, going over everything she'd had at work, wondering if she'd left anything behind. She'd like to think one of the training guys would let her have her own equipment if she had missed something, but she knew the owners wouldn't let her return to the property without an armed guard. Even though the police had arrived directly after her departure, it was a sad end to a very depressing day. And it wasn't even eleven o'clock yet.

Thinking of which, she would have to get Todd some groceries soon. Now she bought groceries for her house-sitting locale and for Todd. She thought about stopping and picking up something now for Todd, but that would involve detouring Tanner at the same time, since he was following her home. Her mind skated through all the items she had left at Todd's place to determine if she could dredge up anything for a lunch for three.

And realized the old standby of sandwiches would work.

They were another good five minutes away when she looked in the rearview mirror and realized she'd lost Tanner. She frowned and went slower, hoping he would pick up her trail again. But, even as she turned into the parking lot for the shop, there was no sign of Tanner. She frowned and wondered if he got a work call and had to go. In his position, she knew it would happen sometimes.

She wondered how he liked that. She wouldn't have a problem with it herself, as long as she remained busy in her life. As far as she was concerned, each person should do what they felt called to do. But it was hardly cool to become so immersed in a relationship where you couldn't be alone and where you couldn't let your partner do what he needed to do.

She'd had several relationships where the guys thought she would eventually stop paragliding, and she didn't understand where that came from. It wasn't like at any point she said, "Hi. I'm Wynn, and, if you love me, I'll stop paragliding for you." Because, of course, that was not who she was. She needed somebody like Tanner, who was off doing his own dangerous work until he was done and home again. He wouldn't put up with a nagging wife wanting him to quit. She laughed at the thought.

Yet women were expected to quit their dangerous jobs when they married. She shook her head.

For all she knew, he was recently out of a relationship or looking for one a whole lot different than what he had had. Like she was. Last night they hadn't gotten that far. Their "date" was an interrogation first, then just a couple friends at a car show second. But they'd had so much fun at the racetrack that she couldn't wait to go out with him again. He was a lot of fun to be with. He wasn't pushy; he wasn't slimy. He was great to talk to, knew a hell of a lot about all kinds of different subjects and was willing to just go at a pace she was comfortable with. There was a lot to be said for that.

She chose the first of two driveways onto the property and parked her Jeep outside at the far end. When she hopped out, she grabbed her duffel bag and small backpack and dragged them toward the workshop. The big double doors to each end of the shop at the back of the house were open. She expected to see Todd's truck and trailer pulled in here. Plus, their small tarmac—at the opposite end of this side of the workshop, off the second driveway—was empty. There was no sign of the trailer. Frowning she walked inside the workshop, dropped her bags by the wall and called out, "Todd, where are you?"

A holler came from around the corner.

She walked in that direction to see him straddling a back door that faced the second driveway, where he had parked his truck and trailer. He must have stood there, looking for her.

"There you are," he said. "I wondered if you'd had a problem after I left. I almost left but parked on the driveway, thinking you may have just stopped for food. But your hands are empty."

"No. I forgot I had to go into the main office and grab my personal stuff from the locker."

He nodded. "Did you get everything?"

"I hope so," she said. "It'll be a little hard to get anything else now."

"You got the gear, and you got all the inventory, so that's what counts. They weren't going to pay you. We've been asking for payment for months now. We had to pay for all that up front. It's hard enough when we have to carry our own expenses but not theirs too," he said resentfully.

"It's a done deal now," she said. "Although we hardly needed this much stock."

Todd shrugged. "We'll use it up fast enough. Not to worry on that score." He looked around. "Are you alone?"

"I didn't think so, but I lost Tanner somewhere along

the line."

"You didn't lose me," Tanner called from behind her.

She spun around, and, when she saw him turning the corner, entering the designated offices area of the workshop, she smiled.

"I like how you live in a square doughnut with a hole in the middle, giving you a completely private garden. Plus your workshop takes up two sides, I see. So the house must be on the remaining two sides. Nice setup for you guys to work from home and yet keep it separate." He held up a bag from a local sandwich franchise and a tray of coffees.

She looked at it and said, "You know? I was just figuring out on the drive over what to feed you guys when we got here. I was hoping we had enough sandwich fixings to make a meal."

Tanner shook the bag. "No need. We passed this place on the way, and I thought I'd go in and grab a few."

Todd walked forward, a big grin on his face. "Thanks very much. Anybody who brings food is always welcome here."

Tanner handed a coffee to him. "I don't know how you take it, so I got some creamers and sugar."

"Black," he said. "It's the only way to drink coffee." He took off the lid and set it down on a desk to the side, tossing the lid in the can. "I don't know about you, but I'm hungry. So, if you don't mind, we'll dig into those sandwiches right away."

"Todd, where are your manners?" Wynn asked, laughing in horror.

He shot her a look. "You didn't bring anything to eat. At least he did."

She groaned. "I was planning on making something

when I got here."

"Good, you can probably still make it," Todd said. "I didn't get very much in the way of dinner last night. Weren't you supposed to pick up stuff and bring it this way?"

"I said I would *if I could,*" she corrected. "Instead Tanner and I had ribs for our dinner and then went to the racetrack for the car show."

Todd stared at her in mock outrage. "You didn't get an order to go?"

"If we had, we would have eaten them at the track," Tanner said. "I gather you like their food too."

"Love it. I'll have to get up there this week. Now I've got a taste for ribs in my mouth." He looked at the chunk of sandwich he had just unwrapped and smiled. "This looks great." He took a big bite.

With a heavy sigh, Wynn walked around to the far side of the desk, pulled up two chairs and said, "I guess we're eating here in the workshop. Don't mind Todd when it comes to food. He's about as Neanderthal as you can get."

Tanner just grinned. "Hey, a healthy appetite is nothing to sneeze at. Our brain doesn't function if we don't get enough food." He handed her a sandwich, grabbed one for himself and placed the remaining three on the desk. "I wasn't sure how much to get, so I got large subs and had them cut in half and wrapped separately."

She smiled as she unwrapped hers. "We pretty well eat anything, so you're safe there."

He glanced around as he prepared to eat his sandwich. "You've got quite the deal here, don't you?"

She mumbled around her bite of food, then waited until she swallowed to speak. "Yeah, we've been doing this for quite a few years now. We started thinking, creating, tweaking designs almost as soon as we got into competitions but didn't set up shop seriously until about four—maybe five—years ago."

"Why did you take the job at the school anyway?"

"I really liked the idea of teaching," she said. "I was tired of traveling the competition circuit. I wanted to settle down. We needed an income to keep up our patents and to move forward with our research. The IP part is expensive. The materials to create prototypes are expensive. You have to have steady money coming in, if you intend to keep doing this."

Tanner nodded. "And, of course at that point, Todd had his accident."

"That was just before I started working. When he stopped competing, so did I. Once I knew he would be okay, I started teaching."

Todd never said a word, just reached a hand toward the three spare sandwiches, looked over at Tanner with a raised eyebrow.

Tanner nodded. "Two each."

Todd snatched up the closest one to him, unwrapping it. "Yeah, my accident changed everything. But it is what it is."

"You seem to be getting around not too badly," Tanner said cautiously. He'd seen an awful lot of men injured in the line of duty, and their various reactions to their injuries were always a tough one to predict. Some were stoic; some were ready to rant and rave at the first sign of anybody willing to listen, and others just laughed and shrugged it off.

"I am now," he said, "but it's been a few years. I didn't handle it very well in the beginning. I was young and cocky and stupid. When I slammed into the ground, all that youthfulness and cockiness and stupidity got slammed out of me. But then you don't know who you are—not when you're that young and especially not immediately after an accident like that. It takes time to figure it all out. It's been a slow process, but I'm getting there."

Tanner said, "That's admirable."

Todd shook his head. "Not really. Sometimes life's a bitch, and sometimes she's your bitch."

At that, Tanner chuckled. "I like the sound of that."

Todd glanced over at Wynn. "She said she was teaching you and another SEALs unit. So you're always in the line of fire yourself. Have you had any bad accidents?"

"Well, I've been shot. I've been stabbed. And I've been partially run over," Tanner said with a grin. "But I'm still here, still standing strong."

The other two stared at him.

He shrugged. "They weren't major injuries. And getting run over was because one of the guys on base didn't know his reverse gear from his drive gear. He hit the gas and roared backward, knocking me down. But that was something I got to tease him about for a long time."

"That must have been tough," she said.

He shrugged. "I wasn't badly hurt. I was more pissed at the time." He glanced over at her. "What about you?"

She sighed and shook her head. "A couple minor injuries, hard landings, things like that. But nothing major."

"Broken collarbone, a couple busted ribs," Todd said, looking at his sister. "And what? You broke your right ankle or was it the left?"

"Left leg," she said quietly. "But everything is healed and doing fine again."

"That's the trick, isn't it?" Tanner said. "Not to get hit so bad that you can't get back up again."

They finished the sandwiches and sat in companionable silence. Finally Wynn said, "You don't have to worry about me, you know? We've been looking after ourselves for a long time."

Tanner looked at her with amusement.

She glared at him. "What?"

"I can't tell if you're trying to get rid of me for real or if you're just giving me an out in case I'm feeling responsible and you don't want me to feel that way."

Todd chuckled. "It's the latter. She's obviously interested. Otherwise she would have cut you dead the first time." His sister shot him a look. But he just chuckled and waved at her. "You know it's true."

Tanner watched the sibling exchange with interest. He was an only child and always felt like he'd missed out on something major by not having a brother or a sister to grow up with. It was one of the reasons why he'd taken to the naval life and to the SEALs teams with a vengeance. He had brothers now. Something he'd never had before. And, just like these two, Tanner had a similar rivalry between the guys on each unit. But there was also trust and caring and respect. He could see that here too. "You're both very lucky," he said.

Wynn looked at him with raised eyebrows.

He shrugged. "I don't have any siblings. And you two look like you really love and care for each other."

"Oh, we do," she said. "And then sometimes I want to kill him."

"Ditto," Todd said cheerfully.

"As long as you don't try, it's all good," Tanner said. The conversation died there. He gave a half wince. "I didn't mean to make that sound like you were a suspect."

"Are you looking into the sabotage?" Todd challenged

him.

Tanner nodded. "Unofficially, yes. But now that the police are involved, I'll make an official witness statement." He turned to Wynn, hoping to get an explanation now that she wouldn't give him at the school.

She sighed. "Yeah, about that. Todd called the police. Not me. So I guess I need to make an official statement too about my near-death experience. I'm still afraid the police won't think that a break-in and these three random *accidents* are hardly anything to be worried about. Maybe we should have the cops just focus on the sabotage."

"And what if they don't stop with those?" Tanner asked. "You said at the river that you thought that particular *accident* was supposed to be the finale. Well, you lived through that attempt. What if somebody continues to try to kill you?"

She stared at him. "That's not likely, is it? What with you involved and now the police? Surely not?" Her voice got fainter. "I was hoping to not go in that direction."

"Regardless," Todd said, shaking his head, obviously frustrated with his sister, "you have to give the police your statement of the events. I've already given them mine." Todd turned to Tanner. "Why is she being so stubborn, so uncooperative?"

Tanner nodded. "Until you find out why somebody is trying to kill you in the first place, how can you tell when he's ready to walk away? Tell me about the first incident in greater detail."

She shrugged, her palms up. "We were going for a drive up the coast. I wanted to get out and think about my life and what I was doing. Todd wanted to just get out of the city. I took some back roads that kept leading to more back roads.

With the Jeep's top off, we went out to enjoy the day."

"When did you realize you were in trouble?"

She turned and looked at Todd, frowning. "We passed a truck parked on the roadside on the way up. And when we went as far as we could, we stopped, went for a bit of a hike, got back into the vehicle and headed back down the road again. When we passed the truck the second time, maybe an hour after the first time, we honked and waved and carried on. But I think it was the same truck that tried to run us off the road shortly thereafter."

"What kind of truck?"

Todd answered, "I was sitting in the passenger's side. It was an F-250 black crew cab, slightly lifted."

Tanner pulled out a notepad and wrote it down. "Any idea what the license plate was?"

"It had a *J* in it, but that's all I could see," Todd said.

"You never even told me that you had looked long enough to get that," Wynn exclaimed.

"Well, it was a little odd seeing the truck just parked there out in the middle of nowhere."

"Did you see anybody?" Tanner asked.

Both shook their heads. "No," Wynn said. "I didn't see anybody there."

"So you didn't stop to see if the guy was in trouble? The vehicle didn't have a flat? It didn't look like it had been abandoned?" Tanner frowned at them. "I'm just trying to figure out why that truck might have been there in the first place."

"Honestly I figured some guy was there for the same reason we were," Wynn said. "Just out for the day."

"Did you tell anybody ahead of time where you were going or why?"

"I told a couple people at work," she said in a low voice. "Just that we were heading up the highway and seeing where it took us."

Tanner looked over at Todd. "Not a pleasant thing to consider, but have you ever checked your sister's Jeep to see if a tracker is on it?"

Todd stared at him, his jaw dropping, and then he shook his head. "No. No, I never did. But I will now."

Tanner held up a hand. "In a few minutes. Let's get this line of questioning taken care of first. So nobody knew where you were going, and, even if some guy did know, he wouldn't have gotten ahead of you and parked on the side of the road so that you passed him twice."

"No. And that's not very likely even with a tracker, is it?" she said in relief. "So it was just some random guy being a bit of an asshole."

"Was there anything suspicious about him being there? Or could he have left the truck to go on a hike?"

"Why would there be something suspicious about him being there? There was nothing suspicious about us being there," she said with spirit. "Think about it. What if the guy went for a drive and a hike, like we did?"

"I saw something just off the side of the road," Todd said. "But I'm not sure what it was now."

"On the same side of the road where the truck was?"

He nodded. "Maybe he was digging or doing whatever off to the side."

Tanner stared at him for a long moment.

Wynn leaned forward. "I don't think I like the sound of that. You never mentioned it before."

"I wasn't being questioned before either, now was I? We were just talking about it but not really realizing there could have been anything important in this."

"And how about now?" Tanner asked in a dry voice.

TANNER SAID, "ALL of this could have started with that truck."

"In what way?" Wynn asked.

"What if he was digging? What if he was burying a body?" Tanner had a dark smile. "For want of another suspicious activity, he could also have been burying weapons. He could have been burying all kinds of stuff, evidence that pointed to him in various criminal activities. So, when you passed him once, he got nervous. Then, when you passed him the second time, he hunted you down. And maybe he was worried you'd seen something. So he ran you off the road."

"Sure, but then wouldn't he have hung around and made sure his *accident* did the job?" Wynn asked.

"Yeah, that would make more sense, unless he panicked and took off."

"And then how could it possibly have been this same guy in the second incident?"

"Yeah, that didn't seem to be all that clear either from what Wynn had told me before." Tanner looked at Todd. "Were you with her for the second event?"

"No. That happened at work. She'll have to tell you more about that. Some beam fell or some stuff from the loft in the warehouse fell and narrowly missed her."

"I already told Tanner about that."

"That was scary. Coming from that high up, even just a few lightweight items hitting her could've been a bad deal." He sent a warning glare to his sister. "But, two weeks ago, we had an intruder here," Todd admitted. "It's one of the reasons she moved into her friend's apartment for a few weeks. Just to do a rethink as to what and how she wanted to live."

"So that move was recent?"

She nodded. "Yes. My girlfriend's back East for a couple months and wanted someone to house-sit while she was gone."

It looked like this B&E had very little to no connection between the other incidences.

Only that felt even more wrong.

From the looks on their faces, they thought he was off his rocker. *Wait until I say this next part.* "If I'm right, it's not just Wynn who could be in danger."

"That makes no sense," Wynn argued. "Think about all the ways there are to kill people. Sabotaging my equipment is hardly the easiest."

"Sure, but it's almost foolproof." He studied her face, watching for the upcoming twist in her features. "I know it's not something you want to think about, but you need to do just that."

"If that's the case, this asshole's not giving up," Todd said in a stark voice. "And does this guy know there were two of us in the vehicle that day or just saw one of us?"

"He'd know there were two of us," Wynn said. "The top was off, so we were both easily visible."

"And it's your vehicle," Tanner continued. "So he's likely tracked the license plate. Meaning, he doesn't know where you live now but could know about this place. Hence the break-in."

Todd then shook his head. "But really, isn't that foolish? Why risk coming inside and getting back out? He could have lit the place on fire and been done with it. If he's been in this place, it's obvious from the adaptations that someone in a wheelchair lives here."

"And maybe that's why he didn't carry out any further plans," Tanner said. "As much as you may not like the implication, being handicapped might have saved your life."

CHAPTER 7

WYNN KNEW HOW sensitive her brother was about his condition, how determined he was to get back on his feet and to live some semblance of the life he used to have. He hated to be called "handicapped." He refused to use the word himself. It didn't change the fact that he *was* currently handicapped, but he probably figured, if he kept saying the word, defining himself as "handicapped," the more his mind would accept it, and it would slow down his progress. She wasn't sure she agreed with him, but, since it was his life and his rehab, and he'd made so much progress on his own now, she figured there couldn't be any harm in continuing to do things his way.

She was a little bit worried about what Todd's reaction would be to Tanner's statement. What she did appreciate was the fact that Tanner spoke in a matter-of-fact tone of voice. He wasn't judging. He wasn't mocking. He was stating the facts. She glanced over at Todd and said, "That would be a change, wouldn't it?"

He gave half a shrug, as if unsure how to take Tanner's comment.

She smiled. "That's not something we considered, but, to go along with that, you were probably wearing your glasses on our drive, right?"

Todd looked at her, puzzled.

Tanner asked, "What about his glasses?"

She smiled. "They're heavy, thick glasses that somebody with very poor sight—or severe light sensitivity—would wear. They wrap around the side of his head and don't let in very much light."

Tanner nodded. "And that would go along with the intruder's possible assumption."

She nodded. "Exactly."

"So you think he thought maybe I wasn't a threat?" Todd asked. This time there was a note of anger in his voice.

Tanner gazed at him, but his gaze was flat, calm. "So prove him wrong. He probably came to the house, saw you were likely handicapped, possibly blind, and figured you were no threat. And he's focused on Wynn now."

Wynn nodded. "Prove to him that you are somebody to be reckoned with. That you aren't something to be discarded like the wheelchair you're working so hard to leave behind permanently." Wynn held her breath. She loved the angle Tanner had taken. It was just the right note. But, since Todd didn't know Tanner, she wasn't sure how well this would be received from a perfect stranger. Sometimes, however, that was the best way.

Todd nodded slowly, though his gaze never left Tanner's face. "I'm not terribly good at the self-defense thing."

"Maybe it's time to look at that then," Tanner said quietly. "I don't know where you're at in your recovery program, but I can see you're not back to full health and to full strength. In self-defense, any weight lifting you can do within the capabilities of where you're at will help you."

Todd looked down at his desk for a moment. Wynn walked to the kitchen—near the end of the first driveway and abutting the garage—to throw out the trash from their lunch and to start some coffee. The men drifted toward her, talking quietly. She was happy Tanner was the kind of person who could do that, who could reach Todd, who could speak openly yet without criticism. Todd had always been supersensitive. Having been a professional athlete like herself, their fitness was incredibly important to them. But, when you lose all that, it's hard to get it back. It was also hard to deal with what you had left to work with. She understood because she'd been there.

In Todd's case, he had been even more stubborn and a whole lot more unreasonable. He'd walked away from his physio a few months ago. She'd been quietly urging him to go back, but he'd been all the more resistant every time she addressed the subject. But now, as she listened to him and Tanner talk, she marveled at how easily Todd was contemplating physio again.

"You don't have to go to the same physio," Tanner said with enthusiasm. "Make sure you go to one who's got experience with where you're trying to go. They can take you to a whole new level of fitness."

The two of them sat down at the kitchen table, heads together, discussing weight-lifting fitness programs and which parts of his body he had to really work on. She hadn't heard so much enthusiasm out of Todd since his injury. She was both delighted and sad. Why couldn't he be like this with her?

She understood it was something guys could talk about a lot easier with each other, and maybe Todd just needed somebody who didn't know what he'd been through to come into this at a fresh angle. Maybe even just somebody who was a complete stranger to all of it, who made Todd feel like he wasn't being looked at as something less than he once was, comparing this Todd to the old Todd.

She didn't understand it all, but she was grateful.

"I tend to avoid public places these days," Todd said.

"Understood," Tanner said. "Or at least understandable. But you're walking almost normally. You shouldn't feel bad at all."

"It's these things." He lifted the crutches he used to support himself.

Tanner nodded. "I hate crutches of any type, but my buddy and I were once both down with injured ankles at the same time and put on crutches for a couple weeks by the doctors. And we still had a lot of work to do with being in the navy." He grinned. "We used to race each other up and down the stairs. Sometimes with crutches. Sometimes just hopping on our healthy foot. It was all good, until I tripped and fell flat on my face and broke my nose," he confessed.

Wynn stared at him, trying hard not to laugh.

He glanced at her and rolled his eyes. "Go ahead and laugh. Everybody else did."

She chuckled. "Good for you for taking it. But that must have been pretty rough."

He shrugged. "It was all in good fun. Competition with support makes all the difference in your life. It makes you reach for things you didn't think you could do." He glanced from one sibling to the other. "You guys know all about that. There's no way having both siblings in professional sports, the same sport at that, didn't command a certain amount of a competitive spirit."

Todd laughed. "So true. For me especially. The last thing I wanted was for my kid sister to come out and smack me down in place rankings."

"Like I'd do that," she scoffed. "It also helped that we

were two different sexes, so we never competed against each other. We did mixed doubles and teams together. It was all fun though."

They sat here, drinking coffee, their conversation more about things in general, mostly about their lifestyles.

Wynn said, "It wasn't a normal lifestyle, that's for sure. Our grandparents didn't agree with us doing competitive sports but were happy to see us happy and let us do our thing."

"As long as we didn't return to them broken and injured," Todd interrupted. "Hence why we're living where we are while I recover."

"And while I was injured before," Wynn reminded him, "you looked after me. Just because your recovery is taking longer than any we've had up until now doesn't mean I'm bothered by it."

"No, *I'm* bothered by it," Todd said. "But Tanner's right. I have come a long way. I tend to forget to look back to those early days after the accident, so I can see how far I've traveled. I still look in the mirror and see where I was before my accident and think how far I have yet to go."

Tanner nodded. "I don't think that's necessarily wrong. I think that's human nature. We forget to appreciate what we've already accomplished. We're too busy counting our failures."

"Speaking about failures, you guys do realize I just got fired today."

"You'll find something else," Todd said comfortably. "Or don't. Help me work on the designs, sell privately, set up the website like we always talked about, go into business for ourselves."

"The whole point of me getting a job," she said in exasperation, "was because we didn't have enough money to do that otherwise, remember?"

He nodded. "But we could also move out of town, change locations to something cheaper, and potentially we'd do just fine anyway."

"No money coming in is scary," she snapped. "The bills just don't stop. We've got all the gear the school never paid me for, remember?"

"So we build them into paragliders and sell them on our own website with our own logo. I mean, we do have a hell of a name."

"True, and you did get good money for the last couple gliders you custom-built." She remained thoughtful. "We wouldn't have to sell very many in a month to cover our cost of living."

"See? You can do the bookkeeping and the office stuff now, and I can do a bunch of the marketing and PR stuff. Between us, we've got it handled. I hate paperwork."

She made a face at him. "And I hate marketing. But both are necessary evils. We already determined which one of us was better at which."

"You know how I am with paperwork. As far as I'm concerned, the round filing cabinet is where it all belongs."

She chuckled. "I hear you. The trouble is, the government doesn't agree. Still, we can't pull any wages. We'd be pulling only expenses for now."

"You're still hot in the industry. I'm still getting endorsements," he said. "We can drag this out for a while. And I think, if we started building our own gear, maybe get into a clothing line, we'd do really well."

"A clothing line? Have you been thinking about that for a while, or did that just pop up?"

"We'd start with something like sports apparel. Not necessarily wind suits, although I can't see anything wrong with starting with those," he said with a quirky grin. "But hoodies and jackets—lightweight, heavyweight, rain-weight, all that stuff—but with our own logo, our own badge. You know? Like Summers and Summers did."

"Sure, but remember they went broke," she said drily.

"They did, and they deserved to. They drank and drugged their way through whatever they intended to do anyway. They dropped their business, which had been doing extremely well, right down a deep hole and followed in after it."

She had to admit that was a fair assessment. She caught Tanner studying her intently. She frowned. "What's that look for?"

"Nothing, just an interesting concept. I think going into business for yourself would be a good idea for you two." He glanced around. "Do you own this place, or is it leased?"

"It's leased. I have a flat of my own in San Diego," Todd said. "But it wasn't wheelchair friendly. So it's rented out for a decent amount that's covering the flat's mortgage. She has one as well."

"Sure, but mine is in New York," she said with a laugh. "For whatever reason, I bought a place a long time ago when the money first started rolling in."

"Both locations are pretty pricey real estate," Tanner said. "Sell them both and buy a place a little bit out of town, and you'd probably do just fine with the leftover money."

The two looked at each other and shrugged. "It's possible," she said cautiously. "But those are also our bolt-holes. They're the only things we have in life."

"No," Tanner said gently. "You have each other. And

that's worth a hell of a lot more. You also have this business you've already invested a ton in, not just money but blood, sweat and tears. It sounds like it's time to make it or break it. You've lost your job, Wynn, but you still have a lot of connections in the industry. Contact them and move forward. Forget about the school you just worked for. Be their competition. You'll take over in no time."

Todd laughed. "I really like the way you think." He got up, stumbled to the coffeepot, carefully brought it back, set it on the table and refilled their cups. "I think he's right though. It's time we did this on our own. Full-time."

She sagged back in her chair and muttered, "I think so too. But that doesn't mean I'm comfortable doing it."

Tanner chuckled. "Doing the right thing is never easy, and doing the hard thing is often the best way forward, especially because it's hard. If you wanted to play it safe all your life, you would never have gone into this sport."

She looked at him and smiled. "You're so right."

TANNER WAS FASCINATED by his further insights into the brother-and-sister duo. He'd done a little research before he had showed up at the school earlier this morning. He found out how well the two were known in their own field. "With your names, you could launch all kinds of things. I think you'd be a big success in no time."

"Maybe," Todd said cheerfully. "But I'd be happy with a chance to continue doing our research and keeping us afloat."

"You may be happy with that. I'm not. I want more for us," Wynn said. "We have a lot of potential. Tanner's right. It's just scary taking that first jump off a cliff."

"And you know how it feels time and time again," Tanner reminded her. He smiled. "I've never seen anybody quite so eager to take that first jump. So what's holding you back right now?"

She stared at him for a long moment, her eyebrows raised as if she hadn't considered that. And then a slow smile dawned across her face. "Nothing, I guess. I still have to deal with whoever sabotaged my equipment though."

"True and that could mean he's coming back here, now that your Jeep is here too."

She shook her head. "Doesn't mean he knows where I currently live."

Tanner hopped to his feet. "One thing we should do is make sure you don't have a tracker on your car."

"I don't like the sound of that." She frowned at Todd, who got up and followed Tanner out.

But Todd got what Tanner was worried about. "Good Lord, Wynn. You can't lead this guy to Elizabeth's apartment."

"But he doesn't want Elizabeth," she said.

"But that doesn't mean he'll leave her alive," Tanner said gently, standing at the kitchen door leading to the garage. "So you need to change locations, and you need to change it fast."

"I don't have any other place to live."

"Come back here," Todd urged. "This is your home."

"I suspect," Tanner said, "if this guy isn't someone directly related to the school and already in the know, that he'll be following the media. If there isn't any mention of your *accidental* death, and he sees your Jeep running around town again, he'll try again sometime in the next week or two. Even if he works at the school and saw the cops converge there earlier today, he may at least lie low for a week or two. But with these four incidences in what? Two months?"

"Three," Todd said.

"Three months' time? He seems to be escalating," Tanner said, looking directly at Wynn for emphasis.

She shook her head. "I don't like this. What the hell does he want?"

"If it isn't the same guy in the vehicle you passed on that back road, it muddies this up," Tanner said. "That brings us right back to the fact it could be professional jealousy or any other number of crazy ideas. You sure you don't have an ex-boyfriend who was pissed off or upset when you broke up with him?"

"I told you, no." Her tone was short. "It makes no sense that anybody would be after me."

"And yet, do you think that's what this is all about, or do you really think your gear was *accidentally* sabotaged?"

She glared at him. "Okay, so there was nothing accidental about it."

He nodded. "Exactly. And, therefore, you have to find out the reason behind it. It can't be that hard."

"Well, it's not that easy either," she snapped. "It's not like somebody jumped up and said, 'Oh, damn, you're not dead. I'll have to try again.'"

Tanner chuckled. "No, it's never that easy. But eventually you'll get to the bottom of it. While you're thinking more on that angle, in the meantime, you have to stay safe, and you have to make sure you don't put anybody else in harm's way."

She glanced around at their home, at the garages and their workshop. "He obviously knows about this place, if he's the guy who broke in weeks ago."

"So maybe move back in here with Todd again, make sure you've got a good security system in place, especially addressing the ways the intruder got inside the last time, and a guard dog wouldn't be a bad idea either," he said thoughtfully. "Or do you know anybody else you can move in here with you for a bit?"

She glared at him. "Why would I want more people here? Todd doesn't like company as it is."

"Granted, with the police notified, they should be making more drives by this place, which is something at least. But I was thinking about a bodyguard or somebody who would be a deterrent for our would-be assassin."

Todd said quietly, "It's not a bad idea, even though I don't like having people around."

"It's big enough." She was thoughtful. "But how much of a deterrent will another person be? If this asshat lights this place on fire, it's not like he's worried about whoever else is inside." She shook her head. "We'll think about our options." Her tone of voice said the matter was closed. "We have lots to think about anyway."

Tanner opened the rear kitchen door, leaving it ajar as he headed to her Jeep.

From the kitchen, in her line of sight, she could see Tanner at her Jeep, running his hands over it. "How can you even find anything like that?" she asked him.

He shot her a look. "Remember the unit you took up for training?"

"Oh, right." She felt stupid.

With her and Todd both watching, Tanner went over the entire Jeep. He nodded and said, "You're clear." He watched the relief wash across her face.

"See? All for naught," she said cheerfully.

"Not really," Tanner said. "Since you no longer work at the school, it just means they'll center in on accessing this place again." Tanner walked around the set of large garages that sprawled along the back of the house that they used as a garage and a workshop. "How long have you guys lived here?"

"Close to five years, I think," Todd said. "A friend of ours owns it."

"Do you want to move or would you want to buy it from him?"

"Depends on the price," Todd said. "Like you stated, real estate here is pretty pricey."

"But you already have an apartment you could sell."

"Sure, and it's a penthouse. Because, in my heyday, I was making good money," he said cheerfully. "But it's amazing how quickly my savings can disappear when I'm not flying as high as I once was. With the medical bills and the rehab and all the other expenses, plus with the endorsements dwindling, it's pretty rough to see it go down."

"Yes, but we both invested well," Wynn reminded him. "So, if we did sell our bolt-holes, we could possibly buy this place and live frugally, just off of our investments."

"But we're running a business too," Todd added.

"So we have to make the business solvent," she said. "I guess I'm having a change of heart, realizing this really is a gift."

Tanner nodded. "It so is." His phone rang. He pulled it out, checked the screen and groaned. "I need to head back. We've got meetings this afternoon. It was supposed to be my day off. But when duty calls ..." He walked toward his Jeep, turned to look at them and said, "Both of you stay safe."

He hopped into his Jeep and pulled out. He hated to

leave them, but, when he got called out, he got called out. That was just the way the naval life was. What he wanted to be sure of was that they would still be here when he came back.

He drove to Coronado Base to the meeting that had been called. As he walked in late, the commander looked up at him and said, "You're flying out at 0800 in the morning."

He nodded, keeping his face calm and quiet. He'd missed the beginning of the briefing so he'd catch up from the guys. Apparently they were doing an extraction. Someone in Iraq who the military wanted badly.

The only good thing was it appeared to be fairly open and shut. Rebel leaders had taken the hostage from a convoy. Depending on how heavily armed the rebels were would tell the navy how smooth and how fast they would be getting in and out. As Tanner glanced at his watch, he realized, chances were, they should already have left tonight. He frowned, his fingers drumming on the desk.

"What's the matter, Tanner?" Mason asked.

"I'm just wondering why we're not leaving tonight."

"We're still gathering intel on his location," Mason said.

Tanner slumped back. "Okay, that makes sense. But, Mason," he added.

"Yeah?"

"Can you get one of the guys to stay with Todd and Wynn while we're gone?"

"Already on it."

Tanner sighed in relief. One less thing on his mind.

But, even though Tanner hadn't left yet, he was already looking forward to being back. That had never happened to him before. And he knew it all centered around Wynn and her brother Todd. But mostly Wynn.

CHAPTER 8

T HE NEXT FEW days were full of heavy discussions between Todd and Wynn, with lots of reorganizing in the workshop, time spent on their new company website and organizing the paperwork already accumulated here. And every day, for at least a four-hour shift if not an eight-hour shift, one of Tanner's SEAL buddies showed up and took a watch inside and sometimes outside the house. They were like silent sentinels, who ate whatever Todd and Wynn ate, whenever they ate. She could almost forget they were here. On the morning of the third day with rotating bodyguards it was not so uncomfortable anymore.

Today, with apologies, their guard had to leave with no replacement at the ready. "Be back as soon as I can or as soon as the next available guy can be here. Lock up behind me. Watch your sixes."

Shortly thereafter, noting the time on the clock in her office read 10:59 a.m., she got up from her desk chair and stretched. "Todd, I can't do a desk job like this all the time," she yelled to him in the workshop. "This is brutal. How can anybody work in an office, sitting on their butt all day long?"

"Lots of people do it," he called out.

She walked to the open shop section, where he was working on compiling components again. Todd had a hang glider apart on the floor. She preferred paragliding but had done plenty of both. They were very different experiences. From the designer perspective, improvements could be made to both. "What are you doing?"

"Just looking at these joints on the curry straps for the harness," he mumbled.

"Is this that new design?"

He nodded. "I just thought it would be easier to handle. The ultimate dream, of course, is to stay up there longer, having more control to fly up, not just down. Catching the wind is one thing but controlling the wind—now that's a whole different story."

She smiled. Her brother had always been like this. He was never a glass-half-empty type of guy. He was less into competition and more into the feeling of flying. And she understood because she'd caught the bug with him. If their parents had lived, she often wondered what they would have thought of their adult kids' accomplishments.

"I've got these mocked up to scale," he said. "I'm testing how much pressure these aluminum alloy airframes can take."

"There's got to be something stronger," she said.

He nodded. "There is, but, with what we gain in strength, we add in weight."

"Right back to that fine balancing act. I was also thinking better channels in the silks that would hold more loft." She bent over her favorite part of the design work. She'd been sewing wings for her and her brother for a long time.

He glanced at it with interest. "And again we're back to the fact we need a certain amount to hold and a certain amount to float. But if we're carrying any kind of weight …"

"Then we have to have more air pockets. It's fairly well balanced now …" she muttered to herself.

For the next hour, she and her brother sat on the shop floor, smiling, working away, the same as they always used to. This was their dream—to design new products and to run their own company. "By the way," Todd said suddenly. "I forgot to tell you, but a rep called this morning. I asked him about a clothing line. He had a couple suggestions, wanted to know if he could come by this week."

"Depends on how much money we have to invest."

"Actually he was looking at it the other way. If they carry a line of our products, with our name, our logo, as long as they think the line of products is any good, they'll endorse them and sell them in stores."

"And what do we get for that?"

He named a figure that had her rocking back on her heels, staring at him in shock. "Really?"

He glanced at her and laughed. "You've forgotten the figures we commanded in endorsements in our heydays."

"I haven't forgotten," she said. "I just hadn't realized some of those numbers were attainable again."

"You know? I think they really are. When everybody retires, they have to do something. In our case, if we go into research and development of sports gear, honestly I think that's where we belong."

She tucked that away in the back of her mind. She thought she heard the front doorbell and glanced at him. "Did you hear the doorbell?"

But he was already muttering to himself.

She walked to the front of the house and opened the door. She stepped out to see several delivery boxes had just been dumped on the front porch. Obviously no signature required and nobody still here to reveal who had dropped them off. She sighed. "Next time let me know you're coming," she said to the empty air around her. "I'd have you bring them back around to the shop."

Instead of carrying them all individually on her own, she returned to the shop, grabbed the hand truck, rolled it to the front door, stacked up the boxes and wheeled them back to Todd. "Delivery. I presume you ordered some more stuff."

"I'm always ordering things," he said, only half paying attention.

"I know," she said. "I'm telling you some of it's here."

He glanced at the boxes and grinned. "Great. Do you want to move it all over there?" He pointed to his workbench.

She moved it all and said, "We have to start keeping track of inventory. What comes in needs to be entered, and what's used up needs to be recorded."

"I think there's software for that."

"Sure, but somebody still has to enter and remove things."

He glanced at her and smiled. "Remember? That's your area."

She walked back to her office and frowned. "Hey, were you in here?"

His head was back down again.

She thought about this. She'd gone from her office to spend an hour with Todd in the workshop. From there, she had heard the bell, went to the front door of the house, but had to return to the workshop for the hand truck. And then back around to the house for the front porch delivery. She'd maybe been gone ten or fifteen minutes for this delivery run. Otherwise she had been right with Todd on the workshop floor, just a stone's throw from her office. Surely she would have heard somebody in her office if she was nearby. Yet, she swore that the papers she had left on her desk had been moved. She sat back down on her chair and frowned. It was farther away from her desk. Normally she just stood and then stepped around the chair and the desk.

She reared back and then stood. With icy fingers of dread creeping up and down her shoulders and back, she walked to her brother, sat down beside him and whispered, "Hey, I think we just had an intruder in here."

His head popped up, and he stared at her.

"Did you hear anything nearby?" She wiped a finger across her lips in warning. "I went to the house for the delivery at the front door. When I got back, the papers on my desk had been moved, and my chair shifted."

He narrowed his gaze at her and opened his mouth.

She placed a finger against her lips again and whispered, "He could still be here."

He settled into his wheelchair that he always kept close by and moved toward his own office. She watched what he was doing and realized that, depending on where Todd sat and where he looked—whether in the actual workshop or in his own office—he wouldn't have seen her office at all. The side entrance, the actual front door to the shop, was around the corner. If somebody had sneaked in and crept along the side, they could have slipped into her office while Todd muttered to himself. And he would never have noticed. She loved her brother, but, when he got into his work, everything else faded.

He acted very casual. He swept into his office, and, from where she was, she could see him do a slow visual search, then go to his desk and remove something from his drawer. She watched as he logged onto his computer or appeared to be searching. And that was a good point. She hadn't even considered if somebody had gotten into her computer.

As she walked back to her office—searching the large workshop on her way, wondering if some intruder was still here—she tried to log on to her desktop computer. When the screen came up, it showed her normal log-in. She signed in, typed her password. Then she went to her recent history to check documents, but nothing appeared to have been opened. Nothing had been downloaded; nothing had been copied. She sighed. *And why would anybody be here in the offices anyway?* This was her office computer. Like, for paying bills, keeping track of orders, expenses, taxes even. Bookkeeping crap.

But, of course, her laptop was the one with all her early IP designs. Their later improved ones were under tight security here. But no one knew that.

And the laptop had been at the school.

She bolted to her feet. Some of her stuff was still in her Jeep. Granted, it was in the locked garage, but a lot of good that did if the intruder came in via the workshop which also served as their garage. She'd come home from her last day at the paragliding school, unpacking all the stuff from Todd's trailer. But not everything had been unpacked from her Jeep. Most of it had, but some of it was still left there. She hadn't really worried about it, what with it being locked up in the garage. Until now with their newest intruder. She grabbed her car keys, walked around to the garage side of the work-shop, and saw several cardboard boxes still evident in her Jeep. That worried her even more. In a Jeep, everything was so damn obvious. There was no hiding whatever you put in a Jeep.

She went through the boxes, and, on the bottom of one, she found her laptop. Sighing with relief, she pulled it out, putting it directly on top of the two boxes, then carried it all back into her office. Making several more trips, she emptied the Jeep. Back in her office, she took her laptop, put it into the filing cabinet and locked it. At least it would be obvious if somebody was after it now.

But, considering that, what if somebody *was* after it? She needed to have a copy of everything on it. She pulled it back out, put it on her desk and copied over everything to her desktop as a backup and put another copy into cloud storage. By the time she was done, Todd joined her.

"I did a full search, but I don't see anyone. Are you sure?"

"Of course I'm not sure," she said tiredly. "But I swear to God that I didn't move these papers, and I don't push my chair all the way back."

"No, you don't. It always drives me nuts because I have to pull it out in order to get in myself."

"Right? So it just doesn't feel right. But that's when I realized my laptop and a bunch of the other boxes were still in the Jeep. I've just unloaded everything, and I've copied a backup from my laptop to the desktop and now over to cloud storage."

He nodded. "That's something else we'll have to get. We need a big upgrade in our computer security. We've been foolish. And that's something we have to stop. Especially if we want to make a go of this. We're going to have espionage almost as a right because we're going into the business of designing. People will always wonder what we're up to, what we're creating, and they'll do whatever they can to find out. To steal our designs."

She shook her head and glanced at him. "The world sucks."

That startled a laugh out of him. "It does. But it doesn't have to continue to suck."

She stared around her office as she logged off and shut down the computers. She picked up the laptop, put it in the filing cabinet and locked it once more. She walked out of her office and locked it. She turned back to her brother, her shoulders slumped. "I don't even like to think about how much we have to lock up now on a regular basis."

"The other thing is, we need to put alarms on every one of the doors and windows, so we know when somebody is coming in."

"That's for sure, whether we just continue to rent but especially if we buy this place. We'll take a look at that after lunch."

"Lunch. Now that's a good idea."

Together, with everything secured behind them, they headed toward the main part of the house, into the kitchen.

"Did you hear from Tanner?" he asked.

Startled, she glanced at Todd. "No. Why would I?"

Todd shrugged as he moved to the refrigerator to pull out sandwich stuff. "He seemed very interested in you."

"Did he?" she asked drily. "Or is he just feeling responsible?"

"Either way, I think he's a good guy," Todd said. "You could do much worse."

"Maybe, but he didn't get ahold of me recently, so whatever."

"But then again, did you try to contact him?" Todd asked with a snicker. "The world's changing. Girls get to ask guys out too, you know."

"That's only if I care," she snapped. She slapped some mayonnaise on the bread. "We also need to get more groceries. We can't live on sandwiches."

"I can," Todd said with a cheerful smile. "No changing the subject."

"I'll change the subject if I want to," she said mutinously. "No discussions about Tanner and me because there is no Tanner and me."

At that, Todd laughed out loud. "There so is. But that's okay. You can keep your secrets to yourself for a little while longer."

She shot him a hard look. "A lot longer."

He shook his head. "Nope. Tanner is all over you. That says something about who he is too."

In spite of herself, she asked, "Why is that?" She added cheese to the ham on the bread and started slicing tomatoes and onions.

"He's got good taste," Todd said cheerfully. "And some of the guys you've gone out with, well, they've been pretty ugly."

"Ugly?"

"Very ugly."

She laughed, cut the sandwiches in half, put them on a cutting board and put the board in the center of the kitchen table. "How about you sit down and eat and get off the subject of Tanner."

"I'd love to. I wonder how long it'll take before he gets back to you."

"Probably weeks, if ever." But inside she hoped she was wrong.

"HEY, TANNER, ARE you missing your new girl?"

"She's not my new girl," he called back good-naturedly.

He was certainly interested in getting to know Wynn a whole lot better. But, since he was here in Iraq, it would be safer for him and for his unit if Tanner stayed focused on what he was doing than to worry about what was happening to her. He had to trust that Mason had somebody with her and Todd 24/7. Of course, this was an off-the-book mission and had to take a back seat to any ongoing op. That had him a bit worried.

Tanner had told the guys about the *incidents* she'd had. But outside of everybody agreeing it was suspicious as hell, nobody had any answers or any new directions to consider. He'd done his best to run down everything he could, but there just wasn't anything else to go on right now.

He knew that the brother and sister were working on setting up better security all around the house and the workshop, but that wouldn't be enough. If somebody was determined to get at them, either at home, in their vehicles or in the cyberworld, then they would make it happen. Tanner walked into the tent, dumped his kit on the bed and plunked himself down, dropping his boots on top of his bag. He really missed Wynn, something he hadn't expected. She was a breath of fresh air, not only bright and cheerful and comfortable in her own skin, in her own profession, as he was in his, but—he hoped—the attraction between them was mutual. It felt very natural to him.

Hard to work on a relationship while here though. He was really worried about Wynn's paragliding accident. He wondered if anybody had considered Todd's accident in the same light. Maybe someone was after both siblings?

"Dinnertime. Up and at 'em," Mason called out.

Tanner bounced to his feet and walked out of the tent. A bunch of the guys were waiting for him. The chow line was brutally long. While standing in line, Tanner thought about his own future. He'd been saving up his money since forever. Always in the back of his mind he had planned that he would get married, buy a house and start a family. Like that standard dream everybody had. But it hadn't happened yet. And then he came up against Wynn and Todd and saw what they were building, what they were doing for themselves, and it made Tanner wonder when he would go down that road. What did he want to do after his time in the navy? He had never really considered that, thinking he would retire from the navy in his sixties. But life happens …

"Hey, you still thinking about her?" Shadow gave him a light punch in the shoulder. "That's a good sign, right?"

Tanner looked at him and said, "I don't know. Is it? Somebody is trying to kill her. I need to solve that problem, or I won't be able to take her on a second date."

"Not only do we protect the old and the innocent and the injured," Shadow said quietly, "but we also protect those we love."

Tanner shot him a shuttered look. "It's not there yet."

Shadow tilted his head, undeterred. "Given that, you'll need to stick close. As in move-in type of close."

"But it's not there yet," Tanner repeated.

Shadow's lips quirked. "Oh, yeah, it is. You're just in denial."

"I hardly know her."

At that, all the men fell silent and turned to look at him.

Tanner raised both hands in frustration. "What?"

"None of us knew our women very well before we ended up more or less hitched, but we knew the important parts," Mason said. "When it's right, it's right."

Tanner thought about that as they waited in line for

dinner. Was it that simple? He'd met a lot of women who he had liked. But none who kept him awake at night. None that worried him quite the same way as Wynn did. He loved the fact that she was following her passion and that she was doing so well with what she wanted to do. That she might have made some big enemies just meant she was doing some big things. Nothing like power and competition to get other people on edge.

Rarely did people come up against somebody who tried to kill them though.

He pulled out his phone and sent her a text.

The answer came back soon. **Hey, thought you forgot about us.**

He winced. **Sorry. Out of country.**

Immediately her response was **Sorry. I know. I didn't mean to make that sound accusatory.** And she sent a happy face emoji.

He chuckled and texted **Just thinking of you.**

Ditto.

He pocketed his phone and looked up to find all the guys grinning crazily at him. Tanner growled. "What?"

They all shook their heads.

Mason said, "Wynn is good people."

"She is. And I already feel half responsible for her. But is it because I saved her life or because I really care?"

"You already know the answer to that," Shadow said. "Don't take something pure and fill it with excuses or doubts. It is what it is. Just move forward."

"Easy for you to say. You're on the other side."

"Sure, but all of us have been through it," Shadow said quietly. "There's only one person you're lying to, and that's yourself. So open your heart, figure out what it really wants and go from there." And with that profound statement, Shadow stepped ahead of Tanner in the line, snagged a plate and started filling it with food.

CHAPTER 9

FOUR DAYS LATER Todd said, "Have you still not heard from Tanner?"

"Just the once," she said. "I'm hardly a priority for him right now when he's on an overseas mission. And we still don't have a bodyguard replacement after the last SEAL got called to duty last night. Just so you know." But Todd didn't pay much attention to things when he was working.

Thankfully Todd left her alone after that. It was Friday, nine days after her accident. She walked into the office, unlocked the door, turned on the lights and headed to her computer to boot it up. As she sat down, her phone buzzed. She lifted it to see a message from Tanner.

Surprised, she stared at it, but inside her heart warmed. He'd been here it seemed like constantly for the majority of the forty-eight hours after her accident. Just about to respond to his text, her phone rang. And it was also Tanner. She picked up the phone and answered. "Hello?"

"Are you angry at me?"

"Of course not." But of course she was. A little. She sighed. "At least not very much. Besides, you were working. It is what it is."

He laughed. "I didn't get a chance to contact you again. I got in late last night."

She smiled. "So are you off today?"

"I am. I was going to swing by and see if you wanted to go out for lunch."

"Absolutely I do," she said. "What time?"

"How about noon?"

"See you then." Smiling, she ended the call, glad to have Tanner as her assigned bodyguard now. She felt bad that those other guys had given up their free time to be here. And wouldn't you know it? There had been a break-in when one guy had to leave with no backup guard for them. Made her wonder if her house wasn't being watched. But she really didn't want to consider that.

She put down the phone and tried to log in. But she couldn't. She tried again and again. She got up and walked out to the shop, but Todd was in his office, along the same side of the building as her office, yet on the opposite end of the workshop. She walked in and said, "Have you been able to log into the system this morning?"

He was working on his big tablet, making design changes. He shook his head. "No. I was going to ask you when you arrived."

She groaned. "So is this the usual bullshit with computers, or have we been hacked?"

Slowly he lifted his gaze, and a look of horror crossed his face. "We better not have been hacked."

She returned to her office, picked up the phone and called the IT security company. "I can't log in. Can you see what's going on, please?" While she was on the phone, the IT techs went through her system.

"Yes, there was an attack. Somebody trying to get in, too many log-ins within a short time. We locked down all the accounts."

"How many attempts?"

"Seven."

Dazed, she raised her gaze to Todd, now standing with his crutches in her doorway. "Somebody attempted to log in seven times before the system shut him down."

"In that case make sure that's changed to three," Todd snapped. "The hell anybody gets seven tries."

"The system was locked down after three tries," the guy at the end of the phone said. "But we didn't put up an error message, so they continued to try."

"Oh, good." She explained that to Todd, who was surprised.

"That's interesting. Can they tell what passwords were tried?"

She asked the tech that.

"Yes, we do have a list of variations of passwords tried. I'll send those over by email. That was forty-seven minutes ago."

She stared at Todd. "This happened forty-seven minutes ago." She glanced at her watch. "It's eight o'clock now. So we would have been having coffee in the kitchen about seven-fifteen."

Todd shook his head. "No, we probably weren't even up yet. We were late getting around this morning, remember?"

"How long did all those attempts take?" she asked the guy on the phone.

"It took eleven minutes and thirty seconds," the voice on the other end said. "Now if you want to run through the security log-ins, as soon as I get the right answers I can get your system back up and running so your password is allowed in."

By the time she ran through that double-check and entered her log-in and password, the system booted up. "Okay,

I'm in." She released a breath. "Thanks. What I would like to do is have a message alert, something sent to me if this happens again."

"We can set that up," the tech answered. "Is a text message okay?"

"Text message is perfect." Getting off the phone, she turned to Todd. "They'll text us an alert anytime somebody tries to access the system from now on."

"Also have it set up so, if anybody accesses the system outside of regular working hours, we get an alert then too."

"I told them you and I both work evenings and often from our rooms," she reminded him.

Frowning, he thought about that and nodded. "Anything else in here touched?"

She glanced around and realized the filing cabinet lock looked odd. She pulled the key out from where it was taped behind the filing cabinet and unlocked it. The key wouldn't go in. "Somebody has jimmied the lock on the filing cabinet," she announced. "All three break-ins happened when we didn't have a bodyguard on the premises. Granted, the first time we didn't know we needed a bodyguard. Do you think somebody is watching the house now that we both work here full-time?"

Her brother started to swear. "You know? It's got to be somebody after our designs," he said. "There's no other reason to break into our workshop and to try getting into the computers and the filing cabinet."

"I know, but they didn't succeed in breaking into the filing cabinet. And my laptop was in the bottom drawer."

"But your desktop has the same designs backed up to it that are on your laptop, right?" He didn't wait for her to answer. "Presumably we're heading into more and more of this kind of espionage."

"I hope not," she said. "We've been pretty lucky. I don't really want to start living in a world like this." She replaced the key in its spot and sighed. "I guess I need a locksmith in here to change out the lock and key so that I can get into my own filing cabinet." She sat back down, hoping to get some work done. She heard Todd not very far away. She got up and poked her head out of her office door.

Todd stood in the workshop in front of the inventory of raw materials, glancing through everything.

"Was anything taken?" she asked sharply. "I didn't even think about that."

"It doesn't look like it," he said. "But how did they get in in the first place?"

"Who knows?" She ran a hand through her hair. "Just because the police drive by more now, and we have SEALs for bodyguards as often as they can possibly swing it with their real job, we are here alone at times too. I mean, we have locks on the doors, but we don't yet have security alarms on all the windows." She pointed to one of the windows that was open about a foot and a half.

Swearing even more, Todd made his way over and peered out. "Footprints outside," he said.

She raced to his side and stared out. Sure enough this window looked upon the interior courtyard between the L-shaped house attached to the L-shaped workshop. The courtyard could only be accessed via the shop or the house. It was one of the reasons they'd left it open all the time. There was always a nice breeze. "So, somehow he gets in this way. Did he paraglide in or climb over the two-story-tall roof? Regardless, he had free access to everything in the workshop. He gets into my office but can't get into the computer or the files."

Todd nodded. "Sounds about right. So what does he do now?"

"He leaves before we get up, but now he's planning and plotting when to get back in and what he needs to get the job done right this time." She shook her head. "And I really don't like the sound of that."

"So we need to ask somebody who's a specialist in this field," Todd said.

"Security alarms on the windows might help, but a glass cutter would easily take care of that," she said. "Anybody with any skills in breaking and entering would be able to pick the locks and bypass security alarms. They got into my office, but they didn't get into the computers—this time. As for the filing cabinet, he either thought he didn't have time or wasn't too concerned about what was in it."

"Since there's a hand truck right here in the shop, why not just load up the filing cabinet and take it away with him?"

She turned and stared at her brother in horror. "Is that seriously what we're looking at? I came out here to suggest we digitize all our files as it is. Now you're making me think I need to do that today."

Todd straightened and looked at her. "Honestly I'm afraid it *is* something we need to look at today. We also need to look at a better alarm system before nightfall. Somebody is after our designs," he said slowly. "I wonder if it's somebody from your former employer."

She shook her head. "Tanner asked me the same thing. Particularly after the latest accident, I just don't understand why anybody would give a damn. We've been designing new prototypes for several years, and I've worked at the school for two of those."

"Sure, but it's only in the last few months we came up with the best ideas of all, and don't forget. Just because we were designing for years, we weren't building them for anyone else but ourselves. It's only recently that we've put them together. A physical prototype. And you know they're damn good paragliders. The harness system is better than anything else on the market. And somebody else knows it."

"It really breaks my heart to think anybody who I worked with over the last two years is involved in breaking and entering into my place and stealing our intellectual property information that we worked so hard to develop."

"And I don't think they give a damn," Todd said sadly. "Somebody you know, somebody you worked with, someone somewhere has probably been keeping track of your progress with these designs all this time. When you were fired, he realized he would have to come here and take the material you had removed from the warehouse. He didn't get a chance to steal anything, or maybe he just needed the last bits. Who knows? Maybe he figured you were fired because you wouldn't share your designs. I can't say. But what we can say is, we're now on somebody's radar. And we have to do whatever we can to make sure they don't get all our hard work and leave us with nothing."

TANNER HAD A couple days off, and he needed them. He was tired. He hadn't slept well in Iraq, and the pace had been brutal, as always. He got out of the shower, leaving the door open for the steam to vent outward, and, with the towel still wrapped around his hips, he walked into the small kitchen of his apartment and put on a pot of coffee. By the time that had finished dripping, he was dressed. When his phone rang, it was Mason. At least it wasn't Wynn canceling lunch.

"Hey, Tanner. How are things at your end? You at Wynn's or at home?"

"I'll be at Wynn's place soon. I wanted to do some research into Todd's accident in the meantime."

"Well, that's partly why I'm calling. You wanted Tesla to research background info on the two owners of the paragliding school and to do a full rundown on everybody who worked with Wynn. Well, she has that for you. But she says you have to come here and have coffee with us before she'll hand it over."

He chuckled. "Now that's devious. But I accept. Are you sure you're ready to see more of me though?"

"Doesn't matter if I am or not. What Tesla wants, Tesla gets," Mason said with a note of good humor.

But Tanner wasn't fooled. Mason was so head over heels in love that it was stupidly scary. "Be there in ten minutes."

MASON AND TESLA were waiting for him, both with warm grins. She handed him a sheaf of papers she'd printed off. "This is what I've accumulated so far."

He sat down and looked it over while she poured him a cup of coffee. "The school is in financial trouble?"

"Yes, they brought Wynn in, thinking it would bring them big sales. Instead the market itself has taken a hit. The cost of the gear has gone up, and some of the cachet has gone out of the industry—the accidents in this sport are gaining more press coverage, for one. So, instead of getting increased revenues, they ended up with less."

"So firing Wynn made financial sense then."

"Well, it does until you realize there was a life insurance policy on her."

"Who holds the policy?"

"Hartman Insurance," Tesla says. "The benefactor is her brother."

"Well, Todd didn't try to kill her. I know that for sure."

"We can never know anything for sure. Remember that," Mason said. "We can assume, but we can't ever really know."

Tanner lifted his gaze and smiled at Mason. "He really loves his sister, and he's got lots of his own money. So I don't think that's an issue."

"No, but what you don't know is," Tesla said, "Charlie's school is insured, so, if any of the staff dies on the job, the family gets a rider, but so does the school itself, to help cover the bad press."

"Isn't that a very unusual policy?"

"It's incredibly unusual. But, when you consider what a death would mean to the school, it might make sense."

"I'm surprised someone took that on. What insurance company issued that policy?"

"Hartman."

Tanner lifted his head and looked over at her. "Now that doesn't sound right."

"Especially not when you consider Hartman is a very small insurance company, and it's owned by friends of the grandparents of Todd and Wynn."

"I can see the company covering Todd's and Wynn's life as a favor to the grandparents, but why would the company cover the paragliding school?"

"Because that's where Wynn worked. Apparently the grandparents have been upping her life insurance coverage the entire time she's been out competing. Started when she was a teenager, and they haven't stopped. Same thing with Todd."

"Interesting," Tanner said. "Of course Todd was injured, but he didn't die. Wynn too. She didn't die. Her gear was badly damaged, and maybe that's covered somewhere, but she didn't die, and she didn't need any medical care."

"And she's been incredibly lucky the whole time," Tesla said. "So Hartman has continued to cover her."

Tanner tapped the table with his fingers. "Interesting concept. I'm not sure I really like the idea though."

"So we're back to the case of who benefits if Wynn dies."

"The grandparents, the school and Todd."

Cut and dry, just like that. He frowned and looked at it. "She doesn't compete anymore. She's still doing endorsements, but they have dropped off a lot. So keeping her alive wouldn't bring anybody any money. I just wonder if anybody else would benefit from her death."

Tesla shrugged. "I can only tell you what the computers can find, not what people have for intrinsic values. If somebody hated her, there's no better thing than to know she's dead."

"Unless it's to see her suffer every day," Tanner said. "As in the death of her brother or him being crippled, like he is currently."

"That's not very nice to think about," Tesla said, "but, as we well know, human nature isn't always very nice."

CHAPTER 10

A N HOUR LATER Wynn was still muttering over her files when the front doorbell rang. She walked through the shop to the house and into the main entryway. When she peered through the glass window, she was surprised to see two police officers. Those assigned to her sabotage case had told her that they were still working on it and that they'd call with any further updates. That had been seven days ago. And these were not the officers assigned to her sabotage case.

She opened the door and smiled. "Hi. What can I do for you?"

They stood, a frown on their faces. One said, "I thought you contacted us?"

A voice behind her called out, "Yes, we did."

She turned to look at Todd. "You phoned the police?"

His face was grim as he nodded. "Yes, absolutely. It's time to bring in more help."

She stepped aside, though she frowned.

The cops looked from one to the other, and one asked, "What's going on here?"

Todd said, "Come to the kitchen, and we'll explain."

In the kitchen Wynn put on coffee while she listened to Todd explain the nightmare the last few months had become. Once the cops realized her paraglider had been sabotaged, and she and Todd had had two earlier break-ins and now a third one earlier today, where the office had been accessed each time, they got more interested.

"My brother already reported the sabotage, about nine days ago," Wynn said. "We can give you the names of the detectives running that investigation, but they told me that they'd call with updates, and I haven't heard from them since."

"Yes, we'd like their names."

Todd pulled out two business cards and shared them with the two officers.

"But you didn't report the B&Es at that time?"

"Well, there was only one then," Wynn responded, instantly feeling lame.

The two officers confirmed that with their cold stares.

When the coffee was done, Wynn brought the pot to the table with four cups, then pulled out cream and sugar. She sat down by her brother and pitched in as the questions were asked. And they came strong and steady. By the time she was done, she felt worn out. In fact, these two asked way more questions that the detectives on her sabotage case.

Laid bare like that, she wondered if maybe Todd had been correct in calling the police. Again.

"Ma'am, I don't understand why you would wait so long to report any of this when you seemed to be having multiple problems for over three months now."

"I kept pushing it off," she confessed. "Not wanting to believe there was anything serious about this."

Both cops just stared at her. Finally the older one spoke. "Maybe not for being run off the road. Maybe not even for the pillar falling near you at work. But it shouldn't take three B&Es here before you call us. Yet, I have to say, it's the sabotage that almost killed you that has me shaking my head.

You have ten years professional paragliding experience, and, when your own equipment is tampered with, you don't think it's serious?"

She winced. "Okay, so I was in denial. Then I got fired, and that just overtook everything else."

The other cop raised an eyebrow. "You do realize how your own actions are making you look very suspicious to us, don't you, ma'am?" He paused but only for a second, not really expecting her to answer. "And how we are the professionals as to these criminal activities? And how we need all the information, not the things *you* feel are pertinent? Maybe that's why you haven't heard from the detectives on your sabotage report. You didn't give them all the info to work with. Because we will decide what is pertinent and what is not."

With a tiny shrug, she didn't answer his question.

"Why did you get fired?"

Clumsily she tried to explain that too. But she eventually fell silent, saying, "I know it sounds pretty lame."

The older cop wrote down some more notes, asked her for the school's contact information.

She gave him both of the owners' names and several of the other people involved.

"I want the name of the person who drove the bus of students and who drove the equipment there too. I want the names of the other trainers who were up there with you instructing these SEAL units. And whoever else we can contact to confirm the events of that day."

Todd snorted. "You can contact the local SEALs units out of Coronado. Mason was there, as was Tanner, and at least another four or five of them, I believe."

Wynn smiled and nodded. "We had sixteen SEALs that

day, two teams of eight."

"Well, that helps with your credibility," said the older cop.

The other policeman looked at her and asked, "And one of them helped in your rescue?"

Again she smiled and nodded. "Yes. I have to admit that I'm very grateful I had experienced men who knew what to do in emergencies. If it had been any other of our groups that I take up all the time, the outcome would have been very different."

"Would it have been fatal?"

"Ninety-nine percent positive, yes," she said. "Depending on three things—when the glider collapsed, the speed I was traveling and the impact zone—I probably wouldn't have regained consciousness. However, there are some crazy stories of people who have survived all kinds of things, so it's possible I would have survived. But, I think, in the general population, the impression would be that that would have been an instant death."

"Instead you had a SEAL student help you, and, with your instructions, he redirected you both to the river, and you were both saved."

"Yes, but at a cost," she said. "I almost drowned as I was caught between the two wings."

The men frowned as they contemplated what she'd been through.

She sat back, tugged a cup of coffee closer to her and said, "But, if somebody was trying to kill me, that should have done it."

"And then the break-in this morning?"

She pointed to the window. "The footprints are still in the garden outside the window."

They nodded. "We want to look for fingerprints too, plus take photos."

"Do whatever you need to do. I'm happy to help in any way." With the cops' doubtful looks, she added, "Really. Finally. I'll cooperate fully." Restless she got up and paced the small room. "Do you need me, or can I return to my office?"

He nodded. "Go on to your office. We'll catch up when needed. We'll take a look around, get an idea of the layout, take some photos, and, if we think there's enough need, we'll call in a forensic ID team to take the next step."

The corners of her mouth turned down at the thought. It was such an odd thing to consider everybody poking around in their private lives. But Todd was right. When it was laid out like this, there was definitely something going on. She gave a curt nod and walked back to her office.

She glanced at her watch and realized she was supposed to meet Tanner for lunch. As a matter of fact, her phone, which she'd left in her office, was ringing as she entered. She picked it up and said, "Hello?"

"Are you okay?" Tanner asked. "I've been calling for the last ten minutes."

"Sorry, the cops are here."

She tried to explain, but Tanner interrupted. "Change of plans then. I'll pick up lunch for three and bring it there." And he hung up.

She sighed. She glanced up and around, but the room was empty. Todd hadn't followed her. She dropped the phone on her desk and sat down. For a moment, just a short moment, she buried her face in her hands. She had no death wish and certainly no plans to continue dealing with some intruder here. It was all very unnerving to consider somebody had targeted her. She'd spent her life being very focused on her passion. Sure, there had been people who hadn't been terribly impressed with her climb to glory, but it wasn't like she was getting mega-million-dollar endorsements either. She and Todd did fine, but it certainly wasn't enough for both of them to retire on.

Distracting herself with business, she brought up her email program and went through the pending ones, responding to each one as she came to it. Anything to keep her mind busy, not on the police doing their thing or on Tanner, who would blow through the place, larger than life as he was, and would ensure that the cops knew exactly what was going on.

There was just something about alpha males. And yet, it was nice that everybody had stepped up, doing what they felt was right. As much as she had argued with Todd about calling in the police, *both* times, she knew Tanner would back her brother in that decision 100 percent.

"Just what I need," she grouched.

More emails poured in. She focused on work and felt a little better as she got something done. When there was a cough at the door, she looked up, found Tanner standing there, holding a couple brown paper bags in front of him.

She smiled. "I don't know what your long-term plan is, but you'll break Todd's heart if you keep bringing him food and then suddenly stop."

"It's not just Todd I'm bringing food for now," he said. "It's you too."

"I was hoping to go out for lunch," she confessed. "Anything to get away from this nightmare."

"Understood. But, if I need to talk to the cops, it's better that I'm here."

"Your name is on their list, so, if you can confirm with

them everything I already said, then that would be good."

He laughed. "Depends on what you said. But I'll give him the truth."

She followed him back out to see one of the cops talking to Todd, asking more questions. When Tanner and Wynn entered the room, the cop looked up, narrowed his gaze at Tanner and said, "And who are you?"

Tanner placed the bags on the kitchen table, turned and shook the cop's hand, explaining who he was and that he'd been there that day of Wynn's paraglider *accident*. That started off the questions and the comments as Tanner gave his version of the events.

She found it hard to listen to him. It was one thing to explain what she'd been through, but she'd been in such a state, dealing with the problems at that moment, that she hadn't considered how his view would be slightly different and a little more graphic. By the time he was done, she felt more shaken than ever.

To keep busy she unloaded the paper bags and put on fresh coffee. When the cop was done with Tanner, the policeman walked back out to find his partner.

Tanner turned and looked at her. "Can we eat now?"

"Absolutely." Todd rubbed his hands together. "Is that butter chicken I smell?"

Tanner chuckled. "Indian food all the way."

There was fresh naan bread, rice, curry and the yogurt dish she loved so much. She sat down with a happy sigh. "Considering it's been such a shitty morning, this works just fine."

"Now that we've all dealt with the cops, you need to tell me what happened this morning,"

She shook her head. "After we eat. I'm too damn tired of

repeating myself right now."

She ate while Todd explained. Tanner's questions were hard and fast.

She finally raised her hands, palms up, and said, "Obviously this is just one long nightmare that won't go away."

"It'll go away," Tanner said, "but it has to get solved first. You need to check your cell phones and make sure there are no trackers. You need to check your vehicles on a regular basis to make sure nobody's tracking you. You never take the same route home twice in a row. If there's something you do now, a routine, like, going to the gym every Monday, Wednesday, Friday, that stops now." His voice was curt. "And you go nowhere alone."

Her jaw dropped as she listened to his instructions—no make that *orders*—and she could feel her temper building.

And he knew it. He narrowed his gaze and pointed his fork at her. "No arguments. You've already done it your way. And that's not working. Now we do it my way."

She slowly lowered her knife and fork. With her temper bubbling up within her, she asked, "Who died and made you boss?"

"The fact is, if we do it my way, you don't die, and your brother isn't left alone," he snapped.

That was a hell of a reminder. She cast a sideways glance at Todd, but he was busy eating his butter chicken, a big smirk on his face. "Oh, you like this, don't you?" She glared at him.

He nodded. "You've needed somebody to stand up to you for a long time," he said. "And I have no intention of being an only grandchild, thank you very much. I've already lost Mom and Dad. I don't want to lose you too."

The look in his eye was too real. There had been just the

two of them for so long that she understood.

Todd covered her hand with his and said, "Remember how you felt when I had my accident?"

That did it. The rest of her temper slid out. She sagged in place and nodded. Then she leaned over, dropped her head onto Todd's shoulder and said, "The worst day of my life. I figured for sure you were gone, and I was so angry, so hurt that you'd leave me."

"Exactly. There's just been us, and, if anything happens to you, there's just me. Don't do that to me."

She lifted her head, turned her attention back to her plate, more to give her something to think about instead of the tears threatening to drop, and nodded. "Okay, fine. But he doesn't have to be so arrogant."

"*He*," Tanner said for emphasis with a note of wry humor, "isn't being arrogant. *He's* making a point."

She shot him a resentful look. "Conceited, arrogant *and* a know-it-all."

He thought about it and shrugged. "Oh, well, deal with it."

At that, Todd burst out laughing. He attacked the rest of his food with cheerful enthusiasm.

She shook her head, her lips tightened into a thin line. "I think you like this way too much."

"If the shoe was on the other foot," Todd said gleefully, "you would too."

She could accept that. Laughing slightly, she resumed eating again. By the time she was done with her plate, she realized the men were serving up seconds. When Tanner held up the dish for her, she shook her head. "I'm good, thanks."

By the time they had all finally finished eating, and the

coffee was poured, the older police officer came back in and said they had finished here and were leaving.

"I do have one thing to report that should set your mind at ease," the older cop said. "Your latest intruder, from this morning, seemed to have used the delivery to your front door to gain access to the house. Not the window." He paused and looked at Wynn. "By your account, you did not lock the door when you left it to get the hand truck."

She nodded.

"From the footprints outside the garden window, and the foreign fingerprints we found both inside and outside that window, we've reconstructed the intruder's movements. He both raised and lowered the window. He seems to have used the window to prevent being caught inside and crouched in your garden. Then he climbed back through the window into the house to escape, probably via the front door. He didn't bother to put the screen back on the window, so we figure he was in a hurry. Either he has been watching your movements or just caught a very lucky break to drive by when the delivery man was here and took advantage of that."

"So," Wynn spoke, turning to her brother, "the intruder *was* here when we searched for him earlier. But we were looking for him in the workshop, not in the house." She visibly shuddered, turned toward the police officer. "Doesn't make me feel any better overall, but at least we can still keep that window open. It helps to cool that one side of the workshop."

"We'll give you further updates as we find out more details. And we'll increase our drive-bys past your house, both day and night. Otherwise"—he stared directly at Wynn—"do not hesitate to update us with any more odd occurrences in your life."

Wynn sighed and seemed properly chastised.

"We will, Officer." Todd nodded. "I'll come and lock the door behind you." He followed them out to the front door.

She sat and waited until she could hear the *click* after he said goodbye. Then she started to relax. "I really don't like having very many people in my space," she said.

"It's always hard, isn't it? Strangers coming and going, feeling the invasion, the lack of privacy."

"A sense of violation," she added. "To think somebody came in here, deliberately trying to hurt us, not physically, but business-wise, it's just a creepy feeling. I didn't have a ton of girlfriends growing up, so I didn't have that real close connection with others in a group. It's always been just Todd and me. Such a horrible feeling to think somebody in the outside world is trying to harm us."

"And it may not be so much trying to do you harm as trying to line their own pockets. Greed is a powerful motivator for some," Tanner reminded her. "So let's hope that, A, we're only dealing with one asshole, and, B, he decides it's not worth his time and effort."

She brightened at that. "I like the sound of that. It would really suck to think I had two of these guys up against me. But then what's the purpose of trying to kill me?"

"I was going to ask you about that." Tanner waited while Todd refilled his coffee cup. Tanner's gaze going from one sibling to the other, he said, "Is there any chance Wynn's *accident* could have been minor sabotage that went crazy, so he just wanted to scare you, maybe get you to quit? But not actually kill you?"

Todd stared at him. "I hadn't considered that. I suppose

it's possible though. But, if you're going to sabotage any-body's equipment when they're one thousand feet aboveground with very little in the way of safety gear ..."

"Which brings us back to the missing parachute." Tanner looked over at Wynn. "It didn't open, and yet, we know that one in every thousand chutes doesn't open based on statistics alone. Could they have known it wasn't going to open?"

"So you're saying, they would have sabotaged my para-glider, but, because I had on a parachute pack, they assumed I'd be fine. And maybe a good hard scare would make me quit this sport?"

"We know it happens," Todd said to his sister. "Look at Amber. She had that bad accident. She ended up with a rough landing after a mishap in the air. She broke an ankle, cracked a rib as she came down, but she never flew again. Everyone said she lost her nerve, and, when I asked her about it, she just gave me that sad smile and said she had lost her passion for something that would eventually kill her."

Wynn sat back and thought about it. "I guess it's possi-ble. It's certainly a little easier to stomach too. I'd rather think somebody was only trying to scare me into quitting, not trying to kill me."

"It's still not great, but at least it isn't as malicious."

She sighed. "Yes, considering the alternative, I'll take this one."

Tanner's phone rang. He pulled it out, checked it and laid it on the table beside him.

Todd looked up. "Where were you this last week or so?"

Tanner's face stilled. Then he said, "I was in Iraq on a mission."

Todd was prying, but he studied Tanner's face while

Wynn watched them both with interest. Then Todd nodded. "Top secret and all that stuff, huh?"

Tanner gave a quick nod. "Most of my work is."

"Okay, I can accept that," Todd said. "Glad to have you back in town now." He turned toward his sister. "Do you get calls and have to get up in the middle of the night and leave?"

Tanner tilted his head slightly as if looking for a good answer. "I usually get a few hours' warning. Sometimes it's less than four though. It depends where in the world the strife is and how many skilled units they need."

"And, being one of the elite, I suppose you only go in when it's ugly."

Tanner chuckled. "If that's what you want to call us, yes."

Wynn filed away that information. "That must be hard on relationships."

He shot her a glance and nodded. "It is. My work is dangerous. It's sometimes pretty hairy. I can be gone for long periods at a time, and then sometimes I'm home for months and months, when it seems like all the world is at peace. And then I get a call, and I'm gone."

She liked that about him. He didn't make any excuses. "Thank you for serving our country."

He gave a slow nod. "You're welcome. I do what I do for people like you."

She thought there was a ton of emotion and a lot of stories and pain behind that statement. She smiled slowly. "And that's why I'm saying *thank you.*"

IT WASN'T OFTEN that he was thanked for the job he did.

These two were good people. They deserved to have a life that was fun and enjoyable, even while they were working hard but doing what they wanted to do. It was hard to imagine somebody was out there trying to kill them—or at least her. And that brought up another factor.

He turned to look at Todd. "So we didn't really discuss your accident. Is there any chance your accident was also sabotage?"

Todd looked at him in surprise.

"Sabotage, attempted murder, scaring you into quitting the sport, whatever you want to call it," Tanner said. "I know it's been a few years, but, if somebody was doing this to torture your family, as in they really, really, *really* hated you, there's a good chance they wouldn't have stopped after your accident but would be looking for another opportunity to go after your sister as well. So I guess that's what I'm asking. I know it's not something you want to contemplate, but to have taken you out and made you suffer for years and then to take out your sister, well ..." He shrugged, his palms up. "I had to ask."

Todd just stared at him.

Wynn answered him with slow words. "He was in a paragliding competition. There was no real way to understand what went wrong. His frame snapped. We were in Hawaii. He came crashing down. He was too low for his parachute to open fully. Although he did crash, the partial-chute drop helped stop him from a complete blow into the cliff edge. It was bad. But, if that chute hadn't opened, it would have been way worse."

Todd nodded slowly. "The frame itself was smashed into the rocks, and there were only pieces afterward to collect."

"Any idea why the frame snapped?"

"I broke my own rule," he said. "I always retire a frame after so many hours of flight time. And I was past it. But I had won every other competition with this glider, and I wanted to use it as my lucky charm that day."

"And, any other time, would you have considered that number of hours to have been an issue in terms of equipment fatigue?"

Todd shook his head. "No. But it was my own rule. So, when the accident happened, I figured I had just pushed my luck once too often."

"And now? Considering the sabotage to your sister's equipment, how do you feel about your own accident as you look back?"

He was silent for a long moment, his hands hugging the cup of hot coffee. His face went white, as if the memories were difficult.

Tanner could understand that. He'd been through enough ugly scenarios that even the mention of one was enough to make his system chill to the point of being frozen. He worked long and hard on not having things like that incapacitate him. And so had Todd. But Tanner suspected this was the first time anybody had suggested that Todd's accident was anything other than an accident. Tanner looked at Wynn. "Who won the competition with Todd out?"

"Nobody. When Todd went down, several other people immediately went down to help, and the competition was called off."

"And is there any chance that, by not winning that competition, somebody else lost out?"

"Like endorsements?" Todd asked.

Tanner turned to him. "I suggest we look at it from all angles. If you had won, would somebody else's nose have been out of joint? If you had lost, would another somebody's nose have been out of joint? And, with your crash, did that boost anybody up in the rankings? Did somebody get endorsements because you were now out of the picture? Things like that. Money is power, and, in competitions, everybody wants to win."

"I was less about winning," Todd said, "and more about just enjoying the sport. Wynn and I are very similar in that way. We mostly competed against each other. However, we really competed against ourselves. We kept wanting to best our own records. When we went up in the sky in these competitions, it was us against Mother Nature. And that's how we felt. It wasn't about competing. It was about flying."

Tanner pointed at Wynn. "You said something to that effect earlier."

She nodded. "And I meant it. But not everybody feels the same way," she said in a wry tone. "That particular competition of Todd's was the last of the season. The others wanted the competition to be run again, but, after Todd's bad accident, it was just canceled. The year was finished by tallying up all the runs until that point."

"And did that make sense to you?" Tanner asked. "Would you have thought there was a better way to do it?"

She shook her head. "No. I think that was the best way to handle it. But my brother had accumulated so many points that he still retained top status. If anybody had wanted to beat him that season, well, it was pretty much a no-go."

"He had already been winning pretty steadily?"

"Sure," Wynn said, "but two others were winning steadily too. Really only the three of them were at the top of the pack. And that left an awful lot of guys who just didn't have the skills yet to challenge them."

"That's pretty egotistical to say," Todd said quietly. "An incredible number of very talented men were coming up behind me. But, that season, three of us were in competition for the overall championship."

"Since you had that accident, the next year, of course, you weren't even in the play. Who won that next year?"

Todd looked at him. "Steve Catcher. He was one of the two other men."

"Fascinating," Tanner said. "And did he have an accident at the end of his year too?"

Wynn stared at him this time. "I really don't like the way your mind works."

"I've heard that before." Tanner gave her a grim smile. "It doesn't change the fact that these questions have to be asked."

"And I really wish they didn't," she said. "That's a pretty sad way to go through life."

He nodded but repeated, "It doesn't change the fact."

Todd answered the question with a frown. "I'm not sure I can answer that. I know he was awarded the championship. But he dropped out of sight afterward. I don't know what happened to him."

"Are you a good-enough friend that you can get in touch with him and ask? Or were you never really friends?"

"We were really good friends," Todd said. "It's partly because of Steve that I recovered as well as I did. He wouldn't let me give up."

"Now that's interesting. Maybe you should contact him, ask him about his competition win, why he's not out there anymore. Ask if there are any rumors about the third guy. What was his name?"

"His name is Roger. We called him Rog." Todd pulled

out his cell phone and flicked through his contacts. When he got to Steve's entry, he sent a text. **Hey, stranger.** He looked up at the other two, then added **You dropped out of sight. Is everything okay?** He read his text out loud for Tanner and his sister, then Todd hit Send. He put the phone on the table beside him. "No idea if I'll even hear back from him."

"Have you had any contact with Rog since your accident?"

Todd shook his head. "Rog and I weren't exactly friends," Todd said, his voice short. "He was one of those win-at-all-costs kinds of guys."

Tanner stared at him. "And you never considered or it never crossed your mind that *win at all costs* could easily mean sabotaging the man at the top?"

"Well, it didn't do him any good," Wynn said, "because, if he did sabotage Todd's rig, Todd still won, and then Steve won the year after."

"And this year?"

Todd looked at him, his face turning slightly gray. "I believe Rog is in the lead."

Tanner nodded. "Maybe it took him three tries to get it right, but this year he'll win regardless."

Wynn grabbed Todd's hand and squeezed it. "It wouldn't hurt to make a few inquiries. We know a lot of the people in the competition circuit. We know a lot of the judges. If anything is off out there, maybe somebody will let us know."

Todd nodded. "I can look into it. But I tell you, I can't say I'm terribly impressed with the concept of opening up that part of my life."

"No," Tanner said, "but you'll do it to keep your sister safe."

CHAPTER 11

L ATER THAT NIGHT Tanner and her brother had a few drinks, then heard a noise outside. At that point, Tanner declared in a solid hard voice that he was staying, and nothing they said would change his mind.

She hadn't minded. Although he certainly wasn't drunk, she didn't want to see him leave and definitely not to drive. He laughed and told her that he never did anything stupid like that. One DUI and his navy career would be over. She was glad to hear that, but, at the same time, it was a little awkward at bedtime. She'd taken away any opportunity for further questioning when she dumped blankets and pillows on the couch for him.

Todd chuckled and said, "Well, she put you in your place."

Tanner had given her that hot look she'd recognized a couple times before and said, "You could be nice and let me sleep in your bed."

She shook her head. "Not happening."

"Have you moved out of your friend's place?"

She nodded. "I did. It's the two of us here now."

"Well, for tonight, it's the three of us," Tanner declared. "Go grab some sleep. I'll keep watch."

She snorted. "Not necessary. We should be fine after having all the cops crawling over this place all day long.

Surely the bad guy will take the night off. You're here as a friend. Just sleep." And she walked out, headed up to her room.

Her brother had followed suit at a slower pace. His bedroom was on the main floor, so he didn't have to navigate stairs.

It was a large house, and she'd often contemplated that maybe they should look at purchasing it. There was really no need to keep her apartment in New York, except it had always been hers, her little piece of something. But she hadn't been to New York in years and had no intention of living there ever. So why was she holding on to it?

As she lay in bed that night, she tried to remember what the real estate value on it was, but the figures escaped her. She'd look it up in the morning.

WHEN WYNN GOT up the next morning, her mood was dark and gray to match the clouds outside. Then she remembered how Tanner had spent the night here. That brought a smile to her lips.

Now that she was up, with a full cup of coffee in her hand, and both men still sleeping, she headed to her office. She was relieved to notice the office door was still locked and her computer off. Nothing appeared to be changed in any way. She sat down at her computer, booted it up and brought up the tax bill she'd paid on the New York property last year, to find the market value on her apartment. And, sure enough, it was a figure that made her gasp. And she could sell it for even more than that. With that money she could probably buy this rental property outright. If her brother sold his San Diego penthouse apartment, then potentially they would have enough money to do what they were doing, as long as they were careful, for another five years. At least hopefully until they could get off the ground floor and make some profits in their business.

She'd have to remember to talk to Todd about that this morning. His property probably wasn't as valuable as hers, but then she didn't know what his penthouse would get right now nor what would be the price to buy this place—or even if their friend was willing to sell this place. She sent their friend an email and just asked about any interest in selling.

Then she checked her emails and the cat meme of the day, which always put a smile on her face. She stood and walked to the window in her office, opened the curtains and found the sun shining through the earlier cloudy gray skies. It felt weird not going to work anymore. After a couple years of going out in the sky every day, she didn't really miss it at the moment, but she knew she would eventually.

Sitting behind her desk again after her short break, she typed Roger's and Steve's full names into Google to see if anything came up. There was nothing on Steve. Rog, however, had a lot of press saying he was the new sweetheart of the industry. She frowned, wondering if something *had* happened to Steve, now that he apparently hadn't been in the season at all this year. She had found contact information for him as well online, but what she had was even better: a number and an email address for his sister.

She looked up the email and sent off a message, asking if Steve was okay. She'd barely sent it off when she got a response telling her to call. She picked up her phone, dialed the number.

When Tanya answered the phone, she said, "Hey, this is a voice from your past. How are you?"

Wynn was happy to hear Tanya's voice. The two women laughed and greeted each other like old friends.

"That was quite a surprise getting that email from you," Tanya said. "And good timing. I was just about to go for a run when I saw it."

"Good for you," Wynn said enviously. "I pretty much gave up running."

"It's still the only way I stay fit," Tanya said morosely. "I'm not long and lean like you. And I have a tendency to put on too many pounds too quickly."

Instantly an image of Tanya's voluptuous figure filled her mind. "And yet, it was you the guys always looked at," Wynn said with a grin. "You had one thing I didn't have."

"Yeah, what was that?" Tanya asked curiously.

"Curves," Wynn said. "I could paraglide with the best of them. But, man, when it came to walking into a room and getting all the men's attention, you had that hands down."

Tanya's laughter pealed through the office.

When there was an opening, Wynn asked, "What happened to Steve?"

Tanya groaned. "He was at the top of his game. And then something happened. He went to pieces. He's not paragliding at all anymore. He stays in his big paid-for home, plays in his pool. He is doing a lot with his music now—as long as he's recording at home, that is, no live performances—but he doesn't go up in the sky anymore."

Wynn sat back with a feeling of shock. "Can you tell me why or what happened?"

"He sometimes won't even talk to me."

"Why? He was, as you said, at the top of his game. He was doing great." Wynn didn't understand. The Steve she knew would never have ended up like that. She wanted to know what happened. Usually there was an accident in the air. And then she knew. "He had a close call, didn't he? One that scared the crap out of him."

"Oh, he sure did. He was up with a couple friends, and something happened to his gear. He survived, fairly safely. Like, he didn't break anything. He was really sore for a long time. He ended up coming down pretty rough, and I think he just saw his life passing before his eyes and realized he needed to make a change."

"Is it a good change though?" she asked. "Or is he hiding, just not wanting to do anything?"

"That's a good question. It'd be really good if you guys could come and see him." And then she went silent for a long moment before she tentatively asked, "If Todd can't … That is … I'm so sorry. I forgot he was badly injured."

"He was, but he is slowly recovering. He's walking again, although with crutches to keep his balance, but he's getting there."

"Oh, I'm delighted to hear that," Tanya said warmly. "Todd was always the best. When he crashed, we all thought for sure he was a goner."

"I know. I had a crash myself here just a few days ago," Wynn said ruefully. "It was only because of the quick actions of one of the people I was with that I didn't have a repeat of Todd's accident myself."

"Oh, my God! That would have been terrible," Tanya cried out. "Were you hurt?"

"No." She laughed. "I don't know how or what good deed I did to deserve it, but I didn't get injured in any way. I was pretty terrified though, and I have to admit I haven't been up since then but mostly because of other circumstances. It's not because I'm scared."

"Yeah? You know? That's what Steve said to me too. He said that he'd go up. He just needed a day or two. But then that day or two ended up being more than a day or two, and, by the time I realized he hadn't been up at all, I think it was too late," she said quietly. "So make sure you do get back up because I know how much you love it. You were teaching, weren't you?"

"Yes, for the last couple years."

"You two were the brother-and-sister duo nobody could catch up to." Tanya laughed. "I was always jealous, even though I didn't paraglide. I hated that sport. But you guys were crazy about it."

"It was in our blood. But now we spend most of our time on the ground. I guess life's like that. It's cyclical," she said with a smile.

"I guess," Tanya said. "We're not very far away. We're outside San Diego. Steve's got one of those fancy million-dollar homes on the ocean. Why don't you come down and visit?"

"I'd like that," Wynn said. "I know Todd would too. I think it's important to stay connected to the friends we made. Recovery is hard enough. But, when you do it alone, it's a bitch."

The two women set up plans. Wynn wrote the date down on a notepad beside her, knowing she'd have to confirm it with Todd first. With a quick promise to call back with their answer, she got up and headed to the kitchen. Todd was there, holding a cup of coffee, looking a little worse for wear after an obviously bad night.

"Don't you look like shit after a late night of drinking," she said cheerfully.

He just glared at her.

She chuckled. "Is that what I look like when you say that to me?"

He nodded. "But you look worse."

She grinned at the typical-brother response. "So you want to go visit Steve?"

He looked up at her in surprise.

She held out her phone and wiggled it in the air. "Just got off the phone with Tanya."

Todd leaned forward. "How is he?"

Wynn shook her head. "Not good." Her tone was brisk. "He did have an accident after the season. He was up with friends, and his equipment failed. He did survive, but it scared the crap out of him."

"It scares the crap out of all of us," Todd said with a sad smile. "But he didn't get hurt?"

"Banged up and bruised but not too bad. It was more the experience. He hasn't been up since," she said quietly.

Todd stared at her. And then the corners of his mouth turned down, and he nodded. "I understand exactly how that feels."

She grabbed her brother's hand. "I'm sorry."

"Nothing you can do about it," he said. "I'm not sure I'm capable of going up again anyway."

It was the first time he'd ever said that. She'd thought for sure that was what drove him with his research for a safer glider. And now she had to wonder. "I tentatively set up a visit for Thursday at noon."

Todd considered that and nodded. "It'd be really nice to see Steve. Apparently we have lots to talk about."

"I know. How sad is that?"

"Did you mention anything about our problems?"

She shook her head. "No. I thought it was enough of a

shock just to contact her out of the blue. And I figured it would be best if we explain it once, and that it should be in front of Steve and his sister."

Todd nodded. "Good idea."

Tanner walked in just then, running a hand through his hair. His face lit up at the sight of the coffee.

"Hungover?" she teased.

"Last time I was hungover I was sixteen," he said. "You learn in the military to never let things get that far. But I'll never say no to coffee." He poured himself a cup and sat down at the table. "Did I hear Steve's name mentioned?"

She nodded and filled him in.

He stared at her. "Another accident, one that killed another career?"

Her face grim, she nodded. "Exactly."

"So can I be invited to lunch that day?"

"I thought you had a job to do," she said.

"I'll take that day off," he said, sending her a long look. "You know somebody else needs to be there. Not only does somebody else have to make sure the right questions get asked but you need a witness to whatever Steve says."

Her stomach started to knot. "You can't possibly think he had anything to do with Todd's accident?"

"No, probably not," he said slowly. "But that doesn't mean Steve doesn't know something and has stayed quiet for the last couple years."

"If that's the case, why would he speak now? To me? And especially in front of an unknown witness?" Todd asked. "Nobody wants to admit something like that after the fact."

"Probably because he had a bad accident himself. Maybe he has a suspicion about what went down with you that he hadn't realized before it affected him personally. It's one thing to suspect something. It's another thing when that suspicion is confirmed."

"Then why wouldn't he go to the police?" Todd asked.

Tanner turned to Wynn. "You said he's housebound. What do you want to bet it's more than just a fear of flying that's keeping him that way? What if he's afraid of a second attempt on his life?"

THURSDAY MORNING TANNER pulled up in front of Wynn's house and walked inside the open workshop. There was no sign of either brother or sister. As he wandered past each office, one at one end, one at the other, he found each inside their own office, each on their computers. He ended up at Wynn's office and knocked on the door. When she looked up and smiled, he walked in. "Are you guys ready to go?"

She gasped, looked down at the clock on her computer and nodded. "I didn't realize it was so late." She stood, grabbed her sweater off the back of her chair and picked up her purse.

Although she might not have been aware of the time, she was prepared. They walked together over to Todd, who was working away on his computer.

He groaned when they walked in and said, "I just need another hour."

"Well, you're not getting it right now," Wynn said firmly. "We're going to see Steve. He needs us too."

Todd shot her a look, but he logged off the computer, pushed back his chair and grabbed his crutches. "Fine, but I don't want to be gone too many hours. I want to get this finished today."

Tanner kept his grin to himself. He knew several other people just as dedicated to their work. Mason's partner, Tesla, was one of them. Often Mason had to drag her away from her work in order to eat. Devlin's partner was another one. She was an inventor and computer programmer and God-only-knew-what-else, but her current specialty was drones. And, when she got into a project, nothing got her out. Devlin had been known to pick her up and carry her away from her workstation, kicking and screaming.

Tanner could imagine Todd was of the same ilk. Dedicated to his work, so caught up that he ate, lived and breathed every bit of it. It wasn't a bad way to be if you had a passion like that. But, for those around them, Tanner wondered just how easy those people were to live with.

They were a little late pulling up to the beautiful waterfront property. Tanner stood beside his Jeep and whistled. "Wow, isn't this something?"

"Yeah, it is."

He looked over at the two of them. "Did you get this kind of money from endorsements?"

They both shook their heads. "No, but Steve came from a wealthy family to begin with. I think this is the family home. No, the other one was small, wasn't it?" Todd looked over at Wynn in confusion.

"His family did have waterfront property, but I believe they sold it when they moved to Europe and split the money between the kids, or so I'm thinking. Steve added to his pot and bought this place."

They walked down the big wide Spanish staircase. As they came around the corner, there was a massive swimming pool with an infinity-edge hot tub and a fantasy backyard.

Wynn called out, "Tanya? Steve?"

There was a cry from inside the house, and large glass doors opened up. A voluptuous young woman stepped out, her smile huge and bright as she raced toward Wynn. The two women hugged. Wynn introduced Tanner to her, and they shook hands. Then Tanya turned, looked at Todd and smiled. She gave him a gentler hug and said, "Damn, it's good to see you two. Steve is inside."

They followed her through the walkway between all the glistening blue water. Tanner marveled at what money could buy. The ocean went on as far as they could see. Neighbors were a long way off on the sides—at least a long way off compared to some city lots—and everywhere was this gorgeous luxury. Tanner had never had an opportunity to have something like this. He wasn't sure it was for him anyway.

He could do with twenty acres twenty minutes out of town. He'd much rather have privacy and a little less luxury than luxury and a whole lot less privacy. He stepped inside the gourmet kitchen to see a man leaning against the fridge.

Todd hobbled forward. "Steve?"

Steve studied him for a long moment, and then there was almost a visible relief as if he finally recognized him. The two men hugged each other. Tanner watched their mannerisms curiously. They were normal except one thing was evident—Steve was afraid.

He saw Tanya catch Wynn's gaze. She shrugged and mouthed *See? He's like this a lot.*

Wynn gave Steve a big hug and said, "It's so good to see you."

Steve looked at her with a heavy sigh. "I figured you guys would be coming and looking for me. I swear I didn't know." And then tears formed in the corner of his eyes. "And I'm so damn glad you're here now. I haven't been able to sleep. I haven't been able to do anything for fear of what you would say, fear of what you would do. And, even now, even though I know I deserve it, I'd much rather have it over with so I can sleep again and know it's done and dusted, and I can maybe finally move on. But, right now, damn it, I'm just a wreck."

Wynn looked over at Todd. He stared back at her. They both turned to look at Tanner. He turned to look at Tanya, but she stared in shock at her brother.

"Dear God, Steve. What have you done?"

CHAPTER 12

WYNN BARELY RECOGNIZED Steve. He used to be a tall gangly guy. He was still tall, obviously, but the gangly part had shifted to being bone-rack skinny. He moved with sharp, stark movements, as if he never rested, as if he was never at peace. When they all finally sat down in the living room, coffee served by Tanya, Wynn managed to say, "Steve, what happened?"

He looked at her with haunted eyes. "I don't even know where to begin."

"At the beginning." Tanner used a calm, steely voice. "In a case like this, that's really the only place."

Steve gave a small nod. He gripped Todd's arm. "I'm so sorry. I hope you can forgive me."

Todd frowned at him. He wasn't saying yes, but neither was he saying no. "Tell me," he said.

"It was after your accident," Steve said. "We were all still in shock. I remember sitting there in the bar, thinking that could have been me. Wondering how much I really wanted to continue with this lifestyle. I'd seen accidents before, but I hadn't seen the men involved immediately afterward. But I had seen you. I saw your twisted legs. I saw the blood. I saw the open bone." He shuddered. "It was the worst I've ever seen."

Wynn watched the young man's face, the myriad expres-

"

sions crossing it. She couldn't believe the change in his demeanor either. Steve always used to be the guy who stood up straight, gave you a big smile, had a great big belly laugh. He lived large, and he loved life. Now he looked like a shell of the man he had been. As she stared at him, she realized he wasn't even thirty years old. He looked over fifty now.

"Keep talking," Wynn urged when he fell silent.

He shrugged. "It's hard to know what to say. I was at the pub that night, drinking my sorrows. I raised more than a glass or two in your honor, Todd, as I knew you were in the hospital, fighting for your life. I thought about going home, but then I grabbed my beer, and I went and sat in the corner. I didn't want to talk to anybody. I didn't want to have anything to do with anyone. Life sucked. Just seeing what had happened to you, well, it was like seeing my life pass before my eyes. And I don't mean to demean what you went through, but it was … it was pretty rough." His voice broke.

Wynn was amazed at the depth of how Todd's accident had struck Steve. Maybe it was a good thing, but seeing the man he was now, there had to be so much more to it.

"The thing is, the way the pub was arranged," he continued, "there were booths. I was sitting in mine, huddled down, moping, trying to forget what I'd seen of you after your accident. I could hear voices behind me." He fell silent again.

Todd gripped his hand. "Tell me."

Steve gave him a haunted look. "It's hard."

Todd nodded. "I know. I was there."

At that, Steve winced again. "I could hear the men in the booth behind me talking. I thought I recognized one of the voices, but I wasn't sure."

"Who was it?" his sister asked, moving to sit beside him.

"Why did you never tell me about this?"

He gave her a shuttered look. "Well, you were wrapped up in your latest boyfriend."

She winced. "Yeah, that's when I was sleeping with as many of the paragliders as I could," she said in a dry tone. "Let's just say, I was young and stupid."

Wynn stared at her. "You *were* doing a lot of partying. Not still?"

She shook her head. "Actually the partying led to drugs, and the drugs led to a really bad experience. I'd always kept to light drugs, usually in a party scenario. But I ended up with a little too much. I think it came in one of the drinks. I never did find out for sure, but I woke up in the hospital with my stomach being pumped. I made a change of lifestyle right then and there," she said quietly. "Went off men, went off booze, went off drugs."

"I'm so glad," Wynn said impulsively. "You scared me back then."

Tanya nodded. "I scared myself. I was lost when Mom and Dad moved away. I gave off a tough and capable exterior, but inside I was anything but. … I wasn't suicidal, but I didn't really care what happened to me. This guy," she said, pointing her thumb at her brother, "was doing so well on the circuit and having such a ball, it seemed like he was such a success, and I was such a failure." She gave her brother a sad smile. "The things we do to ourselves and to each other without intending to."

"I hear you there," Todd said. "My sister and I have been to hell and back since my accident."

Tanya nodded. "Both of us had our own journeys, and they were difficult enough in their own way. But when you add in a sibling who's going through a rougher journey, well, it's hard to make any comparison and not feel bad."

Wynn smiled. "And yet, at the same time, you want to be there for them, and you want to grow from this so neither of you ends up stuck behind, but it's hard."

"I kept telling Wynn to carry on and to forget about me," Todd said. "She wouldn't listen. I wanted her to leave and to have a life and to not hang around her crippled brother. She used to get so angry with me."

Tanya smiled. "I think that's what pulled me through too. When Steve had a good year, I was having a great year. When he was having a bad time, I was having a worse time. But when I finally woke up and smelled the roses and realized I was on a downward spiral, Steve and I reconnected in a big way."

Wynn turned to look at Steve. "What were those men saying? And who were they?"

"I thought it was Rog, but I wasn't sure. He was talking about how pissed he was that, once again, he'd missed the title, and he thought for sure that, after you fell, Todd, that he'd take the title the next year. He sounded fairly fanatical about it, to tell you the truth."

"Did he make it sound like he'd had anything to do with the accident? Or was he just capitalizing on somebody else's bad luck?" Tanner asked.

"It wasn't him that worried me," Steve said. "It was the guys beside him. They were talking about how they could fix it so he won the next time. They were joking, but, at the same time, it didn't seem like they were joking."

"What was Roger's answer?"

Steve shrugged. "I'm not sure he gave them one. He was almost as drunk as I was. I was incredibly upset over your accident, and I think Rog was just as incredibly upset that the competition had been canceled. He was in good standing, and he would have moved up the ranks and probably would have taken the championship the next year."

"Except you did," Tanya said. "You won last year, and then you quit."

"I did," he said, "and I suspect I'll never go back up in the sky again, and maybe that's okay too. For a long time I worried it wasn't okay. I worried I had let the sport get to me and let the fear cripple me. And I think I'm out. I think I'm still afraid. But I'm afraid of different things now."

"You're afraid your equipment will be sabotaged, not that you'll be killed," Wynn added.

Steve lifted a shaky hand and wiped his brow. "The thing is, I don't know who the other two men were, but, as the conversation went on, it sounded like they were trying to convince Rog to take a deal."

"What kind of a deal?" Wynn asked, hating what he was implying.

"I don't know. What I do know is that, at one point, as I got up to leave, one of the men said, 'We can fix it. Just like we fixed Todd.'"

Silence fell on the group. Wynn's brain went black for a moment. To think of someone having done that intentionally to her brother …

Tanya covered her face with her hands.

Steve leaned over and put an arm around Tanya's shoulders. "I'm sorry I never told you, Sis. I never even thought about it at the time. I was too horror struck and too devastated by what I had just heard. I wasn't sure what to do. What I didn't do was, I didn't tell the cops. And I know I should have."

"Yeah, you should have," Todd said. He shook his head.

"The question is, were these guys just being asshats and implying that, or were they talking about something they'd done?" He swallowed hard. "It's one thing to consider my injuries being from an accident but another thing altogether to consider that the crash was deliberate."

Steve shook his head. "I stumbled outside, not really sure what I'd just heard. But, when I woke up the next morning, I was even more confused. I thought for sure nobody would have done that. But then I couldn't handle the consequences, and I just refocused. That winter I took off, and, by the time the season started the next year, I'd firmly convinced myself I had imagined it. But, at the same time, I was constantly aware of my equipment. I hired somebody who stuck with it at all times." He looked over at Tanya. "Remember Pedra?"

Her face flushed. "Of course I remember him," she snapped. "I'm pretty sure he's the asshat who gave me the drugs."

"It's quite possible. I think he was selling drugs on the side. But I did trust that he was looking after my gear. Maybe I shouldn't have hired him, but it seemed like there were no mishaps for the entire season, and, as I gained confidence, I did better and better. I only beat Rog by a couple points," he said slowly. "And there's a funny thing about that day. I was going to use my regular gear, and then I decided at the last minute to use my new one. Even as I was getting ready to take my last run, I was thinking it was a foolish thing to do because there wasn't time to test it. But instinct kept telling me to go on, to *use the new one*. And, as it is, I did just fine, and I won."

He took a deep breath and continued, "A few days after the competition, I took out my normal paraglider, and I did have a bad accident. But it was nothing like Todd's. It was bad enough though that I know, if I'd taken that glider up on competition day, where I'd have pushed the gear to its limits, I'd have crashed and burned in a bad way. As I found out afterward, my gear had been sabotaged." He said it so simply and so clearly that nobody was left with any doubt that at least he believed what he'd said.

Todd let out a deep slow breath and sank against the chair. "Dear God."

Wynn wasn't sure those were quite the right words. But she was too shocked to say anything.

"Do you think Rog did that?" Tanya asked, her voice rising. "Or whoever he was talking to that night?"

"I don't know."

"But the police can ask him that," Tanner said in a no-nonsense tone of voice.

Steve said, "After my accident, I tried to contact Rog. I wanted to ask him if he knew anything about it. But he didn't answer my calls."

"He's pretty well winning now," Todd said slowly. "He could just be busy, or maybe he feels guilty."

"Yeah, we're coming up to the final competition," Steve said. "And I don't know if he'll win or if it'll be three times lucky."

"You mean, if this third year in a row, the lead person has an accident, only this time it's a fatality?" Wynn asked, her voice deathly soft. She couldn't quite believe they were talking life and death here.

Steve looked over at her and nodded. "That's what I'm worried about, yeah."

"When is this final competition?" Tanner asked.

It was Wynn who answered. "This weekend. The championship is this weekend."

TANNER LISTENED AS he considered all the things they knew so far. "We need to go to this competition to make sure Rog doesn't become the hat trick."

"It's not a place I want to go," Todd declared, shaking his head.

"What we need to do is ask him who was at that meeting in the bar," Wynn said. "Rog knows me quite well. I could possibly get him to talk to me."

Tanner felt a spike of jealousy in his belly. "How well do you know him?"

She slid him a sidelong glance. With her lips twitching, she said, "Well. But not that well." She glanced over at Tanya. "But you do."

Tanya shrugged. "I did. But then I must have slept with fifty other paragliders. They all just rolled into one, and not one of them stood out."

"Ouch," Todd said.

Tanya glanced at him. A hot red flush washed up her neck.

Tanner stared at the two of them and realized what she'd said and what Todd's response meant.

Steve looked from one to the other and said, "Really?"

Tanya shrugged. "Sorry, Todd. I didn't mean that quite in that way."

"The thing is, that's how you did mean it." He stared moodily at the table. "And that was before my accident."

"Maybe it would be better now," she said quietly. "We were both pretty full of ourselves. Now we'd be a lot more real."

He looked at her, smiled and asked, "Take two?"

At that, she burst out laughing, her joyous sound pealing

across the room.

Tanner grinned. He had to give Todd full marks for trying. He didn't know that Tanya was quite ready for that, but, if they'd been there once, maybe this would be a good time to reconnect. Todd was definitely much more physically capable than he'd been since his accident. The fact that he'd felt strong enough and confident enough to make that move here today was interesting. Tanner was happy for Todd. It was hard to consider a lifetime of loneliness ahead of him.

Wynn patted Todd's hand gently, then spoke to Tanya. "Anytime you want to come and visit, Tanya, feel free. We're not very far away."

Tanya nodded. "Ditto. I'm sorry it's taken us so long to reconnect."

"I ended up quitting at the same time as Todd. I won my season. He had won his, but his accident completely changed everything for us," Wynn said. "I no longer cared about competing. I just cared about keeping my brother alive."

"You two were always close," Tanya said softly. "The same as we were, just different."

Wynn looked over at Steve. "You have no clue who was in that pub with Rog?"

He shook his head. "I don't. But, after my accident, knowing that my rig had been sabotaged, there's a part of me that thinks, if I even show my face again, I'm likely to be up for round two myself, and not in a way that would put a smile on my face."

"I had an accident just over a week ago," Wynn said quietly. "My gear was sabotaged."

Steve paled and Tanya gasped.

Wynn nodded and picked up Tanner's hand in hers. "Tanner saved my life."

And then she gave Steve and Tanya a quick rundown of what had happened.

Steve was visibly shaking in front of them. "Whoever this is, he's after all of us," he cried out. "There's no way I can go back up in the sky again."

"You don't need to," Tanner said quietly. "Think about it. That was one stage of your life. You're allowed to change and do something different from now on."

Steve stared at Tanner, his brain obviously working, as if trying to latch on to the logic, to find a place in there that made sense. Something he could accept and move into.

Tanner tried again. "Your life has had three stages so far. Before you did paragliding, during paragliding, and now this is after paragliding. Create a life that makes you happy. Don't be a prisoner in your house. Don't be a prisoner on the ground, with fear keeping you there. Find a way forward. Just because paragliding was what you did, doesn't mean it's what you should be doing or what you can be doing or what you will be doing in the future."

Steve looked at him and said, "But that would mean making peace with my past. I'm not sure I'm ready to do that."

"It is time though," his sister said. "You can't live like this. You hate to leave the house. You're a shell of the man you used to be. You don't sleep anymore. You wake up in the middle of the night, crying out with nightmares."

Self-conscious, Steve looked at the coffee table. "It's hard to forget some of this stuff, and it sneaks into your mind in the night when you're at your most vulnerable."

Tanner nodded. "I've been there. I understand. But, if

we go to the championship this weekend, we'll make sure nothing happens to Rog."

Steve lifted his gazed and looked at him. "And what if it was Rog who took care of Todd's accident and mine?"

Everyone was silent. Tanner nodded. "In that case, we better make sure he doesn't take out yet another competitor."

Wynn looked at him. "It'll be pretty hard to do. Like Steve did, a lot of people hire someone to stay close to their gear. You're not supposed to have the public anywhere near your rig."

Tanner nodded. "I understand that. But, if somebody's already managed a number of accidents, the last thing we want is a yet another one. And we certainly don't want a fatality." He tilted his head and frowned. "Do either of your ex-bosses ever go to the competitions?"

"Of course," she said. "They're sponsors."

Tanner gave a grim smile. "In that case, we're definitely going."

CHAPTER 13

W YNN STARED AT Tanner in surprise. "You can't really think Charlie and Curtis had anything to do with it, do you?"

"Not necessarily. But I did get some information pulled up on the school. I haven't shared that with you yet because I hadn't really seen anything that linked the staff or the owners to what was going on with this latest angle on your accident, Todd's accident and Steve's accident. But, if the owners are connected to the competition in any way, and there have been more accidents, then what we need to do is take a much deeper look." He stood. "And the sooner, the better."

Tanya protested. "Hey, we've got lunch ready. Stay at least long enough for that. Then, if you have to run, you have to run. Hopefully it won't be so long before you guys come to visit again." She looked at her brother. "It's good to see them, isn't it, Steve?"

For the first time since they arrived, Steve gave them a solid smile and, in a quiet voice, said, "Yes, actually it is. It's nice to reconnect. I hadn't realized how much I had isolated myself. How much this house had become a cage that I couldn't release myself from."

Wynn walked over and gave him a hug. "And that's what friends are for."

"I felt so guilty," Steve said as they walked to the dining room. "I heard that conversation, but I never told anyone. It was just too unbelievable. I couldn't consider it."

"And that's understandable too," Wynn said firmly. "Don't think about it like that anymore. And, if anything else comes to mind, anything at all, then text me or give me a call. Something may help us put the pieces together. I don't know if Rog is behind it or if Rog is a victim or if it has nothing to do with him. For all we know, we have somebody who likes to torment people."

They all entered the dining room, the table already set up buffet-style for lunch. Wynn looked at it and smiled. "This is beautiful," she exclaimed. "Really beautiful. Tanya, you've gone to a lot of work."

"My new hobby is cooking," Tanya said with a self-conscious laugh. "I really enjoy it. Staying home, being a bit of a homebody, is quite nice."

Wynn looked at her with new eyes. "Who knew?"

Tanya nodded, realizing just how different her life back then was as compared to her life now. "I didn't."

Everyone took a seat at the table and soon filled their plates. "Whoever is responsible for this has a motive. There's always a motive," Tanner said. "Power is most likely."

"In what way?" Steve asked.

"In this case, money. Money gives people power. When the ego is involved, then you can get revenge motives too. People do all kinds of things to each other for some of the simplest reasons. But here a lot of reasons could be involved and some very powerful motivators." He looked down at the make-your-own-nachos buffet and smiled. "This is lovely and making me hungry."

Wynn nodded as she topped off her plate and dug in.

"Me too."

About twenty minutes later Tanner picked up the earlier conversation. "Are there any groupies or particular people who hang around competitions all the time who might get too attached to a potential winner or a returning champion and want to see their favorite win at any cost?"

They all had to stop to consider it.

"That would probably be a question I could answer," Tanya said slowly. "I was certainly part of that groupie scene. Except that, because my brother was actually competing, I had a little more power. As you might say, I could get people into the back of the restricted areas, could get them in to see the insider scoop. The media was always pumping me for the goods, the latest details," she said.

She reached for her water glass and took a big drink before setting the glass down. Her gaze wandered to the four of them at the table. "But I can't think of anybody like that. People got very defensive about who was best, what gear was best. But I don't think anybody was so crazy as to sabotage somebody else to make sure their favorite won."

Her face twisted, and she stared down at her plate. "At least, I would hope not. A lot of those people I knew pretty well. But not any of them struck me as the kind of person who would hurt another."

Wynn said to Tanner, "Very few people have access to the gear. Chances are you'd have better luck if you were a cameraman, judge or even a stealthy spectator."

Todd agreed. "The cameramen are all over the place. So are the judges. A certain amount of media covers the competition too. And the sponsors are there. It's less about spectators and more about the people hooked into the competitions."

"Good to know," Tanner said. "I hadn't considered that. So then consider this. Is there any rivalry between the sponsors?"

"All the time," Todd exclaimed. "But not to the extent of killing somebody. They might offer better contracts, but I don't think they'd ever kill one of the stars. It's the stars who make them money. Whether it's for them or for someone else, money flows in this industry."

Wynn understood that. Tanner was just turning over all stones, but she thought he was wrong there. "This has a personal feel to it," she announced. "Look at my accident. I can't imagine how many people had access to my gear."

"That's what I mean though," Tanner said. "Just your bosses and your coworkers were around your rig. You said yourself that no other training was scheduled for that day, except for the units I was a part of. So how many people had access?"

"Only staff, like you said," Todd said. "Unless you consider the fact that the place is left empty overnight. It's all too possible that somebody jumped the fence, went into the hangar, did whatever they needed to do and left again, without anybody being the wiser."

"There is security though, isn't there?" Tanner asked Wynn.

She nodded. "There is, but it's not that great. And it's only on the windows and the doors on the ground floor of the warehouse."

"Are there other doors?"

She nodded. "One that goes up to the top of the shop for loading. It's got a large double door, so gear can be loaded up there without having to go through the main part of the hangar."

"And that door should be kept locked, but, of course, it's only a door, so who knows what might have been done." Tanner nodded his head. "Something else to think about then."

"The perimeter gate is always locked though," she noted. "But, like Todd said, it wouldn't be that difficult to climb a gate and jump over. It's not like it's an electric or barbed wire fence. I don't believe there's perimeter security at all either. The place is not high-tech, and it's not full of anything that's terribly important. Sure, there are supplies, and there's gear, but it's all insured. It's not design work or cutting-edge materials that people want a sample of—except for my two gliders and laptop. Not the typical stuff that we would think espionage revolves around."

"I DON'T THINK we can make any assumptions at this point," Tanner said as he picked up a tortilla, filling it with some of the leftovers on the table. "I have to admit, I'm really enjoying this lunch. Thank you very much for inviting me." Although he'd more or less invited himself.

Tanya laughed. "Well, you can put that down to Wynn. She really wanted to bring you."

He glanced at Wynn.

She gave him a bland smile. "Hey, why not?"

"We've been doing a lot of lunches together."

"So how serious is it between the two of you?" Tanya piped up, her gaze curious as it flitted from one face to the other. "It's been a long time since Wynn had a relationship."

Wynn looked at her. "How would you know?"

Tanya gave her a small smile. "I've been keeping track of you on social media."

"Good luck with that," Wynn said. "The only thing I ever post is about upcoming classes I'll be teaching. I never put anything personal on there."

"Why is that?" Tanya asked.

"Because I don't think it's anybody's business but my own," she said. "I've always been like that."

"Whereas I've been the opposite," Tanya said with a smile and a heavy sigh. "There are more pictures of me partying with every Tom, Dick and Harry than you could shake a stick at."

"But that's the old you," Wynn said. "Not the new you."

Tanner loved that. It was a great way for Tanya to look at her new life.

Tanya stared at her friend for a long moment and then gave a slow nod. "So very true." She glanced over at her brother. "And that was the old you too, Steve. This is the new you, and you get to make whatever you want of it," she added gently.

He nodded, picked up his coffee cup and held it up for a toast. "To friends reuniting after a long time apart."

They all clinked glasses together and had a drink.

Not long afterward Tanner stood. "I need to be going."

Todd and Wynn stood too. They said their goodbyes, thanked everybody for a wonderful time and then headed outside to the Jeep.

"You sure we couldn't stay a little longer?" Wynn asked as she climbed into the front passenger seat, watching Todd as he made it into the back seat without her help.

Tanner sat behind the wheel and glanced at her before shaking his head. "I have a lot of research I need to do. And, if this competition is this weekend, I think it's important we do some work ahead of time, so we're prepared when we arrive."

"I gather you're planning on going?" Todd asked, leaning his elbows on the two front seats and peering at Tanner and Wynn.

Tanner nodded. He knew they needed to be there. Chances were good this whole mess centered around these championships. "We have to find out what the hell's going on. If any answers lie in that competition, then I need to be there."

"Well, you're not going alone," Wynn said. "I know a lot of the people who will be there. That will help us get to where we need to go."

He looked at her and smiled. "Sounds like teamwork to me."

"Maybe," she said with a supersweet smile. "As long as you remember that I'm the boss."

Todd chuckled. "*That* sounds like fun. Too bad I'm not going, as that alone would be entertaining to watch."

"I'm the boss," Tanner said, "in all things related to security. You can be the pro at the paragliding, with the people, the competition. I'll need to know how it all works. But the minute there's any sign of danger, it's my lead, and you follow."

The two of them stared deep into each other's eyes.

Then Todd whispered, "Could you drive please instead of just sitting there looking googly-eyed at each other?"

Tanner laughed, turned on the Jeep and pulled onto the highway. "Absolutely. But I still need to hear your sister acknowledge when I'm the boss."

"I don't have a problem with you taking point in any dangerous situation," she said smoothly. "As long as you give me the chance to be point when I need to be."

"Absolutely," he said with a big grin. "I can't tell you how much I'm looking forward to the weekend."

She snorted. "We probably should book a hotel, since we'll need to be there late Friday and up early Saturday, plus it's a little way out of town. And drinking to be social might be required."

"I think it's a good idea anyway," Tanner said. "We won't want to drive back and forth if we're drinking." He glanced in the rearview mirror at Todd. "You should come."

Todd shook his head. "I'd much rather not have anything to do with that entire scene anymore. Plus, as long as I'm hobbling around on crutches, I'd be holding you guys back."

"No, you won't," Wynn exclaimed. "If you want to come, then come. But, if you don't want to come, then believe me, I understand."

"Then I won't come," Todd said. "Just like Steve, that feels like a bygone era. I'm happy to be doing what I'm doing now."

Wynn glanced at Tanner, catching his questioning look, and shrugged. "That's fine, if that's the way you feel."

"Besides," Todd said, "I hate being a third wheel."

She gasped. "There aren't two wheels yet, let alone a third."

He chuckled. "I mean it. Whatever you guys have going on here, it's heading for some serious alone time. So get it out of your system before you come back, okay?"

She glared at her brother and fell silent. Once they got home, she exited the vehicle and stormed inside.

Tanner stopped Todd. "Do you have a problem with us having a relationship?"

Todd shook his head. "Hell no. I don't have a problem

with the two of you getting together, but you might have a problem with her. She's been a little too long on her own. Yet, you're good for her. But it might take a little to get her to moving toward that next step."

"Any upsetting history I should know about?"

Todd shook his head. "No, it's usually about me. She hates to have anything to do with anybody if it takes her away from me. And it's definitely time that she got over that problem."

"She would have gotten over it a lot earlier if you had gotten over your problems sooner," Tanner said beside him.

"I know," Todd said. "Believe me. I know. But I've come a long way. As a matter of fact, I think she has too. It's good to see her dating again."

"I can hardly say it's been *socially correct* dating so far. She literally fell in my lap."

At that, Todd laughed. "Then ensure you make the most of it. You don't meet a girl like my sister very often. She is solid gold all the way. But don't think I'll stand by and let you hurt her."

"Believe me. I know that. And I wouldn't, not intentionally. But I really like her. And I want to see where this goes."

Todd smiled. "Then go get 'er, tiger."

CHAPTER 14

FRIDAY EVENING, AFTER finding no vacancies at the third hotel, Wynn turned to Tanner and said, "I hadn't expected this. But I should have."

"Neither did I," he admitted. "I know Todd said we should book ahead of time, but we didn't have any significant lead time to do that. I didn't think securing a hotel room thirty hours earlier would've made any difference."

"I knew this would be a popular weekend," she said, "but I hadn't realized no hotel rooms would be available."

He glanced at the list in his hand. "We have one more to check."

She blew the loose hair strands off her face. "I'm not holding out much hope."

They got back into her Jeep, and, following his instructions, they arrived at the parking lot of the very last hotel on their list. "I suppose we could still try some B&Bs," she said doubtfully. "Yet, I imagine they're pretty full too."

"Worst-case scenario is we have to drive home."

"I know, but that's not what we planned."

They walked into the front reception area. The woman at the desk looked up and smiled. "I suppose you're booked up this weekend too?" Tanner asked nicely.

"I just had one cancellation," the woman said. "For tonight only though."

"We'll take it," Wynn jumped in, already pulling out her credit card. "I don't care where it is or how big it is, but we've checked other hotels and haven't had any luck."

"I know. This event has gotten more and more popular every year," the woman said with a big smile. "It's also the Blues Festival this weekend. For whatever reason they have them at the same time, making it almost impossible to find a room anywhere."

"Well, that explains it," Tanner said.

Wynn, feeling lighter now that they'd found a room, said, "I'm sure the city planners must wonder. It would make more sense to spread these events out over several weekends." She finished the registration before Tanner had a chance to.

When they were handed the room key, the woman gave him instructions on how to get there.

Wynn looked around, asking, "Do you have a coffeehouse or anything here?"

The woman shook her head. "But there are a couple restaurants across the road. There's a coffee shop beside us, so you won't starve."

Tanner chuckled. "Is there a bar?"

The woman nodded. "Both of the restaurants have alcohol licenses, and there's a pub a block away." She pointed in that direction. "And I think they're open till one o'clock on Fridays and Saturdays."

Walking back outside to the parking lot, feeling a whole lot better, they grabbed their overnight bags. Following the instructions, they headed up to the room. Wynn unlocked the door, stepped inside and smiled. "It looks better than I thought it would."

"What did you expect?" he asked. "A flea-infested rent-by-the-hour place?"

She laughed out loud. "Interesting description. No. Did you?"

"Thankfully I've never had to go that low, at least not in this country."

His grin told her that there was a lot more to the story behind his comment, but he wasn't prepared to tell her about it right now.

She walked through to the bathroom, quickly used the facilities, washed her face and hands, then stepped back out again. Seeing the one large bed, she felt the heat as it fired up her blood. "I guess we should have double-checked if there was one bed or two."

"Unless you have designs on me, I don't think it's an issue," Tanner said, his grin several watts higher. "Besides, if we were fussy, we wouldn't have this room."

"Maybe I do have designs on you," she said, loving the banter. "And you're right. At least we're here."

"We've got what we've got. It's better than driving home again."

On that cheerful note, they headed out to the front of the hotel. Wynn looked around and said, "I think we should head to the competition area, see if I know anybody there."

"Is it within walking distance?"

She took a moment to orient herself and then smiled. "It is indeed. It's about four blocks from here. Of course, the jump off points will be a long way away. We'll see the landings, and, if the visibility is good tomorrow, we'll see them taking off." She led the way, adding, "I never did have much in the way of lunch today, did you?"

"No," he said. "And then I ended up working out for a few hours this afternoon."

"Does your job change a lot?"

"All the time," he said, "but the one constant is the physical training component."

"Makes sense to me. It doesn't matter what field we're in, we have to stay at the top of our game. Anything less than that can be fatal." She felt his glance on her face but kept on walking. "The question is, I guess, do we want to stop here and get something to eat first?"

"I'd rather see the layout, see who's there, see what we're up against. Maybe see if Rog is there. His reaction to seeing you, things like that. And I presume there'll be a lot of food at the site."

"There's probably a beer garden close by. There could be food trucks. This area is well known for its cafés and pubs."

"Well, let's take a look. We can always step away and grab some food later."

It was a good ten-minute walk by the time they entered the park where the base was set up. She turned and studied the area carefully. Over several hundred people appeared to be here already, some sprawled out on the grass, others wandering around with food and friends, or still more just standing and talking, enjoying the beautiful day.

"Are all the competitors here in this area?"

"They're cordoned off on one side." Her voice was low. Determinedly she wove a path through the people. She'd been to so many of these that she knew to keep going deeper and deeper into the crowd. Eventually she'd find where the media crew were setting up. She could hear the music from the Blues Festival, but they were still a long way off.

"Was there any competing today?"

"Tonight will be the gala event," she said. "Lots of promo, lots of media, lots of attention, lots of sponsors. There will be a lot of autograph signings, talking with the competitors, things like that. They will be out there with their gear, but the stuff they'll be competing with won't be here tonight."

"Good thing," he said with feeling. "No way you'd be able to keep that secure here."

"Everybody has their own vehicle. They'll all bring their own gear. They'll have their own team. It's not just the outside people—you have to watch the people on the inside too."

"I think that's always the way it is. Nothing's more dangerous than those you trust most."

She shot him a look, realizing in his line of work that was probably a death sentence. Then she thought about her own work and realized it was the same thing. "I think you're right." Just then she caught sight of somebody she knew. She put her fingers to her lips and let out a whistle.

The woman in question turned. Catching sight of Wynn, her face lit up. Maneuvering through the crowd, she came over and threw her arms around Wynn. "Oh, my goodness. You look absolutely fantastic."

"Thanks," Wynn said, grinning. She introduced her friend Cindy to Tanner. "We came to see how things were going. I haven't been competing now for a couple years. I wondered if it had changed at all."

Cindy laughed. "The groups come and go, but I think the same style, the same flavor always remains."

"Rog is up for the championship this year, huh?"

"He is. He's pretty cocky about it too," Cindy said with a grin.

"Who is running up close behind him?" Tanner asked.

Cindy looked at him, her smile brightening a few watts and said, "Chris is. But then Frank is not far behind."

"Are they all here tonight?"

"Normally they would be. But we just got an announcement saying they were delayed."

Wynn nodded. "That figures. It was good seeing you again, Cindy." Saying goodbye to Cindy, she grabbed Tanner's hand, and, looping her arm through his, she led him on a trip around the entire section so he could see the lay of the land.

"As you can see, it's really just a huge crush of people tonight. Tomorrow morning the targets will be set up. All of them will be beach landings. Nobody will be allowed on the beach but the teams, and everybody will be camped out on the parkland around us." She turned and pointed.

"See how everything is on a hill, so people can gather around in a half circle on the grass? That's what makes this spot so great for a paragliding competition. People can sit out back there and still view everything going on at the beach level from almost any point in the entire park. Everybody will have some kind of a view from up there." She turned and twisted to look at the water. "And rescue boats will be out in the water, just in case."

"I guess they have this pretty well down to an art after so many years."

She laughed. "You'd think so, but there's always the potential for something to go wrong." She said impulsively, "Let's walk over there." And she headed toward a large group standing around talking.

One man turned, took a look at her and called out, "Hey, look who's here."

As soon as they arrived, she was engulfed in hugs from the many people she'd known from the circuit. Judges, team members, the volunteers who made all this happen. When she got a chance, she turned and introduced Tanner. The others shook his hand, and there were smiles all around. She loved that sense of camaraderie, that sense of being here, belonging with the group. She smiled and said, "I haven't been here for a couple years. Thought I'd pop by and see what's changed."

"Nothing has changed. It was Todd back then, followed by Steve, and now this year it looks like it could be Rog," said Dan, one of the longest-serving volunteers.

She glanced at him and smiled. "That's not a bad thing. All good things come to he who waits," she joked.

Off on the side was another group of male volunteers. She recognized a couple from the school she'd just been fired from, including Kirk and Tom. She stayed and talked here with this first group for another ten minutes, then headed over to the smaller group.

Kirk saw her, and his face lit up. "Hey, we wondered if you would be here. It's good to see you again."

Tom refused to even look at her.

If he didn't want anything to do with her, she was fine with that. The others from the paragliding school gathered together here greeted her with a wave or a head nod or a personable "Hey."

"Just popping in to see how things are. Haven't been to one of these in a couple years." After a bit of chitchat among the group, shortly thereafter she said her goodbyes.

With Tanner still in tow, she moved from group to group, saying hi to those she knew—some friends, some associates. She had recognized an incredible number of faces, now noticing a lot of the crowd had dispersed. Those still here were mostly organizers. Some were tourists, enjoying the chance to sit on the beach and to watch the sunset.

"What else would you like to do?"

"Well, it'd be nice to go up to where the jump-offs will be. But it might be too late and too dark to see anything."

"Yes, with the sun setting, it will be. And it should be all secured off at this point too."

"So then I suggest drinks and food, or food and drinks," he said with a grin.

"Did you see anything or think of anything you wanted for dinner?"

"I saw a seafood place we passed when we came down to the beach."

"Right. That's Rossellini's."

"I thought it was seafood, not Italian."

"It's both, but they're really good." She turned and headed back the way they'd come.

She hadn't realized how far they'd walked. By the time they hit the sidewalk again, the sun was completely down, and the streetlamps were on. "It's really beautiful here," she said with a smile. She tilted her face up, letting the cool breeze wash over her skin. "I'd forgotten how nice it was to be here."

"You don't seem like the crowd type, but you seemed to really enjoy yourself."

"You're right. I'm not the crowd type. I'm one of those people who does well in crowds, but then I have to recharge in privacy away from everyone. I've known lots of people who seem to absorb the energy from those in a group and light up like a Christmas tree and stay that way until an event is over. I'm not like that. I'm good for a couple hours. Then I get tired and want to go away and be alone."

"I'm more like that too," he said. "I'm not great in big crowds but happy to do an hour of socializing. I'd rather have a smaller group of friends and a barbecue than a big fancy sit-down dinner with people I hardly know."

She glanced at him. "I bet you and your unit do that a lot, don't they?"

He nodded. "Absolutely. Some of our best events are backyard barbecues."

It was just after nine when they approached the restaurant. "Do you think it's still open?" Tanner asked.

"Oh, it certainly will be with the Blues Festival and the paragliding competition this weekend," she said. She headed inside, and luckily they got a small table in back. As she sat down, a candle was lit on the table for them. She smiled. "This reminds me of how long it's been since I've been on a real date."

"How long has that been?"

"Before Todd's accident." She laughed. "After that first year of his recovery, as he got better, I went out with some of the people from work—as a group, you know?—just to get Todd off my back about not having a social life. Early on, one guy got the wrong impression, but I shut him down really quick. It's not wise to date your coworkers. Then another guy and I did stuff together, apart from the group, but just as friends."

"Was it Tom who got out of hand, the guy who didn't want to look at you today?"

She lifted her gaze. "Wow, that's very astute."

"It was pretty hard to miss. Everybody else was friendly and talking, and he had a sneer on his face most of the time."

"Yeah, he's like that a lot. I don't think he ever forgave me for refusing to date him, but Tom wasn't my type. His brother is much friendlier."

"One of those guys was his brother?" Tanner asked in

surprise. "I saw Tom arguing with Kirk at the warehouse. Remember? I told you about that. Is that his brother?"

She grinned. "Yes, and they do fight all the time."

"Wow, I didn't see that coming."

"They don't look anything alike. They're always competing with each other too."

"Not a lot of companies will hire brothers," he said. "I never understood that nepotism policy myself."

"Well, the school can do whatever the hell it wants, considering those two brothers belong to Charlie."

Tanner lifted his head from the menu and slowly placed it on the plate in front of him. He leaned forward. "Are you saying that they're the boss's sons?"

Hearing something odd in his tone, she looked up and nodded. "Yeah, so?"

"*So*," he said, "that would have been nice to know *beforehand*."

"What difference does it make?" She really didn't get it. "It's a fairly common practice to have your children work for the family business."

"Yes, it certainly is, although generally they're in an elevated position, not a mere grunt on the bottom level. But it's a good place for any kid to start in and to work his way up."

"I don't know about *working their way up*, as those two prefer to be in the warehouse rather than doing any paperwork, and they're not salesmen types. Or finance wizards. In fact, I'm not sure they have had any formal education at all." Something was still off in Tanner's expression. "I don't understand, but you're acting like there's something much deeper to this."

He shrugged at Wynn as the waitress walked over then, bringing a cutting board with a loaf of sourdough and pots of different butters. He looked at it appreciatively. "This looks lovely."

The waitress smiled and asked, "Are you ready to order?"

With a nod from Wynn, he waited while she ordered the mixed seafood pasta, and then he ordered the shrimp fettuccine for himself.

Wynn returned the menus and waited until the waitress was just far enough out of hearing before cutting the sourdough bread and said, "Please explain."

"This just hits me as wrong. Tom doesn't like you, and Kirk is friendly to you."

"What's that got to do with sabotaging my gear?"

"Opportunity and motive."

Picking up her buttered bread, she sat back and studied his face. "But they don't have motive."

"Well, you spurned the one, right?"

She shrugged. "He got the wrong idea and tried to kiss me. Made a move on me out of nowhere. I explained to him that I don't date coworkers."

"Right. That's a motive right there. Did either of them ever paraglide?"

"Both of them did," she said shortly. "They competed for a while."

"How good were they?"

"Not good enough."

TANNER'S MIND WAS trying to fit all the different pieces together. At the moment they wouldn't, but he knew they would eventually. These two men worked at the same paragliding school she'd been fired from. That was a connection he hadn't known of before, and yeah—damn it—it did make a difference. It connected the owners, as sponsors of these competitions, and one owner's sons from her former school to her paragliding accident and to these two other paragliding accidents with her brother, Todd, and her friend Steve. What Tanner didn't know was the whys or the hows.

His thoughts still working away, he cut another slice of the sourdough bread. It was really, really good.

Wynn leaned forward and whispered, "What are you thinking?"

He shot her a glance. "A lot of things but nothing's fitting yet."

She thrummed her fingers on the table and settled back for a bit. "I don't think Kirk or Tom would have anything to do with that."

"Yeah? Why not?"

She shrugged. "Basically they're lazy. I don't know that they would have jobs with other companies or that they'd keep them for very long if they continued to work the way they do at their father's school."

"I think that's a common problem with a lot of family members working at a same company. They aren't expected to maintain the same standard as all the other employees. Resentment builds, and all kinds of problems come out of that unjustified favoritism."

She nodded. "They were better at paragliding though. But they weren't competitive level."

"How high up in the rankings were they?"

She shrugged. "I'm not sure they made it to the ranking level. I never looked into it." She stared at Tanner in horror for a long moment. "You're not thinking they might have tried to reduce the numbers above them, are you?"

"Well, somebody sure was," he said.

"It could be that somebody just hated the winners. Figured somebody was flying so high that they needed to be proved they were nobody," she exclaimed in a low voice. "Resentment, jealousy, envy, whatever you want to call it."

He took a big bite of sourdough bread. "That's a very good point," he mumbled. He tilted his head. "I'd never considered it from that angle."

She sighed and raised both hands in frustration. "Nothing about this is normal," she said. "You can't look at it from a normal perspective."

The waitress returned with their meals and placed the steaming hot plates in front of them.

Tanner sniffed the air appreciatively. They hadn't chintzed on the shrimp either. At least fifteen big ones topped his pasta. He smiled and thanked the woman as she walked away. He leaned forward and asked Wynn, "I forgot to ask, but did you want a glass of wine with dinner?"

She shook her head. "I rarely drink."

"I do like a good glass of wine every once in a while, but I'll be fine without one tonight."

"Don't avoid it on my behalf," she said. "I don't mind if you want to drink."

He shook his head and dug into the pasta. At his first bite he stopped and just savored the mouthful. And when he could, he said, "This is great food."

She gave him a cheeky grin. "It sure is. Haven't eaten here since the last time I competed. It's not that far away, but, at the same time, a lot of other places are closer."

"It's all about location, location, location," he said.

The rest of their meal was eaten with small talk and great companionship, like a real date, a normal date. She seemed really comfortable around him, and he was happy about that. That he had Todd's permission to carry on in this direction was also interesting. He felt like he'd asked Wynn's father for permission and been granted it. The trouble was, he hadn't asked Wynn, and he had an idea she'd prefer to be asked herself, not her brother.

He decided to bring it up. "When I was joking with your brother earlier, he told me how you're a great person."

She chuckled. "Did he try to set you up on a date with me? For some reason he's got it in his head that I need somebody in my life. Otherwise I'll waste away just looking after him. Todd's really afraid that he's holding me back."

"That's probably a normal way to look at life when handicapped, like he is right now."

"But he won't stay that way. He's made a ton of progress already. It'll continue to get better."

"You're a very positive person, aren't you?"

"Yep, sure am," she said. "It's way better than being negative all the time. How depressing is that?"

"A lot of people would say it wasn't depressing but that it was being realistic."

"Well, realists can be positive thinkers too," she said with a smile. She put down her fork and knife and pushed away her plate and then sat back. "I forgot how big the portions were here."

"We can get yours to go, if you want."

She nodded. "You never know. That might do for a nice breakfast."

He shook his head. "I'm not sure I could stomach seafood pasta for breakfast."

She chuckled. "Maybe a midnight snack."

"A midnight snack, yeah, if you exercise between now

and then," he said drily. "But otherwise I can't imagine what would give you the munchies in the middle of the night." He lifted his gaze and caught the heated and teasing look in her eyes. Instantly his body responded. He settled back, letting out a slow breath. "Wow."

She raised an innocent eyebrow and said, "What?"

He shook his head. "You are dangerous. You're damn dangerous."

She chuckled. "Sorry. I shouldn't tease you."

"Well, it depends if it's a tease or a promise," he said.

"Good question," she said honestly. "No doubt I'm interested. No doubt we're spending some time together to get to know each other. But I do have to admit that I haven't been able to get my mind off that single bed we have to share tonight."

He closed his mouth and tried to control his breathing. He needed everything in his system to calm down, as it was all on high alert, especially his groin. When he could finally talk again, his voice was still strangled. "Neither have I. Neither have I."

She leaned across and gently stroked the fingers of his hand just lying there on the table. Her fingers slid up and down his heavy fingers, her soft skin smooth and silky against his. He wasn't sure just what was going on, but he was more than willing to see where it went. He wanted to believe they were heading down this particular path together.

When she slid her fingers once again down his, he slid his through hers and gently grasped them. "Your fingers are really soft," he commented. He scooped up another big shrimp, yet studied the plain but neat and tidy nails at the end of her fingers. "Do you ever wear nail polish?"

She smiled. "Sometimes. But not very often. I find it

chips too quickly."

"I was wondering how women could keep it all looking so neat and tidy," he said.

"Lots of work, lots of touch-ups. When you're active all the time, nail polish isn't something easy to maintain."

He finished off his plate and set it aside. His stomach was happily full. He glanced around, loving the atmosphere, the candlelight, the murmured conversations in the far corners. "This is a lovely restaurant, especially at nighttime."

She squeezed his fingers and started to withdraw her hand. But he held it tight.

He asked her, "Are you ready to go?"

She stared at him, and then she licked her lips.

Instantly his blood boiled again. He shook his head. "You *so* have to stop doing that. As far as I remember, the hotel is a good four blocks away yet."

Her face crinkled up in a laughing grin. "What's the matter? Not sure you can go the distance?"

At the double entendre he grinned. "I know I can. But I hate to hit the finish line before I even get started."

She squeezed his fingers and this time pulled her hand away. "I don't think we've hit the starting line or the finish line yet."

"No, but I have high hopes." He motioned to the waitress for his bill, and, when she brought it, he snagged it up. When Wynn tried to pay for her dinner, he shook his head and said, "You wouldn't even let me pay for the hotel."

"Nope," she said. "That's a rule of mine. I always pay for my hotels."

"Well, I consider this a date, and I always pay for dinner on a date." He signed for it, left a generous tip, stood and held out his hand.

Without hesitation she rose, but, instead of grabbing his hand, she slid her arm through his and snuggled up close. When they had to separate enough to get through the tables, he motioned her ahead. Outside in the cooler air, he wrapped an arm around her shoulders. When she came willingly, his heart beat that much faster. They stood for a moment, just holding each other, staring out at the lights.

They were out of the way of the restaurant's main entrance, around the corner. He smiled and said, "You're so beautiful."

She tilted her head back, smiled up at him and said, "Thank you. You're not too bad yourself."

That startled a surprised laugh from him. He leaned over, kissed her on the nose and said, "I don't think you're quite right there, but I'll let it slide for now."

"You do that," she said. "But I'll remind you again later."

With his arm wrapped around her, they meandered toward the hotel.

Lots of traffic still traveled up and down the road. He waited to make sure no cars were coming, then led her across to the other side where the hotel was.

Another set of headlights came toward them. The vehicle slowed down when they reached the sidewalk, then suddenly veered toward them and gunned it.

Tanner didn't have time to do anything but react. He quickly shoved her to the side and dove after her. The vehicle bounced off the sidewalk, raced to the corner and turned superfast, its tires squealing. That had been as deliberate of an attack as any he'd ever seen.

He hopped to his feet and raced to Wynn. "I'm so sorry. Are you okay?"

Dazed, she sat up and looked at him. "He deliberately tried to run us down," she cried out. "He drove up on the sidewalk and tried to hit us."

"I know. I figure he must have seen who we were in his headlights, made a sudden decision and then gunned it."

"Did you recognize the vehicle?" she asked.

He shook his head. "It was a white Dodge pickup truck. But I didn't catch the license plate."

"I don't know anybody who drives a white Dodge truck," she said.

"A lot of people are here with rigs like that. Not to mention the driver might not be the owner."

She nodded. "All of a sudden I'm not feeling so good about being here."

He helped her to her feet and waited until she tested her weight on both ankles and was relieved to see she wasn't in any pain. He wrapped an arm around her, held her really close in a hug and then whispered, "I'd feel better if we got back to the hotel."

Silently the two hurried to the hotel. Back inside the building, he led the way to their room. Checking to make sure nobody was loitering around the hallway, he unlocked the door, held up his hand to stop her from entering and did a quick search of the room. Finally he returned to the door and let her in.

"Was that really necessary?" She searched his face. "Are we really expecting to be attacked in our room?"

"No way to know but better safe than sorry," he said quietly. "What I won't do is take any chances with your life. I had thought that potentially whoever had sabotaged your gear might have moved on. But tonight says that not only have they not moved on but they definitely are targeting you.

That was no random act of violence back there. We were seen, and somebody made an impromptu decision to go on the attack."

"And that's damn scary," she said. "I mean, there was hardly time to react. If you hadn't pushed me out of the way …"

He wrapped his arms around her and held her close. "Don't even think about it. Brush it off for the moment. Otherwise it'll take you down that path of fear."

She pulled back and announced, "Too late. I'm already terrified." She walked to the bed, kicked off her shoes and flung herself crosswise onto the huge king-size bed. "It's not every day I have somebody trying to run me over," she mumbled, facedown on the comforter.

"I'm glad to hear that," he said. "It's pretty horrific for it to happen once, but the last thing we want is to have it happen more than that."

She flipped over, laying on the bed on her back, now staring at the ceiling. "It makes no sense," she murmured.

"I know, but we have to assume you were recognized."

She sat up slowly and frowned. "It could have been you they were after. It could have been somebody who recognized you from your work or from one of your missions."

"Possibly," he said, "but given the circumstances, it's not very likely. And let's not forget that the reason we came here was because you know so many people. And that means, not only do you know many people but many people know you."

CHAPTER 15

WYNN DIDN'T KNOW what to think. The effects of the lovely dinner had worn off. And the seductiveness of the evening, together with a promise of the night to follow, was a distant memory. And that made her feel really sad. Instead she was lying on the bed, dressed and by herself, trying hard to calm the butterflies in her stomach and the shaking in her fingers. She held out her hand and tried to hold it steady, but it wasn't having anything to do with that.

Tanner's words about the *many people here knowing her* rang in her ears.

He tugged her into his arms, lying down beside her, twisting her so their heads were on one pillow. "You're fine," he said. "I'll do everything I can to keep you that way."

She rolled onto her side and looked at him. "You think I'll feel any better if you get hurt protecting me?" She stroked his cheeks and nose. "No way I want that to happen."

He smiled and kissed her fingers. "Ditto. No way I'll let anything happen to you while I'm here."

"In that case, we have our work cut out for both of us …"

He lowered his head and kissed her gently, his mouth moving across her lips, more soothing than loving, trying to ease her fears. She wrapped her arms around his neck and held him tight. The last thing she wanted was soft loving.

What she wanted was passion to overtake them and to give her an hour of distance, an hour of something else, something entirely disconnected from what she'd just been through. An hour that would make her forget everything that had happened over the last few months.

She lifted his head, gently tilted his chin, and then tugged him down to her, sealing her lips over his, kissing him like she really wanted to. When she finally let him go, he took a deep breath, then a second one. She smiled as her fingers drifted across his lips, and she whispered, "Give me a night to remember and let me forget the horror of all we've learned over the past few weeks."

He dropped a kiss on her nose, her forehead, her cheek. Then he shifted back so he could look at her face again. "Are you still in shock?"

"If I am, does that mean you'll administer medical first aid?" she said in a teasing manner, running her fingers lightly up his arm and shoulder. "And, if you're really worried, no, I'm fine."

He smiled, lay down, tucked her closer into his arms and closed his eyes.

She stared at him a moment and then shook her head. "Oh, no you don't."

His eyes popped open. There was a teasing glint to them.

She shook her head. "No sleeping. We have all night." She moved her hand up to his shoulder and down his chest, playing with each of his ribs as she came to them, then down to where his jeans met his shirt and pulled his shirt from his jeans, sliding one finger inside at the hip. His eyes became smoky, deepened in color. The look in them made her heart race.

"Yeah? What for?" There was a wicked grin in his eyes.

She slowly drifted her finger inside his waistband, around to the front and back to his hip again. "Oh, I don't know," she said in a silky tone. "But I'm pretty sure we can come up with something." She dragged her finger back to the center and slid several fingers inside, going deeper.

He gave a strangled gasp as he rolled onto his back. "Yes, I think so."

She climbed on top of his frame. She gently grabbed his hands and pinned them above his head. Surprise was in the depths of his gaze. She grinned. "I know you could overwhelm me with your strength, but I would like it if you kept your arms up here."

He frowned and whispered, "I will for a second or two. But beyond that I make no promises."

She chuckled and sat up until she was astride his hips, and then she pulled her T-shirt over her head. His eyes darkened yet again, and he licked his lips.

She undid her jeans and pulled down the zipper. Standing up on the bed above him, she quickly dropped her jeans and stepped out of them, kicking them to the floor. Dressed only in purple panties and a purple bra, she dropped back to straddle him. Then she tugged his shirt fully out of his waistband and moved it up his chest. Obligingly he leaned forward so she could pull it over his head. As soon as she had it free, she tossed it to join her clothes on the floor.

Her breath whispered out of her throat in awe. She studied the heavily muscled body before her. "Wow. You do work out."

"No, I work for a living in a physical job," he corrected. "I'm not a gym junkie. I'm somebody who must call on the strength when I need it."

She stroked her fingers across his impressive six-pack, her fingers reaching up to gently pinch his nipples. "It's a fine difference, I guess, but a very important one, given the work you do."

She gently stroked his chest and his ribs, her fingers sliding into the grooves and moving around back and forth. She was fascinated by the muscles, fascinated by the size of him. She was long and lean, and there wasn't a whole lot to her. She was small-breasted, small-waisted, whereas he was big in the shoulders; even his waist was massive.

"It's amazing how very different we are." She slowly stroked her hands down his belly, watching with a smile as he sucked it in.

She again slid several fingers just under the waistband of his jeans and gently stroked back and forth. Then she shifted so she sat lower on him and reached for his belt buckle. Immediately his hands came down to help her. She stopped, looked at him and said, "Your arms."

He gave her a half glare but put his arms back up over his head.

She proceeded to unclasp his belt, then opened the button to his jeans and undid his zipper. She got up to walk to the end of the bed. There she grabbed his shoes, pulled them off, tossed them to the floor. Then she took off his socks and pulled at the legs of his jeans. He lifted up so they came away easily.

When she had them off, she smiled. "That looks much better."

He looked down. Of course his body had already heavily reacted, the evidence lay pulsing inside the soft cotton boxers he wore.

She ran her fingers up his lower leg. "All of you is heavily muscled," she said in delight. She gently stroked the definition of his thighs—first one, then the other. "Sometimes Mother Nature just does a bang-up job, doesn't she?"

That startled a laugh out of him.

She grinned. "You might laugh, but I mean it. You're perfect. Instead of a lean, mean sports machine, you're a massive, mean sports machine."

"Look at you. You're the lean, mean sports machine. Not a whole lot of spare flesh on you anywhere."

"Unfortunately you're right there," she said, crestfallen. "Particularly not in the chest. And I don't have a big butt either."

"From my viewpoint," he said, "you're absolutely perfect."

She gently drifted higher up his body, letting her fingers explore, sliding under the elastic of his underwear, feeling her own body clench and warm with passion as she realized what a joy it was to be with him. She'd been so very much looking forward to this, and she had wondered if they would get this far—knowing it would be a question she had to face and already knowing what her answer would be. She couldn't wait to have him inside her.

Only she wanted their first time to last, at least for a little bit.

With a smooth execution of her hand, she stroked up his hips and around to the inside of his thighs. Then she came back around and up again, gently exploring, always avoiding the large bulge in his underwear. He was massive, the same as he was everywhere else.

Finally she couldn't wait anymore. She slid her hand down to gently grasp him over the cotton material. He groaned, his back arching. She moved to kneel beside him, her left hand stroking his belly, his chest, soothing, calming, even as her right hand slid up and down his shaft, his body arching with every motion.

He groaned and whispered, "When do I get my arms back?"

She bent down and gently kissed him, her tongue laving over his lips, soothing, stroking, sliding inside to explore his mouth, dueling with his tongue. "Well, I'd say anytime, but …"

"Done," he whispered. He flipped them—so she was suddenly lying on the bed beneath him—kneeling between her legs, his body raised above hers.

She opened her thighs wider, but he wasn't having anything to do with it. He slid his hands under her back and gently undid her bra, pulling it off, throwing it down. His gaze latched on to her breasts, and she watched with rapt attention as he studied them. He reached out with both hands and cupped her gently. She might be small, but they were still a handful, and, with both of his hands on her, she arched her back into his touch, loving the feel of those big caring hands, moving, sliding, massaging, caressing her body.

It had been a long time since she'd had sex, and she loved it dearly. But she had to know and to like the person she was with. She didn't want to have sex with a stranger. Tanner had passed that stage when he'd saved her life.

His thumbs moved across her nipples, and her hips shifted restlessly. He leaned over one breast, his elbow on the bed, and took her nipple in his mouth, suckling it gently. She reached up and caressed him, her fingers sliding through his hair as she twisted gently under his ministration. But then he moved right down a center line to her belly button and below. He caught the band to her underwear with his chin, and, within seconds, he had them off. His followed. Before she had a chance to acknowledge that, he had her opened wide and spread out, his tongue busy tasting, exploring, as a finger slid inside her.

She cried out. Her hips lunged upward, but he captured her with both hands and held her in place while he tasted and teased until she was weeping with joy. Then, once more, he gently slid one finger deep inside, stroking upward. She cried out and came apart in his arms, trying to pull him up to her, only to collapse back as sensations washed over her and through her. He withdrew his finger, gently coated each of her nipples and then proceeded to suckle hard.

She wanted him as close as he could get before she exploded a second time. She wrapped her thighs tight around his hips, stopping him from leaving her. Or trying to.

He chuckled, gave her a hard kiss and slowly kissed his way back down.

She grasped his hair, whispering, "I want you inside me. I want you inside me now."

He looked at her as he moved back up her body, aligning them. He held her hips in his hands, positioned himself at her center, and then slowly eased himself inside. Filled, and stretching, and so damn tight, he slid deep inside, coming to rest at the heart of her.

She lay shuddering, barely hearing his worried question.

"Are you okay?"

Waves and waves of tremors racked her body, sending her arching and shivering, completely overwhelmed with the moment. "Fine," she whispered. "But it's never been like this before."

He leaned down, whispered words against her lips and then kissed her lightly. He slid one hand underneath her buttocks, positioned her where he needed her, and, holding her steady, he started to move.

She couldn't speak, her body focused on responding to him.

He held her body in place as he pulled out and then slowly slid back in again. Over and over, faster and faster, stronger and stronger, he drove her once again to the edge and held her there until she begged and pleaded with him for more. Just when she didn't think she could handle any more, he slid his fingers down between them, touching the sensitive button at the center of her folds, and she cried out as her climax ripped through her yet again. But he didn't stop, nor did he slow down. He rode her through it as the orgasm tore up and down her body.

Finally she heard him give a hoarse shout, his body freezing above her, and then surging over and over again as his own orgasm ripped through him. She groaned as he slowly lowered himself, gasping above her. He shifted to his side and tugged her with him, holding them still connected hip to hip.

Held in his grasp, connected in all ways, his arms tight around her as if he would never let her go, she laid quietly, her body, her heart, her mind completely overwhelmed with what had just happened.

She'd had orgasms before. She'd had lots of great sexual experiences before. But this? ... This was something special. It took several long moments before her body stopped trembling. And, when it finally did, she took a deep breath and then another one.

Above her, he whispered, "Better?"

She nodded. "Although I can't say anything else will ever be as good again," she whispered back.

Why shouldn't he know how good this had been for her? It wasn't like she wanted to hide it. She wanted to stand on the rooftop and shout it to everyone who'd listen. She gave yet another deep happy sigh as the last of the quakes and the shivers passed away, and she relaxed into his arms.

"That was magical," she whispered as she let her eyes drift closed.

TANNER GENTLY HUGGED her close, stroked the back of her neck and her shoulders and whispered, "If you're tired, go to sleep."

"I was hoping to do this again," she murmured. "Sleep seems like such a waste." She smiled at the rumble of laughter coming up his chest, rolling just underneath her ear. She lifted her head to smile at him. "But a nap would be good."

"Sleep," he said. "I'm not going anywhere."

She frowned, looked at him intently and said, "Promise?"

He pulled her down for another deep, mind-drugging kiss, and, when he released her, she sagged against him as if all the stuffing in her had completely drained away. He loved it. "I promise," he said. "Just rest."

She decided to close her eyes and let herself sleep. But she wanted him rested as well. "Make sure you sleep too," she cautioned. "No point in you staying awake on guard, looking after me. We're safe here. And we both need to rest. Tomorrow is a new day, a new dawn. And, for all we know, all kinds of new trouble."

He gave her shoulder a gentle squeeze. "I'll be fine. You just need to sleep."

She chuckled. "That's not normally what guys say when they're in my bed."

"It's what I'm saying," he said firmly. "It's all about your health and all about whatever it is you need to do to be okay, to handle whatever tomorrow brings."

She yawned again, snuggled deeper into him, appreciating the warmth that came from a blanket he drew over her shoulders, and she whispered, "Good night."

"Good night," he whispered against her temple.

Her breathing slowed, deepened.

He smiled and held her close. No way would he let anything happen to her. Not now that he'd finally found her.

Several moments later he shifted to reach his phone.

Time to call in reinforcements.

CHAPTER 16

THE NEXT MORNING Wynn woke up drowsy and warm, not wanting to move. A heavy leg was flung across hers, almost holding her in place, and, from the even, heavy breathing behind her, she realized Tanner was still asleep. She tried to slip out from under his leg, but he mumbled and tucked her up closer. She laughed softly. She twisted to look down at him, dropped a kiss on his nose and said, "I have to go to the bathroom."

He rolled to his back, his leg flopping onto the bed. She slid out from under the covers, walked to the bathroom, used the facilities, looked at the shower and decided that was a perfect next step. She turned on the hot water and jumped in under the spray. When she was showered and ready, she headed out to the bedroom to find Tanner waiting for her. He was on the phone. She waited until he was off and asked, "Any news?"

He shook his head. "I gave the make of the truck last night to my buddies, but, because we didn't catch the license plate, nobody has any idea who it belongs to. Given that a lot of trucks are here in town right now, it could take a bit to track it down. And could be a stolen truck."

She headed to her carry-on bag and pulled out some fresh clothes. "If you want to grab a shower, I'd love to hit the competition early this morning. I don't know if we're staying all day or not, but it would be nice to at least take in some of the sights and sounds." She straightened and looked over at him. "There should be a lovely coffee shop on the beach where we can see everything."

With his eyebrows raised, he said, "Now that would be wonderful. I'll be five." He walked into the bathroom and shut the door.

She heard the shower water a few seconds later. She dressed quickly and repacked her bag. She didn't know if there still was full occupancy for this hotel tonight, but she wouldn't mind staying another night. It could be an idyllic holiday. She hadn't forgotten the reason they were here, but, at the same time, it was a lovely reminder of her previous life. Yet, she didn't miss it anymore. She'd been more than ready to walk away.

Tanner was done in the shower faster than she'd seen any other man do. When he came out with a towel wrapped around his waist, she seriously wondered if they should just go back to bed. He saw her gaze and waggled his eyebrows.

She grinned. "Hold that thought. We have things to do, places to go, people to visit today, but tonight ..." She left that thought hanging.

"Message received," he said regretfully. "But don't think I'll forget that last bit."

Once he was dressed, they walked downstairs and checked out. Then, with their overnight bags packed into the vehicle, he asked, "Do you want to walk?"

She nodded. "The parking down there will be terrible."

Arms looped together, they walked several blocks toward the beach. She couldn't help analyzing the wind, the sky and the weather. "It'll be a beautiful day. At the moment it seems like the air is completely still."

"Which is a good thing for the competitors, I presume?"

"Actually it's the opposite. The winds give us an awful lot more we can do. If it's still, sure, but we're down to the equipment then. When there's wind, then we can do magic."

"*Magic*? I like the sound of that."

"We'll have to go up again," she said. "Have you done any paragliding since we were up together?"

He shook his head. "I haven't had any time."

"Exactly. I've been a little busy myself," she said with a laugh.

At the beach she led the way through the gathering crowd of sun-seekers and competition attendees to a small coffee shop at the end of the beach. It was just far enough away from the main traffic that she hoped it wouldn't be too busy. It was plenty busy, but they still snagged a small table. They sat and enjoyed a good breakfast and coffee. Then, armed with coffee to go, they headed back outside.

They walked along the beach until they had to cross the road because of all the barricades erected to stop people from getting too close. She smiled at some of the people here, and, with Tanner at her side, they crossed over and took a detour around. "It's odd being on this side," she commented.

"I imagine."

She noticed his gaze was always searching, always moving. "What are you looking for?"

"Well, that truck from last night would be nice," he said. "Other than that, anything that feels wrong."

"Such as?"

"Somebody else who might want to attack you."

"Makes no sense to attack me at all, and I don't know what the hell it would have to do with the other attacks. I thought we were here more because of my brother's accident."

"Your brother's accident and your accidents and any connections between them."

Up ahead she thought she saw Tom from her old job. But he wasn't looking at her. Instead he was walking, his head bowed, his collar pulled high, his gaze staring down. She frowned. "I wonder where he's going."

Tanner followed her gaze. "Good question. If he's trying to hide, he's doing a good job of it. I almost didn't recognize him."

"Right."

At his urging they fell into step behind Tom and kept an eye on him. At a large crowd of people ahead, he skirted around the back and then stepped up beside someone. She studied the other man and said, "I don't think I've ever seen him before."

As they watched, an envelope was passed between them. She straightened indignantly. Tanner patted her shoulder. "It looks bad, but it could be any number of things, *including* a drug deal."

She frowned and calmed down slightly. "I still want to have a talk with him."

"Well, you might, but you'll only get a chance after my turn at him." His voice was hard.

She turned and glared at him. He dropped a kiss on her nose.

Then their world exploded as a vehicle slammed into them.

She was lifted and flung to the grass, crying out in shock. Cries all around them rang out as people rushed to help her. Because she'd landed on the grass—and the vehicle hadn't had much momentum because of so many people milling about—she was okay. But she couldn't see Tanner. She made her way to her feet with the assistance of several people. She stood there shaky for a long moment and cried out, "Tanner? Are you okay?"

He appeared at her side, his face furious.

She realized he was short of breath. "Did you chase after it?"

He nodded and wrapped her in his arms. "It was the same truck from last night."

"Did you see who was driving it?"

He shook his head. "But I got the license plate number."

She leaned back. "How long will it take to get the owner's name?"

"Mason is on it already."

"Do you guys get access to stuff like that? Isn't that secret?"

He shook his head. "The DMV database has it all. And, if Mason can't get it, we have plenty of friends in law enforcement who can."

She glanced around at everybody standing nearby, making sure she and Tanner were still okay. She thanked several people and took several tentative steps.

Tanner studied her walking pattern. "Your ankle?"

"It's a little tender," she said. "I don't think it's major."

He led her to a bench and helped her sit down. Then he walked back over to the crowd, and, while she watched, he spoke to several people and wrote something down on a notepad. When he returned, she looked up at him in confusion. "What was that all about?"

"Names and addresses, contact information for witnesses of the accident."

That kept her quiet as she thought about him having the

presence of mind to do that while she sat here, still in shock.

Just then a young man came toward them. "I saw what happened," he said. "I work over at the coffee shop. You guys were just in there and lost your coffee, so I brought you two more. Please sit and relax."

And, with a brief smile, he took off, not even giving her a chance to thank him. She laughed. "Well, this certainly shows us another side of humanity, doesn't it?"

He smiled and nodded. "That was nice of him."

At his concerned look, she smiled. "I really am okay." She gave her legs a bit of a shake. "It was just the shock of being upended and finding myself suddenly on my back on the grass."

"And yet, we're both here. Thank heavens," he said with a chuckle, giving her a gentle hug. "Maybe we can have a talk with Rog, give him a warning, make sure he takes extra care to go over his equipment, see if we recognize any of the same people around the place. Do we need to stay right through to the end, to the last run?"

"We probably should." She took several sips of her coffee. "I wouldn't mind getting closer to where everybody is. If we head that way"—she pointed—"we should find a place to sit down and to relax until things get started."

With him at her side, the two made their way. She felt a little rougher than she expected. By the time they got to a bench close to the proceedings, she plunked down with relief. "You don't realize just how much an incident like that can wipe you out." She drained the last of her coffee and tossed the empty cup into the garbage can. He did the same. Together on the bench, she said, "I feel woozy. Maybe I landed harder than I thought."

He twisted and looked at her, his hand going to her

forehead. "Did you hit your head? Are you okay?"

She stared at him, feeling her energy drifting away. "What's happening to us? I didn't think so."

He turned to look around them. "We're in trouble," he managed to choke out. He pulled out his phone, and, as she watched, he typed in a short word and pressed Send.

"What … was that?"

"A code word for … help." But even as he tried to get the last word out of his mouth, his head lolled to the side, and slowly he slumped over.

It took a moment for her to understand what was going on, and then she slowly fell to the side too.

Dimly, in the back of her mind, she realized people had grabbed her, lifting her, carrying her away, but the world was spinning around her. She couldn't fight. She couldn't struggle. As the gentle words in her ear whispered, "Calm down. You're fine," she sagged in relief and let the unconsciousness take her.

TANNER WOKE UP abruptly. It took him all of ten seconds to understand he was in a van, rattling around in the back. It only took a couple more seconds to realize he was not only tied up but that Wynn was tied up beside him. Instantly he became alert, his mind searching for answers, realizing they'd been drugged and kidnapped. The back of the van they were in was empty but for the two of them. It wasn't the truck that kept trying to hit them, so obviously another vehicle had been brought in to kidnap them.

He had managed to get off his Help message, so he could only hope his friends were coming to the rescue. It was still daylight. *Good.* He hadn't been out that long. He could barely see up to the front seat where both the driver and a passenger were. Tanner rolled over ever-so-slightly and whispered to Wynn, "Wake up."

A soft moan came from her. With his mouth against her ear, he whispered, "We've been kidnapped. I need you to wake up. I need you to wake up now."

Her eyes fluttered open. She twisted slightly and looked at him, and he nodded. He motioned toward the front of the van. She was moving very little. She twisted enough to look up at the front, but they could only see the back of the driver and the passenger. She glanced around, but there wasn't much for her to see since the van was empty except for some gear and tools. She looked over at him in horror. They weren't gagged, but they knew not to bring any attention to themselves or risk getting them both in more trouble. She whispered, "Who?"

He shook his head.

"Where are we?"

Again he shook his head. The question of why was in her gaze, but he had no answer for that either.

The van took a turnoff then and climbed. She opened her eyes wider as if understanding the route.

He frowned.

She whispered, "We're climbing. I bet we're going para-gliding."

He stared at her. "Do you think they are taking us to the competition launch point?" Although why they would, he didn't know.

She shrugged and twisted her hands, tied behind her back, trying to get free.

As he watched, she folded her body up small and tight and managed to get her arms around her butt, over her feet, so they were in front of her. She lay back down, both of them still waiting to see if their actions had been noted.

In the front seat was a little conversation and some music, but nobody in the front seat seemed to care what they did, or didn't hear them, now moving around in the back of the van.

She stared at the knots around her wrists, her fingers working them. He knew he couldn't manage the same maneuvers she had, but he studied her knots and then realized how they worked. He leaned over and, with his teeth, unraveled hers. It took a lot of effort and a lot of muscle, but he had no trouble finally untying her.

With her hands free, he whispered, "Get your legs."

When she got her feet untied, the van took another turn and headed up an even steeper road. He rolled to his side, and she went to work on his hands, also tied behind his back. It took her a lot longer because the knots were tighter, but finally she managed it.

Just in time because he could feel the vehicle slowing as it rose to the top. He quickly untied his ankles.

He didn't think anybody involved in this mess had plans he would be happy about. He took a look out the van's rear window and saw they were cresting a hilltop. Quickly he opened the back door, pulling her out with him. He heard the shouts from the guys in the front seat, but Tanner didn't care and took off running, pulling Wynn with him.

Up ahead he saw several paragliders already stretched out and stopped. He motioned at them and said, "What the hell?"

He backed up, but a warning shot fired over his head had him freezing. He turned, pulled her into his arms, and saw the passenger holding a gun on them. "Tom, I presume?”

His face twisted. “You piece of shit,” he snapped. “You don’t get to know my name.”

“Kirk and Tom. Loser sons of Charlie, part owner of the paragliding school that just fired Wynn. Assholes that.”

Tom shrugged. “It doesn’t matter. You won’t live long enough to do anything about it.”

“What the hell are you doing, Tom?” Wynn cried out. “You kidnapped us.”

He nodded. “And now I’m going to kill you. Unlike before, I’ll make sure you die. No way you should have survived last time.”

Tanner froze. “You’re the one who sabotaged her rig?”

“Of course I did. And her brother’s.” He laughed. “Todd and Miss Snot Nose here think they are better than everybody. Both needed to be brought down to earth like the rest of us.” He laughed at his own joke.

“What’s the point of us having another accident then?” she asked in confusion. “What purpose would that serve?”

“You’re sniffing around all the accidents in the competition. Don’t you realize how rigged this competition is? We get to choose who wins and who loses. It’s got nothing to do with skill. You always thought you were so good because you won. And because your brother won. But that’s bullshit. We *let* you win. There’s a group of us, and my dad has been involved since the beginning. Now me and Kirk are a part of it too,” he said. “I was way better in the sky than you any day.”

At that, Tanner smiled. “So you’re really jealous, huh? Because you weren’t good enough? You weren’t good enough to make it pro like Todd and Wynn were? Did you see us walking on the street last night and couldn’t stop your jealousy from taking over and had a try at running us over?"

"I was good enough," Tom said with a snarl. "I just didn't want to go any further. Too much effort. Not when it was all rigged anyway. And I might have lost my temper last night in my truck, but, if I'd wanted to kill you then, I could have."

Tanner glanced down at Wynn, who stared at Tom. "Why the gun?"

"Just in case. But I can hardly shoot you, can I?" he said with a smirk. "At least not unless your body is so badly damaged from the emergency landing that they won't give a shit, and they'll put down the cause of death due to the crash when you smashed into the ground."

"So you didn't expect her to live through the last event? Were you also the one who broke into her house?"

"No. That was Kirk. We were looking for her designs. We told our father we had better designs than they did. But of course our designs weren't quite as good because we didn't come from the same background and the same history. So we were going to steal them and make them ours. Our father would at least let us move up in the family business, maybe hand it over to us finally, like he promised all those years ago. But we couldn't find her latest designs." Anger raged through him. "But, once you're gone, we'll take care of Todd. That'll be a break-and-enter that went bad, and we'll take the computers so we don't have to rush to get the information we want before we're caught." He motioned with the gun. "Get over to the paragliders."

Tanner led her to them. "Are they rigged to crash?"

"Maybe, maybe not. If you're lucky, you'll survive this crash. If you don't cooperate, I'll shoot you both dead. It'll be a murder-suicide then. I'll find a different way to dispose of your body. I could just throw you over the cliff and toss the gun too. It won't make any difference. I'll have wiped it clean."

Tanner swore inside because that was too often the case anyway. He looked at the paragliders. "And what did you do to these?"

"Rigged them both of course. Would have taken care of your reserve chute but, of course, you're too good to want to fly with that extra weight," he said. "We will paraglide along with you, witnesses to your terrible accident," he said with a laugh. "We'll make sure you go down. No matter which way it happens, you're going down."

Tanner looked at Wynn; her face was pale, but she was calm, even if her bottom lip trembled.

"So you really want to kill me? Then you'll kill my brother, just for some designs?"

"Not *just* for some designs. To take you down. Your ego was too big after we let you win. These competitions got nothing to do with how good you are. They are all about the sponsors and who wants to help you be what."

"This has nothing to do with the competition. It's all because I turned you down, didn't want to go out on a date with you, isn't it? Because I liked hanging out with your brother instead?"

His face flushed red. "Get the hell over to the paragliders. You want your little boy toy, whatever he is? Well, he's going down with you. Hopefully getting laid was worth dying for."

His brother finally came out of the van then, a gun in his hand, as he walked nearer and directed Tanner to a particular glider and then pointed Wynn to hers.

"So, Kirk, you're totally okay with a double murder too,

huh?" she asked.

He shrugged. "Gear up."

Angrily she picked up her designated harness and strapped it on. Tanner had already geared up himself. The other two parachutes and the paragliders were for Kirk and Tom.

Under their kidnappers' orders to jump, Tanner took a final breath, called out to her and said, "You know it'll be okay, right?"

She turned and smiled at him. "It will be what it is." And she leaped off the cliff.

He watched her tilt her face up to the wind, possibly accepting this was her last flight, and he had to admire her for having so much guts.

With the men pushing him, he jumped off the cliff behind her. He expected a bullet in his back at any time.

There was a lot of wind picking up. He watched as Wynn caught a thermal and rose up higher. He caught one himself. Caught on that turret of air, they both rose. He twisted to look behind him to see the brothers in the air as well.

She glanced at Tanner, a worried smile on her lips. He could see she'd been busy checking out the rigging. He wanted to make sure she was ever-so-slightly above him, so he could help catch her. He didn't have any expectations that another rescue like the last one would work here, but he'd do what he could. **Of course, there was no guarantee they wouldn't sabotage both of them midair.** As he caught sight of her pack, he frowned. Why the hell did this one have a *T* on it? He glanced over at her and called out, "What letter was on your glider?"

She looked at him and shook her head. She couldn't

hear him.

He wondered at the chance that maybe Tom had the wrong pack. If she got his instead of hers, maybe she'd survive this after all. Of course the *T* could be for *Tanner* as well, and that didn't make Wynn's chances any better at surviving with a sabotaged chute and glider.

Just then her wing ran into trouble. She struggled to so it would fill with air again. She hadn't pulled her chute yet. If she got the pack intended for her, he knew it wouldn't open. No reason to give her a good parachute if they wanted her to crash.

She pulled her parachute cord, hard. It opened. As she popped up, the relief on her face made his heart warm. But they weren't out of trouble yet. He sailed closer toward her, motioning for her to stay away from the brothers. He watched as the brothers struggled, then heard a shot fired, and Wynn's parachute whipped about helplessly. Damn. That was a lucky shot. The silks shouldn't be that badly damaged from a single hole but if they caught part of the rigging…

Higher than he was, she dove toward him.

And sailed below him. She screamed in panic.

Scrambling, he caught her damaged chute as it whipped past, the jolt and extra weight taking him down faster. But he wrapped it several times around his arm and held on tight—and saw Tom, his own parachute failing to deploy, heading straight down to earth.

Tom screamed and cried out for his brother.

Tanner caught the look on Kirk's face as he stared at his brother, with almost maniacal glee. More shots were fired. Tanner maneuvered to the far left, getting as far away from the brothers as they fought it out in front of them.

Another bullet was fired, and Kirk's glider ran into trouble now.

Tanner realized that Tom knew he was going down and that his brother had given him one of the bad chutes.

Kirk's glider deflated, the wings flapping helplessly in the air. He opened his chute—and one more single shot was fired. Kirk hurtled to the ground after his brother. Screaming, Tom hit hard and bounced, then lay still.

Wynn and Tanner—falling faster than they should have been because of the double weight, her dangling helplessly and him clutching the ungainly damaged chute—watched helplessly as Kirk landed not far from his brother.

Neither man moved. Prepping for a hard landing, Tanner felt the weight release as she hit the ground first and rolled down the slight slope. He dropped the silks and landed hard, falling to his knees and rolling to take the blow. He came to a stop only to have her throw herself on top of him, crying out for him. He hugged her tight, both of them wrapped up in each other's arms. He whispered against her ear, "Are you okay?"

She nodded and whispered, "I'm a whole lot better than they are."

Shouts reached his ears. He lifted his head to see people racing toward them, and he realized how much of the fight up above had been seen by everybody below. They were surrounded very quickly with helping hands, unhooking and detaching their gear as medics raced over to the other two. Once he and Wynn were both free, Tanner stood and hugged her tight once more.

His phone went off. He pulled it out to hear Mason's voice. "We got six men on the way."

"I see two coming toward me right now," he said.

"Macklin and Jackson."

"Good. Are you okay?"

"I'm okay, but both Wynn and I were almost smashed into a pulp. Instead, the two men who attacked us, Kirk and Tom, the sons of Charlie, one of the co-owners of the school she used to work for, killed each other." He quickly gave a rundown, then said, "Neither of us are feeling great. Still under the effects of whatever drug they gave us in the coffee. And, man, I sure would like to get that asshole who doped us picked up," he said heavily. "But you know what? Maybe because we were drugged, we escaped any real injuries here, like a drunk driver in a car wreck. We lived, so we're okay."

Jackson and Macklin reached them. They forced Tanner and Wynn to sit down and to get fully checked over by the medics and to have blood samples taken to prove what drugs were in their systems. Jackson and Macklin listened to Tanner and Wynn tell their story and then called the cops.

Jackson said, "I'll secure the van. We'll need the forensic evidence on that one."

Tanner nodded. "Thanks. Honestly I just want to go home. The last two times I've been paragliding, it's been total shit."

Wynn, still in his arms, laughed. She tilted her head back and said, "Well, you know what they say. Third time is the charm."

"Does that mean the third time is an easy flight, or the third time we don't survive?"

"Third time we have an easy flight," she said firmly. "In both cases, these accidents were man-made. That's got nothing to do with the sport."

He stared down at her and grinned. "True enough. I don't know about you, but I think we deserve a couple days in bed, just resting."

She wrapped her arms around his neck and whispered, "Hear, hear. But how long until we can get there?"

Jackson snorted, envy on his face. "It'll be a couple hours yet. Not only do you have the police to deal with but, Wynn, you have to talk to your brother."

Her face wrinkled up in a grimace. "True enough."

It was six hours before they arrived in her driveway and parked. She got out slowly. "I didn't realize how sore I would be."

"It'll take a lot of hot Epsom salt baths and some muscle relaxants for us to feel better in a few days," he said. "Not to mention, we have to wait for the drugs to leave our system."

She smiled. "*But* we will be taking relaxants and baths. And Tom and Kirk won't be."

<h1 style="text-align:center">CHAPTER 17</h1>

TODD MET THEM at the doorway, the worry on his face breaking her heart. She walked closer, and her brother enveloped her in a big hug. "You really know how to scare a brother."

"I was pretty damn scared myself," she whispered.

He looked at her. "Kirk and Tom, really?"

"But then Kirk pulled a fast one on Tom. Kirk gave Tom one of the bad parachutes, and I got one of the good ones. Until one of the brothers shot it up."

"So Tanner saves you—again—and Kirk throws Tom to the wolves. Then Tom turns around and shoots his brother's paraglider after realizing what's happened."

"Yeah. Kirk figured that, at the end of the day, he could probably blame everything on his brother and walk away free and clear, possibly getting half of the school all to himself." She walked inside with Tanner. "It's not very late, but I'm beat."

"Time to rest. No more accidents, no more break-ins. It's over with," Tanner said quietly. "Maybe, just maybe, it'll all be good from now on."

She gently stroked his cheek. "Thank heavens for that."

Todd looked at Tanner and asked, "So are you moving in, or is she moving out?"

Tanner's eyebrows popped up. "I'm not sure. We haven't discussed it."

"Well, *you* may not have," Todd said, "but I cleared out the other wing of the house for all your apartment stuff. I figured you might as well move in. At least part-time. Considering you're gone on missions all the time, this just needs to be your home." And he hobbled off.

Wynn, a surprised look on her face, turned to Tanner. "Don't feel like you have to by any means," she rushed to say. "I've never heard him talk like that before."

"We already cleared the air," Tanner said with a big grin. "Todd's just given me even more signs of his approval."

She hesitated. "Are you renting?"

He nodded. "I am. And Todd's right. I am gone a lot."

She nodded. "Of course you are. Heroes are like that."

"What the hell are you talking about, *heroes*?"

"You're a man of honor, and there's no way you would give up your job, serving your country, even for a girlfriend," she said gently. "And that's the way it should be."

He looked at her, shoved his hands in his pockets and said, "You've been talking to Mason?"

She raised her eyebrows. "No. What's that got to do with anything?"

"Nothing. Just this thing about honor among the group."

She nodded. "Of course. You're an honorable band of men. I'm just very happy you're mine."

He leaned over and gave her a hard kiss. "Ditto."

Laughing, their arms wrapped around each other, they slowly moved into the living room.

"I don't know about you," she said with feeling, "but I need to take a couple pills and lie down. And if you say ditto …"

He chuckled. "You head on up to your room. I'll bring in the bags and grab the medicine."

"Perfect."

As she headed upstairs, she couldn't imagine what the next few days would be like, better than the last few for sure. They had to find out about Charlie's arrest and someone needed to warn Rog and update Steve. She knew the police and Mason would handle most of it so she and Tanner could rest. The two of them had time together now… honestly… she hoped they had a lifetime together. She had no intention of letting Tanner out of her life again. You only found a hero like him once in a lifetime.

JACKSON

SEALs of Honor, Book 19

Dale Mayer

PROLOGUE

J ACKSON PEARSON WALKED to the front of the military
rig full of equipment, now on the roadside with steam
pouring out of the engine, and popped open the hood.
Damn truck. He was part of a convoy, heading from training
back into Coronado. A smaller navy rig pulled up in front of
him. The driver walked toward him with a smile. He looked
at her and asked, "Can I help you?"

She chuckled. "The question really is, can I help you? I
was instructed to see if you were in trouble when you fell
behind. Truck problems? I might be able to fix your rig and
get you back on the road."

While he watched, she clambered up on the bumper and
took a look under the hood. She frowned and muttered. He
was about to check it out himself but hadn't had a chance
before she got here.

"Your engine obviously is overheating," she said. "Looks
like you've got a hole in the radiator." She continued to
check underneath the hood for a moment, then slid off the
bumper and stood next to him. She frowned and asked,
"Where were you stopped last?"

He motioned back up the highway. "Popped into the gas
station to get water."

She nodded. "Interesting."

"Why?" he asked, staring at her, then at the steam. She

was small, maybe five feet, two inches, tiny, and didn't look like she knew the front end of a truck from the back end. But, not only was she knowledgeable, she appeared to be all business.

"Because I've seen that hole before." She turned to look around. "I'm thinking this vehicle needs to be towed back."

"Why? What is it?"

"Did anybody know you were going into that store?"

Exasperated, he put his hands on his hips. "Are you going to tell me about the hole?"

"When you went inside the store," she said, without answering him, "did you see anyone outside, hanging around your truck, anything unusual?"

Slowly realizing something was seriously wrong, he said, "No. Why? What was I supposed to see?"

"Not see," she said firmly. "But hear."

He stared at her, confused, looked at the radiator and shook his head. He frowned at the rig and turned to her again, recognition now in his gaze.

She nodded. "Yes, that's a bullet hole."

CHAPTER 1

"**S**HOW ME," JACKSON snapped, his voice hard. Why the hell hadn't he seen that? Well, of course he hadn't. She'd gotten in the engine first. "What's your name?"

"Dahlia Montgomery." She wore a big smile. "My friends call me Deli."

His eyebrows shot up. "That's a … nice name."

She shrugged. "I make a mean sandwich. What can I say?"

That startled a broken laugh out of him. "Okay, Deli—if I may call you that?" he asked, one eyebrow up.

She nodded. "Sure. We're friends until I have a reason not to be," she said cheerfully. "If you come around to this side, you can see what I'm looking at."

It took a bit of twisting and bending to see what she pointed out, but, indeed, a nice neat little hole was very apparent in the radiator. "We can't see if it went out the back, can we?" he asked, straining to look.

"Not without some help." She took out her cell phone, turned on the flashlight and used it to direct a beam of light into the hole. And, sure enough, it came out on the other side.

He swore. "What the hell?"

"Missed the grill," she said. "Lucky shot there. The grill would have deflected it a little more off to the side, but, as it is, the radiator is history. This vehicle is going nowhere until I can plug that." She frowned and looked at it. "Any chance we can find the bullet at the store you stopped at?"

Jackson shook his head. "The shooter would have retrieved it, whether intentional or a stray shot."

"Well, if the bullet bounced around in the engine before exiting the rig, she's definitely not going anywhere."

"Got anything to plug the radiator with?"

She nodded. "But, in this case, I think we're better off to have forensics look at it."

"Nobody was killed though," he said jokingly.

"No, but what if it was an attempt to kill you?" She turned to look at him. "Do I need to rethink my decision about letting you be my friend?"

He could tell from her tone of voice that she wasn't serious, but the subject matter definitely was. "If you're asking whether I have any enemies or any reason to consider why somebody is trying to kill me, the answer is no. At least I don't think so. I have no idea what's going on here."

"Tell me what happened when you went to the station."

He organized his thoughts. "I pulled in, didn't need gas, so I parked right in front of the restaurant side of the building, went into the convenience store, picked up coffee and a couple bottles of water."

"How was the coffee?" she asked curiously.

He slanted her an odd look and then shrugged. "It was gas station coffee. How do you expect it to be?"

He then went through his next steps. "I went into the men's room, used the facilities, washed my hands, went through the cash register, came back out to the truck and drove to catch up."

"You fell behind the convoy," she asked, "but not so far

back to look like you did it on purpose?"

"On purpose? … As in hoping to shut down the vehicle myself, so I couldn't make it into the convoy or to separate me from the convoy?"

"Who can tell at this point," she said quietly. She reached up to close the hood, then turned to look at him, and he realized just how short she was.

"What do you know about all this?" he asked.

She beamed a great bubbly smile at him again and said, "Nothing. I don't like to play cops and robbers. I like to play with cars and motorcycles and planes, anything mechanical. But, when they break down or are damaged like this, I get really pissed. In this case you should be pissed because your rig took the bullet."

"But it wasn't intended for me," he argued.

"Yeah? What's your evidence of that?"

He stopped and looked back the way he'd driven. "It's more likely it was a wayward bullet," he announced. And yet, even that didn't make sense. The path looked to be straight through and through at that height. He stepped back, dropped his hand. The trajectory of the bullet meant someone had shot from the hip. "Why would somebody shoot in at this angle?"

"No clue," she said. "Depending on where you rank in the military, it could be somebody else's job to figure out, not yours or mine."

He snorted. "Oh, I'll be on the team that handles this."

She turned to look at him. "Really?"

"If I can, yes." He pulled out his phone and made a call. "Hey, Swede. Mason anywhere around?"

"Yeah, hang on," Swede's booming voice announced.

The phone was shuffled, and Mason came on. "Where

the hell are you, Jackson?"

"In a spot of trouble, sir."

"Damn it, knock off with the *sir*."

Jackson grinned. He did it mostly to rile Mason. They were the same age, but he knew it made Mason feel old. "It's that age thing, sir."

Mason said in exasperation, "Then spit it out, young'un."

At that Jackson started to laugh. "Well, I could use a hand."

"What do you need?" Mason's voice turned businesslike.

"My rig picked up a bullet hole. Two rather, as the bullet went through the radiator."

There was silence for a brief second, then Mason exploded. "Where exactly are you?"

"Four miles past the last rest stop. I went in to get water and coffee, then to use the bathroom, came back out, hit the road again. I've got Deli here, who was sent to see what was causing me trouble."

"Dahlia? That's awesome. She's great. Is she the one who found the bullet holes?"

For some reason that rankled Jackson. But he admitted it readily enough. "Yes, she's the one who found the bullet holes."

"Yeah, she's good that way."

"It'd be hard not to see it," he said in exasperation. "It's a through-and-through shot."

"We'll get you towed back here then."

"I believe she's got that already organized."

Mason's voice warmed again. "She would. She's really efficient."

"You know her?"

"Best mechanic on the base. Don't tell the guys in the garage that, but she's got the feel for it. When I went to buy that secondhand vehicle for Tesla from her uncle, I didn't trust it. I had Deli take a quick look at it. She found all kinds of shit going on. But we got it fixed, and now it's the safest it can be."

Jackson smiled. Mason wouldn't leave his wife unprotected. "Can you insert me into the investigation team?"

"You know the MPs will be all over this one. They'll probably tow it back for a forensic visit and then conclude it was just something to note in the files and to not worry about. As long as there are no casualties and not too much vehicular damage, then it won't get very much publicity or investigation hours."

"But somebody shot at the vehicle," Jackson said in exasperation. "Were they shooting at me? Were they shooting to stop the vehicle down the road so they could hijack us? I don't know."

"Don't worry about that right now." Then Mason hung up.

When Jackson put away his phone, he turned to look at Deli. "Mason doesn't seem to think anybody'll give a crap."

At the name *Mason*, her face lit up. "Are you friends?"

He nodded. "Yeah. I'm relatively new to the unit, but all of us in that group are friends."

"You're a SEAL then?" She smiled. "But a green one."

His hands went to his hips, and he glared at her. "Hardly green," he snapped.

She chuckled. "We all have to start somewhere. What you don't know is, I started at about age six with a wrench in my dad's garage. I've been wrenching ever since."

He just rolled his eyes.

At the sound of a vehicle they both stepped out of the way. A black pickup truck drove past at a crazy fast speed.

When Jackson realized something had been stuck out the window, he grabbed Deli and pulled her to the ground.

Gunfire shattered the windshield of his rig, as the pickup drove right past them.

Jackson tried to identify the plates, but the truck was going too fast.

"Did they just try to kill us?" Deli gasped.

He nodded. "Looks like it. Or to scare the crap out of us at least."

"Why the hell aren't you armed?" Deli asked Jackson.

He pointed to his rig. "I had plenty of firepower when on assignment or on these exercises. It's in back of this rig and the others."

"You don't even carry a knife?" she asked, incredulous.

"You are talking to a trained SEAL," he informed her.

A second and third vehicle came down the road just then. This time there were two military rigs, one the tow truck.

Deli raced to the second vehicle and explained about the pickup that had just fired on them. It took off, giving chase as the tow truck pulled a U-turn and worked to hitch up the front of Jackson's military rig. He had it ready to move in about five minutes, while Jackson kept watch on the road, alternating with checking his watch.

She turned to Jackson and asked, "Are you okay to ride in the cab of the tow truck? Or you can catch a ride when a driver comes for my rig."

He still stared at the road where the others had gone. "Did you hear back from them?"

"No, not likely to either," she said. "I don't know who

they were. But they could have caught the asshole already."

"Shouldn't they be back by now?" He didn't like this at all. He pulled out his phone and called Tanner. "Are you around?"

"Yeah. Mason called me. I'm heading in your direction, buddy. You got a lift yet?"

"If I want to be a threesome inside a tow truck, I've got a lift, yeah," he said with light sarcasm.

"I got your back. I'll be there in ten."

Feeling much better, Jackson turned to Deli and said, "Tanner is about to pick me up."

She nodded, walked up to the tow truck and said, "Good for you." She opened the door and started to climb in.

He walked over to her. "Hey, if you want to ride back with us, that's cool too."

She smiled but shook her head. "I don't wanna let your vehicle out of my sight. We've got this." And, with that, the tow truck pulled away.

Jackson sat on the side of the road with just a backpack, water bottle, and a now-cold cup of coffee in his hands. He turned to look in the direction the other vehicle had gone after the pickup. It bothered him that they hadn't returned yet. If the black pickup had been happy to shoot at them parked on the road, there was no reason they wouldn't attack another military vehicle coming up behind them.

While he was still musing, a big black Jeep Wrangler drove up. And there was Tanner. Jackson crossed the road, hopped into the passenger side and said, "Are you doing anything right now?"

Tanner raised an eyebrow and looked at him. "You mean, outside of picking you up?"

Jackson told him about the pickup truck that had shot at them and the military vehicle that had gone after the shooter but hadn't returned. Before he'd finished speaking, Tanner had the Jeep heading down the road after the vehicles of interest.

"How long since the pickup drove by?"

"Twenty minutes, maybe thirty," Jackson said, his voice dark. "I can't imagine what the hell will be on up ahead."

They found out soon enough. They went around a corner, followed by a hairpin turn and another corner. Off to the side of the road, the military vehicle was upside down in the ditch, its front wheels still spinning. Jackson and Tanner jumped out as soon as their vehicle stopped, raced down the hillside to find both men unconscious but alive.

Tanner made the necessary calls while Jackson removed the passenger from the vehicle, laid him out gently on the side of the road, checked him over and realized—outside of a goose egg already forming on his head and a badly broken leg and potentially some rib injuries—he didn't appear to be critical. He went to check the driver, and this time he found one bullet had grazed alongside the man's temple and another had gone through his shoulder.

Swearing lightly, Jackson checked for a pulse, cut the man's seat belt and gently eased him from the vehicle. He didn't appear to have any injuries to his arms or legs, but the bullet wounds were bad enough. Jackson ripped off a chunk of his T-shirt and wadded it up against the slowly welling blood coming from the man's shoulder. He'd need another one to stop the bleeding on the man's head.

Tanner raced down with his phone going back into his pocket. "Help is on the way."

"Cut off more of my T-shirt. We need to stop the bleeding on his head."

With the bulk of his T-shirt now in strips, they wadded it up and used light pressure on the driver's head and shoulder to slow down the bleeding.

"My water bottle is in the Jeep, I should have brought it down with me," Jackson said.

Just then the driver reached up and grabbed his hand. "Water," he whispered.

Jackson patted him gently and said, "We'll get you some. Hang on."

Tanner shook his head, scrambled up the loose rocky terrain of the ravine to the Jeep. He pulled out the water and came back down. When he held the bottle to the man's lips, Jackson lifted his head and gently helped the man get into a better position to drink.

Tanner joined the passenger on the other side of the vehicle.

When the driver had had enough water, Jackson asked him, "What happened?"

"Chasing a truck," he whispered. "But they were waiting for us."

"Did they run you off the road?"

"They shot at me first. I couldn't control the vehicle at that point. We spun around and went over the edge. I was afraid they would come down here and put another bullet in me, then one in my buddy, killing us both."

"But they just left you?"

The man didn't answer.

Jackson asked him another question. "Did you see the men?"

"No, not clearly. I thought I heard footsteps, but they must have thought we were dead already."

Jackson compared the wounds he could see now versus that first impression of when he'd approached the vehicle. They had looked dead if not mortally wounded. It would have been a risk to shoot them at that point, given their open position and the traffic that could come at any moment. "It sounds like you got lucky," he said. "If nothing else, you're safe now."

"How badly hurt?"

"Hopefully you'll be fine," Jackson said quietly. "Better to not talk right now. Your buddy is unconscious with a possible head injury from the crash and has a broken leg. I'm not sure what else. You've been shot high in the shoulder and grazed by a bullet along your head. But I think you'll recover just fine."

At that the man's head slipped to the side, and he fell back into unconsciousness. Jackson checked his breathing, finding it steady, rhythmical. "How is the other guy?" Jackson asked Tanner.

"Still unconscious and that's probably the way he should be. His leg looks like a bitch."

Another good five minutes passed before they heard a vehicle up above, and with it came two paramedics. Both injured men were quickly transferred to stretchers. It took the four of them to get the injured men up the hill. The ground was rough, and the gurneys bounced getting to the ambulances.

The military police vehicle was on the side of the road, and, sure enough, local cops were up there with it too. After Jackson and Tanner explained what had happened and had given their statements, they were allowed to head back to the Jeep.

As they waited for everybody else to leave, Jackson asked,

"What do you think?"

"I think there'll be a full investigation on both sides," Tanner said, fatigue in his voice. "And I don't think either will find anything."

"But this sounds like it was a setup," Jackson said. "I don't know if the bullets fired into the windshield of my rig were directly intended for us as much as to get somebody to follow them."

"Meaning, the shooter wanted to be followed? So he could attack a second military truck?"

"It's possible. What have we got then? Military killers? And for what reason?" Just the thought made his blood boil. Military men served to protect—not to get ambushed, especially not at home.

"It could have just been a prepper, who thought we were encroaching his territory," Tanner said quietly. "As much as we like to think all the bad guys live on foreign soil, we should know that's not the case. We have enough home-grown assholes here that we don't need to go looking for anybody else around the globe."

"True enough. But, if that's the case, it'll be a local police matter, not a naval investigation."

"Yep. It already is," Tanner said. "But there's also a good chance it'll be a joint task force. I don't think they'll let you be on it because you were one of the men shot at."

"That's so not fair," Jackson snapped. "I have every right to track down this guy, particularly after being shot at."

"You keep talking like it's only one guy in the pickup. Is that correct?"

"Only one shooter, that I saw, and he was the driver. But he had a passenger with him."

Tanner nodded. "We have two days off coming up."

Tanner looked at Jackson. "What were you planning on doing for those couple days?"

The thought of beer at Mason's backyard pool party flew out the window. "I guess I'll be tracking down an asshole's black pickup truck," he muttered. "In which case, we should check out the gas station where I picked up the bullet holes to my radiator. Maybe it was behind the sabotage of my rig in the first place."

Tanner turned off the Jeep and looked at him. "My lady isn't in town until tomorrow, so I'm available today."

"Really? Are you sure?"

Tanner hopped out and walked across the road. "You know we'll never gather better forensic evidence than we can right now. The teams that just left already looked but ..."

Jackson knew, while they were waiting for forensics, the expected rainstorm could come and wash away evidence left behind. Plus the shooter could come back, looking for something in particular.

Jackson and Tanner drove first to the gas station and searched the area. But too much traffic had passed for tracks, and there was no evidence to collect at the parking lot that they could see. Further questioning of the gas station personal proved fruitless as well. No one saw or heard anything and they didn't have a working video security feed outside of the store.

On the way back the two men searched the road for evidence where the pickup truck had been parked. It was farther down the road than they expected—a good 150 yards away from the accident scene. There they could see the tire tracks on the shoulder. They carefully photographed them as Tanner walked around, looking for any evidence the shooter or his passenger may have scattered when opening the pickup's doors. "Did the shooter really lie in wait for these men? Were he and his buddy just happy to kill anybody, or were these two targeted?"

"They didn't kill them," Tanner said. "Remember that. They could have put a killing shot in both of them."

Jackson didn't want to think about it, but it was hard not to. Both men had been completely vulnerable at that point. It would have been easy enough to kill them.

"Aha," Tanner said as he squatted down. He glanced at Jackson. "I don't suppose you have any evidence bags, do you?"

Jackson checked his backpack and found a couple small grocery bags from the treats he'd picked up earlier in the day. He dumped one out, turned the bag inside out and handed it to Tanner. And watched as Tanner carefully used his hand inside the bag to pick up a cigarette butt on the ground. "Is it fresh?"

"Yeah, I can still smell it," he said. "One of the men is a smoker."

Feeling buoyed by the possible DNA collection which could yield fast results if the MPs were to run the tests against all navy personnel, Jackson continued to walk along the roadside. "There isn't a whole lot here," he said. He stood and glanced around at the rural road. "There won't be any street cams, nothing for us to get information from." He thought back to the gas station. "We already know they have no working cameras outside either. Hazards of small out of the way stations."

The two men hopped into Tanner's Jeep and headed back to the gas station.

DELI SAT QUIETLY in the tow truck. She'd spent many a happy hour in tow trucks. Her brothers had the tow truck company, and her dad had the mechanic shop. She'd loved going out with her brothers on service calls. Her brothers had found her presence easier for the customers too. It had worked well until she had joined the military. That had been the one thing her family hadn't agreed with. But she'd wanted to do her part, wanted to do something for her country. She was still doing the same type of work, just for a different employer.

She wondered where Jackson went. She knew he wouldn't leave this alone. She didn't like the idea of being attacked at home either. Gunfire had been sprayed at her too; only Jackson's fast reaction had saved them both, and she wouldn't think about how close she'd come to dying today.

The truck driver looked at her. "What the hell happened to the vehicle?"

She just shrugged and smiled. "Radiator leak."

He snorted. "Sure it is."

She understood his reaction because it was a simple thing to resolve if one had water. But, in this case, it would involve a little bit more than water.

The tow truck driver drove her back to the meeting place, where a military tow truck waited for them. Her driver pulled up to the side and said, "I guess you guys need your own ride for this stuff, huh?"

She didn't say anything, just hopped out, watching carefully as he unhooked Jackson's shot-up transport. The driver was a talker, but, at least, he was a good driver, and he took good care of his cargo. As soon as it was unhooked and lined up over the hoist, she could feel the relief in her gut. She'd been worried about getting the truck back without another ambush. It would just be her luck today.

But she needed to check out this rig. Why had it—or Jackson—been targeted? The answer lay in the truck.

Unfortunately she wouldn't be assigned to give it an in-depth examination. That wouldn't stop her from taking a quick look at it when she got the chance. She thanked the driver, offered him a tip, which he refused, then he hopped back into the civilian tow vehicle and took off.

She recognized the military tow truck driver waiting for her. "Hey, James. How are you doing? I didn't expect to see you here. Looking for an excuse to get out of the garage?" James Carville was another mechanic she worked with. Like her, he loved any chance to get out and about.

"Same, and always," he said with a grin. He motioned at the vehicle to tow. "I'm doing better than you obviously. Were you driving this thing?"

She shook her head. "I was sent to see if the guy driving it needed a hand. That's when we realized it had a bullet through the radiator."

He motioned at the windshield. "And what about that part of it?"

"While we were standing there, a pickup truck came whipping past and shot at us. So I'm not exactly sure if that was the original shooter who damaged the radiator or somebody else."

James just stared at her.

She shrugged. "It's been an eventful couple hours. If you get this hooked up, we can get going."

At that, James jumped into action and had the rig's front end lifted into the sling. He motioned at the cab. "Let's go. I believe we're taking this back to our garage to take a look at it."

"We are. Although I'm not sure who'll be assigned to the case. I want to take a closer look, see if a second bullet was fired and if it's still in the engine."

"Well, if it's not yours to work on …"

He left his thoughts hanging, but she didn't need to fill in the blanks. They both knew that everything done in the garages had names assigned and then checks and balances done for all the work they did.

They were on the road in minutes. He kept up a light conversation. She answered as best she could, but she didn't want to be too social. She was more concerned about what the hell Jackson was doing. Because she knew in her heart of hearts that he'd gone after the black pickup truck. She'd wanted to go with him, but, at the same time, she was no hero. She was all about working in the background, keeping things running, so other people could be heroes. Still, she wouldn't mind keeping track of him. And, if he knew Mason, well, maybe Jackson was a good guy. She didn't have any reason to not think so because Mason's group was fairly elite. But she hadn't met any of them who she didn't like.

Her phone rang. She looked at the number and smiled. "Mason, I was just thinking about you."

"Ah, now that's a good sign," he said. "The guys followed the black pickup, by the way."

"Jackson did?"

"And Tanner, who volunteered to pick him up."

"Did they find it?" she asked eagerly.

"No, but they found the military vehicle that went after them, flipped in a ditch. Both men are badly injured, and a bullet grazed the head of the driver, and he'd also been shot in the shoulder."

She gasped silently. "Were they waiting for them?"

"Yes. They were ambushed."

CHAPTER 2

DELI WAITED FOR James to unhook the vehicle. She knew the forensics team would come soon, and she wouldn't be allowed anywhere close to the rig. She was a mechanic, but that didn't make her high up on the pole, particularly a brass pole. James was an equal when it came to pole-climbing.

She'd been in the military four years, and she was damn good at her job. But she had no wish to be a lifer. At some point she wanted her own mechanic shop, like a small mom-and-pop place, where she could raise kids and just work on the vehicles she wanted to.

A pipe dream she knew. But she also had some dreams of designing. She was a huge fan of tricycles and knew a lot of people would laugh at her for that. But she thought they were fun and a safer alternative to motorcycles. She could ride those two-wheeled versions too, and she thoroughly enjoyed hitting the highway on her Harley. But she kept thinking about kids and safety and longevity of the sport. Which brought her back to trikes.

Jackson's vehicle was parked off to the side in one of the slots. She pulled out her cell phone and started taking pictures. She captured everything on the outside first; then she took pictures from the inside, looking for another bullet that may have been lodged in the vehicle. After all, who is to say the shooter just shot the rig once? She really wanted to get a look at what was behind that radiator. Had that through-and-through bullet caused more damage in the engine? She bent down, took a look underneath, but it was getting dark, and she couldn't see anything. She used her cell phone's flashlight, but the machinery was too tightly packed under the hood to get a better view.

"So did you find anything?"

Surprised, she looked up, banging her head. Swearing softly, she pulled herself out from under the vehicle and glared at Jackson. "Did you have to do that?"

He motioned at her underneath the vehicle. "Did you have to do that?"

She hopped to her feet and brushed off her pants. "Yes, I did. I'm not likely to be assigned to any of the forensic investigations, and I wanted to see for myself just what happened."

A curious light lit the depths of his brown eyes. He stared at her. "Well, give then."

She shook her head. "Give what?"

"What did you find?" he asked in exasperation. "Come on. Share. Pretty please," he said in a wheedling voice.

She stuck out her jaw, and he just grinned, charming her. She reached up and rubbed her temple. "I couldn't see anything, to be honest. I took pictures, but, if I can't get this rig on a hoist and take it apart, I can't yet see if any more shots were fired at the rig. I was hoping to find a bullet is still here."

"Let's find out if we can get you assigned to the case then," he said. "I bet Mason could pull some strings."

"I wouldn't ask him though," she said. "You know there's a time to pull strings, and this might not be it.

Besides, the investigators won't tell me anything now."

"No, but we do know people who could help us with that," Jackson said.

"*You* might," she muttered. "But I'm a mechanic, remember? I'm not one of those dashing-hero types. I don't have all these networking connections you do."

He walked around the vehicle, but then he stopped and turned to look at her. "You know Mason. He's one of the best networking guys you can have in your corner. How well do you know him?"

She shrugged and said, "I know Tesla better." She watched that same curious light warm his gaze again.

"Tesla is a sweetie," he said. "We all want a Tesla for ourselves."

She laughed. "I can see why. She's a good friend. But I personally wouldn't want a Tesla for myself."

At that, he burst out laughing. "Nice to know you're looking for someone, and it's not her," he said smoothly.

She frowned, wondering if he'd suddenly jumped the conversation to a personal level or if she was only imagining it. She gave a headshake and walked around the vehicle to the other side. "I don't see anything else that indicates what the hell went on," she said. "I wish I'd been at the accident scene."

"Why?" he asked.

"Because I've done some accident reconstruction, and that would have been nice to see."

"Would photos help?" he asked in a low voice. "Because I took lots."

She spun to look at him and nodded with a sharp movement. "Absolutely. But I need a laptop to look at them, to enhance them. Did you happen to take a look at where the shooter's pickup might have laid in wait for the vehicle following them?"

He nodded. "Don't tell anyone, but Tanner picked up a cigarette butt too. And it still had the aroma of cigarette smoke on it."

She rubbed her hands together. "You know something? We're on this."

"And you also know that we don't have the right to. At least not per military protocol."

"True," she whispered, frowning. "But how long before NCIS gets on this or the military police? I'm not sure exactly who would handle it. It was a military training exercise but with naval officers involved. And, of course, you were there, were part of one of the groups too, weren't you?"

"Absolutely I was," he said, "and so, in theory, was NCIS. But also the local civilian authorities have jurisdiction for the shooting, because it didn't happen on base."

She shrugged. "The brass will have to sort out their own branches. What I want to do is make sure the evidence is preserved."

"Exactly," Jackson said. "Which is why we picked up a cigarette butt."

"Will both men be okay?"

"I think so," Jackson said. "I did speak with the driver. However, he doesn't remember much."

"But it was an ambush," she said softly. "They probably would have come around the corner, been shot at, then the wheel would have spun out of control, and maybe it was just luck on the part of the bad guys that had the military truck flipping down a ravine."

"The driver thinks as least one person walked down to them, and yet, didn't shoot them."

"So they didn't finish them off." She chewed on her bottom lip when she thought about that. "That's an interesting thought. Because that would have been two sure kills."

"Unless the two guys in the pickup weren't trying to kill them, or they were hoping the men would die anyway, and there wouldn't be an investigation because it would have been labeled an accident."

She nodded at that. "Except for the bullet holes in your transport and in the driver of the other military truck," she reminded him. "Hard to ignore that. Maybe the shooters were just out causing trouble."

"What kind of a world do we live in," Jackson said in a hard tone, "that ambushing a military rig with two innocent men is considered fun?"

"Worse happens," she warned. "And you know it."

He nodded. "I know it, but I haven't seen it recently. Not here at home."

"There was that case of the preppers a few years back. They decided to start World War III by shooting a couple civilian law enforcement officers. Remember that case?"

He frowned, then shook his head with a shrug. "No, I can't say I do."

"It was down in the South. They took out a couple black officers. Then they took out a couple white officers, hoping it would start some racial kerfuffle. I think ultimately what they really wanted was to test their prepper storage emergency plans."

"I remember something about them converting old bomb shelters into war bunkers," Jackson said thoughtfully. "One of the cops lived, right?"

"Yes, one of them did. But three died. Three preppers were basically bored to death, waiting for something to happen so they could start fighting back. So they decided to incite something themselves."

"And you think this might be something like that?"

"Who the hell can tell?" she said. "It could be one of our own, a handful of veterans mad at our armed forces, like Timothy McVeigh, but focusing on military personnel." She took several steps back to look at the vehicle. "There's nothing quite like firing on a military rig to get some national attention."

"But, in this case, they didn't get any attention, did they?"

"And maybe they thought they would and are surprised right now. They could be making plans to create more chaos."

Jackson frowned and thought about it. "I'm not sure I like the way your mind thinks."

"Doesn't matter if you like it or not," she said. "Shit happens. And more often than we like to think."

JACKSON HAD TO agree with Deli, but he didn't like the idea of somebody ambushing military personnel in the States. These men and women went to battle for their country every day. To think the actual enemy came from their own part of the world was devastating. So many military personnel survived untold horrors, terrible rigors and psychological trauma from missions in Iraq and Afghanistan. Then they came home and, during basic training missions, were shot at for no decent reason that Jackson could see. And that made it so much worse. He watched as she walked around the vehicle again. "What's bothering you?"

She shot him a look but ignored him.

He crossed his arms and waited. He'd heard Mason say she was a hell of a mechanic, and she was certainly looking at his rig from a different perspective than he was. When she squatted and studied the underside of the carriage, he walked to the area and squatted beside her, trying to see what she saw. "It would help if you would explain."

"I can't really explain. I have to get it up on a hoist, but I think the front axle is off."

"Off?"

She nodded. "After you have a really bad accident, the alignment goes out, and the axle can get damaged. Some of them have to be replaced. This one doesn't feel like it's that bad, but I'm wondering if it was tampered with."

"Likely done on base then? Wow, that makes our bad guys closer than I like. When we theorized 'one of our own,' I really didn't think it would be someone we may know."

They shared a worried look.

"And," Jackson continued, "seeing as how that initial sabotage didn't work, they came by and put a bullet in the vehicle?"

She turned to look at him. "How was it you ended up driving this rig?"

"Good question," he said, casting his mind back to this morning, when they'd all been assigned their duties for packing up from their training exercise. "They needed a relief driver," he said thoughtfully. "And I was looking for some downtime and thoughts-to-myself time. So I volunteered."

"So it would have been random?"

He shot her a hard look. "Random as to who took the driver's place. Maybe not random about the assigned driver backing out. A line had been drawn through his name on the duty roster."

"Then we need to find out who that driver was and see if this attack was really directed at him. You could have been an innocent bystander in all of this."

"Or he could have been part of the setup. Neither is a nice way to look at it. I wonder who that original driver was."

"You can't remember?"

"His name was something unique. Something you don't see often." He paused, then suddenly said, "*Chester*. It was Chester, but I don't know his last name."

She straightened slowly. "Chester Parks," she said, her voice low, deep. "I know the name. There was some trouble with him a year or so back. He got into a couple arguments, and a man died."

"A year later is a long time to exact revenge," Jackson said, interpreting her comment. "If that's what you're thinking."

"I don't know what I'm thinking," she burst out.

But Jackson already had his phone out, sending a text to Mason, asking if Chester Parks had been the man assigned to drive the rig. Then he added a line about asking someone to find out why Chester couldn't drive the truck.

"But," Deli continued, "about that same time, we had some thefts in the garage. One of our mechanics was found on the security tapes at odd hours in the garage when not scheduled for duty. The tapes didn't confirm he stole anything, but I turned them over to the MPs to investigate. Never heard anything afterward and the thefts supposedly stopped, plus the mechanic still works here, so I guess the matter was resolved."

Jackson's phone rang, interrupting their discussion. It

was Mason, but it was likely too early for answers.

"Hey," Mason said. "Chester was injured today. Remember hearing about the guy who shot himself in the foot?"

At that, Deli leaned in to hear both sides of this conversation.

"No, I didn't hear about that," Jackson said. He started to smile and then realized it was likely this guy. "Are you saying Chester shot his own foot?"

"Yeah, he was taken to the closest hospital to get medical treatment. That's why they needed a driver."

"Wow," Jackson said. "We were just wondering if Chester was part of the ambush. If so, he seems to be pretty dedicated by shooting his own foot." When Mason didn't say anything, Jackson continued, "Of course we considered that he himself had been targeted, and I just happened to be the unlucky substitute, but the shooters didn't know there had been a change of driver."

"It's possible. In that case, maybe they were looking to waylay you and take you prisoner."

"Whoa, whoa, whoa," Jackson said. "That's quite a leap. Why would you even go in that direction?"

"Because none of the bullets hit you," Deli said. "Hi, Mason. Deli here."

Mason's voice lightened as he said, "Hey, Deli. Glad you weren't hurt in the spray of bullets. Sorry I forgot to say that earlier."

"Thanks. I'm pretty damn happy about that myself," she muttered. "The thing is, I *was* there. A couple bullets were fired, but they were aimed at the windshield. So warning shots."

"Could they have seen Jackson?" Mason asked Deli.

"And, if they didn't see him clearly, they may have thought Chester was there instead. Maybe they have an old beef with him and just wanted to rattle his bones a little bit."

"Then why shoot the two military guys who went after them?" Jackson questioned.

"It's possible they were too close, and the shooters were in danger of getting caught," Mason said. "So they turned around and attacked instead. That would also explain why they didn't kill them. It wasn't their intent from the start."

"But they did shoot them—one at least," Jackson said. "That driver had a bullet hole in his shoulder and a graze alongside his head."

Deli nodded. "But I bet no bullets were found there, were there?"

"I did a cursory look but didn't see any," Jackson said. "Of course the head shot grazed him, and that bullet could be somewhere along that road or down the hills off one of those tight turns. But the driver's shoulder shot was through-and-through. The bullet didn't enter his seat. So it's got to be somewhere."

"Maybe we should go on a drive," she said suddenly. "Take a look …"

"Whoa," Jackson said. "You did hear me say that thing about getting removed from the investigation since I'm a witness?"

"I did. But you and Tanner already picked up that cigarette butt and took photos of tire tracks," she reminded him.

He glared at her. She glared back at him.

Mason started to laugh. "You can't go tonight," he said. "It's pitch black out there, and you won't be able to see anything. However, if you're both up to it, I suggest—if you feel that strongly—that you go at the crack of dawn, before that storm is supposed to hit. Take a look, see what you can find. But I would also park a long way away and walk in. You don't know if anybody else will be watching. Or if the shooters are returning to the same crime scene."

"Why would they?" Jackson asked curiously.

"Hard to say," Mason said. "But, for all you know, they're seeding forensic evidence to lay the blame for this elsewhere."

"Meaning, they could have found a way to blame Chester?"

"I don't know how or why that would be," Mason said. "But, considering Chester is the one person who couldn't have been involved because of the accident he had earlier …"

"But do the shooters know about that?" Deli asked. "Still, it's a bit of a stretch."

"All this is a bit of a stretch," Mason said in exasperation. "If you have to go, don't take anything or remove anything from a crime scene," he warned. "There will be a formal investigation into this. But, as you know, sometimes the brass's wheels move slowly."

CHAPTER 3

WHEN SHE GOT home later that night, Deli walked straight to her shower. She had a small one-bedroom apartment to herself on base. She preferred living on base, but, at the same time, a part of her wanted to find a place out of town. She'd only been in Coronado a year, but somehow that year had come and gone, and she hadn't done anything about moving. But, even more so now, as she was living and breathing the military life, it was important to get some sense of balance. And living away from base would help in many ways.

She quickly scrubbed down, taking extra time on her hair. She had auburn hair that stopped just below her shoulders. She kept it in a braid, but, for washing, she took it out of the braid and gave her head a good scrub, almost moaning as the hot water poured over her body. When she came out, wrapped in a bathrobe and her hair in a towel, she made a cup of tea and sat down in front of her laptop.

She downloaded all the images she'd taken with her cell phone. While she waited for them to load, several emails came in, and they were all from Jackson. He had sent her the photos from the crime scene: the photos he'd taken of the tire tracks and of the overturned military truck. She appreciated his thoroughness. She searched through them and found some amazingly close-up pictures of the accident.

Obviously one of the two men had been pulled from the vehicle and was lying to the side of it as they awaited medical assistance. Jackson took the pictures as he had tried to help the two injured men. Photos of the side of the vehicle, the top, the undercarriage—basically he'd done a three-sixty inside and out as much as he could. She slowly went through them one at a time, looking to see what damage had been done. Because it had flipped end over end, an awful lot of the vehicle's metal damage came just from its collision with the ground.

She sat back and sipped her tea as she slowly pored over the pictures. When her phone rang, she knew it would be Jackson. Although how he'd have tracked her down, she didn't know. But, if he was part of Mason's unit, he'd have no problem doing so. It was a little disconcerting though. They all seemed to know so much and to know how to do so much. Made her feel like she didn't know near enough. "Yes, Jackson, I'm home, and I'm fine."

"Good, but no *hello*?" he asked. "How did you know it was me calling?"

She chuckled and said, "I half expected you to."

"I just wanted to see if you got the photos."

"I did. Thanks. I gave them a cursory look but haven't had too much time to go over them. You were very thorough."

"Good. Anyone discuss the shooting with you? Get too curious? Anyone acting odd?" he asked smoothly.

"No, it was quiet," she said. Just then she heard the weather outside—predicted to begin farther east, past the ambush site, then hit the base—which would change their plans for the morning. "Can you hear the storm outside? So much for our crack-of-dawn start."

"That's one of the reasons I'm calling. No point in going with the heavy rain pounding outside. And this particular weather front covers all the way to the accident site and beyond. I checked the weather forecast overnight, and this isn't letting up."

She winced, glancing at the clock. "So I get to sleep in tomorrow after all. Well, a little, as it's still a workday," she said, trying to inject a note of positivity to her voice. "If we could have seen something, it's already too late."

"True, so forget about it. Have a good night." And he hung up abruptly.

She stared at the phone and asked the empty room, "Like I'd forget about it? How could I?" She got up, made herself a simple ham-and-egg omelet for dinner and would have liked to eat it on her small balcony, barely wide enough for her small barbeque at the end, and a chair, but not in this weather. So she positioned a chair in front of her French doors and, balancing the plate on her lap, she slowly ate her dinner as she watched the storm. She'd planned to go to bed early too but hadn't realized how late the day had gotten.

Her phone rang again. She looked down but didn't recognize the number, so turned it off rather than answering it. She'd had any number of odd phone calls lately—shortly after her boyfriend moved away—and she had no intention of engaging with that repulsive person. The fact that Jackson had tracked her down just showed it was way too easy for somebody to get her number, and, in fact, someone had. Maybe she was putting out the wrong vibes. The only vibe she wanted to project was *Get lost*. Not to everyone, not all the time. But she wasn't really in the market. She wasn't *not* looking, but she wasn't actively trying to find a partner either.

She and her boyfriend had broken off about four and a half months ago. It had been good while it had lasted, but they both realized they were ready for other things. He'd moved back East, and she'd stayed in California.

No way was she trading sunshine and vineyards for snow six months out of the year. He'd just laughed and told her that the snow was great, and, if she'd learned to snowboard like he did, she'd learn to appreciate what winter had to offer. But he hadn't been able to convince her. They realized that, if they weren't interested in staying in the same area of the country, they really had nothing strong enough to carry on with. It had been a sad parting, but, when it was over, she hadn't missed anything about him, even though he'd been the person she'd done everything with before their breakup.

Their weekends had been filled with hikes and traveling around the state, exploring different corners. They used to go for long drives because they enjoyed it. And, with him gone, she'd tried to do the same things alone, but they didn't have the same appeal. Now, four months later, she had stopped going on those drives altogether. She'd been looking forward to going out with Jackson tomorrow morning for their evidence-gathering expedition.

He was different, jovial, lighthearted, big, but he apparently didn't know a whole lot about mechanics. Then not everybody could know everything about everything, she had to keep reminding herself. She worked in a man's world, and often they knew or thought they knew a lot. But she knew a whole lot more about mechanics than most.

In that way Jackson was refreshing. He didn't pretend to possess knowledge he didn't have. He probably knew the basics of a vehicle and likely more than that, but she was the one who would tear apart the engine and put it back together again.

She frowned as she got ready for bed, wondering what the morning would bring. As she was about to fall asleep, her phone rang again. Without thinking, she answered it. "Hello."

"There you are," the sleazy voice said. "I caught you again, didn't I?"

"Leave me alone," she snapped. "I don't want anything to do with you, so stop calling me." She hung up on the caller.

When it rang again, she refused to answer. When it didn't stop ringing, she shut it off and set the phone on the charger. She stared at it for a long time and wondered what the hell she could do about that caller. He was a pain in the ass and really affecting her moods, not to mention had her more than a bit worried that he might escalate his interactions with her. She rolled over and, with great difficulty, finally fell asleep.

JACKSON WALKED INTO the hospital. He understood the two unconscious men were held under guard in case anybody came back after them; plus they needed to still be questioned. He wondered about the security here. Surely it would be enough to keep them safe in the hospital until they woke up. But, since there was suspicion of an ambush, the authorities wanted to make sure these two men were questioned before another attempt happened.

Jackson shrugged and headed up to the third floor. As he approached, he saw that Commander Fielding stood talking with Sergeant Mitchell and a man Jackson didn't recognize. He turned as Jackson approached and nodded. "Jackson."

He stepped forward. "Yes, sir."

"You found these men at the accident site, is that correct?"

Jackson gave a clipped nod. "Yes, that's correct."

"I want the details, please. Tell me exactly what happened. Start from the beginning."

Jackson's face twisted slightly as he figured out what the commander would consider the beginning. "I took my vehicle to a rest stop to get some water. When I came back out, I was a little farther behind the convoy than intended. I pulled onto the highway, picked up speed, could see the convoy ahead of me, but my engine died. I managed to get off the road onto the shoulder, but steam came from the engine. I hopped out, opened up the hood as a military vehicle came to check on me. Dahlia was driving."

"Deli?"

"Yes, Deli or Dahlia," he added. "Dahlia, the mechanic." He shrugged. "Sorry. I don't really know her full rank and name. She was sent to give me a hand. Somebody had seen my vehicle in trouble."

Several other men nodded. "We know Deli," they said. "She's a character."

Jackson's mouth kicked up into a slight grin as he had to agree. She was that.

"So she came back, and what did she say?"

One of the men in the group interrupted before Jackson could answer. "Why are you here, Jackson?"

"I came to see how the men are doing, sir." He looked to the open doors to their rooms, where he could see the two men. The one closest to him appeared to be sound asleep, and the other man with a bandage on his head and his arm in a sling was restless, potentially awake.

His gaze zipped back to the others. "Have they been questioned?"

The man slowly shook his head. "Did you want to question them?"

"Of course I do, sir. I want to know what happened and who did this to them. My vehicle was shot up just before theirs. I would love to be part of any investigation."

The man frowned, but Sergeant Mitchell nodded. "We'll get back to you on that, son." He motioned at the second door. "We've just spoken to him ourselves. Go in and say hi. You may ask a couple questions but don't get him riled up or upset."

Jackson nodded and made a quick exit into the room. With a bright smile he said, "Hey, I'm Jackson. I'm the one who found you upside down on the side of the road."

The man's face lit up, and he reached out a hand. "I'm Max. Thanks so much for the assistance."

"I don't know how much assistance I was," Jackson said. "You went after the pickup because it was my vehicle that got shot up."

Recognition locked into Max's face. "That's where I know you from. You were standing beside the rig with that cute mechanic and the shot-out windshield."

Jackson nodded. "And before that, somebody, though I can't say it was the same somebody, shot the radiator in my vehicle while I was at a stop getting water." He pulled up a chair and sat down beside Max. "Did you have any idea who came at you?"

Max shook his head. He stretched on the bed a little bit, wincing with the movement. "We came around the corner, and there they were. I jerked hard to avoid them, and I heard shots, but, at the time, I didn't register what was happening.

I think it was my quick turning of the vehicle that saved my head from a bullet hole," he admitted. "But then we spun out of control, and the vehicle flipped. I don't remember anything after that."

"He shot you high in the shoulder, and a bullet grazed your head. Maybe turning the wheel like you did saved your life. However, you told me at the accident site that you heard footsteps down in the ravine, while you both were still trapped in the overturned vehicle, and yet, nobody shot you then. Interesting that your buddy didn't get any bullet holes either."

"As I remember he was bent over, trying to find something in his pack," Max said. "Not sure what. So, if his head was down low enough, he would have escaped detection completely."

Jackson thought about that, visualizing how the man was probably huddled over, trying to locate something. "Good timing on his part."

"Good timing on both our parts," Max said. "I'd sure as hell like to get out of here and go after that asshole."

"One asshole or more than one?" Jackson asked curiously. "I would think more than one."

"I can't say for sure. I never got a clear-enough visual to determine that." He looked at Jackson. "What about you? Did you see them when they drove past?"

"I did," Jackson said. "I could swear two people were in the truck. The driver was firing in our direction, but I don't know what the passenger was doing."

"He wouldn't have been able to fire past the driver, unless the pickup's rear window was open. Then he could have fired out of there."

"I don't know what happened at that point, as I was

ducked down behind my rig," Jackson said.

"So one vehicle, out of the blue, attacks a parked military rig obviously in trouble and then waits to ambush a vehicle coming after it?" Max asked. "Doesn't that just beat all?"

"The problem is, they had a reason. I just don't know what it is."

"And was it personal? Were they after anybody in particular, or did we just happen to be the unlucky ones who ran into their bullets?" Max asked.

"I can't see how I'd have been targeted," Jackson said. "I was a replacement driver for a guy who got hurt."

"So maybe he was targeted?"

"It's possible," Jackson said in a neutral tone. "It's something we're looking at."

Max's gaze narrowed. "Are you part of the investigation?"

Jackson snorted. "Not officially, no. But I really don't like the idea of getting shot at or ambushed in any way without being able to find out who the hell it was and what the hell is going on."

"I wish I could join you," Max said, raising his arm and then freezing in pain. He took several deep breaths, then whispered, "Damn it, I forgot." He shifted gently in bed, then grimaced. "It'll take a day or two for me to get mobile enough to drive again."

"Not to worry," Jackson said. "If you give me your number, I'll stay in touch. And you can text me if you remember any other details."

"Happy to," Max said. "But honestly it happened so fast that I don't remember any details."

"I know the feeling." At that, Jackson and Max exchanged phone numbers, and then Jackson stood. "Have you talked to your buddy yet?"

"No. He was unconscious when they brought him in, and, as far as I'm aware, he hasn't woken up yet."

The two men exchanged worried glances. Head wounds were notoriously difficult. They could be simple and appear like nothing, only to kill a person later. Or the patient could be unconscious, like this man was, and the head wound could end up sending the man into a deep coma that could take him days—or never—to wake up from.

With a goodbye, Jackson turned and walked out. As he stepped down the empty hallway, he thought he heard another voice. He stopped and turned around, but no one was here. All the men he'd seen earlier had left. In fact, the guards were no longer here either.

He frowned, shoving his hands into his pockets as he contemplated that. Was that deliberate? He stepped back into Max's room. "Security was here earlier but aren't now. Any idea why?"

Max looked up and nodded. "As far as I know, they were just keeping an eye on me until everybody got a chance to talk to me."

"Okay. I guess that makes sense then," Jackson said with frown. "But I have to admit, it feels odd out there."

"Odd in what way?" Max asked, his voice sharp.

At the sound of approaching footsteps, Jackson flattened against the wall next to the doorway and held a finger to his lips.

Max lay still in the bed and closed his eyes but seemed to be peering beneath his lashes, trying to watch.

The footsteps grew stronger and louder, but they came from the opposite direction that Jackson had taken to get here. He didn't even know what was at that end of the hall. He thought an exit was there, and that would make sense because that would be an alternative set of stairs in case of fire or whatever.

He waited as the footsteps slowed. He glanced over at Max.

"You awake there, Max?" The man's voice was soft, and he stopped just outside the doorway.

But his voice didn't sound friendly. There was something dark to it. If this was a friend, why would he act like that? And, if not a friend, how would he know Max was in here?

The nameplate on the door. Jackson had seen it when he'd come in but hadn't thought anything of it. It was Max's name. The nameplate on the other door had been *Barney,* the passenger riding with Max. The intruder stepped in enough that Jackson could see his feet over the threshold. But he wasn't far enough in that he could see Jackson standing there.

Then the intruder raised his hand, and both men could see the gun with a silencer on the end.

Jackson slowed his breathing and focused. ... He'd get one chance ...

He lunged—surprised to see a three-hundred-pound masked man—grabbed the shooter's arm, spun, knocked the gun out of his hands. It skated across the floor, but the gunman wrapped his other arm around Jackson's throat in a hefty chokehold. Jackson dropped to his knee, tossed the man over his head to the floor in front of him, then quickly flipped him facedown on the floor and pinned him to the floor.

"Woot, nicely done," Max crowed from the bed.

Jackson grinned. "It was, wasn't it?" Suddenly he flew through the air as the man bucked straight up and tossed Jackson like he was a fly. He landed hard but bounced to his feet and spun, only to face the intruder with the gun again. The gun bucked in his hand, but Jackson had already slid sideways. He felt the burn on his leg, but he lunged forward, knocking the gun away before a big-ass boot came up and smashed into his face.

As he lay here, he heard footsteps, many sets coming toward him and another set racing away to the left. He groaned and sat up to see Max peering down at him from the edge of the bed.

"Sorry, Jackson. He's gone."

Jackson collapsed on the floor and stared at the ceiling. "Shit."

CHAPTER 4

DELI WOKE SUDDENLY. She'd been exhausted and had gone to bed right after dinner. Now instinct said something was wrong. She bolted upright, slipped out of bed and softly raced so she was flat against her bedroom door. She cocked her head, listening for any sound. She didn't know what had disturbed her, but something sure as hell was going on. And it seemed to be inside the complex.

She was on a ground-floor apartment, something that had never bothered her before, but now that she could see all the what-if scenarios running through her mind, she realized it was not the best choice for a single woman, especially one with a stalker. Sure, she had a lot of self-defense skills and had the same military training as everyone else on the base. Plus she lived where hundreds of other men and women with the same skills could help her out when needed. However, when it came down to flat-out comparing muscle to muscle and skill to skill, it was pretty damn hard to beat somebody twice your body weight. Only so much Deli could do, given her petite build. But she did the best she could with what she had.

She waited with bated breath to see if the sound repeated itself. And there it was, but like a gentle knock to her front door, as if somebody was afraid to disturb her or just checking to see if she was in and awake already.

But then she heard them trying the doorknob.

She slipped into the living room and ran to the front door. She didn't have one of those peepholes to see who was on the outside, and that was just too damn bad right now. She peered down at the floor and could see shadows of two feet on the other side of the door, projected by the hallway light outside. As she watched, the footsteps turned and walked away.

With her senses strained for anything unusual, she walked around the living room. She wasn't exactly sure what she wanted to do. But, if that person had been serious about getting ahold of her, they should have knocked louder. She contemplated her options, then raced to the French doors and slipped outside onto her patio with its wrought-iron fencing and hopped over it into the grass. Keeping close to the building, she ran around to the front of the building, where the main entrance was. There she stood in the shadows and watched as a man dressed all in black moved away from the building.

She didn't like anything about this now. She didn't recognize him, but then she couldn't see his face. He had a dark hoodie over his head and was in black track pants. He stepped out and moved toward the parking lot. She followed at a distance, hoping he'd get into a vehicle, and she'd have a chance to grab the license plate. But instead he picked up his pace and then, in a burst of energy, bolted to the far side of the parking lot and between the two buildings. Had he seen her? Had he heard her? Or was it just his normal modus operandi?

Still, it made him look guilty as hell. But of what?

Disturbed, she returned to her apartment the way she'd come. As she approached her French doors, she stopped and realized she'd left them open. In fact, if this man had been working with somebody, there was a good chance her apartment had already been breached by her own negligence. Staring at her patio doors, she stopped and listened but couldn't hear any sounds on the inside. After a moment she stepped back into her apartment.

She did a careful walk-through to make sure it was empty. As soon as she was sure it was secure, she closed the French doors, locking them behind her. But it would take a hell of a lot more than a closed door to make her inner sense of insecurity calm down. Somebody she didn't know, suspicious as all hell, had come to her door. She'd heard them try the doorknob, but it was locked. What had they expected? Of course it was locked.

But then she remembered several girlfriends who were nonchalant about locking doors. Maybe he'd hoped he'd get lucky. And what would he do now that he knew her door was locked? Would he come back with tools? Or try for an easier victim?

Perturbed and not sure what to do about it, she brought out her journal and jotted down some notes. Maybe her unknown caller might have stepped up to something more.

After the day she'd had, she really didn't need this. She got up and went to her laptop, transferred her written notes to a digital copy, then emailed them to herself to make sure they didn't disappear. There wasn't a whole lot of information she could send because she didn't know very much. She described the voice she had heard on her most recent phone call, the dates when he had called and now the event that had happened tonight.

But she knew it was not enough. If anything happened to her, there would be no leads. Her notes said very little.

They would know somebody had bothered her. She didn't have any girlfriends to contact, and she wasn't sure who of the men in her world she could trust to take this information and to not laugh at her. Her brothers would go bonkers and want her to call the cops. But she lived on a base. The military police would be brought in, and that wasn't something she was prepared to do.

She didn't want to closely examine her reasons for that. But, being on base, doing the work she did, being part of this crew, a certain self-sufficiency was required of her.

A certain independent I-can-take-care-of-myself attitude. But, alone at night in the dark, it was pretty easy to forget all those skills she'd learned and to forget about all the men around her who would be on her side. And then she thought about Jackson.

What if she told him?

She sat back from the computer and contemplated the idea for a long moment. And then, without questioning herself, she copied the information, titled it In Case Anything Happens But Don't Freak Out and fired it off.

The response came back less than three minutes later. She had already stepped away from the laptop when it dinged. She sat back down to read the message. All there was to his email was *WTF?* And then her phone rang. She groaned and answered it. "I was trying to find someone who wouldn't freak out over something like this, someone who would be completely reasonable," she snapped.

Silence came.

Shit, was it even Jackson?

Then she double-checked the phone ID and groaned in relief. "Damn it. I figured it was you, but, when you didn't answer, I was afraid I was talking to somebody else." She walked to the couch, flinging herself down full length across the green plaid material.

"How long has this been going on?" Jackson asked, his voice rising in anger. "And please tell me that you've told other people besides me."

She didn't know what to say, so she said nothing. She could hear his growl into the phone, one of frustration and disbelief.

"Why?" he asked, his tone ominous.

"Because it hadn't escalated to the level it did tonight."

"From the beginning, I want all the details right now," he snapped.

She pinched the bridge of her nose and muttered, "I shouldn't have sent that email to you."

"Well, you did, so now you deal with the consequences. No way in hell are you giving me this little tidbit of information and then expect me to walk away without making sure you're safe. How do you think I'd feel if something happened to you?"

She didn't know what to say again.

And then his voice changed. It became more persuasive. "Did you consider how that might have impacted how we viewed what else happened today? Maybe it wasn't me they were shooting at. Maybe it was you?"

She gasped.

"See? We can't ignore this," he said. "Every plot has multiple threads, and we often don't know what shit is coming down until it's all out in the open."

"I don't think my caller has anything to do with today." She rushed to justify her actions and then tossed it all out in the air, saying, "At least I don't think so. There was no need or reason for anybody to come after me like that. And it wasn't me they shot at in the vehicle chasing them."

"And what if they were just trying to stop somebody from tracking them down?" Jackson said. "Maybe they hoped they'd hit you and took off only to find they had someone on their tail faster than they expected and realized they couldn't outrun the military rig?"

"Nobody hates me enough to do that," she stated boldly. "I have great friends."

"But you didn't contact any of them, did you?"

She groaned. "No, and now I wish to hell I hadn't contacted you."

"If you get hurt because of this, you'll be damn glad you did," he said. "If you die because of this, I'll be more than pissed."

She chuckled. "If I'm dead, I won't care, will I?"

"But I will," he growled. "So think of somebody other than yourself."

That silenced her. Pain and shock slid inside her gut. She was now forced to consider how her brothers would feel if they received a phone call saying she'd been murdered. Finally she gave Jackson the truth. One she rarely admitted herself.

"You know what the mentality is in the military." Her voice was soft, quiet. "We're supposed to be tough. We're supposed to be know-all capable people. I didn't want anybody to think less of me."

This time it was his turn to be silent for a moment. "I don't think this situation applies," he finally said, obviously trying for a neutral tone of voice. "It's one thing if you're on a mission or you're training. Obviously you don't want to appear weaker or to be less than the others. But you are a woman alone in your apartment, and somebody not only has your phone number but now knows where you live. The world over has seen some of the most capable women taken down just because they were physically smaller or caught unaware by a man who was more determined and of a darker nature than they could have suspected. I don't want somebody to find you dead in your bed because a predator got into your apartment when you thought he couldn't."

"That's not a thought guaranteed to make me sleep tonight," she snapped. "How about we talk about sunshine and roses instead, so I'll at least get some sleep."

"How about we talk about reality."

She could hear him take a deep breath and then another and another one.

"Okay, look. I'm sorry. I'm not trying to terrify you," he said in a more persuasive voice. "But I want you to be sensible. I don't want you taking any chances. And I don't want you brushing off any of these incidents as not being important. Especially in lieu of what went on earlier today."

"Okay, fine. I won't," she said. "I'm back at work tomorrow morning anyway."

"Good," he said, "because I've got some days off. I'll meet you at the navy garage tomorrow. I'd like to see what's happening with that rig."

"I'm not sure I'll be able to tell you anything because I don't know if the rig will still be there when I arrive," she said. "I work as a mechanic. I'm not the brass. And, when they move things around, we're just puppets on a string."

"I know," he said. "But you need to also know that I was at the hospital tonight, and we already had an incident there."

She bolted upright. "What kind of an incident?"

"A huge gunman walked into the driver's hospital room.

I managed to stop him from shooting Max, but, in the process, I got into a hell of a fight. I ended up losing him," he said in disgust. "Believe me. I'm not feeling too decent about my own defensive techniques."

"Hand to hand?"

"Kind of. I took a bullet burn across my thigh, but it's minor, and a boot to the jaw, and, with people racing to our assistance, he booked it. I did manage some good moves on him, and he'll feel our dustup as much as I am," Jackson said with a note of humor. "He'll be damn sorry he picked me. But I'm pissed I didn't get him myself. I did search, but there was no sign of him. The security videos are being studied, but, even if they see him, it won't tell them much— other than he is a giant of a man. He had on a lab coat and a black ski mask."

"Jesus," she said. "Are you all right?"

"Yeah," he said. "I am. Just goes to show you that even a guy my size can sometimes come up against someone even bigger." He sighed. "I'm pissed he got the better of me." And then he chuckled. "So was Max. He was awake and wondering why the hell somebody would try to kill him in the hospital."

"They should have had security twenty-four hours a day on them."

"They did until the brass talked to him. They figured it was just an ambush, and he happened to be the unlucky fly caught in the web."

"I wonder if they still believe that," she said. "So how bad is the bullet burn?"

He dismissed it. "It's nothing, just a scrape. I'd have taken a bullet right through my leg if it meant I'd caught him."

"Sorry."

"Nah, it's okay. I was protecting Max. That's what counts. Unfortunately, by the time I got the door open again, the intruder had already bolted down the stairs. My fault but he won't get a second chance." Jackson's voice was determined. "That's enough of that crap. And, from now on, Max has a guard."

"And the other guy?"

Jackson's voice dropped lower. "Chances are he would have gotten a bullet too, but he's in a coma, hasn't woken up from the accident yet."

"And maybe that fact alone saved him," she said softly. "Because, if he'd made any move, he probably would have taken a bullet right in the head."

"That's quite possible," Jackson admitted. "But the bottom line is, neither man can be left unattended now. Somebody is after them. We don't know who, and we don't know why, but we have to make sure the attackers don't get a second chance."

She agreed.

And then he said it. "What we also have to make sure of is that the guy who came to your door tonight is not connected. Because it just occurred to me that, if they tried to take out those two, maybe they're coming after you as well."

"NOT LIKELY." *CLICK.*

Jackson frowned, not appreciating her response. He slowly replaced his phone in his pocket and relaxed on his big easy chair. They'd been shot at on the road, the backup team attacked in a hospital and then an intruder had come to her apartment. How could she *not* consider these were all connected? It didn't mean they were for sure, but it was definitely something that had to be investigated.

He thrummed his fingers on the armchair for a long moment while he thought about his options. Would she sleep tonight? Was she even safe tonight? She'd shown she was capable of handling the situation herself, but he knew everybody, no matter how strong or how good, when coming up against a faster or bigger or more subtle foe—or multiple foes—or someone who had the element of surprise, greatly limited what she could do.

He grabbed his phone from his pocket and dialed her number. When she answered, her voice hard, angry, he snapped right back at her, "Do you have a couch?"

Surprise made her gasp. "Yes, I do. Why?" she asked.

"Because I'm coming over and spending the night on it." He hopped to his feet and walked into the kitchen, where he snatched up his keys. His wallet went into his pocket next, and, just for good measure, he grabbed a jacket. As he walked out the door, he locked it and said, "We're not taking any chances."

"You don't need to come here," she said in exasperation. "I told you that he's gone."

"What if he returns?"

Silence.

"Can you really tell me that you'll sleep tonight?"

"I don't know," she admitted, fatigue threading through her voice. "But I sure as hell was hoping to."

"Which is why I'm coming over. If nothing else, having me on the couch will make you sleep better."

"What are you now, a knight-in-shining-armor? Do you lie on the couches of every damsel in distress around the world?"

"That's a lot of couches." He laughed. "If anything happened to you, I'd be kicking myself forever. And I can't live with that."

"That guilt complex of yours needs to be pruned down," she said, her voice gaining strength.

Not that he cared. He was already in his Jeep. As he pulled up at the corner, he said, "One thing though."

"Yeah, what's that?"

"What's your address?"

At that, she laughed, great big waves of laughter, as if not only was what he'd said funny but she had needed the release. Finally she settled and gave him her address. "You know you don't need to come here though, right?"

"You know I'm going to anyway, right?"

"I live on base. How dangerous can it be?"

"I live just off base, and you've already had an intruder once tonight. What do you mean, how dangerous can it be?" he asked in exasperation. "Did you contact security? There's a whole military police force at your disposal, you know."

"I know that," she said. "And, no, I didn't call them." With that she hung up.

He tossed the phone onto the bench seat beside him and drove in the direction of the base. He cleared security and headed toward her apartment, which should be close to the main entrance. He parked in the visitor parking area and walked to the building, realized she was on the ground floor, adding to the danger level, and approached the main entryway to the complex. Checking the resident roster hanging nearby, he rang her door bell. There was a quick *buzz*, and she let him in.

He walked in her apartment building. She was waiting for him outside her front door, her arms crossed against her chest, her shoulder on the door jamb.

"You don't look like a knight-in-shining-armor," she said with a quirky grin. "No armor."

"Just a thick skin," he said good-naturedly. "Particularly when I'm around people like you."

She shrugged. "I told you that you didn't need to come."

He motioned at her to get out of the way. She turned around and walked back into her apartment. He followed, closing the door, noting she had only a simple dead bolt. "You could use better security."

"Tell the super. It's not like anybody thinks we're in a danger zone."

"No. There's an awful lot of base housing. It's quite a nice area."

"It is," she said. "I've been happy here for a year."

"When did you stop being happy?"

She shot him a look. "What makes you think I stopped?"

He chuckled. "You haven't been sleeping well for a long time."

She spun around, fisted her hands on her hips and growled. "Are you kidding me? How would you know that?"

"When I first saw you today. Bags under your eyes, that weary expression on your face, your shoulders slumped instead of standing straight up like somebody who jumps out of bed every morning with a great attitude to start the day," he said.

She shook her head. "That's just reading too much into it. Maybe I broke up with a boyfriend, and I'm really upset. Or maybe I'm dealing with some sort of a flu or cold?"

"It's possible," he said. "But, on the other hand, chances are I'm correct. Am I?"

She glared at him, walked to the closet and pulled out a

blanket, which she tossed onto the couch. "I'm only giving you a blanket because I feel like it," she muttered.

"Appreciate it," he said to her retreating back as she walked into her bedroom and closed the door.

He figured from her attitude that he had been right. That wasn't cool because, if there were any other incidents, he needed to know her backstory.

CHAPTER 5

S HE WOKE UP feeling surprisingly refreshed. She lay in bed for a long moment, wondering what was different. She remembered the intruder, and how she had tossed and turned in bed afterward, trying to get to sleep and not being able to.

Jackson. She had to smile at the thought of the big guy stretched out on her small couch. She really should have warned him. It would turn him into a pretzel in a very short time. On the other hand, she should be nice to him, at least feed him breakfast, because he was responsible for her getting some sleep last night. He was right; she hadn't been sleeping well for days.

Now she wasn't sure what to do. She couldn't see how her *visitor* could be connected to the ambush-related incidences, but enough crazies were in this world that she couldn't be too sure. Being shot at and then having an intruder at her apartment in the same day had played on her nerves. The scenario hadn't drained from her mind until she realized Jackson really was stretched out on her couch, in protective mode. She hopped out of bed, had a quick shower and dressed.

As she walked into the kitchen, she found he wasn't on the couch at all. He'd stretched out on the floor. She tiptoed as quietly as she could into the kitchen to make coffee.

His deep growly voice whispered, "Good morning."

She stopped, walked back to the living room and stared down at the big man. "Good morning. You opted against the couch?"

"My back wasn't meant to be twisted in as many tight corners as that thing would have insisted upon," he said humorously.

She grinned. "I did think maybe you would end up pretzel-shaped this morning."

"The least you can do is offer me coffee."

She turned her back on him and returned to the kitchen. "I was just about to put it on." She put a pot on to brew and then checked out the fridge. But she hadn't done any shopping in days, so her offerings were meager. She did spy bacon and eggs. She slammed the fridge shut and turned to look around the corner. He was folding the blanket and laying it on the arm of the couch. "I have bacon and eggs," she announced. "Not very much of either but enough for the two of us, if you're up for it."

His gaze lit with warm appreciation. "I don't know any guy who would turn down that offer," he admitted. "Do you have toast to go with it?"

"Of course. You want carbs, don't you?" She opened a cupboard beside her. "I have a bit of bread. Actually the bagels look better."

"Perfect. Toasted bagels to go with that would be great." He disappeared into the bathroom.

She smiled and set about making breakfast. She had the bacon simmering nicely and two cups of coffee poured when he came back out, looking a little more refreshed and awake.

"Did you get any sleep?" she asked as she turned the bacon in the pan.

He came up behind her and sniffed the aroma coming off the stove. "I did indeed. The question is, did you?"

Feeling well enough to give him that point, she nodded happily. "Absolutely, thank you. I hadn't realized how much it was all wearing me down."

"You were shot at and then had an intruder all in the same twenty-four hours," he said with a gentle squeeze of her shoulders. "It's to be expected that sleep might be hard to come by." He walked to the table, moving the coffee cups. "All set. Shall I set the table?" And with that they prepped the breakfast for the two of them.

As she sat down to their full plates, she said, "So what's next on your agenda?"

"Grilling you," he said cheerfully.

Instantly her stomach soured. She glared at him.

He motioned at the plate in front of her. "Eat. You need food."

"Then don't ruin it by saying things like that."

"Okay," he said amiably. And he plowed into his breakfast happily.

By the time they were done, she knew what was coming. It didn't diminish her enjoyment of her breakfast, but it did make her wonder if there was a way to get out from under the discussion.

She glanced at her watch. "I need to leave soon."

He reached over and covered her hand with his. "No, you don't. We need to get some answers. Just a few questions."

She groaned, then hopped up, grabbed the coffeepot and refilled their cups. "You've got less than ten minutes." She sat back down, crossed her arms over her chest and waited.

He fired questions at her. "How long have you been

bothered by this guy? How did it start? Do you have any idea who it is?"

The questions had enough variety that she realized he didn't have a clue who and what was happening here. But then why would he?

She explained about her caller, that he'd been calling for a couple weeks now.

"Do you have the phone number he's calling from?"

She pulled her phone out, brought up the number, showing it to him.

He wrote it down. "Have they increased in frequency?"

She nodded.

"Any reason to suspect your caller is your intruder?"

"No more reason to suspect that," she said, "than to suspect it might be connected to the shooting yesterday. I don't have any reason for any of this."

He nodded. "Then that's something we need to lock down. Any intuitive feeling or worry it might be somebody who has bothered you in the past? Anybody been a pain in the ass? Anything like that?"

She shook her head. "No, I've never experienced this before. Not the calls. Not the unwanted visitor."

HE WASN'T SURE if he believed her, but she obviously wasn't willing to offer any more information. He'd questioned her about the issue several times now, and she didn't budge. He shrugged and stood. "Time for me to leave." He grabbed his plate, washed it under the running water with some soap and a quick rinse, placed it in the rack, then repeated the motions with his cutlery and cup. When he was done, he finally turned around and said, "You won't be working alone today, will you?"

She turned, startled, almost dropping her cup in the process. "Do you really think it's that bad?"

"I don't know," he said. "You're not really talking. All I have to go on is you—we were shot at on the side of the road, carrying out the duties of your job, and now you have an intruder where you live. Not to mention a stalker on the phone." He gave her a hard glance. "From my perspective, that's adding up to some serious danger."

"And all three incidences could be completely unrelated," she said carefully.

He continued to stare at her. When she didn't say anything more, he shrugged and walked toward the front door. "Text me when you get to work so I know you're there and safe." He let himself out of the apartment.

She didn't say goodbye, but then neither did he.

He walked to his Jeep Wrangler—a favored personal vehicle among the SEALs—and considered his options until his phone rang. "What's up, Mason?"

"You've been unofficially assigned to the investigation," he said abruptly. "But it'll cost you a few days off."

"That's fine," he said. "What about the men in the hospital? How are they doing?"

"One is still unconscious. The other is recovering. He's under heavy guard now. There have been no new incidences."

"Well, there has been, just not one you know about." He filled in Mason on the things going down in Deli's life.

"She really thinks all that could be coincidence?" Mason asked in amazement.

"I know. Hard to believe. I'm sitting outside her apartment complex right now, waiting for her to go to work."

"You're to head to the military police station."

Jackson could hear paper rustling on Mason's end.

"You're to meet two MPs by the names of Brown and Billings. And I'm giving you advance warning. They're not impressed that you're joining them."

"What else is new?" Jackson said with a smile. He turned the keys forward in the Jeep's ignition. "I'll let you know how the day goes."

"You do that."

Just as he was about to pull into the traffic, he hit the brakes and watched Deli hop into her vehicle, reverse out of her slot and tear off toward her job. He pulled a U-turn in the middle of the street and followed her. Since he'd been keeping watch on her all night, he might as well keep watch on her a little longer.

When she pulled into the large garage where she would be working for the day, he honked the Jeep's horn, then headed on toward the military police offices. He parked, hopped out, walked into the large room and identified himself. The woman at the front counter nodded and motioned at a chair for him to sit in.

He took a seat and waited. And waited. And waited. Finally he pulled out his phone and called Mason. "Still here. I've been sitting in the front lobby, waiting, for two hours. Nobody's even willing to talk to me. I've got better things to do with my time than take this crap."

Mason snorted a short expletive. "Yeah, you might as well leave then."

After hanging up with Mason, Jackson rose to his feet, walked over to the receptionist and said, "Seeing how the two men aren't willing to even talk to me, I'll take it up with the brass when I walk out of here." He pulled out the cigarette butt and the photos of the tire tracks and laid them on the desk. "I figured they'd want these. At least I am doing something to track down the shooter."

And he turned to exit. He could hear shouts from behind him, but he ignored them and headed to his Jeep. The last thing he planned on doing was getting shafted in an investigation from supposed members on the same team. They either wanted his help, or they didn't, but he had no intention of letting the investigation go, either way. He needed to figure this out. He'd do it with their help or without. He reversed the Jeep out of the lot as men ran out of the station. He ignored them and took off. He watched in his rearview mirror, lifted a particular finger and laughed. Sometimes being a bit of a rebel felt good.

CHAPTER 6

W ORK HELD NO surprises this morning. It was Friday. Usually the best day of the week. Only not today. Too many odd scenarios from yesterday for her to have any feel-good moments today. Deli kept looking around to see if anybody was watching her. Odd, it wasn't that she felt like she was being watched, but that sensation remained, what Jackson had been talking about, that somebody was after her. And that just meant it was prudent for her to keep an eye out.

At midday, Moe, who worked alongside her, said, "What the hell is wrong with you today?"

She shot him a hard look, lay down on her dolly and slid under the vehicle, ignoring him. When she came back out looking for a different wrench, he leaned against the grill of the rig, staring down at her.

"Are you expecting an ex-boyfriend to show up or something?"

"Like hell," she said good-naturedly, sliding back underneath.

She kept working on the vehicles all day, but it was hard to focus. Her mind went off in a million different directions. Jackson had to be wrong. None of this could be related. Because, if it was, then something seriously ugly was going on. If it was just a phone caller, that was one thing. The intruder alone was another thing. But no way would she be the target for that shooting on the highway. That had to be completely different.

Maybe they were after Jackson. She knew he'd already considered that. And maybe it wasn't that they were after either of them. Could be they just happened to be in the wrong place at the wrong time. The trouble was, none of it made any sense.

By the time she wiped the grease off her hands and took off her coveralls, Moe still stood there, staring at her. She glared at him. "What's wrong with you today?"

"You," he snapped back. "You're edgy, out of sorts. You keep looking over your shoulder, like you're scared."

Her hands fisted on her hips, her stance widening, then she paused. … She considered what he'd said and then said, "Does it really look like that?"

He nodded.

"I had an intruder last night," she said slowly. "He came into my apartment building. I didn't catch him. He took off on me. I guess I'm a bit edgy."

Moe made an odd sound and straightened. He shoved his hands hard into his pockets. "And, of course, you called the cops, right?"

She just raised an eyebrow, walked over to the paper towels and dried her hands.

"You can't be the big bad female navy mechanic all the time," Moe snapped. "If I had an intruder, you know, sure as hell, I'd have called the cops."

At that, she laughed. "Yeah, you probably would. But, because I didn't have anything to tell them, there was no point in calling them."

"They have to know there's an intruder on base. You

know we've had different run-ins at various times. It's always a pain in the ass for everybody involved, but we want everybody on base to be safe, not sorry afterward."

She nodded. "I know."

"Call Billings at the military police station," he said. "He's decent. He'll talk to you."

"Maybe," she said noncommittally, not wanting to get edged into a corner where she felt like she had to do something like that. Her phone rang. She pulled it out, not sure why she expected to see Jackson's name on the ID, but instead it appeared to be her caller. She groaned, hit Off and shoved the phone back in her pocket.

"And who's that? Your new boyfriend?" Moe teased.

"Stalker," she snapped. "My life is going to hell in a handbasket." She exited the building at a rapid pace.

She hadn't gone more than a few feet when Moe grabbed her by the shoulders and spun her around. "Are you serious?" he asked incredulously.

She brushed her hair off her forehead and glared at him. "Yeah, I'm serious."

"And what's to say that intruder wasn't your stalker last night?"

She shrugged. "I don't know."

"Then get your ass down to the MPs and tell them. All of it. Or I will."

She glared at him, but she couldn't do a whole lot now that she had opened up to him. Not only was he her boss, he was also right. She shouldn't be making light of it all. It wasn't that she was doing that as much as she just didn't want to get involved in this investigation.

He gave her a hard shake. "Now. Do you hear me?"

She glared at him. "I hear you. But what if it's nothing? … Then I'm wasting everyone's time. I'll look foolish."

"Better foolish than dead." He dropped his hands and stepped back. "What if there have been other occasions of such an intruder, and nobody called?" Moe glared at her, twisting his mouth and shaking his head. "I'll be calling Billings later tonight. If you haven't contacted him, you can expect him to hear all about it from my point of view."

She gave a quick nod and angrily headed toward her vehicle. She didn't want to get involved with the police. She pulled out her phone and called Jackson instead. "My superior wants me to go to the military police," she said without any introduction.

"Good. Not sure it'll be of any help, but you need to at least report it. They can't keep data on break-ins and know about similar cases if they don't know about yours. One of the problems with serious crimes like that is so many people refuse to report them."

She listened but could hear the distraction in his voice. "Where are you?"

"Just pulled into the hospital parking lot," he said. "I'll talk to the two men, see if they have anything new to share."

"I could join you," she said instantly.

"No," he said. "You go to the MP station. I was already there. Complete waste of time for me."

"What do you mean?"

"I was assigned to the investigation. The MPs are working the case with NCIS—doing the groundwork," he said. "Yet, they wouldn't even talk to me this morning. They let me sit in the front lobby for two hours until I walked. I dumped my complaint in the brass's lap."

"I wonder how I can use that?"

"What do you mean?" he said, his voice sharper.

"I don't know," she said, warming up to the beginning of an idea in the back of her mind. Feeling better, she headed down to the MP station. When she got there, the receptionist looked up and inquired about the reason for her visit. She explained and was told to take a seat and how somebody would come and see her.

"I was told to contact Billings," she said.

"He's not here right now," the receptionist said.

"Oh. I already spoke to Jackson about this matter, so maybe I'll continue to work with him instead of you guys." She got up and walked toward to the exit.

Immediately the woman jumped up and asked, "Where are you going?"

"Jackson is part of this investigation," she said innocently, "and you guys are unavailable. I'll speak with him instead." Deli shrugged, as if to say, *What difference does it make?* Then she reached for the door.

Instantly somebody from the back room came forward and said, "What can we do for you?"

She turned to look at the man standing there. "I think I'd rather report to Jackson."

A frown crossed his face.

"I understand he's on this investigation as well," she said, "or do I have that wrong?"

The man and the woman exchanged a glance; then the man said slowly, "No, you're not wrong. But, as you can see, he's not here right now."

"He was here for almost two hours this morning," she said smoothly. "And apparently you guys wouldn't give him the time of day. So I came in here to talk to one of you, but now I've decided I'd prefer to talk to him. At least he's cooperative and available and willing to speak to me." And she turned and walked back out.

She would rather talk to Jackson anyway. If the MPs had treated him like that, she expected the same disregard too. And she didn't want anything to do with behavior of that sort either. Especially from other navy personnel. Seems sexism was alive and well in the States no matter who you worked for, but it was more pronounced in the military, she thought. She walked to her vehicle, pulled out her phone and called Jackson. "Well, they did acknowledge you're part of the investigation, but that you weren't here right now."

Jackson laughed. "They can acknowledge whatever the hell they want," he said. "As far as I'm concerned, I'm doing my own investigation."

"Good," she said. "I think I'll join you. I told them that I'd tell you all about it anyway, and, seeing that you already know what's going on, that just saved me the trouble of having to go over everything again."

"Wait. What?" Jackson asked in surprise. "You didn't tell them all the details?"

"Nope. I was asked to sit and wait. Like they did with you. I decided I had better things to do. So I told them that I was speaking to you."

A startled silence hung on the other end of the phone, and then he started to laugh. "And why would you want to stir up a hornet's nest like that anyway?"

"Why did you?" she asked, getting into her car. "We shouldn't have to demand respect from our peers, not in America, and certainly not in the navy," she said in a huff. "I'm coming to the hospital. See you in five."

She reversed out of her spot and headed toward the hospital. She parked beside his Jeep and walked in, smiling at the receptionist. She knew where she was going and took the stairs. When she got to the correct floor, she walked up the hallway to see a security guard standing watch. She smiled up at him. "May I go in and see the men? Jackson is supposed to be here already."

"He is." The guard motioned her inside.

She stepped in to see one man in bed stretched out, still obviously on the mend, with Jackson sitting beside him. "So did you spill the beans and tell him all the juicy details?" she asked the patient.

The man on the bed looked at her in surprise and then grinned. "Deli?"

She nodded. "As I recall, you're Max. I helped you fix a flat on the sly after you took a corner too fast, running into the median. You brought it to me in a panic, knowing you would get shit for it."

Max grinned and chuckled. "Quite a memory you got there, lady. That was at least three years ago. I'll have you know that I'm driving much more carefully now."

"Good to know," she said with a big smile. "Got yourself in some shit this time though, didn't you?"

"So did you," he shot back. "I understand from Jackson that the two of you got shot at before we went after them."

She nodded. "And the MPs—even their receptionist— are pissed off that Jackson had himself assigned to the investigation."

Max nodded. "I know. They don't like to share information with anybody."

"That's all right. I figured we could do a little bit of sleuthing ourselves." She reached into her pocket and pulled out a piece of paper with a license plate of a vehicle written on it. "So not only were the drivers switched out but so were the vehicles."

"Whoa. What driver are you talking about?" Jackson asked.

"Remember the driver who was hurt and you were taking his place? He was assigned a military jeep, only that was switched for the transport rig you ended up driving. Maybe it's nothing but ..."

"Are we thinking that has something to do with the attack?"

"I don't know," she said, "but, as far as anomalies go, that's a big one." She handed the note over to him. "Chester is still not back at work. Maybe we should pay him a visit. That would be the nice thing to do, wouldn't it?" she asked. "I mean, he is convalescing at home after all."

"Meaning, it's a great time to ask him some questions. I like it." Jackson hopped to his feet and turned to the patient. "We'll let you know if we find out anything."

"Do that," Max said. "This is far more interesting then lying in bed, trying to heal."

As she walked out, Deli asked Max, "How many more days?"

"I could be home tomorrow," Max said. "It depends on my ability to move freely."

"What you mean is, your ability to go wee-wee on your own," she said with a chuckle. "Funny how bodily functions always rule our state of independence." She grinned. "Let us know if you get loose of here. We can always give you a ride home."

His face lit up with a smile. "Hey, I appreciate that."

She raced after Jackson, who was already striding down the hall. She called after him, "Wait up."

He opened the door and held it for her. "Why should I wait? You would probably accuse me of being sexist and that you could open your own damn doors."

"There's never a sell-by date for manners," she said.

He chuckled. "So now we have two vehicles. Why don't you drive yours back to your place, and we'll go in my Jeep?"

She considered that, then nodded. "Sure. You can pay for the gas."

That startled a laugh out of him.

Back at her car, she hopped in and drove home. She parked in the space designated for her apartment, walked over to the Jeep as Jackson pulled up and got into the passenger side. "Do we have his address?"

"Yeah, we do. And a recent photo. He's just a block or two away from here."

Jackson pulled onto the main road and took a left, then a right. A series of apartments were up ahead.

She looked at them and said, "A friend of mine used to live here."

"Yeah, which one?"

"An old girlfriend," she said, "but she moved back East a few months ago."

He led the way to the second-floor apartment. At the door he rapped hard enough to make sure it was heard. But there was only silence inside. He rapped again and again, still getting no answer. Frowning, he pushed on the door gently, and it appeared to be closed tightly. He tried the knob, but it was locked. He glanced at her. "If he was hurt enough to stay home for two days, you'd think he'd be here."

"Or maybe he's sleeping?" she suggested. "Particularly if he is on the mend."

He nodded slowly, thought about it and then pulled a small tool kit from his pocket. He glanced left and then right, and then very quickly pulled out a thin tool and unlocked the door.

She gasped as he pushed it open.

He shot her a look and ordered, "Stay here." And he shut the door with a hard *snick* in her face.

HE KNEW ALMOST instantly. The smell of death didn't change. Always recognizable, it didn't matter what corner of the world he was in. But what he didn't know was if the man was alone or not. Careful to not touch anything, he walked through the apartment to the bedroom. There he found the driver, Chester, deceased, a nice circular bullet hole in the middle of his forehead. There were no signs of a struggle, as if maybe he had been in bed, sleeping, when the shooter arrived. Jackson walked back out into the hallway, closed the front door behind him, took his T-shirt hem and wiped the areas he had touched and said, "He's dead."

"Seriously?" She gaped at him.

He nodded. He pulled out his phone and called Mason. "Hey, the driver I switched out for? I came to ask him a few questions. I knew he shot himself in the foot, so should be home, but he didn't answer when I knocked. I picked the lock and entered the apartment to find a nice round bullet hole in his forehead."

He heard Mason's breath suck into the back of his throat. "Seriously?"

"Yeah. Now I need to get Billings and Brown in here because we have a murder to tie all this together."

"Doesn't sound like it ties anything together," Deli said from beside him. "More to the point, it's blowing things further apart."

"I'll make the phone call," Mason said. "You disappear

first."

"Okay, we'll be off the property in less than five minutes."

Jackson pocketed his phone, grabbed Deli's arm, hooked it with his, and they walked down the stairs, back out of the building to the Jeep. As soon as they were inside his vehicle, he reversed it and pulled in the closest coffee shop parking lot. Deli followed him inside, where he ordered two coffees and sat down at one of the tables near a window, overseeing the street traffic.

She leaned forward and whispered, "Why are we here?"

"Well, no way we weren't noticed at the apartment," he said, "so we might as well have a nice public place for Billings and his buddy to come question us."

"How the hell would they know we were there? Wasn't that the whole point of calling Mason?"

"It was, but, of course, cameras were in the stairwell," he said. "As soon as I saw that, I realized we couldn't hide our presence. I should have just called it in myself."

The length of time it took before the MPs arrived surprised him. It was close to an hour before Billings walked into the coffee shop and sat down across from him.

Jackson lifted the coffee cup to his lips and took another sip. They were on their third refill. "I expected you a lot earlier than this," he said.

"You could have called us yourself."

"We saw how well you do teamwork," Jackson said, nodding to Deli.

Billings snorted. "Look. Okay, so we didn't treat you the best this morning. I'm sorry about that," he said sarcastically. "We really don't like people who have nothing to do with our team nosing in on our investigations. We already have

NCIS involved. Don't need you too."

"Yeah, well, if you were doing your investigation, then you should have found this driver a hell of a lot earlier than I did."

"And you should have reported it yourself, not set Mason on us."

"I forewarned you that I'd have the brass on you. You obviously aren't talking to me anyway," Jackson said.

Just then Billings's buddy walked in and sat down with them. He glared at the two of them. "Are you done with your funny little tricks? Because you just compromised our investigation," he snapped.

"Bullshit," Jackson said. "That guy has been dead at least a day. It'd be interesting to see what the coroner says."

"Why? Cause of death is obvious."

"No struggle, no fight, lying on his back with his arms spread like that. Either he was asleep or maybe drugged."

"Why drugged?"

"Maybe painkillers? He did shoot himself in the foot. That did give him a valid reason for not driving that rig." The men digested that and then nodded.

"We'll track his whereabouts and movements that morning," Brown said.

Jackson nodded. "You do that. I imagine, once he got home, he went straight to bed and didn't get back up again. Made him a pretty easy target."

"Sure, but that still doesn't help us with the *whys*."

"No, it doesn't," Jackson said. "But, seeing as how you were not very open about your case, we won't be very open about other issues that might be related."

The men straightened and glared at him.

He shrugged and motioned at Deli. "You want to tell

them what's going on in your world?"

She sighed, sat back and relayed all the information that she had so far not volunteered.

The men stared at her. "So this might be about you?"

She shrugged. "I have no clue. For all I know, this has nothing to do with me. I've got a phone stalker, and I had an intruder."

"I think the shooter is coming back after all of us in-volved with the sabotaged military rig," Jackson said. "The expected driver was just the first one killed. Earlier last night someone came to the hospital after Max, who chased down the shooter and ended up in a ravine. And later last night somebody came after Deli at her home."

"Has somebody tried to come after you yet?" Brown asked Jackson.

He shook his head. "Not that I know of. But I haven't been home. I stayed watch at her place to make sure the intruder didn't come back. For all I know, my place was broken into."

"Well, that would be first-things-first then," Billings said. "Go home, and check it out. And stay there." His voice was hard as he said that last bit.

Jackson gave him a bland smile. "I'll do what I planned on doing right from the beginning. Getting to the bottom of this—with or without your help."

CHAPTER 7

AFTER THE TWO MPs left, Deli looked at Jackson. "I need to head home and get some food." She lifted a hand and frowned at the slight tremor in her fingers.

He reached out, grabbed her hand and held it tight. "Blood sugar or nerves?" he asked.

"Blood sugar," she said with a rueful smile. "I didn't eat lunch today."

His brows drew together in a thunderous frown.

She rushed to say, "I had it with me, but I was busy. Then, when lunchtime came, I didn't feel like eating."

He glanced at the coffee shop's menu board.

She shook her head. "No, I'm not eating here. Everything will be full of sugar."

"Well, sugar is good at this point," he said, a twinkle in his eyes.

"It is," she said, "if you're two years old."

He chuckled. "Okay, so it's great for a pick-me-up when your blood sugar is dropping, but you're right. A solid meal would be better."

"Which is why I need to go home and make some dinner," she said. "It's already late, and I want to have leftovers to take for lunch to work tomorrow."

"So what are you making when you get home?"

She wasn't sure if he was asking for an invite to dinner

or curious for his own sake. "I'm not exactly sure yet, but I think I have a steak in the fridge."

"A single steak?" he asked in mock horror.

She nodded. "I wasn't expecting company for dinner," she retorted. "And I'm still not."

His crestfallen face turned her outrage into giggles.

"Or we could hit the grocery store on the way home," he said, "and we could pick up a second steak."

She thrummed her fingers on the table as she stared at him. "Whatever we do, we need to do it fast because I'm starting to crash. I won't have much time to get some food into me after we get home."

"Barbecued, broiled, or fried?"

"If you're cooking, then barbecued." She glanced at her watch. "There might be two steaks in my fridge, but they'll be small," she warned.

"Got any rice or potatoes to go with it?"

She nodded and stood. "Come on. Let's go. Otherwise I'll have to get a cookie here to tide me over, and that'll just pick me up and drop me even further."

He was up and ahead of her, leading her to the Jeep within seconds. Flying toward her place, he said, "Do we need to go to the grocery store at all?"

She shook her head. "No, I don't think so. As long as you're not a fussy eater."

"Nope," he said. "But I do like to cook."

"Good," she said. "You're on. I'm so tired of cooking for one. It's taken a lot of the joy out of it for me."

"That's why it's always fun to go to Mason's for a barbecue with a bunch of the guys. It's much more of a social event, kind of a potluck meal, and I enjoy that more than just cooking for one myself," he admitted. "But I make a mean spaghetti sauce and chili. The trouble is, I can't make a little bit. I end up with a huge pot of it, and then I have to freeze it."

"There are worse things."

At her place she went to unlock her apartment door and froze.

He reached around, tucked her off to the side against the wall and whispered, "Stay here."

She watched as he disappeared into the apartment, the door already ajar. He came back a few minutes later as silently as he had entered. He shook his head. "It's empty."

She stepped behind him, a cry of outrage as she saw her couch and coffee table upended and drawers pulled open in the kitchen. She wandered into her bedroom to see the bedding also tossed. She stretched out her hands. "Why?"

"Good question. I was going to ask you that. Is there any chance you're hiding something that somebody wants?"

Bewildered, she turned to look at him. "No, I don't have anything. None of this makes any sense."

"Maybe planting incriminating evidence?" He grabbed her by the shoulders, and her trembling got worse.

Before he asked, she said, "This is mostly nerves now, not to mention anger."

He nodded and led her into the kitchen. "I'll light that babysized barbecue of yours and pull out the steaks. Let's get the food going, and, while everything's cooking, we'll get the bulk of this cleaned up."

And that was what they did. She clenched her jaw and pushed through her anger. She handed him the plate of seasoned and hastily marinated steaks, already had rice in the rice cooker and the beginnings of a salad on the counter when she realized he was taking pictures of everything.

"I never even thought to do that," she said ruefully.

"Doesn't matter. I did," he said. "If dinner is under control, those steaks won't need but four minutes on a side. So let's get started on cleaning this up."

He got the couch and cushions back together and the living room shaped up quickly. The kitchen had drawers open but not much tossed. It didn't take five minutes to put it all back together again.

She stood, surveying the place. "If it didn't take much time to put it back together, why bother in the first place?"

"Maybe to make it look like a robbery," he said.

"My flat-screen TV is still here," she said in exasperation.

He glanced at it and nodded. "It's a little hard to carry for one person and to make it look unobtrusive as to what he was doing."

She thought about that and shrugged. "Whatever."

She checked on the rice, finished making the salad, brought out the plates and cutlery as he walked out to throw the steaks on the grill. While he barbecued, she headed into the bedroom and straightened up her bed again. Things were askew and tossed but no real damage done. If they'd been looking for something specific, they hadn't been very thorough. Most of her dresser drawers hadn't been touched at all.

When he let her know the steaks were done, her room was mostly cleaned up. She wandered back into the kitchen, set the table, brought over the rice and salad as he took the steaks off the barbecue and set the plate down in front of her.

She sniffed the air appreciatively. "Steak is always better barbecued," she murmured.

"I'm delighted you have one," he said. "So often women

don't."

She shrugged. "I do barbecue sometimes but not often. I can't be bothered to turn it on for just me."

"I get that." He sat down opposite her. "All we're missing is a bottle of wine."

"I don't have any," she said. "There might be a beer in the fridge though."

He cocked his head to the side, his eyes alight with interest.

She laughed. "You go look. I'm starting on this steak." She stabbed the steak closest to her, moved it onto her plate, served herself a little rice and a hefty portion of salad, and dug in. The first bite was absolutely delicious. It was medium-rare; exactly the way she liked it.

He came back with the beer, holding it out to her. "Shall we share?"

She shook her head. "Back to that blood sugar thing. I need food more than I need alcohol."

He poured his beer in a glass and then sat down to tackle his steak.

When she was halfway through, she looked up at him. "Why was he here?"

He studied her thoughtfully as he chewed his steak and then said, "Right now I'm thinking, if it was your stalker, maybe he's looking for something to take away, a souvenir of you. If it was related to the other scenario and the murder of Chester, then I'm afraid it might be more of a warning or a distraction—a diversion, so to speak."

"So the intruder came in looking for something to steal and took off when he didn't find anything?"

"It tracks properly," he argued. "You had an intruder. You scared him away before he had a chance to check out your place. He takes advantage of your absence to come back and to make sure there really wasn't anything here, so he could move on and forget about you. Or maybe he took something small, so small you don't know it is missing yet."

She considered that. "I guess it's better than some options," she said.

"Exactly."

An odd thought popped up. "Is it possible that, instead of looking to steal something, he left something behind?" she said abruptly.

Across the table Jackson froze. "Like what?" Jackson's voice turned hard, cold.

"You mentioned how the shooter could be planting evidence." She winced. "I have nothing in mind in particular. It's just, if he didn't take anything …"

He slowly lowered his hands, placing his knife and fork on either side of his plate and stared at her. "What made you think of that?"

She knew he was thinking the same thing she was. He was just waiting for her to voice it. She glared at him then lowered her voice. "What if he planted a bug?"

"And why would he?"

Keeping her voice low, she leaned in closer to Jackson as she explained her thinking. "To get details on the investigation. If it's somebody on base, they could have possibly heard how you put yourself on the investigation. Or had seen us involved one way or another in it. Or had heard you were at the hospital." She waved her hand about. "And may have seen that you stayed the night here."

He cut another piece of steak, slowly popped it into his mouth and chewed it as he contemplated the idea.

"The thing is, I don't have any way to find out if he did

or not," she confessed. "I might live and work on base, but I'm not privy to that level of spy gear." She raised her gaze and studied him. In a lower voice she whispered, "But you are."

He gave a clipped nod, held a finger to his lips, picked up his phone and sent a text.

She didn't know who he sent it to but figured it was Mason.

Jackson pointed his knife at her steak and said in a normal speaking voice, "The salad and rice are delicious, by the way."

She figured that meant she should resume all normal conversation and nothing else. "It wasn't hard to create. It's a pretty easy meal." And she didn't say another word.

When their meal was finished, she cleaned up the table, while he washed dishes, when she heard his phone go off. He checked it, held his finger to his lips again and walked to the front hallway and very quietly opened the door. She peered around the corner to see who he let in. A tall male with dark hair walked in. Ironically it was the hard look in his gaze that reassured her. He knew Jackson and had come with a purpose.

Jackson walked over with his finger against his lips once more and whispered against her ear, "This is Kanen, one of my unit. He'll check out your place."

Her eyes wide, she watched as he walked around the apartment with a small handheld device. It made a funny flashing signal in the living room.

Jackson crushed her against his chest and whispered, "You were right."

She reared back and stared up at him, gasping.

He placed a finger over her mouth and whispered, "Remember, *shhh*."

They followed Kanen through her small apartment and found another one in the bedroom, but that was it.

"Interesting," Jackson said quietly.

Kanen disabled both of the bugs and held them up. "They're our own, standard military-issued bugs. That both narrows and widens the field tremendously."

"What do you mean, they're our own?" she asked suspiciously.

"They were probably taken from the base," Jackson said quietly, "by somebody who knows us."

JACKSON WASN'T SURE what to make of that finding and the fact that they had found two bugs. He studied them, locating their serial numbers.

Kanen held out his hand for one.

Jackson placed it in his palm and asked, "Can we track them?"

"I doubt it," Kanen said in a low voice. "The serial numbers have been scratched off. They could have been stolen. They could have been damaged models and taken from the garbage, then repaired. No way to know."

"And who supplies them for the military?" Jackson asked.

"That's a good point too. Just because they are the same we use doesn't necessarily mean it came from the base."

Jackson was hopeful they had a way to prove that. But the fact that it was even the same kind meant it was somebody who knew them.

"How does that help us?" Deli asked. "I presume there's no way to get fingerprints off this at this point."

The men shook their heads.

"No," Kanen said. "They're too small, and we've already handled them enough to smudge anything that might have been there."

"Of course," she said with a shrug. "But why make it look like a break-in here? That just led me to my bug-planting theory. Wouldn't it have been better to come in and to leave without anybody realizing it? Then I would never have thought to search for bugs. If nobody saw him, why cover up bug-planting with a fake break-in?"

At that Jackson grinned. "Because somebody probably did see him." He walked to the front door, opened it, stepped out into the hallway. He looked at the other doors around and said, "Which one would most likely have seen somebody come here?"

She pointed to the left. "Marsha. She's home all the time." Deli walked over to her neighbor's door and knocked on it. When an older woman with hair in a frizzy beach-wave curl opened it with a big smile, Deli said, "My place was broken into. Have you seen anybody suspicious here lately?"

"Oh, no!" Marsha shook her head. "Not at all. Of course I'm not here watching what happens in the hallway all the time," she said apologetically. "I saw your new boyfriend, but that's it."

Jackson froze. He stepped up beside Deli and asked, "You saw me?"

Marsha's gaze went from Jackson to Deli and back again. She blushed and muttered, "Sorry, Deli. I didn't realize you were playing with several." She tossed her an admiring look. "Takes balls to do that these days."

Deli groaned. "This is Jackson. He's a friend of mine, not my boyfriend," she explained. "And I don't have a boyfriend, so I don't know who this other man was."

Marsha stared at her. "Really? Because he said he was your boyfriend. He was just leaving you a surprise. He had a package with him. But I wasn't sure. It was decorated like a birthday gift or something naughty," she said with a wink.

"I *don't* have a boyfriend," Deli reiterated firmly. "So I have no idea who this guy is. Any chance you could describe him?"

Marsha leaned against the doorjamb, crossed her arms over her chest and stared up at the corner of the hallway, as if trying to remember. "Tall, slim, all dressed in black, a cap on his head, his features were more Slavic-looking."

"What do you mean by that?"

She frowned and said, "He had, like, higher cheekbones." She motioned at hers. "And they were sunk in a little. Dark eyebrows. He had a five-o'clock beard going on already. So maybe not Slavic but swarthy." She got the right word with triumph. "I guess Slavic would have been more regional—or Swedish, right?"

Jackson nodded. "Okay, did you see any distinguishing features? Did he have a big nose? Did he have gross teeth? Did he have anything on his wrists?"

She shook her head. "I hardly talked to him. I asked him what he was doing. When he explained who he was, he was really cute about it. He stammered, almost blushing. I figured he was pretty innocent. Or at least doing something that made him feel special or was hoping to make you feel special." She turned her gaze back to Deli. "This was just a couple hours ago."

Jackson studied Deli's face as she turned to look at him. He gave a clipped nod. "We can certainly take another look. It probably isn't too hidden." He knew exactly what the surprise was—bugging her apartment. But he couldn't place the person Marsha was describing. He glanced around the hall. "Of course, there are no cameras that would have shown his face either."

"Well, there is one," Deli said, "down at the far end at the doorway." She looked at Marsha. "He didn't ring outside the apartment building, did he?"

She nodded. "Yes, but he identified who he was and how he was trying to leave you a present. He had it in his hand." She held her hand up, making the shape of a box about four inches by six inches. "But it was all wrapped up. So I figured it was totally okay."

"How did he get in her apartment?" Jackson asked.

"That's the thing. That's how I knew it was okay too," Marsha said gaily. "He had a key. He said it wasn't working outside on the apartment door, but then half the time ours don't either, do they?" She shared a comical grin with Deli. "But he did get into the apartment with it, so I figured it was no big deal. Then I came inside and made a cup of tea."

"You didn't hear any banging or anything going on?"

Marsha shook her head. "No, but I was doing some vacuuming and had my talk shows on, and you know I get really focused on those. Besides, if there was any banging, I would have just assumed you'd come home."

Jackson caught sight of Deli's face turning beet red.

Marsha just laughed and turned to head back inside. "And speaking of TV shows," Marsha glanced at her watch, "my favorite is about to start. So if you don't mind ..." And she closed the door in front of them.

"How do we get a copy of the images from the camera at the doorway?" she asked as they headed back into her apartment.

"Kanen is probably already on it," Jackson said.

"How can he be on it?" she asked.

"It's just a feed," Kanen said from the living room, where he sat with his laptop open and his legs propped up on the coffee table. "No different than any other. Easy to access if you know where it's coming to or from. But I can pretty well assure you that your intruder's not looking directly at the camera."

"But he would be though, wouldn't he?" she argued. "If he called Marsha and asked to be let in?"

The two men looked at her, and then Kanen started clicking on the keyboard. "If he did, I'll find it," he said. He glanced around the living room. "The place couldn't have been tossed too badly, if you got it already sorted out again."

"It was bad enough that I don't want to see it any worse, but it was doable." She slumped down on the couch beside him. "I feel useless. Isn't there anything I can do?"

"I want a list of everybody in your life, present and your recent past," Jackson said. "Anyone who might have access to the keys to your apartment."

She wrinkled her nose. "Hardly anyone."

"Well, *hardly* doesn't mean no one, so ..." Jackson grabbed a piece of paper from the table, checked the other side, saw it was blank on the back side, flipped it over, handed it to her and gave her a pen out of his pocket. "*Everyone.* Any friends you've given a key to for safekeeping. Any men you've given keys to use at night. Your intruder got a key from somewhere. I want to know where your keys are normally kept, etc."

She groaned and wrote down names. He watched as three made the list, and then she sat back and studied the names and shrugged. "None of these people would care to come into my apartment to plant bugs."

"Of course they wouldn't," he said. "But that doesn't mean other people didn't get access to your keys through them. With that, it's easy enough to get copies made."

Startled, she looked at him. "But that could be just about anybody at work. Because I wear mechanics overalls throughout the day, I keep my purse in a locker."

"Is it locked?"

She shook her head. "No, we're assigned lockers. It's just a few of us. So no need to lock up my purse. I don't keep anything valuable in there."

"Credit cards, money?"

She shrugged and shook her head. "No. Usually only my lunch bag. … And my keys."

"Then write down who you work with as well and put down beside that person's name that he's an employee with access."

She shook her head but obeyed. When she was done, she handed him the piece of paper and pen. "I still don't think any of these men would have had anything to do with it."

"No, I doubt it too," he said. "But the fact of the matter is, you have a stalker, and we have a murderer. We can't take any chances."

"You make it sound like these are two separate people."

He studied her for a long moment. "I can't figure out how they could be related, unless you are holding out on me." He paused, but she only rolled her eyes. "At the same time, if we treat each as a separate person, we'll get a little further in terms of who's doing this. The more they do, the more we see what it is they're up to, and the easier it will be to catch him or them."

"Why?" she asked. "It's not like fingerprints were left

here. So that's a dead end. We found the bugs and turned them off or whatever. As far as you know, they're military issue, the same kind we use on base. That doesn't lead us anywhere either."

"But this does," Kanen said as he flipped the laptop around for her to see.

She leaned forward to see a grainy photograph of a man standing at the front door to the building. His hood was pulled over his head, and he leaned slightly toward the side, where she knew the speaker was for the outdoor intercom. "I don't recognize him, but it might be the man who knocked on my door last night," she said slowly. "Still, I have no clue who that is."

CHAPTER 8

B UT THERE WAS something about him. She had a hard time trying to figure out what it was but considering the number of people she sees on a daily basis that wasn't unusual. "I want to recognize him, but I don't," she added slowly.

"Are you sure?" Kanen asked.

Jackson just glared at her.

She glared back at him. "What? So I don't recognize him, and that puts me in trouble?"

"He knows you," he said. "So chances are you know him. Something about the way he tilts his head, the line of his jaw. Something in there is familiar."

"Maybe," she said. "But it's not triggering right now."

He nodded and hopped to his feet. "How about coffee?"

She shook her head. "Not this late. I'll never sleep."

Kanen looked up and said, "If coffee is happening, I'll have a cup."

Instead of Jackson putting it on, she rose, walked into the kitchen and put on a small pot. The last thing she needed was more stimulation. What she needed were answers. There was *something* about that man in the photo. But she just couldn't place him. "I don't understand why this guy, if he's the stalker, would be planting bugs."

"No, neither do I," Jackson said. "It would make more

sense that this guy was connected to the ambush and subsequent murder." He turned to look at her and held out his hand. "May I have your phone?"

She pulled her phone from her pocket, swiped it to unlock it and handed it over to him. "Why?" she asked.

"So we can track your stalker." He handed it to Kanen, then glanced back at her. "Do you remember any of the phone number?"

She gave him the area code and the first three digits.

Kanen found it almost immediately. He said something about tracking backward for the number.

"How do you guys know how to do all that?" she asked in amazement as she sat down beside Kanen again.

With both the laptop and her cell phone beside him, Kanen busily checked out owners of that phone number. Suddenly he stopped, looked at her and said, "Do you know a James Carville?"

"James? Yeah, I work with him," she said. "Why?"

Kanen twisted the laptop so she could see the number and the name it was currently registered to.

She stared at the name and shook her head. "But I work with him. Why would he be doing this?"

Instead of making her feel better, it made her feel a hell of a lot worse. She stared at the two men in her apartment, then got up abruptly and walked into her bedroom. She threw herself down on the bed and stared up to the ceiling. She thought about all the times she had come across James, when they had stopped and had lunch, or he'd brought her coffee every once in a while. She'd returned the favor. But he'd never asked her out, never made it seem like he cared for her in any way. So why was he tormenting her on the phone? And was it connected with the ambush and the murder, or was it just a sick mind having fun?

She hopped off the bed after a few moments, walked out to the living room and stood, glaring at the two men. "Are you sure there's no mistake?"

Kanen shook his head. "No, there's no mistake. That phone is registered to him. Now the question is whether somebody else is using his phone to call you."

She glommed onto that idea. "That's possible, isn't it?" She smiled at the thought. "Maybe he has no clue."

"But it would have to be somebody close to him, and you did say it was a male caller, correct?"

She nodded her head. "Yes, as far as I could tell, it was a male."

"Does James live alone?"

"I don't know," she muttered. "I don't think we've ever had any personal conversations at that level."

"Maybe it's time," Kanen said. "But don't let him know you're on to him."

She nodded thoughtfully. "We also leave our phones in our lockers sometimes. I leave mine in my pocket, but most of the time I can't access it because of the mechanics' overalls. We're also not supposed to be talking on the phone at work. Hazardous to our job and focus."

"Is he a mechanic?"

She nodded. "He works in one of the garages. But we don't work together."

"But you've been back and forth between the navy garages to see him, know who he is?"

"Oh, yeah," she said. "He towed in the rig that morning after the shooting. He's brought me a coffee every once in a while. I've done the same for him. But it's not like we're friendly outside of work. We're in the same meetings sometimes."

"What about one of the other guys? Any chance somebody might be working with both of you and used his phone?"

She shrugged. "I have no clue. How would I know that? That's something only he could answer. Although some of the calls have been in the evening. So, unless he doesn't have his phone with him, or he's living with somebody, or left his phone somewhere, there's no way it could be anybody but him."

"It might be time to pay him a visit then," Jackson said.

She frowned. "I thought you just said to find out at work tomorrow, without letting him know I know anything."

"I did," he said, "but now I'm thinking maybe it's better if we step this up and put a stop to it right now."

Kanen looked at his watch, looked at the coffee that had just been delivered in front of him and said, "If we could take that to go, we could visit him right now."

Jackson checked the time. "It's past ten o'clock." He frowned, took a sip of his coffee. "Why don't we finish the coffee and then go?"

Kanen nodded. "Like you, I'd much rather find out what the hell is going on with this guy tonight."

Jackson glanced at Deli. "Do you want to come with us?"

She opened her eyes wide in surprise, but inside she was torn about resolving her problem, at the same time not getting James in trouble. What if it had nothing to do with him? "I really don't want to see him."

"In a case like this, it's much better to face him head-on," Jackson said.

HE WATCHED HER face twist in dismay. He understood her reticence, but she was better off bringing this situation to a close. "At least if we can get *this* problem solved, we'll know it's not connected to the rest. We do need to know if he's connected to these bugs too."

She nodded, stood, walked into the bedroom and grabbed a sweater. It wasn't that it was a cold night, but she felt chilled at just the thought of what was coming. She returned to the living room and said, "I presume with your superspy skills, you already know where he lives."

Kanen nodded. He took a big sip of his coffee, finished the cup, set it down and stood with his laptop. "I think Jackson is correct. This is our next stop, even if it is late."

Jackson led the way to his vehicle. With all of them in, he pulled the Jeep out of the parking lot and asked Kanen, "Where to?"

Kanen gave him directions off base.

"Interesting he doesn't live on base. He could be in single quarters, I presume?" Deli said.

"He may not live alone," Kanen said.

Ten minutes later they pulled up outside James's apartment building. As they walked up, Deli looked up and asked, "What floor is he on?"

"He's on the second floor," Kanen said. "Why?"

She pointed up to where a man was sitting with a beer out on the corner balcony. "James, is that you?"

James stood, leaned over the railing and said, "Deli? What are you doing here?"

"Yeah, it's us. Can we come up for a minute?"

He stared at her in surprise, then shrugged. "Sure, whatever. What are you doing here?" When he got no answer, he went inside and hit the buzzer to let them into the apartment building. He was outside his front door when they walked toward him. He smiled at her, took a look at the two men with her and his face turned belligerent. "Who are these guys?"

"Well, I got myself in a bit of a pickle," she said. "Not knowing how else to handle the situation, I asked for help. They're helping me."

Immediately James turned solicitous. "I'm sorry to hear that. Come on in."

With all of them in his small apartment, he motioned at the chairs. "There's barely enough seating."

She grabbed an armchair and sat down. The two men sat on the couch. She glanced around and said, "It's small, isn't it?"

He nodded. "It is indeed. But it's just me here, so whatever." He sat down on the single chair left. "So what's this about?"

She didn't know where to start. She glanced at Jackson, who gave her a slight nod, and he said, "Part of the problem is that we have two issues going on in Deli's life. One—my vehicle was shot in the radiator. I ended up pulling it off to the side of the road, and Deli came back to see what was wrong with the vehicle. While we were there, somebody drove past and sprayed us with gunfire. But you know that part..."

"Yes, I picked her up. Deli, are you doing okay now??" James asked her.

She nodded reassuringly. "I am. But then two guys from the military went after the shooter's vehicle, and they were found, both alive but injured, their vehicle rolled into a ravine. Since then, we found another guy connected to this whole scenario was murdered."

She took a deep breath as James stared at her in confusion. "So we're trying to separate two different problems—one, which is this nasty shooting and murder issue, and …" She glanced at Jackson, and he just stared at her steadily. She looked at James. "And a man who keeps calling me at different times of the day and night and isn't very nice in what he says."

Instantly the color drained from James's face. He stared at her and then at the two men. At that moment Kanen opened his laptop to the page he had ready and turned his laptop so James could see the list of calls he'd made to her phone.

James sagged back against the chair and reached up, running his fingers through his hair. "Shit."

"So you can see why we might be here," Jackson said. "I have to know for sure if you're connected with the murder and putting several of our men in the hospital." His voice was hard. "And I want to know why the hell you're terrorizing Deli."

James just stared at Jackson but didn't say a word.

"James, was that you?" Deli asked. "I went through all the possibilities." She kept her voice in a low tone. "I was thinking maybe somebody else had used your phone. But these guys seem to think it was you. I really need to know the truth. I've got enough going on in my life that I need to at least solve this."

He looked at the laptop facing him but appeared unable to speak.

And she knew. Her heart sank. She glanced at Jackson, and he nodded.

Jackson looked at James and said, "So now that we know

it was you …"

Instead of answering, James bolted out of his chair, raced out the apartment door and out of the building. The three of them sat in his apartment and stared after him.

Kanen said, "Damn. I hate when that happens."

Deli looked at him in surprise. "When what happens?"

"When a suspect does something I didn't count on." He stood slowly. "It's not like he can run anywhere," he said. "We know who he is and where he lives. The rest is just details." He turned to look at them. "I suggest you contact the military police, get them to handle this, and also, contact James again in the morning. I don't know how far he'll run or for how long, but I highly doubt he'll return anytime soon."

CHAPTER 9

THE NEXT MORNING Deli woke bright and cheerful. Just knowing it had been James who had been calling her … Jackson was right, it was a huge relief. To think she'd been worrying about all manner of things when it was a harmless coworker playing mind games with her. She understood James's panic, but he had brought it on himself. That had nothing to do with her. And it was really karma if he was panicked. For he'd caused her lots of worry too. What she really needed to do was figure out if that was related to her intruder and the bugs. Somehow she thought not.

But James did have the same access she had on base. He might have friends, somebody in the supply department. She didn't know.

She hopped out of bed, had a quick shower, walked into the kitchen and found Jackson already up with a pot of coffee started. She smiled at him. "Nice house guest. You help around the place."

He nodded. "I aim to please." He wiggled his eyebrows at her, and, in imitation of Groucho Marx's voice, he said, "You could try my other skills too, you know?"

She chuckled, not for an instant taking him seriously. "Not likely," she said. "I know all about Mason's group. No way I'm getting involved with any one of you."

His lips quirked. "I have to admit Mason's reputation is

pretty impressive. I'm not sure everybody thinks it's a bad thing though."

"Maybe not," she said, "but that doesn't make it a good thing either. At least not in my book."

"You don't want a relationship?" he asked curiously.

She tilted her head, studying his face, looking for any sign of disappointment or some emotion attached to that question, but all she got was a bland, flat tone of voice. That in itself was a giveaway. She smiled at him. "I haven't been looking, but, if I trip over someone who makes me forget where I am and what I'm doing, so I only want to be with him, then maybe."

"Wow, that's an interesting way to look at it," he said. "I can't say I've ever considered a partnership to be like that."

"I'm not sure it always is," she said, "but I want a partnership to be more than what I currently have all by myself. I don't want it to take away anything I have. We need to be as good as or better together than what we have individually."

He nodded. "Agreed there. Just hadn't expected somebody to want to be transported to another world just by being in a person's presence," he said teasingly.

She rolled her eyes at him. "I'm hardly a schoolgirl looking for her next crush." She laughed and opened the fridge, looking inside. "Still didn't go grocery shopping."

"No, but you do have enough to make pancakes, if you're up for that," he said.

She frowned over the top of the fridge door. "You're asking me to make you pancakes?" she asked suspiciously. "You haven't tried my pancakes."

He was at her side in an instant. "Actually I was asking if you'd let *me* make pancakes," he said eagerly. "I love to cook. We already went over that part. Remember?"

She nodded and made a waving motion with her hand. "Be my guest."

He headed for the cupboards where she had bowls and pulled out flour and the last of the eggs.

She watched in amazement as he very quickly, and with no recipe, had a bowl of batter. "You have made these a few times," she said. "I wish I liked to cook more."

"I think being alone tends to diminish our enjoyment of stuff like that. I mean, really, it's hard to make pancakes for one person. You make one pancake. That's a letdown."

"On the other hand," she said, "it's fast."

He nodded "That it is."

As she watched, he had a frying pan heating up and soon flipped golden pancake circles onto their uncooked side. When she realized she hadn't done anything to help, she set the table, refilled their coffee and brought out butter, jam, and honey for the pancakes. Then she turned and said, "I don't have maple syrup."

He nodded. "I know. I saw that. But pancakes with jam and honey are great too."

Within minutes they both sat down to a stack of pancakes each. Another stack was on a plate in the middle of the table. She looked at it and said, "I hope those are for you."

"I hope they are too." He flashed her a wide grin and took a large bite. He sat there for a moment with his head cocked to the side as he chewed, then gave a decisive nod. "They're good." And he cut into the rest of his stack.

She was a whole lot more cautious with her bites. But he was right; they were good. Then she realized that was such a mild word. "They're delicious," she muttered around a mouthful. "It's been a long time since I had homemade pancakes."

"They're pretty simple to make," he said.

She didn't bother trying to keep up a conversation. She was too ravenous. Maybe it had something to do with their evening visit last night; maybe it was just falling into bed dead tired, but she inhaled the pancakes to the extent that she looked at the stack remaining, wondering if he'd split them.

He grinned, took the top two off the stack and put them on her plate. "See if you can eat these before you go after the rest," he said.

She chuckled. "I'll eat these and not any more, so you go ahead and finish the rest."

He didn't wait for her to change her mind. He stabbed his fork through the four remaining pancakes and dragged them onto his plate.

When she was done, she sat back and smiled. "Any update on James?"

He shook his head. "Nope. But we need to go to the MP station and talk to them this morning."

"Should have done it last night," she said.

"Should have, could have, would have. If he'd stuck around, we wouldn't have had to," he said, "unless you want to press charges."

"If he lays off now," she said, "no, I don't need to. But I really don't want him taking off and doing this to somebody else."

"He's already taken off," Jackson said. "What we need to do is make sure he doesn't do something stupid."

As she sipped her coffee, watching him finish the pancakes, she wondered about the stupid men in his world of peers, and then she realized James might feel cornered and could take a step that was seriously stupid. With that in her mind, she pulled her phone toward her and dialed his number.

"James, answer me," she whispered.

She watched as Jackson slowly put down his knife and fork, staring at her in surprise. But the phone in her ear rang and rang. She frowned, turned off the call, looked at the number on the screen and then redialed it.

"Just on the off chance he might answer me," she said. "I don't want to be responsible for him committing suicide."

Jackson nodded approvingly as he reached for his coffee cup and took a sip.

The phone rang again and again. She frowned, stopped the call again and placed the phone on the table beside her. "I don't feel very good about this," she said.

"What do you want to do?"

She stared at him. "I want to go back to his place."

He nodded, straightened up from the table, collected the dirty dishes, rinsed them in the sink and loaded them in the dishwasher. He turned to look at her. "Then let's go."

For a moment she was disoriented, and then she remembered. "It's Saturday, isn't it?" She grinned at his nod. "I forgot. I thought I had to go to work today." As she thought about that, she wondered if it changed the scenario with James. "I wonder if he has a place to run to or to hide or to just get away from it all on the weekends. Because that would make the most sense right now."

She grabbed her purse and sweater, and then the two of them walked out to his Jeep. She got in the passenger side and thought about all the things she knew about her coworker. She didn't know him all that well, but she remembered him talking about going to his mother's and looking after her place. She told Jackson that, and he nodded.

"Most of us have places we like to go to, but, if we don't know where his mother's place is, that doesn't help much."

She was silent the rest of the way to James's place.

When they pulled up to the apartment parking lot and got out, she had a sinking feeling. "I really don't like this now."

Jackson looked at her sharply and reached out a hand, and eagerly she placed hers in his. Then they walked into the apartment building, up the stairs to the second floor. At James's apartment door, she stopped. A yellow crime-scene tape was spread across his doorway. Her breath caught in the back of her throat, and she could hardly swallow.

Just then two men stepped out and stared at them. Jackson stepped forward, identified himself and said, "We came here looking for James."

"Well, you found him," the first man said, his arms crossing over his chest. "What's your business with him?"

Jackson looked at Deli and explained.

"And yet, you didn't call us?" the man said in disbelief.

"We were going there this morning," Deli admitted. "But I had this horrible feeling. I've called him a couple times, and I decided we should come here first."

The men studied her for a long moment. "May I see your phone please?"

She pulled out her phone, swiped it to the right to open it and showed the MP the history of her calls to James.

"You must make a full official report. I also need you to verify where you were last night."

She stared at the open doorway, her stomach sick. "He's dead, isn't he?"

The man nodded. "Yes, he is. But he didn't commit suicide."

JACKSON WALKED A step closer, put his arm around her shoulders and tucked her up close. "You're not responsible. You didn't do this."

She stared up at him wordlessly, tears already forming in the corner of her eyes. "The last we saw of him"—she turned to face the detective—"he raced out of the apartment. Whether ashamed or shocked or he just didn't know how to react, I don't know. We left soon afterward." She motioned at the doorway. "Have you identified him? Could I at least see to make sure it's my friend?"

"Friend?" He narrowed his gaze at her. "That's an interesting relationship you have there."

"I worked with him, saw him occasionally. I had no clue he was my phone stalker," she said. "I could have been friends with him, certainly more than we were, if I'd realized he wanted something more as friends. But I could never have been his girlfriend. I just didn't feel that way about him."

The man walked back inside the apartment, conferred with somebody else and then called out to her to come inside.

She walked in and gasped. Indeed, it was James. He lay on the living room floor on his back, his face to the ceiling and a bullet hole in his forehead. "Oh, my God."

"Can you confirm his identity?"

She looked at Jackson. They both faced the detective and nodded. "That's James."

She covered her mouth with her hands, turned and walked out in the hall.

He knew she had to clear her head, get that image out of

her mind. Hell, so did he. Although she'd asked to identify the body, that didn't make the reality any easier. James might have been playing games that had hurt and terrorized her, but she was all heart inside. She'd not wish for his death.

Jackson watched her with concern as she paced back and forth in the hallway, faster and faster. Finally he pulled her into his embrace and just hung on. And then she started to cry. He held her close and let her bawl.

He looked back at the two men. "Can we go to the station later and give you our statements?"

After handing over his phone number and address, confirming his ID, the police let them leave. Jackson moved Deli along to his Jeep, and, once inside, he sat there for a long moment, wondering what his next move was. And then he knew.

He pulled out his phone and called Kanen. He studied Deli, who sat in the corner, no longer crying but just staring, lost in her thoughts. When Kanen answered, Jackson said, "James was shot sometime during the night in his own apartment."

He heard Kanen suck in a breath and asked, "Did you see him again after last night?"

"No. I went straight to bed, and I've only been up maybe an hour," Kanen said, yawning. "I wasn't alone last night myself."

"Good," Jackson said. "It'll make it easier for the police to believe you didn't have anything to do with it."

"I didn't, so that's not a problem," Kanen said. "But that really tangles things up again, doesn't it?"

"It does indeed," Jackson said, "I was pretty happy with the idea we could at least take the phone calls out of the equation. But for him to be killed just like Chester was …"

"I know. Are you guys heading back to your place or her place?"

"I'm taking her to my place," Jackson said. "We need to get more intel on this James guy."

"The bodies are piling up," Kanen said. "I'll fill in Mason on this."

"Do that." Jackson hesitated, looked at his watch and said, "We'll swing by the hospital first. See if we can talk to Max or if Barney has regained consciousness. We'll be at my house in two hours."

"See you there."

"Will do." He pocketed his phone, started up the Jeep and drove toward the hospital.

As he pulled into the parking lot, he checked out Deli. She looked better now but still upset. "Are you up for this?"

She nodded and hopped out of the Jeep. "Absolutely. But I really hate to think James was involved in the rest of this."

"We don't know that he was," Jackson said. "Last night we didn't think he had anything to do with it. But I have to admit, his murder does change things."

Holding hands, they walked through the hospital and took the elevator up to the floor where the two men were staying. The security guard was still outside. That was a good thing. But did these guys have any idea they were potential links to the case?

Jackson stopped where the officer stood, identified himself and then rapped on the door. When Max called out, "Come in," Jackson opened the door, grinned and said, "You up for visitors?"

Max smiled. "I'm glad you could brighten my day. I can't wait to get out of here. I'm not that badly hurt. Why the hell are they keeping me?" His words came out in a rush, as if hoping somebody would give him answers. And then he caught sight of Deli. He smiled and said, "At least you brought me a pretty visitor."

They sat down on nearby chairs, and Jackson brought Max up to date on the death of the original driver and of James.

"James who? James Carville? I don't have a clue who that is." He stared at Jackson and then at Deli, frowning. "How do these pieces fit together?"

"We're still working on them." Jackson looked around at the room. "I presume you're staying here for security reasons, not for your health."

"To the best of my knowledge, I'm very healthy. Well, outside of the fact my shoulder is still healing. But I could be convalescing at home."

"And where's home?" Deli asked.

"Off base with my wife and two kids. They're concerned as to why Daddy doesn't get to come home." He looked over at Jackson.

Jackson could see the nervousness in his eyes.

"I get the feeling the MPs think I had something to do with this."

Deli jumped to her feet. "What? You crashed on purpose? Got yourself shot somehow? It's not like you could have shot yourself." She was thunderstruck and outraged on his behalf.

Jackson reached out a calming hand, had her sit back down again, so the guard didn't come in and remove them. "I suspect it's more about keeping you safe," he said.

"I hope so." But Max didn't look convinced. He motioned at the door. "And Barney there, he's not even awake yet. I'm not sure he'll ever wake up."

That was a sobering thought. And it would add to their body count unfortunately.

"They weren't able to find that vehicle or the man who shot you, or his cohort, and we don't know who killed the other two men."

"Which really means, we know jack shit," Max said in disgust. "I suppose the military police aren't letting you in on anything."

"I'm supposed to be attached to the investigation," Jackson said, "but they haven't shared anything with me. Now they'll use my visit to James last night as a reason not to. Plus I was the one who found the driver dead. They'll try to put me on the suspect list just to keep me out of the loop."

Max nodded. "You have to admit, from their perspective, that makes sense."

"Only because they're too lazy to look any further."

They left soon afterward. Jackson stopped at Barney's side. The man appeared to be sound asleep. Jackson didn't understand how comas worked, but this man looked more asleep than unconscious. Maybe that was normal. He waited for a long moment, studying the man's eyes to see if he was in REM sleep, but there was no movement. And again Jackson didn't know if that was normal or not.

Frowning, he motioned for Deli to leave ahead of him. Outside he stopped and asked the security guard if there had been any other visitors.

The guard looked at him curiously. "Just Max's wife."

Jackson leaned forward and said, "Two men have been murdered over this incident. Stay alert."

The security guard nodded. "Always."

Jackson and Deli walked outside to the Jeep again. Their

visit hadn't taken very long, and he still had an hour to kill before Kanen came over to his place. He looked at Deli, but she looked the worse for wear. He hopped back into the Jeep and drove around to the Coronado Beach, stopped at one of the parking spots and held out a hand. "Let's walk for a little bit, get some fresh air on our faces."

Eagerly she jumped out of the Jeep, and together they walked to stand at the water's edge.

"I don't hate him, you know."

"Of course you don't," he said. "I don't know what he was up to with the calls, and I don't know where it would have gone. But, because we don't have those answers, remember him as the coworker you used to know."

She squeezed his fingers. "Thank you. That's an easier way to consider it."

And then silently they turned and walked along the beach, neither saying anything, just enjoying the moment. When they got down a good mile from their parking spot, she said, "We need to trace the families."

He stopped for a moment, then walked slowly back toward the way they'd come. "Meaning, to see if there was a connection between Chester, Max, and James?"

"There's an awful lot of *personal* in this. Maybe it has nothing to do with the military at all. Maybe they all knew each other or are related in some way, belong to some group together."

"We should definitely see if they have anything in common," he said.

"We can set up a time line when we get back, and we'll do a family tree for each of them as well."

And that was what they did. Now at his place, which they'd tested and found clean of bugs, he brought out a large poster board. He put it up on the wall and then started genealogy research on each of them.

By the time Kanen arrived, they had already done Max, Barney, and James, now working on Chester. Kanen stepped in, looked at the board and whistled. "Oh, that's a good idea. Should also go into their hobbies and any clubs they belong to."

"I've got Max's phone number. We can call him at the hospital and see if he belongs to any clubs or has any hobbies. Even sports."

Up went another poster board as they tried to track hobbies. Kanen sat down to do computer work on both James and Chester and, through social media sites, found out both were involved in the popular forums, both having accounts and responding to a lot of various posts. There didn't appear to be a trend. Just active on Facebook, active on Instagram, posting a lot of photos of various things they did. But always alone.

"So both of them were alone. That makes Max the odd man out here because he has a wife and two daughters."

"And his wife has visited the hospital, the security guard said," Deli pointed out.

"What about Barney? Anybody know anything about his family history?"

"Single, never married, no children listed," Kanen said.

"What's the chance they belong to a singles club or an online dating program?" Deli asked, turning to look at Kanen excitedly. "Is that possible?"

Kanen shrugged. "Well, I can check a few." And he bent back to his laptop.

She turned to Jackson. "There has to be something that connects them."

"They could be car hobbyists or something," Jackson reminded her. "James worked with you. So obviously mechanics was an interest. What we don't know is what Chester's interests were. And they may have nothing to do with Max and Barney."

"Well, there was the shooting. That's a pretty common thing between them," she said drily.

"But," Jackson added, "Barney was bent over in the truck. The shooter may not have even known he was there."

Deli nodded. "It would be nice if we had the bullets. Will forensics let us know if the shots came from the same gun?"

"I'll give Mason a call to see if he can wrangle that information. But I doubt that type of forensic information will be released until trial." Jackson pulled out his phone and dialed Mason.

When he explained the favor, Mason said, "It's probably way too early, but I'll get on it."

Jackson put his phone back on the table and heard his stomach grumble. "So maybe it's my turn to provide lunch," he said. He looked around the kitchen, realizing he didn't have much food. "When we're at Mason's, we'll fire up the barbecue and throw something on it."

"If we're at my place," Kanen said, "it would be pizza all the way."

"It's my turn to make a meal." Deli turned and walked back into the kitchen. "Provided I can find something, that is."

Kanen looked at Jackson and raised an eyebrow. "Sounds good."

Jackson shook his head at Kanen, murmuring, "Don't go there."

CHAPTER 10

D ELI WORKED AWAY in the kitchen, making sandwiches. There hadn't been a whole lot of choice otherwise. But, with the men talking cheerfully behind her, and everybody pulling together as a team, she managed to create enough sandwiches to fill them up. She carried a large cutting board into the living room and set it down on the coffee table. The men stared at the stack she had created and cried out in joy.

"Oh, wow, there's enough to feed us," Kanen said. "Hey, Jackson, she's a keeper."

Expecting some snappy response back, she was surprised when she glanced over at Jackson's face to see a thunderous frown as he glared at his friend. Kanen, on the other hand, had a big smirk on his face as he picked up the sandwich closest to him. It was obviously an inside joke. She wasn't sure what it would take to become an insider herself, but she was happy to be included at this point and to help solve this nightmare.

James still caused her distress when she thought about him. She knew it was stupid. She didn't even know him that well. But to think he'd been involved somehow and then had died for something he'd done, it was just difficult to process. She really wanted to make sure Max stayed safe. Not to mention Jackson and Kanen.

As she ate a sandwich, she studied the wall full of Jackson's pictures of family and friends. "Are we considering what military groups and teams they might be on?" she asked.

Jackson looked at her and frowned. "Such as?"

"Clubs, sports competitions, that kind of stuff. You know? The base is a whole city in itself. What about medical? It's not that they'd be part of a club, but they could have used the same doctor. For all you know, one of them managed to see a specialist and the other didn't, or one got something paid for that the other didn't. Same for education," she said. "I know James was trying to get training to work higher."

"What do you mean by *higher*?"

"Literally. *Higher.* He wanted to work on helicopters. But he was a truck mechanic."

"So then you're suggesting maybe somebody else also wanted to be a helicopter mechanic and may have gotten there before him?" Kanen asked doubtfully.

"No, I mean, maybe somebody else got funding that he didn't get. Maybe the other guy doesn't even know anything about him. Maybe James just got pissed off and said something to the wrong guy, or said that, you know, the other guy didn't deserve it. Who knows?"

"I would admit that something like that is definitely possible if we were talking about only one murder," Kanen explained. "It just seems like a stretch, considering all the scenarios."

"Let's think back to that day when I pulled into the truck stop and somebody shot the vehicle I was driving," Jackson said. "That seemed very targeted. I highly doubt anybody knew I would be driving it. So it was either targeted at Chester, who is dead, or it was random."

"Maybe they wanted to take Chester out at that spot. Maybe they were supposed to be part of a rendezvous and take him out down the road. He was supposed to drive that rig, not you."

Jackson froze. "Actually," he said, speaking slowly, trying to remember the details of what he'd heard. "I'm pretty sure another guy, a friend of Chester's, was supposed to drive it in his place. At least he volunteered too."

"Do you remember who it was?" Kanen asked. "Why are you just remembering this now?"

"I overheard a random conversation as the truck was loaded. I never heard a name," Jackson said. "But I do remember a face. Tall, dark hair …"

"Then we need to find out who in Chester's circle is tall and has dark hair. Which unfortunately is likely to be a lot of people."

"What was the truck carrying?" Deli asked. "Maybe they were hoping to divert the truck or its contents."

"I don't know specifically what my rig carried," Jackson said. "I was asked to drive it back to base. I hopped into it, started the engine and pulled in behind the convoy."

"And we never checked it the entire time we were there either, did we?" Deli asked.

"No, I never did," he said. He put the half sandwich down on his plate and settled back in his chair. "That would imply that somebody, such as this friend who volunteered, had set up a rendezvous. And, when they realized it was the wrong driver, they shot the vehicle, hoping to ambush it."

"Which they did, but I'd already gone back to help you. So, instead of ambushing you, they would now have to deal with me too. And that might have pushed them a little bit too far. They took off, hoping maybe the gunfire would chase us away. Instead it brought more military down on their backs, which they dispatched quite easily."

"We need to know what was in the back of that truck," Kanen said.

"Even better," she said, "I might be able to get into the truck. I wasn't allowed to be there, but I checked it to see if there was more engine damage. I was concerned with the mechanics of the vehicle," she said in disgust. "I never once checked to see what was in the back of the truck."

"You also can't count on the fact that whatever was in the back would still be there. And we don't know to what lengths people will go to in this case. Maybe they just wanted the rig itself. Maybe it was supposed to be diverted to a whole new chop shop."

"Maybe. But I think what it was carrying is more likely the goal."

"We were on a training mission," Jackson said. "How much in the way of valuable goods could there possibly be?"

"We've seen people murdered for twenty bucks," Kanen said. "Let's not diminish the value of what might have been involved there. If it was our weapons or any new tech, those would be worth a lot of money. And it could have been easy money made. Just sell off the arms. Maybe this is something they do on a regular basis. Maybe the payoff is only ten thousand dollars, pennies on the dollar, like when selling counterfeit money in exchange for real bills. But ten thousand dollars is a lot of money for some people. How do we find out what was in the rig, if its contents have already been removed?"

"The paperwork will have a manifest," Deli said. "Everything is marked down as to who's going where with what."

Jackson grabbed his phone from the table and waggled

it. "Mason again then?"

"You could try one of the others," Kanen said. "Dane is in town. Swede is too. Even Tesla. Depending on what she's doing right now."

"Going directly to Tesla without going through Mason would get us in trouble," Jackson said with a big grin.

"For that matter," Kanen said, popping the last of his second sandwich into his mouth and standing, "I might be able to get into it."

"Hacking the government database?" she asked in mock shock.

"Hardly," he said. "I have somebody in the supply department. We'll see if he can get me any answers." He pulled out his phone, walked onto the small deck and started talking.

Deli looked at Jackson. "Do you guys know everybody everywhere?"

He shook his head. "No. But it does help to have friends in certain places. If somebody is stealing military goods, this is an easy way to find out."

"Not really," she said. "Not if they wanted to get away with the theft. The manifest would have listed everything."

"Well then, the manifest would be a good way to keep track of which vehicle you wanted to put things in. But it doesn't mean what was in that vehicle was only what was on that manifest."

She stared at him in surprise, then slowly nodded. "In other words, there could have been a whole lot more in there that nobody knew about." She thought about it and gave a quick nod. "Smart."

Kanen came back in with a grin on his face. "He looked it up while I was on the phone. There were supplies, mostly camping gear, in that truck."

"And has it all been removed?"

He nodded. "Another vehicle came into the shop where your rig was taken and removed all the gear from it."

"Does he have confirmation that what was removed was actually what was on the manifest?"

"He never assumed anything different," Kanen said. "But, if somebody is trying to steal stuff and get away with it, they wouldn't mark anything that's not on the manifest anyway." He turned to Deli. "Any chance we can look at the security tapes from where that vehicle was emptied, see if anything extra was taken out?"

She stared at him in surprise, then slowly nodded. "Maybe. I do know the security guys. I've hassled them a time or two myself," she admitted.

"Why?"

She winced. "At one point, I thought somebody was stealing tools from the navy garage."

"Were they?"

"We had no proof," she said. "There was some suspi-cion, but nothing that we could ever prove."

"And who was it that you were suspicious of?"

She sighed heavily. "James."

The two men looked at each other, looked at her and said together, "Bingo."

JACKSON STARED AT her. "I guess, until we asked the right questions, it was hard to get the right answers."

"I mentioned it earlier, how it happened like a year ago. I don't think I mentioned James's name," she admitted. "Of course the MPs never got back to me about that initial investigation. And James still worked for the navy in the garage, but no more stolen tools were noticed, so I figured he had been cleared and just dismissed it from my mind." She sighed. "And then with all this here lately, I was so hung up on James being dead, it never occurred to me that he might have been involved in something else. But, of course, we never had any proof of who stole the tools back then either," she reminded Jackson. "The only one we ever caught on camera was him."

"What was he doing?"

"He was in the wrong place at the wrong time, acting weird. But he had nothing in his hands, and we couldn't follow any of his movements to anything suspicious, other than his very own mannerisms."

"Then let's see if we can find someone who can give us a hand looking at the videos of that rig."

"If we go to the base"—she looked at her watch—"I think Carney might still be there."

"Carney?"

"One of the guys who handles security. He is the one I spoke to before, who ran the videos for me."

"No point in sitting here," Jackson said, hopping to his feet. He cleaned off the table, snagged his jacket and cell phone. "Let's go." He looked over at Kanen. "Are you coming?"

Kanen nodded. "Hell yeah. We need everybody on board to make sure nobody else gets killed. I'll be in my truck behind you."

On that note they dispersed to their vehicles. Jackson unlocked the Jeep, waited until Deli was in before he turned on the engine and slowly pulled out. "On to the base then. Which garage are we talking?"

She gave him the number.

"Any idea if the rig's still there?"

"No, no idea," she said. "We'll find out when we get there."

It took fifteen minutes. The traffic was light, the weather dark. And, even though he'd just eaten, he couldn't stop thinking about dinnertime. And maybe he could sneak her away for a real date this time. He glanced at her, but her profile was set, as if she was angry at herself regarding James.

"What's upset you so badly?"

She shot him a look. "I should have remembered. When I realized James was involved with the phone calls, even then I should have remembered."

"Why? What does one have to do with the other?"

"He knew I was the one who had reported him."

"That could explain the harassing phone calls. But why a year later?"

Deli shrugged. "I hadn't really thought about that."

"And," Jackson continued, "if nothing came of your report, and he was off the hook, why bring more attention to himself?"

"But I don't know for sure that nothing came of it. That's the thing. Once you hand over information to the MPs or your superior, you know what it's like. It moves up the chain of command, and you never get any more details. It's like sending an email into cyberspace with the wrong address. It's gone, leaves your hands, and you have no idea where it ends up."

"True enough," he said. "The thing is, it does connect that garage where the rig was with James and your phone calls. So now I think this is all connected. And maybe it does make sense that he ran off when we arrived. Maybe he figured out he'd been made."

"Ran off where?"

"To whoever he's working with," Jackson said. "Because that's what makes the most sense."

"That's a very disturbing thought," she muttered.

They hopped out of the Jeep, waited for Kanen to pull up in his black truck, and the three of them walked in to the navy garage. Deli stopped to survey the vehicles. And then pointed. "It's that one."

"How do you know it's the same one?" Jackson asked.

She just shot him a look.

He grinned and took her word for it. He wandered over to take a closer look, and, sure enough, he could see the bullet hole in the radiator.

Kanen looked at him. Jackson nodded. Kanen's grin was wide and bright. As he walked past, he said, "Like I said, a keeper."

Kanen was lucky he was out of reach because Jackson was ready to cuff him one across the head.

Just then a call came out from behind them. "Who are you, and why are you here?" It was a booming voice.

Deli grinned. "Hey, Carney. It's me."

Carney looked down at her, and a big wide grin split his face. And what looked like a sumo wrestler became a teddy bear in front of them. "Hey, Deli. What are you up to?"

"I came to see you," she admitted. "And I hate that you'll think I only want to see you when I need something, but I do need something."

Instead of being offended, he chuckled, his great big belly rolling up and down in a wavelike motion. "That's good," he said, "because at least then you do come see me. Now what can I help you with?"

"I need to check when this vehicle was brought in," she said. "It was still fully loaded. My understanding is everything was removed, and everything on the manifest was checked off. Do you have this particular corner on video?"

Carney glanced at the vehicle, checked where cameras were and nodded. "I think so, yeah. Why? Is something missing?"

"Quite possibly," she said. "And then there's the fact we have multiple murders."

His expression changed. "Murders?" he repeated.

She told him about James. He shook his head. "Oh, that's bad. That's really bad."

"Why is that?" Jackson asked.

"Because we had those guys in here about a year ago, asking questions about James in regard to the thefts of tools. Remember?" Carney asked Deli.

"Yes, I do remember," she said. "That's why I was wondering if he had anything to do with this more recent activity with the possibility of thefts of government property. And the fact he's now dead."

Grim-faced, Carney said, "Come on. Let's take a look. What I don't want to do is accuse the wrong man, and, because he's dead, he can't defend himself, and that makes him a hell of a scapegoat for others."

Jackson appreciated that viewpoint. Too often people were more than prepared to blame anyone but themselves. And, if James was innocent, it would be good if they could find that out too.

Kanen came up behind him. "You take a look at the video. I want to inspect the inside of the truck."

Jackson said, "If you don't mind, Carney, I'll come with you."

Carney looked at him and frowned.

Deli reached out, patted his hand and said, "He's one of the good guys."

"I am one of the good guys, and I'm very grateful to Deli for saving my life a couple times," Jackson admitted. "Now I'm trying to make sure that whoever was after James doesn't come after her."

Carney's face turned dark, like a thundercloud. "That is not cool. It's bad enough they went after her at all. Best we stop this before it goes any further."

CHAPTER 11

S HE FOLLOWED CARNEY to the security room. "How is the wife doing, Carney?"

His face split with a big grin. "Expecting baby number four," he said proudly. "We're really hoping for a little girl this time."

She was delighted for him. He was such a great guy. "Now that is good news. You two make great parents."

He chuckled. "It helps a lot when you want the kids. The wife and I, we've got twelve siblings between us. We love family reunions. But it's not for everyone." At the door up front, he unlocked it and entered. The room was empty except for computer equipment and a handful of chairs.

She glanced around to see four monitors running off of four cameras. "Okay, so what we need to do is go back to the day before yesterday," she said. She turned to Jackson. "What's your guess?"

"Why don't we run the videos from the time the truck arrived," he said. "That way we won't miss anything that happened here."

She nodded.

Carney sat down, started playing on the keys, bringing up the feeds that had been stored. As soon as he started on Thursday's feed, they fast-forwarded until the vehicle was towed in. He hit Stop, then Play.

They pulled up chairs and sat beside him. There didn't appear to be too much going on. Guys walking around back and forth, but nobody was interested in that particular vehicle. Not too much later she arrived, did a check on the vehicle itself and never checked what was inside the back.

"Is that normal?" Jackson said.

"I was worried about the mechanics," she explained. "I wasn't worried whether it had anything in it. As there didn't appear to be any damage to any of the exterior, I wasn't thinking there would be damage to the interior. I was also on a short time frame, trying to make the best use of my time." She castigated herself now because she should have taken a look at the contents. Even a quick look.

The video feed kept going until all the men left. No mechanics worked on the night shift. But somewhere around two a.m., movement was detected by the camera. Carney leaned forward. "Whoa, that's not good."

"Who is it? Do you know?" Jackson asked.

Carney stopped the feed, backed up slightly, took a frame, moved it off to a different monitor, and there he digitalized it into a larger size, zeroing in on the man's face.

Deli sighed. "It's James," she said sadly. "I don't know what he was involved with, but it was not good."

"No, it sure wasn't," Jackson said.

As they watched, James hopped into the back of the rig in question and, a couple minutes later, came back out, carrying several boxes. He disappeared after a quick glance around and then returned and did the same thing again.

"They aren't very big boxes," she said slowly. "They could be anything. I'll have to double-check what was on the manifest in order to consider what could have come in boxes that size."

James did it one more time, having removed six boxes total.

Jackson asked, "Carney, can you freeze a couple of those frames so we can get the size of the boxes?"

Carney backtracked, picked up several of the feed frames, zeroing in on the boxes. There were no names or labels that they could see. He turned to Jackson and asked, "Who am I supposed to send it to?"

Knowing it was a dicey issue, Jackson answered cautiously, "How about Mason?"

"He's got clearance." Carney sent six different images to Mason.

Deli added, "And Jackson is on the investigation team. Can you copy that email to him too?"

Carney nodded once more.

Jackson thanked Carney, stepped away and called Mason.

Deli could partially hear the conversation as the images went through his email, letting Mason know what to expect. "I guess I don't get access, do I?"

Carney glanced at her and said, "What's your involvement in all this?"

"We were the last ones to see James alive as far as the police are concerned, and both Jackson and I were shot at because of this rig. We figure they were trying to get whatever was inside and were hoping to take the two of us out."

"This is ugly business, it is." Carney thought about it for a moment and then said, "I guess, for the sake of inspection purposes, we should at least send this to somebody to confirm what it is."

"Exactly. Send it to Billings. He's the investigating MP officer," Deli said. "Now that I've seen this, let's go through the proper channels to make sure whoever is behind this gets caught."

"I can do that," Carney agreed.

As soon as he was done, she said, "Would you mind going back to the feed? I just want to make sure nobody else is in the garage."

Carney brought up the feed, and they continued to watch. Just when she was ready to call it quits, another figure moved through the garage. She leaned forward and said, "Is that someone else coming to the truck?"

"Yeah, looks like it," Carney muttered. "I'll have to check and see who was on night shift that evening because, from the looks of this, they must have been sleeping to not see these guys."

Just then, with his face partially away from the camera, the man jumped into the back of the truck. There was no sound on the camera, just the video feed. He jumped out of the back of the rig, looked around, but his hands were empty and his back rigid. He turned and kicked the tire furiously.

At that, Carney sucked in his breath. "I know who that is," he snapped.

"Who?"

"Magnus. He's security too and was on night duty that night."

"Do you think he's involved?"

"Either he just saw the feed and came to see what might have been taken and knows he's in trouble for not seeing what was going on, or he came to take it himself and lost out because James got there before him. Either way he's pissed."

"A double-cross?" she said on a low note. "This is getting more interesting by the moment." She looked over at Carney. "When does Magnus come back on again?"

"Tonight, I think. I'd have to check the schedule."

"Would you mind doing that for me now? And please take several sets of these frames and send them off to the same people."

"But Magnus might not have anything to do with it," Carney warned. "I don't want to get him in trouble for nothing."

She patted his shoulder. "You've got a big heart, Carney. If Magnus was just checking, knowing he would be in trouble because he missed something, then that's understandable. Not everybody would have seen James in there. He knew where the cameras were, and he came for a purpose. But, if Magnus is involved and was trying to get some of those supplies for himself, or was hired to retrieve it and lost it because James got it first, then we need to know."

With a dour face Carney nodded. "Let's go check the schedule." He got up, left the monitors alone, ushered them ahead of him and locked the door as they left. Going into the lunch room, he pulled the schedule off the wall and held it up. "He's due in tonight. But a note is here, saying he called in sick."

"Does it say *he* called in sick, or did someone call in sick for him?" Jackson asked.

Carney narrowed his gaze as he looked at Jackson. "It doesn't say. I didn't take the phone call. Why?"

Jackson looked at Deli.

She stared back, her stomach sinking. "Because we already have a trail of dead men," she said slowly. "If he's involved, or if anybody even *thought* he was involved, there's a good chance he won't be coming in again ever."

It didn't take long for them to roust out Magnus's home address. Leaving Carney with their thanks, telling him to report what he'd seen to the MP investigators, she left with Jackson at her side.

"What about Kanen?" she asked.

"I texted him. If we need him, he'll join us at Magnus's house."

Using the GPS, they located Magnus's address, which was not on base. It was fifteen, almost twenty minutes by the time they pulled up outside a small set of townhomes.

Deli looked at them intently. "This is mostly a family neighborhood."

"He could have a family," Jackson said. "We can't make those kinds of assumptions."

"No, we can't," she said as they drove in to the main area.

They parked and worked their way around to Unit 21. They walked up the front steps and knocked. No lights were on, and nobody answered the door. She frowned and looked around. It was a fairly calm, quiet area, and nobody was outside playing or coming or going.

Jackson knocked again, then looked at her and raised an eyebrow.

She shook her head. "You know we have no right to go inside."

"Except we're concerned friends," he said quietly. He pulled the hem of his T-shirt over his hand and turned the knob. It opened underneath light pressure.

She frowned. "Why isn't it locked?"

Jackson shrugged, poked his head inside and called out.

She wanted to stop him. But, as he stuck his head around the door, he turned back to look at Deli. She frowned and said, "What's wrong?"

"The smell," he said harshly. He pulled the door closed

and picked up his phone. "We need to bring in the police."

"Are you sure he's dead?" She grabbed his arm and squeezed. "What if he's just really badly hurt?"

He shot her a look. Just then somebody at the other end of his phone answered. "I'm at a house with a suspected fatality." His voice was low, harsh. "I need to go in and check to make sure that's the case."

Mason's voice could be clearly heard. "I'm surprised you waited."

"I'm trying to be circumspect," Jackson said. "I've seen too many bodies in the last few days."

"Understood. Walk through very quietly and make sure that's what we're talking about."

She didn't want to go in.

Jackson held up his hands and whispered, "You stay here. I'll be right back." And he disappeared into the house.

She shouldn't have tried to stop him earlier. They should have checked to make sure the man was deceased, but then she smelled the odor as it wafted out the open doorway.

Jackson was back in a second, his face grim. He was no longer talking to Mason. "Mason is marshalling the forces. MPs will be here soon enough." He motioned at the steps. "Have a seat."

She shook her head, pointed to the vehicle where a woman was unloading groceries. "I'll talk to her first." And she bounded down the steps and headed over.

As she approached, the woman looked up and smiled.

"Hi. Any idea when you last saw Magnus?" she asked, pointing to the house. As she glanced back, she could see Jackson sitting on the front step, watching her.

The woman shook her head. "I haven't seen him today," she said. "Though I don't have too much to do with my neighbors, he's been fairly regular coming and going. He's always been friendly enough with a smile. Why?" She turned back to Deli with a frown. "Is something wrong?"

"That's what we're trying to decipher. We can't enter illegally of course. We're just trying to locate him."

The woman nodded. "I have no idea. He doesn't tell me his plans. As far as I know, he goes to work and comes home, like the rest of us." She ended that with a light laugh.

Deli nodded. "Thanks. I was just wondering if you happened to see any of his associates or a girlfriend around."

"There's been one guy back and forth a couple times. I've never seen a girlfriend there."

"Any idea what this other guy looked like?"

"He was big." The woman laughed. "As in really big. Maybe six feet four inches, three hundred pounds, something like that. I never did see much of his face, but he's been here a couple times."

"How did you know it was the same man each time?"

"He drives the same vehicle as I do, which seemed really odd. This is just a small SUV that holds my kids," the woman said. "You expect a huge guy like that to drive a big truck or a Hummer or something."

"So he looked very alpha male–ish?"

"Very. And he was big but not fat. He just looked like a huge brute."

"White skin?"

The woman nodded. "White skin, dark hair, mustache. Tattooed. He had one with a funny flower-snake on his arm. I can't really describe it."

"The police may need to talk to you about that," Deli said. And then seeing the woman's face, she rushed to add, "Only if there's something wrong of course."

The woman's face cleared. "Whatever. I'd probably recognize the tattoo again," she said. "It's hard to describe." She grabbed the groceries, carried them up the steps and walked into the house without another word.

Deli could understand. Nobody really wanted to be questioned about neighbors, but no doubt something had gone wrong in Magnus's life. She mentally sorted through all the men she knew. Six feet four inches and three hundred pounds was fairly discernible. She couldn't remember anybody who might fit that description. Dark hair, tattooed, heavily muscled, big but not fat.

She walked back to Jackson and repeated the woman's words.

"I'll have to think on that," Jackson said slowly. "I know a lot of big guys. Take Swede, for one. But he's not three hundred pounds by any means."

"But she did say muscled, not fat. So when she says three hundred, that could have been just a figure she tossed off. Swede has got to be at least two-fifty."

Jackson chuckled. "I see you know him too. And he is, at least. But he sure as hell would take exception to anybody saying that every inch wasn't necessary."

"There are a couple other guys like him," Deli said. "I see a lot of them coming through with their vehicles. And speaking of vehicles, we have to remember that most SUV designs are similar, so it's easy to confuse one model from the others."

"True enough." He looked over and saw the Ford label on the neighbor's SUV and said, "She's also right about how most big guys like that would be driving something else. For all we know, this guy's married and has four kids of his own."

"Exactly," she said.

Just then two military vehicles pulled up, and Coronado PD showed up as well. Deli saw one officer and smiled. "That's Alex." She lifted a hand and waved.

Jackson frowned at Deli. "You know Alex too? I know her through Macklin, another SEAL."

"Sure. This city is not very big, and the base acts as its own little town as well," she said with a big smile. "After that last set of murders, lots of us knew who she is."

"Interesting. I guess in a small town you get to know people."

"Absolutely."

Alex walked over, planted her hands on her hips, her face sober. "Tell me you two weren't involved please."

Jackson gave her a lopsided grin. "Sorry. It's not so much that we're involved, but we seem to be tripping over bodies these days."

She stormed up the steps and headed inside. The other policemen joined her. Both Jackson and Deli sat on the steps together as the crowd moved upward.

Quickly enough Alex came back out, barking orders. She stepped down and stopped in front of them, pulled out her notepad and said, "From the top."

Deli winced. "Can we go somewhere? It'll take a while."

Alex stared at her in surprise.

Jackson shook his head. "This is only one of three murders so far."

Alex's shoulders slumped. "Coffee shop it is." She pulled out her phone and made a call. When she was done, she said, "We'll meet at the Starbucks around the corner."

Jackson nodded. He helped Deli back into the Jeep, and they rerouted to the coffee shop. It was a cooler day, and the patio section was open in the back with nobody else around. They all grabbed coffees and headed out there.

This time Alex had a larger notepad and her laptop. As they sat down, they glanced around to make sure nobody could overhear them. She opened up a document and said, "Let's go."

Jackson started, with Deli interrupting whenever she felt something was necessary. By the time they had updated Alex, she was muttering to herself.

"Are you guys always like this?"

"Macklin is like this too, isn't he?" Deli asked, chuckling.

Alex groaned. "Macklin is way too much like this. He won't be impressed that another one of his buddies is involved in a police matter."

"I didn't do it on purpose," Jackson said. "I was asked to drive a rig back to base. Not my fault somebody shot the radiator, then peppered the two of us with gunfire."

"Either of you hurt?"

"Not enough to be bothered about," Deli said.

Alex sighed. "Okay, so now I have to work with the MPs again …" She rolled her eyes at them. "I'm sure you can understand how I'm not thrilled with that concept. But this one *is* on my turf."

"Understood," Deli said with a smirk. "This way they get to work with you."

"They're not the best at sharing," Alex said. She closed her laptop, propped her elbows on the table and sipped her coffee. "Are you holding up okay?" she asked Deli.

Deli's smile wobbled. "I am. This whole thing just seems to be going down a deeper rabbit hole right now."

"What are you thinking happened to Magnus?"

"I think he either failed to do what he was supposed to do as security guard, or he got his nose into something illegal that he shouldn't have," Jackson said succinctly. "I'm thinking he was supposed to retrieve whatever was in the back of that vehicle, and he got there too late. So, when whoever it was expecting a delivery didn't get his merchandise, they took out the weak link."

"But then what about James?" Deli asked. "Did Magnus go after him?"

"No way to know," Jackson admitted. "Not yet at least."

"Then the real question is, what were they after?" Alex asked. "And who do you think is involved?"

"That's what we have no clue about. Max is in the hospital. Barney is still unconscious," Deli supplied. "James is dead, and now Magnus is dead. And Chester, who was the one originally to drive the rig instead of Jackson, he's also dead."

"So three murders and two men injured." Alex whistled softly. "That's a pretty hefty body count."

"What worries me most is that these victims were all navy men, all stationed at the Coronado base," Jackson noted.

"Yeah," Alex murmured, "that is unfortunate because the shooter may well be one of yours as well." She tilted her head, first at Jackson and then at Deli. "So watch your backs."

They shared a glance with each other before nodding back at Alex.

Alex continued, "What could possibly be worth stealing—and a possible treason charge—in that truck from a training mission?"

Jackson reminded her, "A lot of people were at the training sessions and packing up. The manifest could have had just the ordinary information, but somebody could have delivered something to the training camp to be passed on. I was delayed in the convoy and was bringing up the rear, but I wasn't that far behind. Maybe the smuggler thought the bullet to my radiator would strand me on the roadside, which it did, but then I also had Deli there and her rig was parked nearby. They wouldn't have known how many people were with us."

"So they just peppered you two with gunfire and took off."

"Yes," Deli said. "I saw them approach but then ducked and was out of sight until they were gone. By the time we could see them, they were speeding down the road, and the pickup was too far away to identify the drivers or the plates," Deli pointed out. "Then two military vehicles weren't far behind them, likely sending the shooters on the run. So, if they had planned to make sure we were dead, they didn't get that chance. Bad timing on their part but good timing for us. And knowing they were being chased, they raced ahead, turned around and managed to take out the rig following them. And that, of course, is where Max and Barney fit in."

"And yet, the shooters, having taken out the men chasing them, didn't go back after you guys?"

"I figured they decided to cut and run," Jackson said. "If there was one vehicle chasing them, chances are more were on the way. Both to come help us and to go after them. It makes sense to escape while they could."

"And sure enough we did get a tow. Jackson came back with Kanen, I believe, didn't you?" Deli turned to look at him.

"Tanner picked me up. We went looking for the men

who shot at us. And found Max and Barney instead. Tanner was only available that day. Then Kanen came over to check for bugs in Deli's apartment."

Alex continued to write notes on her notepad as she pondered her way through the puzzle. "So we're assuming something valuable to the shooter was in the back of that rig. Send me photos to let me know the size and the shape of the boxes. Can you estimate them right now?"

"Rifle size," Jackson said. "And there were six boxes."

"But a rifle case, as in a single gun? Not a large crate?"

Jackson shook his head. "Not a crate but we were testing out brand-new models of HK-416s with a different heat scope, night scopes, and a new cartridge system. They're not on the market. They're not even available for the military yet."

"Wow. Somebody would definitely want those—good guys and bad guys."

"For the firepower alone, of course they would. It's also a brand-new design. So if anybody wanted that information for a competing company, then it would have a lot of value."

"Were other weapons being tested there?" Deli asked. "I remember hearing something about a brand-new semiautomatic with some new reloading system."

Jackson looked at her in surprise. "You know about that? I heard of it, but I never saw it."

"What's the chance a third brand-new gun was being tested?" Alex asked slowly. "Six boxes. I'm thinking six weapons in individual crates, two of each kind?"

"Individual weapon cases, yes," Jackson said. "Of course we're just guessing. An awful lot of hand grenades and a couple other new tech devices were there as well. We were testing them as part of the training exercise."

"What kind of tech devices?"

"Picking up signals off cell phones, triangulating new GPSs faster, better coordinate systems," he said. "Nothing too advanced. And things like grenades, which you can certainly buy almost everywhere right now, if you have the right contacts. If you don't have the right contacts, well then, maybe somebody thought they could utilize that source."

"Which is a little scary," Alex said.

"But you know as well as I do," Jackson said, "that everything can be bought for a price."

"So the best bet is that this was all about some of the new models somebody wanted to get their hands on."

Jackson nodded. "But I can't say that's the only thing that could have been in there. For all I know, those rifle cases were stashed full of money, only used to convey the money."

Deli looked at him in surprise. "Why the devil would anybody do that?"

He chuckled. "People do all kinds of things for some of the weirdest reasons. Cash is very hard to move these days. Money laundering is not as easy to hide anymore with all our digital advances. Maybe that's what they were doing."

"So, with this gear theory, we need to know where that gear came from and how long ago. And has anyone checked to see if they've gone missing?" Alex asked.

"That'll be harder to get information on," Jackson said. "You'll have to work your liaison with the MPs to get it."

She nodded. "Actually I have a better source." She just grinned. "Mason in town?"

Jackson burst out laughing. "Now you're trying to tap him too, huh?"

She shook her head. "Nope. It's Tesla I want."

Deli watched as the laughter died from Jackson's face.

He nodded thoughtfully. "Well, she certainly has some pull on base, if that's the type of information you need."

"It would help. We also need to know how many people knew about it, who brought the prototypes in, how many were brought in and where are they now. Because, if they've shown up and have been tagged as returned from this training session, then we're barking up the wrong tree, and we need to think about a different one," Alex said. She gathered up her laptop and paperwork. "On that note, I'll head back to the office and see what I can find."

"And our statements?"

"I've pretty well got them down here," she said. "I'll email them to you. I want you to sign them, scan them back in and send them to me. If you can't do that, then come on into the office, and I'll get them printed off. We'll get them signed and witnessed."

Deli watched as Alex got up and walked away. Deli faced Jackson. "Alex must have an interesting career, ... the people she deals with, the cases ..."

"Interesting, yes, but I don't think her career is easy," he said. "She helped a friend of mine who was a suspect in a murder investigation. It got pretty ugly there for a while. Not only did the two of them come through unscathed, but they came through together."

"You're talking about Mack, her current partner?" she guessed.

He nodded. "Big Mack," he said with a laugh. "Speaking of more guys who are big and bulky and six feet four inches ... But he's definitely not three hundred pounds."

She thought about Macklin, remembered having met him at least once at Mason's. "No, I think he's probably running two-fifty or two-sixty."

"Exactly. Kind of like Swede. But because they're both so big, it's hard to make a serious estimate." He glanced over at her. "Now what do you want to do?"

She reached up and scrubbed her face. "I'd like to chill out somewhere. Go home, kick my feet up, put on a movie and try to forget about this."

"I need to catch Kanen up," he said. "And it's likely to be close to dinnertime."

They glanced at their cell phones. "It is," she said. "Not sure I'm hungry after that smell from that house though."

He nodded. "So, your place or mine?"

She groaned. "Are you telling me that we have to do that together thing again?"

"Three men are dead. Do you really think it's safe to stay alone?"

She glared at him. "At least we know who my stalker is."

"*Was*. But you don't know who your unwelcome visitor was nor who your intruder was—your supposed new boyfriend. Any chance all three were the same guy? We should at least consider that."

Deli shook her head. "I've worked with James for years. I would have recognized James's walk if he had been my visitor who I followed to the parking lot. So I don't think it could be him. However, with all the focus on navy personnel, do you realize how many different people I see in the course of just one week? Many would be lightly familiar just from meeting them at work but not enough to recognize them. And the guy with the wrapped present, I don't remember seeing him ever. He wasn't James for sure."

Jackson paused for a moment before speaking. "We should test your place for bugs again too," he said. Pulling out his laptop, he again scanned through the images of James in the mechanics' garage. While looking through those, he reminded her, "Kanen also installed a video camera at your place. Remember? We should look at that."

"I don't think I even knew about that," she said slowly. "Although, now that I think about it, I'm not surprised."

"It was directed toward the living room," he assured her. "To catch anybody coming in through the patio's glass doors or by the front door."

"I guess that makes sense. But can Kanen check that without us going in?"

Jackson pulled out his phone, dialed Kanen, put it on Speakerphone and said, "Hey, there's been a lot happening on our end. What's going on at your end?"

"After you took off, I went to the security room and talked to Carney myself," Kanen said. "I've been waiting for you to check in."

"Yeah, about that …" Jackson pinched the bridge of his nose while Deli watched, then he gave a shortened version of everything that had happened during the day.

"He's dead too?" Kanen asked, his voice easily coming through the phone Jackson held in front of him. "Also I did check the video camera at her place. But there's nothing showing. This is getting messy."

"Yes. Alex also is now involved."

Kanen gave a low whistle. "Macklin won't like that."

"No, but he'll deal, like he always has to deal. Nothing like having a cop in the family."

"True," Kanen said.

"Well, she can certainly be a help to us," Jackson said. "Our current working hypothesis is that the prototypes we were testing on the training session might have been stolen. Any idea how we can track down if they got checked back in again?"

"Those weapons? They are state-of-the-art," Kanen said thoughtfully. "That's an interesting concept. I hadn't even considered them. But they'd be worth some serious money to the right people."

JACKSON SNORTED AND stood from their table at the coffee shop. "That's Kanen. Put his nose on the scent, and he's gone." He grabbed their empty coffee cups, tossed them in the nearby trash can, then held out his hand. "Come on. Kanen's off on a chase. Let's go check out your place. Then we'll head back to mine."

He hated to see the fatigue pulling at her face. She was so damn capable, but everybody gets worn down by this never-ending set of events.

"Do you think somebody's been there?"

"I doubt it," he said. "But I did leave something behind in case the front door was opened."

"I don't even think I want to know," she said, her voice low. "I'm getting really, really tired."

"That's your blood sugar mostly, topped off by all the emotional drama," he said. "How about a steak again for dinner?"

"Does it come with all the trimmings?"

"If that means a baked potato, sour cream, green onions, stacks of sautéed mushrooms on the side and a Caesar salad," he said, wrapping an arm around her shoulder and tucking her close as they walked through the coffee shop. "Then absolutely. I have everything already at home."

"Can we eat in twenty minutes before I crash?" She moaned. "Because that sounds absolutely fantastic."

"How about you have some baby carrots now—I've got some stashed in the Jeep—to tide you over for about two hours? If I have food on the table ready for you to eat by then, am I forgiven for everything that's gone wrong today?"

She squeezed his hand, sliding hers in to lock with his. "You're not responsible for anything. It's just a shitty day— or rather a couple of shitty days."

As they walked toward his Jeep, she asked suddenly, "Do you think that's it? Or do you think we'll come across more dead bodies?"

"I'm sure hoping that's it," he said, "but with three dead men and two injured, there's no way to be sure."

"Do we need to check in with Max? Make sure he's okay?"

"He should still have a security guard on him. And I don't know what Max's role in all of this is, or if he was just the unlucky vehicle driver who went in pursuit of the shooter."

"I hope he's not involved," she said. "I really like the guy."

Almost two hours later and now in his apartment— which hadn't been tossed by any intruders—Jackson settled back in his chair. They'd gone to her place, done a quick second check for bugs, found nothing and, feeling better, had headed to his apartment for some much-needed suste- nance. His stomach was full and happy, his mouth still humming joyfully with the taste of steak and baked potato and Caesar salad. He studied Deli's features. "Ready for a nap?"

She shook her head. "No, a nap will mean sleeping right through the night." She glanced at her watch. "But I don't know how it got to be almost seven o'clock."

He reached for the bottle of wine and topped off her glass. "After the days we've had," he murmured, "an early night is exactly what you need."

She smiled. "True enough. But there's still so much to be done."

"Eating and sleeping have to be done too."

"Sleep might have to come next," she said. She lifted her glass of wine and clinked gently against his glass. "To a much better tomorrow."

"To a better tomorrow," he echoed. He took a sip and then added, "Hopefully one that doesn't mean us finding another dead body."

She gave a mock shudder and looked up at him, her eyes haunted.

His heart swelled for her. "I'm sorry you've had to see this," he murmured.

"It's not your fault," she said. "It's just incredibly bad luck we're involved to this extent. You never did get far with the MPs did you? You were attached to the investigation, but they weren't happy about it or something?"

"Something like that, yeah. But we're so involved now that I'm sure we're both suspects."

Her gaze widened in horror. "Seriously?"

He wanted to reassure her somehow that this wasn't the case, but anybody with a brain would have to consider that. "Even if they do, they're not likely to look at us for long," he said reassuringly. "But we were the last to see James alive as far as anyone knows – except for his killer."

"But they were all dead when we got there."

"We know that, and surely the coroner's time of death will prove that," Jackson said, his voice low. "But we could go through some pretty unpleasant questioning first."

"But we have alibis," she snapped.

Apparently the thought of being a suspect made her more angry than upset. He grinned at that. He preferred spitfire over tears any day. "Sure, some of the time we do. Some of the time we were sleeping. And honestly, we're most likely to alibi each other. That's not exactly what the MPs want to hear."

She tapped the table impatiently with her fingers. "Well, that's not acceptable. I've never been called a liar in my life."

"You mean, at least for somebody to get away with it," he said with a big grin. "But I think everybody realizes that you're great at what you do and that you're also honest and ethical. We just have to make sure everybody involved in this investigation knows too."

"Alex should be able to help us there."

"Sure, but she can't have a personal interest in this, or she can't work on the case," Jackson reminded her. "It's one thing to know of us. It's another thing to know us well."

Deli raised both hands in frustration. "Well, that's of no help then."

He loved the fact her brain was always ticking, her mind was always spinning angles, moving forward, looking at things from a different perspective. "I'm not prepared to walk away from this and allow other people to handle it. Are you?"

"I'm not sure there's anything we can do," she said. "Think about it. All we're doing is fumbling around in the dark, finding men after they've been killed."

"True enough," he said. "So maybe we need to find a way to get at these people before they're killed."

He could see from the look on her face just how tired she was. It was hard to make heads or tails out of any of the information they had gathered so far. He had a pretty good idea what was going on, but they didn't know the players.

He motioned toward his spare bedroom. "Look. It's late. If you think you'll sleep through the night, just go to bed now. Have a shower, crash and sleep as long as you need to."

She shook her head. "No, it's too early. Let's get the dishes done." Determinedly she stood, even as he protested. But she was stubborn if nothing else.

As much as he loved her spirit, that stubbornness went along with it, so he was hardly one to complain.

They did the dishes, and he refilled their glasses with wine. He'd be fine, but he could see the red wine made her even more tired.

She laughed when she took a sip of her refilled glass. "This should ensure I sleep through the night." She sat down in the living room and shook her head. "I'm sinking fast. Maybe I will take you up on your offer for a shower and to sleep here in the spare room. I wasn't going to bed yet, but it feels like I'm being foolish not to. I should sleep better here too."

"Come on." He led her to the bathroom, pulled out clean towels, laid them on the side of the sink and said, "This is for your shower, and, over here, this is a spare room." He opened the door to show her the double bed all freshly made and picked up a bathrobe he kept on the hook on the door. He tossed it on the bed. "Go crash into bed. I'll see you in the morning."

He snagged her into a warm hug, kissed her on the forehead, then dropped his arms and stepped back out. He closed the door gently behind him, only hearing her faint thank-you as the door shut and went *click*.

Back in the living room, he picked up his glass of wine,

sat down on the living room sofa with his laptop and went over the information they had. It was a lot, but it wasn't enough. He got up, went over to the living room wall where they had put the boards. He studied the names, the dates, the places and realized the victims probably were compromised into doing something. That had to be a hard decision. Getting caught meant a life sentence. In this case, more than one life sentence.

Max might hold the key to some of this. Jackson pulled out his phone and called him.

Max answered. "Hey, you found out anything?"

"Nothing good," Jackson said. "Another dead man. And he was a security guard at the navy garage, for the night shift after my rig was brought in. Looks like he was sent to retrieve something from the vehicle, but the video showed James had gone in ahead of time and taken the stuff out."

"What did he take?" Max asked curiously.

"Six boxes. We're assuming they were the new rifles we were testing at training. The new prototypes the military was asked to review. I'm not sure how valuable they would be."

"It's hard to say. I've heard murmurs about some new ones," Max said. "If it's those, they might be worth a lot of money."

"It seems like that's what's going on. We haven't been able to figure out how these men were pressured into it," Jackson said.

"Follow the money," Max said. "It's almost always about money. It's either that or they were manipulated into doing it."

"We've got people on the money right now," Jackson said. "You have any ideas about what connects the victims?"

"All navy men who could have been involved in the

same training. They could have served on the same tours. There are all kinds of ways they could have been connected. The basic fact is, they are connected because they're all involved. Other than that, who knows the *whys?*"

Jackson said, "True enough. I just happen to be one of those plagued by wanting to know the *whys.*"

"Then keep digging," Max said. "I want to get the hell out of here, but they won't let me."

"We have three dead men to go along with the injuries you and your buddy there received. I don't think your security is heavy enough," Jackson snapped.

Silence came while Max considered Jackson's words. "Good point," Max finally said. He groaned. "But there's absolutely nothing here to do. You know that, right? I don't even have my laptop. And there's no Wi-Fi, and my cell phone battery is damaged and isn't recharging properly."

"So what are you doing with your time?"

"Watching boring TV shows and reading old magazines," he retorted in disgust.

Jackson chuckled. "Okay, I can get being pissed at that."

"You could always come and visit," Max said. "Fill me in on the latest details."

"I can do that on the phone, since I have Deli sound asleep in the spare room right now. She's pretty wiped out. We've seen an awful lot of death in the last few days. It's wearing her down."

"And so it should," Max said quietly. "Nobody should see death and take it lightly. We should all be affected."

Privately Jackson agreed. And there was no doubt Deli was certainly affected. "How would they have known about the prototypes being in that particular vehicle?" he asked. "Do you have any idea how shipments are divided between trucks?"

"No, I don't," Max said thoughtfully. "But I can get back to you with somebody who might." He hung up, leaving Jackson to sit here and stare at his phone in bemusement.

"Any supply chain clerk might know," he mused aloud.

He looked up as the guest bedroom door opened. Deli walked out with just the bathrobe wrapped around her, but she looked better, tired but better. She held up the empty wineglass, walked over to the kitchen sink and rinsed it out before placing it upside down on the draining board. "Who were you talking to?"

He waggled his phone at her. "Max."

Her face lit up. "How is he?"

"He's doing pretty good. I asked him how and who would have determined which vehicle was carrying what cargo back from the training."

She froze, looked at him, then gave a slow nod. "That's an excellent question. Because somebody had to put the gear in the right truck so these men could retrieve it."

"Or somebody just told them what vehicle it was in, but it would have been packed up as per whatever requirements this stuff necessitates."

"It's fairly regimented," she said. "But, if Max could get us exactly how and who and what, that would be awesome."

"It's the *who* I'm more bothered about at the moment," Jackson said. "And whether that *who* is still alive or has he been taken out too?"

CHAPTER 12

DELI WINCED. "I sure hate to think that yet another person is dead over this. I handle the big machinery with engines, so guns and weapons aren't my wheelhouse. Are those prototypes really worth that kind of money to take these kinds of risks?"

"Whether it's the money or just that somebody wants to make sure they're crossing their *Ts* and dotting their *Is*, whoever is involved is being taken out of the equation."

She nodded. "But still that's pretty harsh treatment."

"The penalty for stealing military secrets," Jackson said, his voice low and gentle, "is very high."

"Meaning death is preferable? Or are you saying they'll do anything to avoid being caught themselves, and that includes killing anybody else involved?"

"Exactly," he said.

She wandered over and sat down on the couch. "I thought I could fall asleep, but now my mind is buzzing again," she confessed. She stared at the poster boards and all the information they had on them. "Somebody loaded it on the truck. Somebody had to know which vehicle held what. And somebody must have relayed that information to James. And somebody then picked up the material from James." She turned to Jackson. "CTV cameras. Has anybody checked the street cameras on the blocks around his place? Surely we could track vehicles that parked in his apartment complex and the people who walked back and forth around his unit."

"The CTV cameras were checked. He has underground parking available at his complex along with the standard outdoor lot. And, from what the security guards there can tell, any exchange would have happened there."

"Then we should still check every license plate of every vehicle that went in there, maybe find the SUV driver Magnus' neighbor told us about. At least then we might either confirm he's involved or check him off the list," she said enthusiastically."

"The line of thought there is that a meet was scheduled in the underground parking garage. So one vehicle arrived, parked underground. Someone either went to James's apartment to get the guns or James took the guns himself to the underground parking. The contraband would have been delivered to another person in another vehicle also in the underground parking garage. The security tapes have a suspicious thirty-minute-long missing segment."

Hearing that, she frowned. "Why would James take the stolen guns home? Wouldn't it have been better to take them someplace else? And surely the navy has security cameras on all its garages, keeping track of all the vehicles entering and leaving. We should have asked about that when we saw Carney."

Jackson nodded. "We need to see those tapes too."

She pulled out her phone, quickly dialed the garage and, when a voice answered at the other end, she asked, "Is Carney there?"

"No, he's gone for the evening. He'll be back tomorrow morning."

She thanked him and hung up. "Carney is off work. He

is supposed to be back in the morning."

Jackson glanced at his watch and said, "That makes sense. It's nine-thirty. We saw him there earlier today."

She nodded. "I don't like this. I have a terrible feeling Carney is in danger too."

Jackson straightened. "Why?"

She looked at him, trouble in her eyes. "Maybe because he spoke with us. Maybe that's all it takes." She stared at Jackson for a moment, her mind grappling with all the thoughts running through her brain. "If we could just find somebody before they were killed," she said, "it wouldn't feel so bad. It seems like all we're doing is coming in behind the shooter, cleaning up after him."

"To a certain extent," he said, "yes. But you have to remember that most of these men were dead right away. We're just now bringing their murders to light."

"So who else is likely to be killed?"

"Anyone connected," he said.

She nodded. "Like Carney."

Jackson stared at her. "Are you really thinking he's in trouble?"

She sagged against the couch. "I'm not sure," she groaned. "But I know I'll never forgive myself if something happens to him overnight, especially if I didn't do anything to warn him."

"Do you have his number?"

She shook her head. "No, of course not."

He returned to his laptop and typed in some information. "His name is Carney Johansen. But I don't find a phone number for him."

"Well, Tesla will have one," she said. "Or one of my supers would have it."

"Let's make a couple calls and see if we can find it then. No address is listed here."

"That's not unusual, is it?"

He frowned. "It's hard to say."

"You can't be thinking Carney is involved?" She shook her head at Jackson. "Why would he do something like that?"

He looked at her in surprise. "I didn't say I thought he was involved. But we have to consider everybody. And Carney works at the navy garage as well."

"But that would be a third person after the boxes in the truck. Isn't that overkill?"

"Potentially, yes," he said with a nod. "But maybe James was working for Carney. Or maybe the other guy was. We don't know yet. However, we need to double-check with Carney that all is well with him."

Just then Jackson's phone rang. He checked his Caller ID and told her, "It's Kanen." He hopped to his feet, answering the call. "Hey, Kanen. What's up?"

"Just running down leads," Kanen said, "although we're not doing so good. I've talked to Max and Mason. Assigned soldiers boxed up the gear found in each tent involved in the training exercise. The boxes were marked as to their intended destination, like the navy's Coronado base or some nearby army base or whatever. The boxes of gear loaded into each truck weren't designated as to its contents by anyone. They were just packing up, moving out the gear, tent by tent, to be returned to the appropriate base. Other individuals were responsible for loading up the trucks. So it's likely that whoever loaded the boxes in your rig, Jackson, didn't know what they were handling."

"Which makes sense from the navy's compartmentalized

approach," Jackson said. "Plus will most likely save some lives from the shooter's viewpoint. We found Magnus dead as well. We're now trying to locate Carney, the security guard we met earlier today at the navy garage, to make sure he's okay."

Kanen's voice turned businesslike. "Last name? Let me see what I can find." He had the name pulled up in a few seconds and an address right after that. "His cell phone is ..." He rattled off a number.

Jackson wrote down the phone number and address, then said, "And Max says we should follow the money. Of course that's the age-old adage."

"Tesla and I have been doing that," Kanen said. "But so far no unusual amounts of money have shown up in anyone's bank accounts, as least the people we're tracking and their known financial institutions."

"So it wasn't for money? If not money, then what?"

"It could have been in order to avoid something coming to the surface. Blackmail is always a great motivator. The other thing is maybe they were killed so they didn't have to be paid. It's much easier to keep the money all to yourself," Kanen said.

Jackson nodded.

She could hear the phone conversation easily in the small room. Jackson was one of those who held the phone in front of him and talked into it. It made the conversations much easier to hear from both sides. She wasn't sure what to make of this. But she'd feel a hell of a lot better once Carney answered the call she was ringing through to him. But it rang and rang.

She hopped to her feet and walked into the guest bedroom while Jackson was still on the phone to Kanen. She dressed again and came out, snatched up her purse and stood beside the kitchen counter, waiting for him to get off the phone.

Jackson spun around, took one look at her and his eyebrow shot up to his forehead. "Uh-oh."

Kanen said, "Uh-oh, what?"

"Deli is fully dressed and looking like she wants to go out. I suspect she wants to double-check on Carney."

"Ouch," Kanen said. "Sorry to ruin your evening. I think I'll meet you there." And he hung up.

Jackson didn't say another word. He grabbed his keys and led the way.

"Can you drive even after all that wine?"

He shot her a look. "Absolutely. You shouldn't be driving. You're much smaller than I am. That alcohol would have affected you more."

"It's hardly a contest because I'm going regardless," she said. "Carney went out of his way to help us. I don't want him hurt because of it."

"Agreed," Jackson said. He pulled up the address on his GPS. "Twelve minutes. Let's go."

He pulled his Jeep from the parking lot and took off. It took longer than twelve minutes because the traffic was surprisingly heavy. They pulled up beside a small ranch house. Several similar-looking houses were on the block. All the lights were off on the one they were interested in.

Jackson frowned and said, "It isn't that late, is it?"

"No," she said as she dialed Carney's number again.

They walked up to the front door. While the phone rang in her ear, they could hear it ringing inside the house. She frowned, looked at Jackson and knocked hard on the front door. No answer. She reached out, grabbed the doorknob and twisted, but it was locked.

Jackson jerked, put a finger to her lips and then pulled her out of the way. He put her against the wall next to the front door and whispered in her ear, "Stay here. Stay low and quiet. I think someone is inside." He bolted around the back.

She watched him go, wishing somebody was here with her. Just as she thought that, Kanen pulled up behind Jackson's Jeep. She held her fingers to her lips and motioned that Jackson had gone around the corner of the house.

Kanen stepped up beside her and whispered, "What have you heard?"

"Carney's phone rings inside. Jackson thought he heard somebody."

Just then they heard shouts from the back of the house. She heard Jackson's voice. Kanen jumped off the front porch, raced around in the opposite direction to where Jackson had gone. And as he left Deli's sight, bullets pierced the front door. She screamed and ducked farther out of sight.

Somebody bolted through the front door, crashing through it like a bulldozer. She reached out with her foot as the man came out on the front porch and tripped him. He fell onto the concrete porch steps, scrambled to get to his feet, but she tackled him on his back. He went down hard again, but then he got up, easily carrying her with him. She reached for his ears, twisting and grabbing, her nails scratching his skin as she tried to get him to stop. He pulled her over his shoulders and tossed her to the ground and kept running.

Just as suddenly Jackson came around the corner and barreled right into him, but the intruder was light on his feet and bolted with Jackson on his heels.

Kanen was behind them, but he stopped when he saw her and helped her to her feet. "Are you okay?" he asked, brushing her off.

"I'm fine," she said. "Go after him. I'll see if Carney is okay."

"We've already called 9-1-1. See to your friend."

She ran inside the house, turned on the lights and found Carney on the floor, groaning. She dropped to his side to see his eyes open and a half smile on his face.

"Hey, little girl. What kind of trouble did you get me into?"

"I'm so sorry, Carney," she cried out. "It's the same damn trouble James and Magnus got into," she said. "Who knew this would still be reverberating around us?" She checked him over. "One bullet high in the shoulder. I don't see any other injuries. Do you feel pain anywhere else?"

"No," he said, "but my shoulder hurts like a son of a bitch." In the distance they could hear sounds of a siren. He groaned. "My wife and kids are visiting her mom for the weekend. Damn good timing, if I do say so myself."

"Oh, that's such a relief," Deli said. "I worried if anybody else was in the house."

"No." He tried to sit up and then fell back down, gasping in pain.

She reached over and patted his cheek. "You stay right here. The ambulance is outside. You'll be at the hospital in no time."

He rolled his eyes at her. "And since when is that something to look forward to?"

EMTs rushed toward her. She was shoved out of the way as they dropped beside Carney and started working on him. She backed up into the kitchen. She did a quick check of the rest of the house, but, like he'd said, no one else was here.

One of the men looked at her and asked, "What the hell happened?"

"Jackson and I interrupted a gunman attacking Carney," she said, pointing to their patient on the floor. "I tripped the attacker as he escaped out the front door and jumped on his back, but he threw me off. However," she said, "I scratched his ears. You should swab and scrape under my nails. I know DNA results will take time but it could be helpful down the road."

The EMT frowned but did as she asked. "Why were you here?"

"It was a hunch." She shrugged. "Carney's head of security for the navy garage where I work. Two other men who worked with us have been killed in the last two days, plus a third navy man." Her voice was a low undertone. "We came tonight because I was afraid Carney was next on the hit list."

Carney turned to look at her as he was loaded onto the gurney and smiled. "I owe you one for that. If you hadn't come when you did, I'd be a dead man right now."

"I'm just sorry we didn't come sooner," she said in a stark voice. "I'd have done anything to keep you from being hurt."

He smiled. "I'm a big guy. I can take a lot before I go down permanently."

She nodded and knew he was right. But bullets would still stop everyone. As far as she was concerned, too many people had died already.

PISSED AT MISSING his man—but with a photo of the getaway car—Jackson returned to Carney's house, slid an arm around Deli's shoulders and tucked her close to him. "Carney will be fine."

She gave Jackson a misty smile. "Thank heavens for that. We still need answers."

"And we're getting there," he said. "Remember what you said? Wouldn't it be nice if we could get there before the next murder was to happen?"

She frowned and stared up at him. "We didn't though, did we?"

His fingers tightened on her shoulder. "No, in a way we didn't, but you might want to consider that, this time, Carney didn't die. He will make a full recovery, and that's because of us. So, although we didn't stop Carney from getting shot, he'll make it through this. Let's keep working on this and see if we can get to the next victim before he's even attacked."

"I'd love to," she said. "Just missing one thing. That's a name as to who the next victim is. Also we have to consider that maybe there aren't any more victims. Maybe the murderer has cleaned up his act or has tied up all the loose ends."

If only it were that simple, Jackson thought.

As far as he was concerned, both he and Deli could be on that hit list. So his words were truer than ever in terms of making the killings stop before it became an issue for him or her. He wished Carney had been able to tell Deli who his attacker was. Being struck from behind inside his own house implied intimate knowledge of who Carney was and where he lived. That could have been anybody he worked with. And that was a consideration.

He turned toward Deli. "Who else besides James, Magnus, and Carney works in that garage with you?"

She frowned at him. "Probably another dozen guys. But that would be way too obvious, wouldn't it? You can hardly take out your coworkers until you're the last man standing and not have the police become suspicious."

"But the killer doesn't have to take out everybody. And he's already brought plenty of suspicion on the garage employees with his first three kills. Plus, if the killer's not planning on sticking around, maybe it doesn't matter who suspects what," Jackson suggested.

"It's possible. But it could just as likely be any of the supers above the mechanics or the security guards who work in that garage. Or it could be the men in the garage beside us. That would be even better cover."

"Do you always go back to the same garage on the same base?"

She nodded. "Yes, mostly." She turned to Carney's house. "But it has to be somebody who has access to personal information, like where Carney lived."

"Unless it was a coworker. You work long enough with somebody, and you end up sharing a lot of personal information. Or it could be a friend, somebody he may have seen at a bar or had over."

"Or somebody who has access to the computer systems or who knows how to find out where somebody lives through the databases, like an HR manager, a personnel director—a hacker."

"Any and all are possible," Jackson muttered. "We may have to sic Kanen on this one."

"All these men dead or hurt ..." she murmured.

"We know it is all about the truck," Jackson said, "and whatever it was carrying—whether authorized navy gear or something smuggled in among the authorized navy gear. As far as Kanen could tell, there was absolutely no rhyme or reason for which equipment got into any particular vehicle. It was all packed up systemically, in one truck after another and sent out. So whoever loaded those boxes in my rig—or just a witness of that—must have radioed somebody else to intercept my vehicle and to get what they needed."

"Which would explain them shooting the vehicle while you were in the store, to keep you from driving off with it. So they could get the material out then."

Jackson shook his head. "That wouldn't work. I made a very quick stop so I wouldn't get too far behind the convoy. Also, I parked right up front by the restaurant next to the store. Nobody could have gotten into the back of the truck without somebody having seen them. Not to mention they should be secure."

"So then they did the next best thing, tried to disable the vehicle so it would die a little bit farther up the road. But when they got there, I was there." She raised both hands in frustration. "And all we're doing is going over old ground."

"No, not necessarily. Besides, sometimes, by going over old ground, we come up with new answers."

"Why didn't they just shoot us dead on the road?" she said bluntly. "I could see that maybe they didn't have the time or opportunity, but, by showering us with gunfire, that certainly made us more suspicious."

"Didn't it though? They might have been hoping we'd take off into the bush, and they'd pull a U-turn and come back to get what they wanted. But it didn't work out that way. They might have been discussing coming back and killing us as a last resort, but Max was on their trail soon afterward, so they took the opportunity to get the hell away and to firm up plan B."

"I think that's pretty shaky," she muttered. "They could have just hopped out, killed us both, gotten what they wanted and carried on."

He held back from saying there was a good chance the bad guys were still planning to do that, but, on the roadside, he had grabbed her and pulled her behind the vehicle as the gunfire had splattered the military truck. And, as the shooter's pickup drove past, they were also being followed, so they didn't have a chance to come back for a second round of firing.

She walked toward his Jeep. "At this point, I just want to put it all away for a while."

He waited until she was back in the passenger side, then he hopped around to his side. "Ready for bed then?"

"I was ready a long time ago," she said with a yawn. "But, right now, after seeing what happened to Carney …"

Jackson turned the Jeep around and headed home. "I'll make a few phone calls when we get there."

She nodded. "Everybody needs to be brought up to date. We also have to see if anybody else is likely to be in the murderous line here."

He didn't share his earlier thoughts, just stayed quiet, hoping she'd fall asleep on the way home.

But, instead of falling asleep, she seemed to stare moodily at the windshield. Her arms crossed over her chest, her body still, she was silent as she pondered these recent events.

"Just remember Carney will make it."

"And so will Max," she said with a heavy sigh. "But we don't know about the current status of Barney, the other guy, do we?"

"No, but I can call when we get back, if you want an update tonight."

She waved her hand as if to say it wasn't important. "He'll either make it or not," she said. "There's nothing I can do about it right now. Max was driving, wasn't he?"

"Yes. Why?"

"Why didn't they shoot Barney?"

"He was bent over, digging to find something." Jackson pulled into the driveway as he thought about her question. "Angle perhaps, opportunity perhaps." He turned to stare at her in the darkness. "What are you getting at?"

She turned to look at him. "What if Max was involved?"

Jackson stared at her in surprise. "I was pretty sure that mentally we had cleared those two. Are you thinking both of them might be involved?"

She shook her head, twisted her hands, palms up. "I have no clue who is involved and who is not. I just don't want to miss out on an opportunity with a suspect only because we like them."

"I get that," he said and frowned. "Come on. Let's get inside." As they walked toward the apartment, his phone rang. He pulled it from his pocket. "It's Kanen," Jackson told her. "Hey, you got any news?"

"Outside of the fact that Carney will be okay," Kanen said in exasperation, "no. Why? What are you up to, and what do you have?"

He stopped, Deli moving a few steps ahead and sitting down on the short brick wall that lined the front of the apartment building. "Deli was just wondering if we've cleared Max and Barney. She's afraid one of them was involved, and the other one was intended to get hurt or killed. Or possibly both were involved. Of course that means the murderer isn't one of them."

First came silence and then a low whistle. "Well, that's

an interesting angle," Kanen said slowly. "I'm not sure we took that closer look, did we?"

"I'm not sure we did," Jackson said. "I've spent a lot of time talking to Max, sharing details of our investigation, and would hate it if he was involved."

"I doubt he is. What would be the point of shooting them and running them off the road then?" Kanen asked. "Then again, we can't knock anyone off the list at this point."

"I should have another talk with Max," Jackson said. "We're back at my apartment now. Deli is exhausted. I need to get her into bed."

Kanen almost snickered.

Jackson sighed. "Definitely not a night for that."

"It's always a night for that," Kanen said, his voice firmer. "Besides, you need a rebirth of life and not a renewal of death." And he hung up.

As Jackson walked toward Deli, his hand out toward her, he said, "Kanen thought we had knocked Max and Barney off the list too. But you could be right. We have to take another look at them."

"And I hate that," she cried out passionately. "I really like Max."

"Doesn't mean he had anything to do with all this," Jackson said firmly. "We can't jump to conclusions just yet. There could be another dozen suspects."

"Like who else might have had access to those security tapes?" she asked suddenly.

"Exactly like that," Jackson said. He sent Kanen a text asking about that. "And we have to keep thinking like this. Keep bringing up possibilities, keep bringing up ideas. Did anybody have no other family, a loner type, our shooter? Or, if blackmail was involved, who had family members to be threatened? Did anybody have money problems? Was anybody seriously in hock to a loan shark or up to their ears in gambling debts to a bookie? Was anybody vulnerable to take a payout and to betray their country?"

"It could take days to find out that information," she said, all her fire and ice gone once again.

They walked up the stairs to his apartment. He checked his door before unlocking it, entered, turned on the lights, did a quick walk-through to ensure there'd been no unauthorized visitors. But, since the hair he'd placed on the outside of his front door hadn't been disturbed, he assumed all was safe inside. But he couldn't make any assumptions anymore.

He led her into the spare room, then said, "Go crash."

She didn't even argue. She walked in, closing the door in his face. He heard some rustling behind the door for a few minutes and then silence. At that point, the light he could see underneath the door clicked off.

He smiled. "Good," he said. "At least one of us will get some sleep."

CHAPTER 13

D ELI LAY IN the bed, too exhausted to sleep, her mind rolling over and over again with all the faces of the dead she'd seen recently. Thank God, Carney would be fine. But she and Jackson had to stop this killer before whoever it was came back after another one. And she had no clue who would be next. If they followed the pattern, by rights it should be her and Jackson. That was a horrible thought.

But it made sense because they were two witnesses left behind. And, of course, Max. Although he was under tight security. She really wanted him to not be involved. But how did one know at this point? He was still in the hospital. Then she thought about it, wondering. She found the number for the hospital and called. She asked if Max was still a patient there or if he'd been released.

"He's still here," the nurse said. "Under heavy security, but he's still here."

Reassured, Deli hung up, curled up in bed and closed her eyes.

When she awoke some hours later, she lay still, figuring out what she had heard that wasn't normal. Besides the fact it wasn't her home, so nothing sounded or felt right.

Thud.

She bolted upright, frowning at the doorway. What the hell was going on out there? She was tempted to call out, but then everybody would know she was in here. Which was already a bad deal because this was a two-bedroom apartment. It wouldn't take long for whoever it was out there to find out she was here. And that was if she assumed it wasn't Jackson.

Her phone lit up. She snatched it off the night table and looked at it. It was a text from Jackson. **Hide.**

She didn't waste any time arguing. She flipped back the blankets on the bed, smoothing them quickly so it looked like nobody had been there, snatched her clothes from the chair where she'd placed everything and bolted to the closet. As quietly as she could, she pulled on her pants over her underwear and pulled on a T-shirt over her bra. If she was going to get attacked, no way in hell would she do it seminude.

She looked in the dark closet, feeling around for a weapon. Nothing was here but a couple shirts hanging on wire hangers. She took the first shirt and wrapped it around her arm, just in case. That was a horrible thought, but knife wounds were often great big slices. At least this way any knife-wielding attacker would have to get through something first to reach her skin. She took the second shirt and repeated it with her other arm, holding a hanger in each hand.

A lot of good this will do against a bullet, she thought morosely.

Then she curled up in a tight ball with her feet under her and waited. Seconds turned to minutes. Minutes multiplied with her heart pounding and her breathing raspy. The phone stayed silent in her shirt pocket. Why wasn't Jackson telling her it was all clear?

She was afraid to contact him in case his phone went off and somebody noted it. She lay here, remaining still and quiet. Suddenly the bedroom door opened. She sucked in her breath.

"Deli?" a voice called out to her. "It's all right. You can come out now."

She frowned and tried to peer through the closet slats, but she couldn't see him. Jackson? Had that been his voice? It had sounded … off. She refused to move.

Footsteps came across the bedroom, first stopping at the bed and then doing a quick circle around to the bathroom. When he came out, she still couldn't see who it was.

Something was familiar about his voice. Familiar but not. Seconds later the footsteps stopped in front of the closet.

He grasped the doors and then opened them. And he smiled—an evil smirk. "There you are."

She stared up at Max—a Max she had yet to see. Anger twisted his face into an expression she'd never seen before. She tried to bolt under his arms toward the main door.

He grabbed her and flung her back at the closet again. "Easy, easy. You're not going anywhere." He slammed her hard against the closet door, which was partially closed, and, with her weight, it snapped fully, sending her tumbling to the ground, dropping the hangers she had. He bent, grabbed her in his arms, pulled her up and headed toward the living room.

As she went through the doorway, she kicked and screamed, hitting, doing anything she could, but he was bigger, his arms longer, and he held her just far enough away.

In the living room he threw her hard to the floor. She rolled over and bounced to her feet, her hands fisted. She glared at him. "Where's Jackson? What did you do to him?"

"What do you care?" he asked. "You're not even sleeping

with him. Like what the hell's with that?"

"What does that have to do with anything?" she asked in confusion.

He snorted. "Jackson should be getting something for his trouble. Then again maybe you're getting enough money out of this deal to make it all worthwhile."

What the hell? She glared up at him. "I don't know what you're talking about. You're the one getting something out of this nightmare. Are you the one who shot Carney?"

He frowned. "I haven't shot anyone. I'm the injured party here. I want to know where the boxes are that were in the truck."

"You knew about the boxes?"

"Not before. But I don't have a choice now. I was sent to get them from you and was told you might not be cooperative about handing them over."

"So you're after the boxes? And yet, you didn't shoot anyone? But were shot yourself…" Still confused, she wondered if she and Jackson had gotten everything completely wrong. "Is more than one group after those boxes?"

"I have no idea," he snapped. "I was sent here to pick them up. They contacted me at the hospital. Good thing I've healed as much as I have. … The assholes on the phone forced me into coming. I'm pissed that you two would be involved, but I can't really give a shit now. … I'm concerned about my family, and, if you get them hurt, you'll be damn sorry you're alive by the time I'm done with you."

"What about your family?"

"You heard me," he growled, his eyes bitter. "They didn't do anything to deserve this."

She began to understand. But she needed to know something first. She opened her hands, her arms still wrapped up in the shirts, and said, "So did you murder all those guys or not?"

His jaw dropped. "*Not.* I've been in the hospital. Remember?"

"But I just phoned to see if you were there," she snapped, "and the hospital nurse said you were in your room under security."

"I was just released. By the time my wife picked me up at the hospital and we got home, then I got that call, telling me that you had the boxes and weren't willing to hand them over. And, if I didn't get them from you, that I'd be sorry and so would my family. Basically blackmailing me into helping them." He frowned at her. "Why the hell would you even want to get involved in this mess? What the hell is in it for you and Jackson?"

"We're not involved!" she yelled as she sagged onto the couch, somewhat relieved at an explanation for his anger. "If you didn't kill those men, and you don't have the boxes, what the hell is your role in all this?"

"I told you already. I was blackmailed into getting the boxes. My blackmailer said you had them."

"I don't have the boxes," she said slowly, studying his face, seeing only real confusion in his expression. "I thought you came here to murder me," she confessed.

He stared at her, his gaze dropping to her wrapped-up arms. "Me, the murderer? Seriously? They're going after my kids. But I sure as hell am not killing you—if you cooperate."

"Shit." She stared at him in horror. "I don't have the boxes," she cried out. "Jackson doesn't have the boxes either. We're trying to get to the bottom of this. We wondered if you were involved from the first."

He slowed his pacing to turn and glare at her. "Hell no. I was just the unlucky one who chased after the assholes in the beginning. I've been watching from the sidelines, but, after the initial chase, my only involvement began once I got that threatening call tonight." His glare slowly eased as he took a deep breath, then another one. "If you don't have the boxes, who does?"

"I don't know," she admitted. "But there have been a lot of deaths because of those damn things, so this needs to stop." Now that she understood his rage, he was much easier to deal with. "Three men are dead, who we know about anyway. Carney was hurt, and you and your buddy were injured too." She took a deep breath. "But neither Jackson nor I had anything to do with this nightmare other than— like you—we were innocents in this whole mess, just trying to figure it out." The two of them stared at each other.

Max's shoulders sagged. He ran his fingers through his hair and let out a heavy breath. "I really want to believe that." He resumed his pacing in the living room. "Where the hell is Jackson anyway?"

"What?" She stared at him. "I should be asking you that. You're telling me that you broke into his apartment and didn't see him?" She bolted to her feet and raced to Jackson's bedroom. Sure enough it was empty. "But I heard a thud." She turned back to Max. "Did you see him at all?" She didn't know if she should trust this man or if he was the real enemy who had killed everyone. She didn't want to believe that of him, but then she had never seen the angry side of Max before.

"No, I haven't seen him." He motioned toward the living room. "Let's sit down and figure this out."

She shook her head. "I'm not sure what there is to figure

out. Jackson sent me a text to hide. Next thing I know, you're hauling me into the living room—and not too gently, by the way," she snapped, rubbing her sore wrists.

"I thought you were part of this. Part of the group threatening to hurt my kids," Max exclaimed. "And whether you are or not, I still need those boxes."

She understood, but now she was worried about Jackson. "Wait. … How did the bad guys know about you? How could they find you?" Then it hit her. "I bet they checked both your IDs at the crash site while you were lying there injured. It would have been a quick call to the nearest hospital to confirm your location afterward and to see if you were alive or not." She paused. "Jackson said the shooters went down the ravine to check on you."

Max stared at her with such surprise that she realized he hadn't considered that possibility.

"Do you know what's in the boxes?" she asked him.

He shook his head. "No. I only know what Jackson has shared. Right now I don't give a shit what's in them or who wants them. I'm just trying to keep my family safe."

"And where is Jackson?" she asked.

"The front door was partially open when I arrived," he said slowly. He walked to the front door, pulled it open and looked into the hallway.

She followed Max into the hallway. "You're not stopping me from leaving?"

"No," he said, "but I'd really appreciate it, if you have the boxes, helping me out to save my family."

"But I *don't* have them. I *never* did," she repeated, understanding the pain and fear in his voice. "Sorry. The last we heard was that James took them. He was at the garage the truck was towed to. Carney pulled out the videotape, so we could see what happened that night, and James had collected the boxes. And then, after that on the same night, Magnus, who has also been murdered, went into the same truck, trying to get them himself. We're presuming he was killed because he couldn't provide his bosses with the weapons. But he might have killed James and taken them himself. No one knows at this point."

"That makes a terrible kind of sense," Max said. "I gather then that they assumed James gave you guys the boxes. Or kept them for himself?"

"Maybe. We didn't find them at James's apartment. Not that we looked. We were a little distracted by finding out he was dead." She tried to be patient and not to panic over Jackson. She sent him a text, asking where he was. As she looked up at Max, she added, "Maybe we should check James's apartment. Maybe he didn't want to hand them over and got killed for it." She stared at her phone. "I'm now starting to panic about Jackson. I can see he might have gone in pursuit of someone, but he's been gone a long time. Surely after sending me that initial text, he'd send me a follow-up one so I didn't worry."

"I don't know," Max said. "His disappearance is very strange. But, if anyone can look after himself, it's him." He pulled his phone from his pocket. "I just got a text from the same person who phoned me to get the boxes." He stared at his phone.

As she watched, the color drained from his face.

His face was grim when he said, "They've got Jackson. And they want me to bring you to them."

JACKSON WOKE SLOWLY. Harsh voices rained over his head.

"You shouldn't have fucking brought him here," a man snapped, his voice hard. "You should have killed him on the spot. Just like the others."

"There was no time, Hobo. You know that," a second voice said. "You said we needed to find out how big this has gotten. The only way to do that was to grab somebody and to question him. I couldn't do that there. There was no time with the foot traffic in the guy's apartment building. I had to move him."

"He's a goddamn SEAL. If we attack one of their own, there'll be no end of the hell they beat down on our heads," Hobo answered.

"I didn't know he was a SEAL. Besides, it makes no damn difference. He's just a navy guy, like everybody else."

"A trained fighter. Part of a tight brotherhood unit," Hobo snapped yet again.

Jackson lay here for a long moment, trying to recognize the voices. But neither rang any bells. Neither did he know the name Hobo. Jackson's head pounded. Luckily he'd gotten that text off to Deli as soon as he'd woken up in his bed, hearing something off. But it hadn't done him any good. He'd come out of his bedroom to investigate the noise only to take a blow to his head, which dropped him to his knees. Then a rag stuffed into his mouth tasted bad—chloroform maybe but too hard to tell with the smell of cigarette smoke overpowering Jackson's senses—and a hood was yanked over his face. He'd fought hard but had been ambushed. Then it all went black.

He could only hope she hadn't been taken too.

"Did you search the apartment?" Hobo asked.

"No, I didn't. I have no idea if he was there alone or not. But nobody else came out."

"Stupid," Hobo yelled. "You know there's no leaving a place like that until we've checked it over."

"I'm not stupid," the second voice said in exasperation. "But I didn't have time. If you'd come and given me a hand, then maybe."

Silence came at that point. Then Hobo said, "I sent a text. I'm hoping that works to bring her here."

"And how much does she know?"

"We'll find out."

"She was on the hit list. So is this idiot here," the voice said, nudging Jackson's leg.

"Sure, but there could be a lot more people involved. As far as we can tell from this guy's cell phone, he's been talking to Kanen and Mason."

"And both are not guys to be played with either," the second man warned. "You didn't like the fact this one was a SEAL. Well, both of those are SEALs too."

"I told you that you shouldn't have touched him, for Christ's sakes," Hobo cried out in anger. "All you had to do was find out where the boxes were. She's the link to James. She has to know where they are."

"I didn't have much choice. He's been on her tail the whole way. It's because of him and that girl that Carney is still alive."

"And that's just bullshit," Hobo ranted. "How the hell did this become such a big deal?"

"You wanted people silenced," the second man said in a dry tone. "Once you start doing that, you look at whoever else might need to be shut up, and there's just no end of people."

"We gotta get the hell out of here before this gets any uglier."

"Any uglier? You've already murdered several men."

"No, I didn't," Hobo said. "You did."

"Hell no. You're not pinning that on me," the second voice said in warning. "No way in hell you'll do that. This wasn't my deal."

"If I turn you in, I can," Hobo said with a devious laugh. "That's an idea, isn't it? I just turn you in, and it'd be all over with."

"Yeah? And how will you stop me from telling the cops everything I know?"

Just then a door opened, and a third man spoke up. "Hobo, take care of him, will ya?"

Jackson heard a hard *spit*. And then a heavy *thud*. Shocked, Jackson lay frozen on the floor with his eyes still closed. He desperately wanted to see what had just happened. But he could guess.

The new man said, "Fool. I never intended to let you live. If I was cleaning up loose threads, why would I leave you around?" He snorted. "Let's go, Hobo. We have more work to do."

Sounds of footsteps stomped farther away. Jackson had no idea where he was, except he was inside because he couldn't feel fresh air around him.

A door opened and closed; then something locked together, surely on the other side. As soon as he heard footsteps walking away, he opened his eyes and looked around. A stranger, somebody he'd never seen before, lie beside him. The dead man was tall, slim, with swarthy features, so he was likely the guy who had been at Deli's apartment, her fake boyfriend, planting bugs in her apartment. He was on his back, his eyes sightlessly staring at the ceiling. A bullet hole between his eyes.

Jackson shuffled to his feet, realizing he wasn't even tied up. That made no sense. Unless they'd drugged him, thinking he' be knocked out for a lot longer. But then he glanced down at the dead man beside him and wondered what he had to do with the theft of the weapon prototypes. Jackson sat down again, feeling a bit woozy, and searched the dead man's wallet and found out from his ID that he was on Deli's list of mechanics she worked with on base. Jackson shook his head.

When things went sour, they really went ugly.

He did a quick check through the man's pockets and found a crumpled piece of paper. He pulled it out, and, sure enough, it was a list of names with a line through those at the top. Several more names were listed below. Jackson's name was there with a question mark and so was Deli's with a question mark. Below were Kanen and then Mason, also with question marks. Jackson frowned, realizing that, just because these people had been on Jackson's contact list on his phone, sharing text messages back and forth, they'd become targets too.

Who wasn't on this list was Max. And that bothered Jackson. Max could be involved with the bad guys after all. Or else the shooter didn't even know the name of the man he had shot? Or did he not care? Or was Max an incidental attack? Not worth noting?

Jackson slowly made his way to his feet again, struggling to stay upright as his body wavered with every step. He wasn't sure what they'd given him, but it was still having an effect on him.

He had the list in his hands. As he went to stuff it in his pocket, he saw something on the back. It was a note, and he could see the name Max. *Max.* Jackson patted his pockets and didn't have his phone anymore. He rolled the dead man over to check his front pockets and found a phone underneath him. He'd had it in his hand when he fell.

Jackson searched through the messages on the dead man's phone and saw a text sent to Max. When Jackson read it, his heart ran cold. Max had gone to collect Deli and to bring her here. Wherever *here* was …

Was this a solidarity effort on the part of the remaining bad guys to question and then kill Jackson, hoping to take Deli out of the equation at the same time? As he surveyed his surroundings, Jackson realized he was in a small construction trailer. There was a desk but nothing else in the room. His gaze landed on the window blinds. He walked over and ripped out one of the cords. He was hoping for a knife or something more deadly, but nothing much was here. As he peered through the windows, darkness peered back. He couldn't see any sign of anybody else around but knew the first man had left with the third guy.

Where had those two men gone?

As Jackson watched, a vehicle drove slowly up a road toward him. When it entered through some double gates, it stopped right in the middle, so the gates couldn't be closed. As he watched, Deli got out of the passenger side, and Max got out of the driver's side. Shit. This was so not good.

Shouts came from his left, likely from a building he had yet to see. He tried to open the door in front of him, but it was locked.

He raced back to the windows. The construction trailer was old and warped. With difficulty he managed to shift the frame on one of the windows and then pop it out. He jumped up and out. Two men approached Max and Deli. Jackson watched as they were both led to another construction trailer.

As the men disappeared, Jackson ran from his hiding spot over to the second trailer and crouched down low. He slid along the side, trying to hear what was going on.

"Why have you brought me here?" Deli asked defiantly.

"Because you keep sticking your nose in other people's business."

Jackson recognized Hobo's voice. But then who was the boss man?

"You keep murdering people," she snapped. "That's bound to bring attention to anybody." After a moment, she asked, "And why Max?"

"Yeah, Max, why you?" The boss man's voice held a sneering quality to it.

"I don't have anything to do with this," Max said warily. "You're just using me as a tool here."

"I need both of you put down like the dogs you are," the boss said. "Hobo, take care of it, will you?"

Odd shuffling noises came, as if a fight had ensued inside the trailer. Jackson raced around to the door, opened it up to see a giant stranger—Hobo, he guessed—holding a gun on both Deli and Max. The boss stood by passively, watching. Didn't appear to be armed.

As Jackson tried to ascertain if Max was a good guy or a bad guy, Max took advantage of the moment of surprise with Jackson's arrival. He slugged Hobo and grabbed the big man as Deli reached for Hobo's gun arm and pulled his trigger finger, firing the gun into the floor—four times by Jackson's count. Chaos reigned as Hobo shifted, trying to rid himself of Max, while lifting Deli right off her feet.

Hobo was a big monster of a man at about six four, easily three hundred pounds. This was the guy the neighbor had described.

Hobo lined up his shot for Jackson. But Deli opened her mouth and bit deep, clenching tight onto Hobo's muscled and tattooed arm. Hobo roared, and, with his other hand, tossed Max off to the side and then punched Deli a glancing blow.

She went down but scrambled right back to her feet again. Jackson raced forward, going for the giant's knees and toppled the huge man to the ground. With Deli again hanging on to Hobo's gun arm and Max pounding his good fist into Hobo's face, Jackson managed to get the gun away from Hobo and pushed it against the man's forehead.

The mountain of a man froze.

"So, Hobo, I suggest you reconsider your plan," Jackson said softly.

With Max now straddling Hobo and pushing against the pressure points on his neck, Jackson raised the gun to face the boss who'd been issuing the orders to kill. And stared at a gun already facing him. "So you do some of your own killing, do you?" Jackson asked in a mocking tone.

"If I have to," he said. "And how the hell did you get out of that damn trailer anyway? I should have let Hobo kill both of you in there."

Jackson shrugged and slowly made his way to his feet. "Are you really planning to kill four of us?"

"Hell no. Only three of you," he said. "Hobo's worked for me for a long time."

"And has Hobo figured out he's a liability yet? Like the man in my trailer was? And that, once this all is cleaned up, which I presume is the killing of the three of us, that Hobo needs to be taken out too? And what about the unconscious guy you put in the hospital?"

The boss man shook his head. "Hobo won't listen to you. He knows how this goes down."

"What the hell do you want with those new high-tech gun models?" Deli asked as she slowly straightened.

The man looked at her in surprised. "You know about those?"

"Of course. James was videotaped removing them from the truck."

The boss snorted. "I'm a dealer. I deal in information and in products. And, in this case, somebody wanted the plans for those guns, but I couldn't get them. But I could get the models themselves. They could do what they wanted from there."

"So you don't care that these weapons will be used against Americans?" Jackson asked.

"I don't give a shit about Americans," the boss said. "I'm taking my money and heading a hell of a long way away. But, in order to do that, I need them first. And James was the last one to have them. Only we can't find them now, so he must have passed them off to her," he snapped in frustration, pointing to Deli.

"You mean, you *were* taking your money and heading a long way away," Max said, holding his injured arm. "If you're the one responsible for shooting the hell out of me and my partner, you won't like where you'll be going now."

"As soon as the government figures out he's a traitor and involved in acts of treason," Jackson said in a low voice, "he'll go to a nice private little jail, and he'll wish he'd never gone down this path."

"You're the ones not getting out of here alive. Have you ever considered how many bullets your girlfriend there fired from that gun? Your gun is empty, and mine isn't."

Jackson eyed him carefully. He remembered hearing four shots, but he hadn't heard six. He just smiled and said, "Let's find out, shall we? There's still three of us against you."

"But, once I put a bullet in your head," the boss man said in a hard voice, "your girlfriend will go to pieces, and your buddy here will lose a lot of that fire and ice. He's already injured. Won't be anything for Hobo to knock him out of the running."

Jackson didn't dare take a look at Hobo, but he sure as hell hoped Max had used some of those nerve points to take Hobo out of business. Even ten minutes with an unconscious Hobo would be a huge blessing right now. Jackson motioned with his gun. "You better either shoot me or hand over that gun right now." He handed the phone he'd picked up from the dead man to Deli. "Make some calls."

She grabbed the phone, and the boss turned the gun on her, only Jackson stepped in front of her as she bailed out the back of the trailer.

"And now you are running out of time," Jackson said. "You've got less than ten minutes until this place erupts."

"I don't need ten minutes," he said calmly. He raised his gun, but Jackson had already barreled forward, firing at the gunman. Max plowed into the boss man from the side as Jackson hit him in the knees. The man went down, his gun firing harmlessly over Jackson's head, but Jackson's gun had fired true. The man lay on the ground with Jackson and Max holding him down, a bullet low in his belly.

He rolled over, gasping in pain.

"Who the hell were you taking those boxes to?" Jackson yelled at him. "I want to know who your contacts are for the sale of these models."

"Fuck you," he said, now groaning louder.

With a glance to Max, Jackson asked, "Is Hobo truly out?" He handed Max the cable from the blinds. "Give me a hand."

Max hopped up and the two quickly tied up Hobo's hands and feet together behind his back, such that they only tightened if Hobo struggled. Even if Hobo did wake up, he wasn't going anywhere.

As soon as he was secure, Jackson went back to stemming the flow of blood from the boss's body. It gushed heavily. Jackson's shot had nicked an artery.

Max appeared with a towel he had found somewhere and handed it to Jackson. Swearing softly, he folded it up and pressed it over the boss's gunshot wound. While Jackson did that, Max searched the boss's pockets and found a cell phone and a wallet.

"Found a name in here. Not that sure we can believe it though," Max said. "We've got a Bruce Bellego."

"Come on, Bruce. Stay with me here. You're bleeding pretty heavily."

"Bastard," Bruce groaned. "You better not have fucking killed me. This was to be my new beginning, my chance to make a life for myself, instead of this bloody drudgery of working nine to five for the government."

"Where the hell do you work anyway? And Hobo? Where did he figure in your new beginning?"

The boss gave a half cough. Blood trickled from the corner of his mouth. "Hobo was never part of that. I would have taken care of him soon."

Max squatted beside Jackson. "Bruce works for the military, in the supply department."

The two men looked at each other grimly. "Well, that explains how he knew about the prototypes and how they were located. He still had to have somebody in his crew at the training camp."

"Unless he was there himself," Max said. "We often have men keep track of all the gear."

Jackson nodded. "That makes sense. But he probably was watched as he loaded it up. So had to send off the coordinates to make sure somebody else collected it. Was it worth it?" Jackson asked Bruce. "You realize, if you live, you'll go to jail and will never see daylight again, right?"

But Bruce didn't waste energy answering him. Instead he gasped an odd groan.

Jackson realized Bruce wouldn't last much longer. He looked at Max. "Make sure Deli's okay. I can't leave Bruce. He needs medical help, and he needs it fast."

Max raced out the door to find Deli. She returned moments later and crouched beside Jackson. "Oh, wow, he doesn't look good. Will he make it?"

"Not for long," Jackson said. "Hobo over there will. But this guy is bleeding out too fast."

They were both crouched in a pool of blood that widened by the second. She went to Hobo and checked his pockets, pulled out his wallet and some papers. "He doesn't have a cell phone on him."

"It's probably on the desk. Or check the chairs around here. We need it to get to his contacts and to make sure everybody in this nightmare is rounded up. Bruce won't be talking anytime soon."

"It doesn't look like Bruce will be talking ever again," she said soberly. "We can add another dead man to the list."

"Let's hope it's the last one. We need to investigate the men they've been talking to. That should roust out any other stragglers in this scheme. Plus we need those prototypes."

"I suggest we search James's apartment, even the complex or the underground parking garage. He was canny and could have hidden the rifle boxes in a lot of places. How much money do you think he got for this?"

Hobo answered, now awake. "One million bucks upon delivery, which never happened," he said. "I was supposed to get one hundred Gs myself. James wanted more money for his part. He got a bullet instead."

"Well, I think that's a pretty damn small payment for spending the next thirty-plus years of your life in jail," Jackson said to Hobo quietly. "There are a lot of dead men. And no way you're getting off on those murder charges."

Hobo stared at him, his eyes black. "You could turn that gun and shoot me too," he said. "I won't last in prison."

Jackson snorted. "Maybe you should have thought of that before you killed three innocent men."

"They were all part of it," Hobo said. "There wasn't an innocent man among them."

Jackson froze and glanced at Deli to find her staring down at Hobo.

"Are you serious?" she asked Hobo.

His eyes turned to her. "Sure. I mean, except Max and Barney. Hopefully Barney will recover from his coma, as he had nothing to do with this. James was involved. Magnus was lying from the beginning. He caught James retrieving the boxes from the vehicle and forced James to tell him what he was up to. James folded like the wimp he was, and Magnus figured he could blackmail us to get a cut of the pie. So he was put down."

"And ..." she asked, her voice hard, and yet, low. "What about Carney?"

Hobo shrugged. "I don't know if Carney had anything to do with it or not. But he sure as hell wasn't doing his job if both James and Magnus were pulling stunts like that shit. Besides, he's not dead, is he?"

She nodded. "You're right. He's not. I just wanted to make sure he wasn't involved."

"Not as far as I know."

"What about the original driver, Chester?" Jackson asked. "The only reason I ended up driving that rig in the first place was because the original driver couldn't make the run."

"He got sick. Sick to his stomach. We said, *No way, not a good enough excuse*, so the asshole shot himself in the foot to get out of driving the truck. That wasn't allowed either. But you can bet he was involved right from the beginning. He took good money to drive that vehicle. Imagine our shock when we found out it wasn't him driving."

"You're the one who shot at Max, who crashed his vehicle?"

Hobo nodded. "But I didn't kill him. They just had shitty luck and crashed. But still, I didn't kill them." He motioned toward his boss, bleeding out beside Jackson. "Bruce here, he did all the killing."

"Bruce says you did all the killing," Jackson said, wondering at the lies they'd each produced to blame the other.

"Of course that's what he'd say," Hobo said. "But I didn't. That's all on Bruce. He gave all the orders, and Manny followed them all the time. Until Bruce ordered me to kill Manny in the trailer."

Bruce gasped, his face turning pale, his body turning cold as he shivered uncontrollably. "Liar," he snapped. "You did the killing. I might have ordered it, but you did it."

Hobo shook his head. "Too bad you won't be around to prove that," he said calmly. "Looks to me like you're a goner yourself. And, in that case, it's my story against yours."

"But we're here." Deli's voice was hard. "And I've got it on tape." She held up her phone, the red light indicating she was still recording the conversation. "And his dying words place the blame on you for those murders that he ordered, but which you executed."

Hobo glared at her. "I'm not behind bars yet, you bitch. You better watch your back."

She smiled, squatted beside him and said, "But you see? I don't have to watch my back. I don't even have to watch my front because you're the one tied up here, ready for the cops to collect like a trussed-up turkey. You'll have fun in jail. Guys your size will be tested to see if you're as big and as strong and as badass as the other inmates are. You know what? You might like that. Might find yourself a nice little boy, have a nice little cuddly life together."

Hobo's face turned furious. "I'm not some fucking fag."

In the distance they could hear sirens. Cops and an ambulance.

"You never know," she said. "Time served for three murders, plus God only knows how many other charges they'll throw at you, so that'll be an awfully long sentence. We'll see how you feel about being all alone for a good fifty years, if not one hundred years for your crimes."

Hobo struggled against his bindings. "I won't make it," he said. "Shoot me now."

"Hell no," Jackson said. "That's way too easy an end for you. You'll get to live a nice long time in a nice small cage just for you." Jackson sent Mason a text. **All over but need to turn James's place upside down for the prototypes. He was the last one to have them.**

On it was Mason's almost instant reply.

Jackson grinned. It was nice to know you had friends who had your back.

CHAPTER 14

"IS IT OVER? Or just this part? I presume the investigation will continue until we can find out who Bruce was selling the prototypes to?" Deli asked, her voice quiet and hoarse. "So much death. So much pain. And for what?"

"Sorry, sweetheart. It's over for us. The investigation will continue, but we aren't likely to ever hear anything more on it. If the military ever learns more. In cases like these, the gun dealers go underground or disappear completely, so there is nothing more to find." Jackson tugged her into his arms. They'd just finished being questioned at the crime scene by the police. The coroner was here, but the ambulance had left. Now they were surrounded by the stark reminders of the aftermath of major crimes. He rubbed her back slowly, her head resting against his chest. He loved the closeness, the connection with her. But he hated that it had come through so much danger. "I was so worried about you," he whispered against her ear.

She reared back, looked up at him and asked, "Isn't that my line? You know how scared I was when Max came into the apartment, and you were gone? I thought for sure Max was a bad guy."

"Hey," a cheerful voice called out to them. "I resent that."

She peered around Jackson's chest and smiled at the

sight of Max. "I wasn't sure what to think when you showed up at the apartment. You were so angry."

He nodded. "With good reason. But all is well that ends well, and I am sorry for treating you so roughly. And, of course, contacting my own commander before coming your way helped us all out. I wasn't heading into that scenario without some backup behind me." And then the smile fell from his face as he watched the ambulance lights drift farther away. "This has been a huge shitstorm over nothing but greed."

"It all worked out in the end. Mason just called to say they found the prototypes hidden in James's secondary storage unit in the complex," Jackson said. He glanced at Max. "And thanks for coming to her rescue."

"You mean, thanks for coming to *your* rescue," Max said with a grin.

Just then Kanen walked over. He'd been standing to the side, talking with the cops. "You sure you don't want to go to the hospital and get checked over?" he asked Jackson.

Jackson shook his head. "I'm going home to a hot shower and then to bed."

Kanen shoved his hands in his pockets. "I'll be here for a while with the cops. I'll stop by tomorrow morning and see how you're doing." He glanced over at Deli. "Good work tonight."

She shook her head. "I didn't do anything except call you," she said on a broken laugh. "Thanks for coming and rescuing us."

Kanen nodded his head slowly. "But, from the looks of it, neither of you needed rescuing. You both did good."

Someone behind Kanen called his name. He raised a hand, turned and walked back over to the cops.

Max said, "I'm heading home. I've got a wife and kids looking for me. I think it'll be a long time before I leave the house again." He gingerly made his way to his vehicle, obviously still sore. Max turned, motioned at them. "Come on. Get in. Your ride is leaving now."

They scrambled into the back of Max's vehicle, and soon enough he dropped them off in front of Jackson's place.

Deli stood on the sidewalk. "I didn't think. I should have asked him to take me home."

"No," Jackson said. "We'll go in, have a nap and then regroup to see what the hell is going on in our lives."

She laughed at that. "I think it's pretty obvious what's going on in our lives. Chaos swept in, destroyed it and has now left us with the aftermath."

He wrapped his arm around her shoulders, tucked her up close, dropped a kiss on her forehead and said, "Sure, but what is this aftermath?"

"It's whatever we make of it," she said seriously. "So the question is …" Her voice fell off as he opened the front door to the apartment building and ushered her inside. Once inside, she turned to him. She studied his face, hating to see the fatigue on this big strong man. But he'd been through a hell of an ordeal too. And what they'd done to him had probably been way less than what he'd done to himself by worrying about her. She pushed the button to bring the elevator to the first floor, and, once the elevator door opened up, they stepped inside.

He continued to watch her all the way to his floor. When they stepped out, he reached out a hand. She eagerly put hers into his, and they walked to his apartment.

"I'm so tired," she said, "but I'm still on a high."

"That's the adrenaline," Jackson said. "When it drains

away, you'll crash."

"That's likely already in progress," she said with a laugh. "I feel like I could sleep for a week."

"You'll probably have a good night's sleep and feel much better, just be very tired tomorrow."

"As long as I get some sleep, that's good." She headed toward the kitchen, pulled two glasses from the cupboard and filled both with water. She drank hers thirstily and then reached for the other glass. She turned to offer it to him.

He drank it down and then said, "I'm heading to the shower. Are you going back to bed?"

"Yeah," she said. "I'm so done."

She watched as he headed toward his room. Moments later she heard sounds from the other side of the door, then the water was turned on.

She sat in the kitchen for a long moment, wondering what she was doing here. She should be in bed, already out. But she didn't want to be alone. She didn't want to be away from him. Waking up to find Max in the house and Jackson kidnapped had been the last thing she'd expected to find. Like part of her was wrenched away. Missing. Potentially with the thought of never getting Jackson back again. It had been heartbreaking. And it made her realize just how important he was to her.

So what the hell was she doing in his kitchen? She glanced down, realizing that, for all of her running around, she felt sticky, hot, and dirty too. She tossed the idea back and forth for all of thirty seconds and then smiled, walked into his bedroom, stripped down and stepped into the en suite bathroom.

Taking a deep breath for courage, she called out, "Is there room in there for two?"

The shower door opened, and his surprised face poked out. He took one look at her, and his eyes opened wide. But a welcoming grin followed. He pushed the door back. "Always."

She stepped into the shower, loving it as the heated water poured onto her body. She moaned in delight.

"Is it too hot?"

Warm hands and a bar of soap slid up the skin of her back, gently massaging her muscles, easing away some of the pain and stress and fear she'd had. "It's perfect," she murmured.

She stood off to one side, intending to share the water, but he tugged her back into the main stream and gently worked her body over with soap. She gasped when his hands slid over her breasts, gently weighing, cupping, measuring, checking out the fit. She chuckled. "Are they big enough?"

He dropped a kiss on her nose. "They're perfect."

"Good," she said, "because I'll never be one of those women who pays for fake boobs to make my real ones look bigger."

His lips curled in laughter right before he kissed her gently, his hands moving to her hips and her waist, gently sliding around in the hot, slick water to cup her buttocks. And then, in a surprising move, he pulled her tight up against his wet, heated skin. She gasped at the full-body contact, her body arching against his. He cupped her buttocks and pressed her belly against his hard and long ridge.

"You're perfect," he whispered, dropping more kisses along her temple and her ear.

She wrapped her arms tight around his neck and just held him close. "I was so scared when I woke up to find out you were gone," she whispered. "It's only then I realized how much you meant to me."

His arms crushed her tight. "I'm here. I'm safe," he said.

"But you almost weren't."

"And you almost weren't," he whispered back. "We're even."

That brought a garbled laugh to the surface. "So, because we both almost died, we're even?"

"Potentially," he said. "But we won't focus on that. Let's focus on the here and now." His hand slid up her back, his fingers kneading as they went. "And on the fact that we both survived."

Her eyes closed, letting his skilled hands work magic on her tensed muscles. When he reached her shoulders, he stopped and kneaded for a long moment as she leaned against him.

"We'll do your hair first." He reached for the shampoo, lathered it on his hands and then stroked them through her hair and massaged her scalp.

"Wow," she whispered on a gasp. "That feels so good."

He massaged for another few minutes, then gently tucked her head back under the full force of the water and rinsed her hair out again.

"Conditioner?" he asked.

She nodded.

He repeated the motion, gently smoothing the conditioner through the strands of her hair.

She opened her eyes, staring up at him. "So is that lots of experience showing up here?"

"No," he said. "First time I've ever washed a woman's hair."

She gazed at him in surprise.

He gave her a lopsided grin. "You can't go by reputation all the time with a navy man."

She thought about that. There was such a reputation to these men. Particularly when they were SEALs. But all navy seamen had a reputation for being womanizers. She just nodded. "There's always a stereotypical attitude, isn't there?"

"Of course."

She grinned, her hands stroking up and down his shoulders. Then she found the bar of soap he'd put back in the cubby. "It's like being a mechanic. Everybody thinks you're good with tools and engines." She stroked lower and lower before she came to his erection prodding against her hip. "There is one thing about it. We learn very quickly, and I'm certainly good with some tools." Her hand closed around his erection, gently stroking up and down, sliding against his soft skin, feeling the heat of him in her hands.

He groaned, pressing against her. "You can play with my tools anytime," he whispered.

She chuckled. "Tools in the water. Sounds like a mechanic and a SEAL got together tonight."

"Don't kid yourself," he said. "This SEAL plans to stay with this mechanic. This isn't a five-minute recuperation under the water. This is the start of something beautiful."

"Well, we did start a few days ago," she said, kissing him, feeling the pressure and tension coiling inside her, tightening to the point where she wanted to be out of the shower and into his bedroom right now. She pulled back ever-so-slightly. "Are you done here? Can we carry this on in the bedroom?"

He nodded, shut off the water, opened the shower door and reached for the towels. He wrapped her up in one towel, and she grabbed another, drying off her hair as she watched him. With their gazes locked on each other, she stepped out, dried her legs down to her feet so she didn't track water through the bedroom.

As she bent over, he slipped a hand up her buttocks and down the soft crack showing. She gasped and straightened. He gently squeezed one plump cheek and pivoted around and crushed her against him. When his lips came down hard on hers, she realized they'd made it out of the shower, but that was about it. She was suddenly seated on the vanity, her legs wide and him right against the heart of her. She moaned deep in her throat as his hands found the soft moisture between her legs, and he slid one finger inside, followed by another. She groaned, her back arching, her hips thrusting against him.

Before she realized it, he was there, replacing his fingers with his erection. And suddenly he was in and home, stretching her wider and wider. It was almost too much, and she shifted her hips to accommodate him.

"Are you okay?"

She shuddered and nodded. "Yes," she whispered.

He grabbed her hips and pulled her up tight, giving her a moment to adjust. She shuddered in his arms, her body on overload just from his entry. And then he pulled back and so-very-gently entered again.

She wrapped her legs tight around his hips as he slipped in and then pulled out. She couldn't do a whole lot in her position but hang on for the ride. And she was never more grateful for that chance to just experience everything exploding through her.

And then suddenly she was picked up, an arm hooked under her bum, and she was carried into the bedroom, lowered to the soft blankets, and he came down fast on top of her, his movements never stopping as he pounded into her again and again. She matched him beat for beat, twisting in his arms, crying out until finally he reached a hand between them, caught her little nub with his fingers and pinched, gently rolling his finger around the top of it. She gasped, grabbed on tight and slammed up against him several times, reaching for something and finding it as her world exploded.

She fell onto the bed as he grabbed her hips once again, held her tight and poured himself into her. Slowly he collapsed beside her and held her close. She lay trembling in his arms, realizing how sweet this union was after all they'd been through. With his hands stroking her back, the two of them cuddling in the bed, she whispered, "I'm so glad we made it this far."

He dropped a kiss on her forehead. "So am I. Now sleep, sweetie. Just sleep."

She gripped him tight. "I want to, but I'm so afraid that, when I wake up, you won't be here again."

His arms tightened around her, almost painfully so, and then slowly he released her, grabbed the blankets, pulled them up and over the two of them and said, "You don't have to worry about that. Not ever again. I'm never leaving you."

She tilted back, looked up at him, feeling the tears clog her throat and her eyes as she whispered, "Promise?"

"I promise. You're not getting rid of me that easy." And he dropped a kiss ever-so-gently between her eyes.

She slid her arms around his neck, one hand gently caressing his cheek. "I don't plan to get rid of you at all," she said. "Kanen is right. You are a keeper."

Jackson chuckled. "He meant, *you're* the keeper."

"Did not."

"Did too," he whispered. "Now sleep."

She closed her eyes, and, in the comfort of his arms, the two of them fell asleep, knowing that the danger was over and that their future had never been brighter.

EPILOGUE

A WEEK LATER, Kanen Larson studied Deli and Jackson, cuddling on the couch, wondering how Mason's magic could have spread for so long and so far. Kanen was happy for his friend. Hell, Kanen was surrounded by men who were so damn blissfully happy it was almost enough to make a guy sick.

But Kanen wasn't jealous—that wasn't part of who he was. Maybe envious. He wouldn't mind finding his soul mate. … But it wasn't why he was here. It wasn't why he was friends with all these men. They were good men—the kind of men to call on when in trouble. The best kind of men to spend time with, whether at work or when it was time to play. He was blessed; and he knew it. These were great guys. And the women they'd met, wow, they were something else. Talk about raising the bar.

Mason had started everyone down this path. They were all helpless to do anything but follow him. And the thing was, not one of them seemed to mind.

Jackson looked at Kanen and raised an eyebrow.

Kanen just shrugged. "You two look good together."

Jackson smiled, wrapped his arm around Deli's shoulder and hugged her up close. "Feels good together too," he admitted.

Just then Kanen's phone rang. He pulled it out and saw

it was his friend Laysa, calling from England. He lifted the phone to his ear and, in a happy cheerful voice, called out, "How is Laysa doing? Trying to whip all those little kids into shape, make them sit up and pay attention?" he teased.

A broken sob was his only answer. He straightened. "Laysa, what's wrong?"

Another sob came and then an attempt to speak. But nothing came out.

"Take it easy. It's all right. I'm here. What's the matter?"

Her voice broke as she whispered, "Kanen."

"Yes, I'm here," he said. "What's the matter?" He could see Jackson staring at him, a frown forming between his eyebrows. Kanen shrugged, not sure what was going on yet. What he did know was Laysa didn't get upset over the little things in life. He hopped to his feet and walked around on the living room carpet. "Laysa, talk to me," he urged. "What's happening?"

She cried again, her tone raspy as if she'd been crying a lot. And it was a tone he recognized. Her husband had been one of his best mates when they'd both served in the navy together for years. But Blake had been killed almost a year ago, and Kanen had talked to her all the time in the beginning to deal with that loss. She'd had a tear-soaked voice all that time then too. But he'd never heard her like this. "You need to tell me what's going on," he urged quietly. "I can't help you if you don't tell me."

Suddenly she shrieked, then sobbed loudly.

"Laysa," he cried out in horror. "What's happening?"

A stranger spoke in a deadly voice. "Laysa can't talk right now. If you want to see her alive again, I suggest you listen very carefully."

Kanen's heart froze. His chest seized. What the hell was

going on?

He spun to look at Jackson, who even now stood in the middle of the living room, his hands planted on his hips over a wide stance, ready to jump in and help. And he didn't have a clue yet what was going on.

"Who is this?" Kanen barked. "What did you do to Laysa?"

"Did you hear me?" the man mocked. "You need to listen to me. And you need to do exactly what you're told to do."

"What do you want?" he asked. "If you hurt Laysa, I swear to God, I'll hunt you down like the dog you are," Kanen growled.

"But that won't really work for me."

"You have no reason to hurt her. Laysa would never hurt a fly."

"No, she probably wouldn't," the man said with casual negligence. "But you, on the other hand, Kanen, would do a lot to save her."

Kanen stared at the phone. He held it out between him and Jackson. It was on Speaker as it was, but the two of them hovered over it. "How do you know who I am?"

"Oh, I know a lot about you. You're one of those who thinks you're better than everybody else. Asshole SEALs. But Laysa's husband never made the grade, did he? He was just a lowly seaman."

"He was a naval officer," Kanen barked. "He was happy to be who he was."

"But he'd have loved being a SEAL with you," the man said mockingly. "But, of course, you didn't stay behind with him, and he couldn't stand up with you, so you moved on ahead of him."

"What's this all about?" Kanen asked, trying to calm down. The shriek that Laysa had let loose earlier had chilled Kanen to the bone. It was obvious she was in bigger trouble than he had originally thought. "What's this got to do with any of us?"

"Blake has something of mine. And I want it back," the man said. "I'm starting to wonder if he planned to keep it—without my permission."

"Impossible. Blake was one of the best men I ever knew," Kanen said. "Besides, he died nine months ago. Whatever he knew died with him."

Jackson stared at Kanen, a question in his eyes, but Kanen had no clue who he was talking to. It was Laysa that he cared about. This asshole was already dead. He just didn't know it yet.

"Blake had something of mine that I want," the man repeated. "It's my insurance." He gave a harsh laugh. "So it's only fair that, if you want to see Laysa alive again, you'll find that item Blake was holding for me. Maybe he gave it to you?"

"What is it I'm looking for?" Kanen asked cautiously.

"Oh, no, no. It's not that easy," he said. "Laysa doesn't appear to know anything. I have been trying to convince her that she should tell me the truth, but it seems like she doesn't really want to talk. So I thought maybe her husband had given it to his best friend, … but, of course, you won't give me what I want without a little persuasion. I'm sure holding Laysa will make you more cooperative."

Jackson sat down hard on the couch. Kanen sat down a little slower beside him. "I don't know what you're talking about," Kanen said in confusion. "Blake didn't give me anything to hold for him. I hadn't spoken to him for weeks before his death."

"Well, that's just too bad then, isn't it?" the man continued in a gentle conversational tone. "Because, if you don't bring me what I want within seventy-two hours, Laysa will pay the ultimate price." The phone went dead.

This concludes Book 19 of SEALs of Honor: Jackson.
Read about Kanen: SEALs of Honor, Book 20

SEALS OF HONOR: KANEN BOOK 20

His best friend's wife is in trouble...

A panicked phone call sends Kanen flying across the ocean to find that she's been held captive in her apartment, tortured for something her dead husband supposedly hid.

Only she knows nothing about it and her husband is, well, dead...

Dead men don't talk – or do they? As they unravel the mystery Kanen has to delve into his friend's life to see what he'd done that put his wife in jeopardy. And find her captor, before he decides to kill her.

Laysa doesn't know what this man wants, but after seeing Kanen again after so long she knows what she wants. But is it a betrayal of her husband? Then why was her husband hiding things?

And why did her captor want them? Even worse, if he got them in his possession, what was he planning to do with them?

Book 20 is available now!

To find out more visit Dale Mayer's website.

https://geni.us/DMKanenUniversal

Author's Note

Thank you for reading SEALs of Honor, Books 17–19! If you enjoyed the book, please take a moment and leave a short review.

Dear reader,

I love to hear from readers, and you can contact me at my website: www.dalemayer.com or at my Facebook author page. To be informed of new releases and special offers, sign up for my newsletter or follow me on BookBub. And if you are interested in joining Dale Mayer's Reader Group, here is the Facebook sign up page.
http://geni.us/DaleMayerFBGroup

Cheers,
Dale Mayer

About the Author

Dale Mayer is a *USA Today* best-selling author, best known for her SEALs military romances, her Psychic Visions series, and her Lovely Lethal Garden cozy series. Her contemporary romances are raw and full of passion and emotion (Broken But … Mending, Hathaway House series). Her thrillers will keep you guessing (Kate Morgan, By Death series), and her romantic comedies will keep you giggling (*It's a Dog's Life*, a stand-alone novella; and the Broken Protocols series, starring Charming Marvin, the cat).

Dale honors the stories that come to her—and some of them are crazy, break all the rules and cross multiple genres!

To go with her fiction, she also writes nonfiction in many different fields, with books available on résumé writing, companion gardening, and the US mortgage system. All her books are available in print and ebook format.

Connect with Dale Mayer Online

Dale's Website – www.dalemayer.com
Twitter – @DaleMayer
Facebook Page – geni.us/DaleMayerFBFanPage
Facebook Group – geni.us/DaleMayerFBGroup
BookBub – geni.us/DaleMayerBookbub
Instagram – geni.us/DaleMayerInstagram
Goodreads – geni.us/DaleMayerGoodreads
Newsletter – geni.us/DaleNews

Also by Dale Mayer

Published Adult Books:

Lovely Lethal Gardens
Arsenic in the Azaleas, Book 1
Bones in the Begonias, Book 2
Corpse in the Carnations, Book 3
Daggers in the Dahlias, Book 4
Evidence in the Echinacea, Book 5
Footprints in the Ferns, Book 6

Psychic Vision Series
Tuesday's Child
Hide 'n Go Seek
Maddy's Floor
Garden of Sorrow
Knock Knock…
Rare Find
Eyes to the Soul
Now You See Her
Shattered
Into the Abyss
Seeds of Malice
Eye of the Falcon

Itsy-Bitsy Spider

Unmasked

Deep Beneath

Psychic Visions Books 1–3

Psychic Visions Books 4–6

Psychic Visions Books 7–9

By Death Series

Touched by Death

Haunted by Death

Chilled by Death

By Death Books 1–3

Broken Protocols – Romantic Comedy Series

Cat's Meow

Cat's Pajamas

Cat's Cradle

Cat's Claus

Broken Protocols 1-4

Broken and... Mending

Skin

Scars

Scales (of Justice)

Broken but... Mending 1-3

Glory

Genesis

Tori

Celeste

Glory Trilogy

Biker Blues

SEALs of Honor

SEALs of Honor, Books 7–10

SEALs of Honor, Books 11–13

SEALs of Honor, Books 14–16

SEALs of Honor, Books 17–19

Heroes for Hire

Levi's Legend: Heroes for Hire, Book 1

Stone's Surrender: Heroes for Hire, Book 2

Merk's Mistake: Heroes for Hire, Book 3

Rhodes's Reward: Heroes for Hire, Book 4

Flynn's Firecracker: Heroes for Hire, Book 5

Logan's Light: Heroes for Hire, Book 6

Harrison's Heart: Heroes for Hire, Book 7

Saul's Sweetheart: Heroes for Hire, Book 8

Dakota's Delight: Heroes for Hire, Book 9

Michael's Mercy (Part of Sleeper SEAL Series)

Tyson's Treasure: Heroes for Hire, Book 10

Jace's Jewel: Heroes for Hire, Book 11

Rory's Rose: Heroes for Hire, Book 12

Brandon's Bliss: Heroes for Hire, Book 13

Liam's Lily: Heroes for Hire, Book 14

North's Nikki: Heroes for Hire, Book 15

Anders's Angel: Heroes for Hire, Book 16

Reyes's Raina: Heroes for Hire, Book 17

Dezi's Diamond: Heroes for Hire, Book 18

Vince's Vixen: Heroes for Hire, Book 19

Heroes for Hire, Books 1–3

Heroes for Hire, Books 4–6

Heroes for Hire, Books 7–9

SEALs of Steel

Badger: SEALs of Steel, Book 1

Erick: SEALs of Steel, Book 2

Cade: SEALs of Steel, Book 3

Talon: SEALs of Steel, Book 4

Laszlo: SEALs of Steel, Book 5

Geir: SEALs of Steel, Book 6

Jager: SEALs of Steel, Book 7

The Last Wish: SEALs of Steel, Book 8

Collections

Dare to Be You…

Dare to Love…

Dare to be Strong…

RomanceX3

Standalone Novellas

It's a Dog's Life

Riana's Revenge

Second Chances

Published Young Adult Books:

Family Blood Ties Series

Vampire in Denial

Vampire in Distress

Vampire in Design

Vampire in Deceit

Vampire in Defiance

Vampire in Conflict

Vampire in Chaos

Vampire in Crisis

Vampire in Control

Vampire in Charge

Family Blood Ties Set 1–3

Family Blood Ties Set 1–5

Family Blood Ties Set 4–6

Family Blood Ties Set 7–9

Sian's Solution, A Family Blood Ties Series Prequel
    Novelette

Design series

Dangerous Designs

Deadly Designs

Darkest Designs

Design Series Trilogy

Standalone

In Cassie's Corner

Gem Stone (a Gemma Stone Mystery)

Time Thieves

Published Non-Fiction Books:

Career Essentials

Career Essentials: The Résumé

Career Essentials: The Cover Letter

Career Essentials: The Interview

Career Essentials: 3 in 1